SELF INFLICTED

Imprint: Independently Published
© Copyright 2024 by Melissa K. Morgan
The characters and events in this book are fictitious. Any similarity to real persons, living or dead, is coincidental and not intended by the author.
All Rights Reserved.
This book is licensed for your personal enjoyment only. Thank you for respecting the hard work of this author. No part of this book may be reproduced, or stored in a retrieval system, or transmitted in any form or by any means, electronic, mechanical, photocopying, recording, or otherwise, without the express written permission of the author/publisher.
No AI was used in the creation of this book.

TRIGGER WARNINGS:

Bullying
Foul Language
Alcohol Use
Alcoholism
Cheating – NOT between main characters
Explicit Sex:
Mild choking
Biting
Praise Kink
Dirty Talk
Emotional Abuse
Divorce
Death of Parent

It is my mission as a romance author to entertain the audience by telling compelling stories with descriptive romance. The characters that I write are human and go through all kinds of emotions. While Rem and Layla's relationship may be read as somewhat toxic and volatile at times, it does end happily and grows sweeter over time. It is never my intention to harm someone with my words or offend in any way. Please use caution when reading. I would rather you DNF than be traumatized by something. I love you.

Enjoy the book,
Melissa

DEDICATION

For the alt rock loving bookworms that read past their bedtime, suffer from book hangovers, and enjoy romantic smut – This is for you and me.

PART ONE

"I desire the things that will destroy me in the end."

Sylvia Plath

CHAPTER ONE

"Condoms."

I glance up from the magazine I'm thumbing through to shoot my best friend, Aly, a curious look. She's standing near the edge of the bed while holding up a box of unopened condoms with a mischievous grin on her face. My eyes widen as I spring up from the bed, wrestling with her to steal the box as she grips it tightly. She laughs when I finally yank it from her hands.

"Why do you think he has those?" she asks while I shove it into the night table drawer towards the back behind the vintage cigar box.

Is that where she found them? I have a few packets hidden in my room at home in *my* nightstand. What else has she been going through in here? The last thing I need to deal with is my future stepbrother knowing we've been snooping in his room. He was supposed to be here and bailed, so I'm left to my own devices. Which means gathering whatever information I can find on him. I'd rather not deal with the backlash should anyone find out we're in here.

"Are you trying to get me in trouble?" I snap, plopping back onto the bed, picking up the magazine again. "If you don't mind, I'm trying to read up on the latest music news." I wave *Rock Digest* at her. She rolls her eyes.

"Do you think he uses them a lot?" My stomach sours when she asks the question.

SELF-INFLICTED

I don't want to consider whether or not Elijah has a ton of sex. That feels...*icky*. "I don't care. Besides, the box isn't open. Maybe he's saving them."

Aly rolls her green eyes. "Or he just used up the last of his supply."

Sighing, I toss the magazine back on the small desk in the corner, pushing it with my index finger until it's slightly crooked, just how I found it. "We should probably get out of here."

It's a good thing Elijah is out with friends tonight. That's what my dad said before him and his fiancée, Bridget went out to dinner. I figured since I have the house to myself, I might as well do a little investigation. Maybe I can work out why my father refuses to let me live with him full-time while happily taking in a stray. That's not fair. Bridget seems like a lovely woman, but I've never met her son. The ink is barely dry on mom and dad's divorce papers, yet they're already set to be married. The only reason I'm spending the weekend at my dad's is because he's been begging me non-stop to visit since they bought the house a few weeks ago. That, plus the fact that my mother basically kicked me out so that she could throw a dinner party for one of her many best friends. The social life of Regina Barlow rivals many of the *Real Housewives*.

I give the bedroom a final once over as we head for the door. I'm disappointed that there isn't any personal pictures on the walls or dresser. The laptop on the desk is password protected and my hacker skills suck. There's two guitar stands in the corner by the closet with one of the instruments missing. All I can glean about that is that he's into music which is pretty cool. Not that I plan on bonding with him. If his mother can sink her claws into a married man, then there's no telling what Elijah might be capable of.

I let Aly walk out of the bedroom before me, closing the door. "That was boring." I mutter as we head down the stairs.

10

"Why did they leave you alone anyway? Didn't your dad know you were coming to stay for the weekend?"

"I didn't ask if I could stay until yesterday." I hadn't known until then that I wouldn't be welcome in my own home. In the eighteen years I've known my mother, I've been well aware that it's her world and I'm just living in it. Whether she makes plans or not, I'm always the last to know. Just like when her and dad sat me down to tell me their marriage, as well as life as I knew it, was over.

"You couldn't have gone to dinner with them?"

I wander into the kitchen to grab a bottle of water. Aly doesn't understand the dynamics of my family. My parents care little about me despite my constant drive to overachieve for them. Although my dad has the sliver of an excuse for bailing on me this time. "They're meeting with a client."

Michael Barlow is one of Massachusetts' top defense attorneys while his soon to be wife is his star pupil. It hurt to discover he'd been cheating on my mom with his legal secretary, but then my mom is no angel herself, so my sympathy is regrettably short reaching.

"Are you still okay with going to Connor's party tonight?" Her hazel eyes are full of hope. I know she's looking forward to this party because Tyler is going to be there. Her new boyfriend of two weeks is slowly infiltrating our relationship.

"Of course." I say, rolling my eyes. "Come on, you know I'm not that much of a Debbie downer."

She shoots me a look that conveys she doesn't believe that. I mock glare at her. "Kidding!" she assures. "It'll be more fun than sitting here. Maybe you'll find yourself a hot hookup."

While the potential of a hookup does sound fun, I'm not sure I'm in the mood to socialize much tonight. The fight I got into with my mom this morning has effectively ruined my mood for the entire day. She never came home last night. After panicking for

SELF-INFLICTED

several hours, she finally strolled through the front door at eleven o'clock this morning. Even though I'm the child and she's the adult, I worry about her constantly. Every time I try to tell her how I feel, it ends in a fight because she can't see she has a problem. The only thing she cares about is the men who keep her company along with the throngs of fake friends she's amassed over the years.

*

There's a quiet chaos associated with life in suburbia. People struggling to have it all while posting their daily life on social media. The truth is buried deep within the pixels of images on the internet for all to judge negatively or be envious of. It's the American dream. We force ourselves to smile for the camera, appearing *hashtag* blessed. Though if you look through the plated glass windows with white trim and farm style shutters, you'll find that in some circumstances – objects are stranger than they appear. There's a darkness lurking in the shadows formed by the recessed lighting against the distressed shiplap living room wall. Travel upstairs or into the basement and you might find the holes in the façade. A secret liquor cabinet in the primary closet where mom decompresses. A drawer in dad's office filled with dirty magazines of women built with plastic, injected with silicone. Step into each child's room to find a treasure trove of trauma and shame induced from years of knowing the truth behind the mask. From witnessing the terror of parents who stay together for the kids without understanding that the break would be a blessing instead of a curse. That's how life has been for me. A quiet violence where I wake each day in distress, yearning for things to get better. Up until the age of ten, I lived in ignorant bliss. Growing older made me realize that the world is cruel and unfair. Now I'm a cynical young adult with a pessimistic brain.

My father didn't love my mom. He couldn't. She was too obsessed with her lover, chardonnay, along with the highs she sought from being the center of attention. I didn't blame him for making the decision to leave. In fact, I only wished he'd done it sooner. How can you trust anyone else when one of the only people you're supposed to rely on is guilty of being deceptive?

I always hoped my mother and I might form a stronger bond if I stayed with her. That I could connect with her like Aly can with her mom. They take a special shopping trip once a month, have dinner together every Wednesday night and talk almost as if they're sisters instead. I'm ashamed to admit I'm more envious than I'll ever let on. It's not Aly's fault that I choose to live with a woman who acts ten years younger than her forty-two years. A woman who cares more about posting to social media than she does about her own daughter. We have nothing in common, which is really sad when I think about it too much. If she gave a single shit about me, she might care that instead of being home on a Friday night, I'm currently at a house party.

I take a sip of whatever fruity drink Tyler handed us when we walked in. It's unseasonably warm for a late June night. The sun set a while ago, yet somehow I still manage to feel sweat bead down my temple despite my tank top and shorts. I scan the large deck with an inground pool - people watching. Some are swimming while others talk around the fire pit which isn't lit. There's another wooden picnic table across from the pool where it looks like some sort of drinking game is going on. The only people I know here are Aly, Connor, and Tyler. Connor is one of Tyler's best friends as well as the drummer in their band. I've only met them one other time so I feel out of place.

Something cold hits me on the chest and I glance down in time to see an ice cube bounce off before falling to my lap.

"What the hell?" I demand, glaring up at Aly who waltzes past me. She laughs, pointing to Tyler who is standing in front of me with a smug smirk.

"That was him!" she quickly replies.

I brush the melting ice off my lap, shifting my angry gaze to Tyler. "What was that for?"

"You're spacing out, Layla. It's a party."

Rolling my eyes, I say, "You're boring me."

He bends his head to kiss Aly on the cheek. "You're just like Rem. He's brooding in the living room with his guitar."

"Connor is trying to get him out here." Aly adds.

Suddenly the back door opens and Remington Paulson strolls out onto the deck. My stomach dips when he glances over at us while making his way through the fellow party goers. Rem is one of the most gorgeous guys I've ever seen. He's nineteen yet seems older thanks to his above six-foot height and the confidence that oozes from him every second. His jet black hair is styled in a spiky, disheveled way tonight. The form fitting black t-shirt he's wearing displays his well-maintained athletic body along with the black and white rose tattoo on his bicep. I automatically sit up straighter when he approaches. Rumor has it that he lived in California before he moved here. Why he left the warm sunshine for the colder climate of the East Coast is beyond me. I'd love to get out of this small town in Massachusetts to disappear somewhere brighter one day, but that's clearance from my parents I'll probably never get.

"Told you I'd get him to join us." Connor says happily from behind Rem.

Rem takes the full beer bottle from Connor's hand, taking a healthy tug off it. His eyes slide to mine for a brief moment before shifting to Tyler. "You want to play?"

Tyler quirks a brow before leveling his gaze on Connor. "Are we playing?"

"Our stuff is in the garage, so I thought we could play a few songs." He says.

"Hell yeah! Let's do it." Tyler gives Aly a quick peck on the lips before they head back into the house.

"Stalker." Aly mutters, sitting down next to me. "I know an eye fuck when I see one."

Rolling my eyes, I take another sip of my drink. "I'm not a stalker. I'm just appreciating the view."

She snorts. "You know if you weren't such a chicken, maybe you could do more than just stare at Rem."

"We've spoken."

"Yeah for all of thirty seconds at the last party we came to. He thinks you're pretty."

"He said that?" She places the straw of her drink between her teeth, smiling with a shrug. "What did he say?" I hate the sprig of anticipation that sprouts because I don't want to be that girl who gets all twitterpated over a guy just because he's hot.

The three guys start bringing out music equipment, capturing the attention of the other party goers who cheer at the prospect of a performance. They did the same thing at the last party we'd come to. Apparently, Remington met Connor at a music camp several years ago before they reconnected when he moved here. I have to admit, they all sound great together.

Connor sits down at his drum set, beginning to beat a steady rhythm. Most of the partiers stop what they're doing to watch the show. Aly leans closer to me to speak over the noise. "I came over here with Tyler after our date the other night to watch them practice. Remington said, '*Where's your friend? That pretty one that's probably a bitch.*'"

Connor counts a beat using his drumsticks as irritation replaces my hormonal excitement. "He thinks I'm a bitch?" Screw him.

SELF-INFLICTED

She shrugs again. "I told him you're a sweetheart. You just have a serious resting bitch face."

I roll my eyes before focusing on the band when a guitar riff joins the drumming. Tyler sings the opening lyrics to a song I recognize. Aly's attention is instantly stolen by her boyfriend's mesmerizing voice. Tyler has this raspy, sultry timbre that captivates you. When Rem joins the chorus, I'm entranced just like the last time he sang. It isn't just that they're good at what they do, it's that they inspire me. That might seem silly to say, but it's true. As a person who loves music and spends what free time I can surrounded by it, I can appreciate aspiring musicians. They have a hell of a lot more bravery than I do.

Luckily, the closest neighbors are a mile or so away so noise isn't an issue. As the song comes to an end, Rem immediately strums his electric guitar, shifting into another one. My gaze drifts from his brown eyes to his square jaw, then down his forearms where the muscles flex as he plays the instrument like it's a part of him. His long fingers move along the strings while heat pools low in my belly. When I slide my eyes back up his body, I find him staring at me. My breath snags in my throat when he licks his lips slowly before dragging the bottom one between his teeth. I'm fascinated by him as he continues playing while Tyler begins singing another heavy rock song.

Aly leans closer to me once they finish their set. "I also told him you were shy."

"I'm not shy. I'm selective."

"Maybe you should select *him* and see what happens." She shoots me a grin that tells me she totally wouldn't judge if I hooked up with him. "You don't have to worry about that asshole, Adam anymore."

I frown at her. "Don't remind me."

It hurt like hell to discover Adam cheated on me right before graduation with Marla Higgins, the cheerleading captain with an ability to captivate any audience. Especially those with penises. Even though I didn't love him because that's not really my style, I enjoyed his company and trusted him enough to take my virginity. It was an added bonus that my mom seemed happier with me for landing a boyfriend of his caliber. Not only was he popular in school, but his parents ran in the same circle as her.

Just then Tyler slides onto the sofa beside Aly. "You were amazing as always." She says, kissing him.

"Thanks, babe." He guides her onto his lap, taking her drink away before setting it on the ground. They begin making out so I finish my drink, deciding to go grab something else. If I'm third wheeling, I might as well catch a buzz. I run into Connor near the sliding door.

"Did you like the drink?" he asks, running his hand through his damp hair. He's probably hot after drumming like a mad man.

"Yeah, it was good."

He smiles, taking the cup from me. "I'll make you another."

I follow him into the house which is far quieter than outside. The air conditioning cools me instantly, the sweat on my skin now making me shiver. We walk through a large rec room to another door that opens into a hall, leading to the main part of the house. I lean against the cool granite countertop of the island, grateful for the calm surroundings, as he begins making the drink.

"You having fun?" Connor is easy to talk to. He's one of those people who can start a conversation about anything. His calm, blue eyes have a way of making you feel secure.

"Yeah. I can't believe your mom lets you throw parties here."

He grabs some ice from the freezer, placing it in the cup. "She's cool with it as long as it doesn't get out of hand. Which is why we make it invitation only and maximum capacity is twenty people." He slides the cup toward me across the counter.

"Thanks." I take a sip.

Connor's gaze shifts behind me. "What's up, man?"

I glance over my shoulder to see Remington entering the kitchen. He moves beside me, pulling out one of the stools at the island, sitting down. "Beer me." He taps his index finger on the counter.

Connor raises a brow. "Fuck you, dude. I'm not your bartender." He turns away to open the refrigerator, grabbing a bottle of beer to take for himself.

I glance at Remington who narrows his eyes at his friend. "Rude." He turns his head to look at me. "Shitty party, right?"

I shrug casually. "*I* got a drink." Remington grabs my cup from me, taking a drink of the cocktail before passing it back.

He looks at Connor again. "I want that."

Connor snorts. "She saw me make it." He shoots me a wave as he heads back toward the hall. "Maybe if you ask her nicely, she'll make you one."

I follow his exit with my eyes, my heart picking up an unsteady rhythm. I thought I'd have time to think of a topic of conversation or get another boost of confidence from Aly before actually engaging with Remington.

"Layla?" Damn. I like the way he says my name.

I turn back around to look at him. "Yeah?"

"I thought that was your name. I've heard a lot about you."

Knowing Aly that could mean anything. "You have?"

He nods as he stands, walking around the island. He grabs a new plastic cup from the package before reading each bottle of liquor as if he's well versed in each type. "Aly was talking about you the other night. You're best friends, right?" his gaze flicks up to mine.

"Yeah, we've known each other since Elementary school." I narrow my eyes at him. "You think I'm a bitch."

He places three different bottles next to his cup, a devilish grin forming on his face that makes my stomach dip. "Guilty." He admits, beginning to create his drink. His eyes lift, pinning me. "You're not though."

"How do you know?" I question, doing my best to look unfazed by the way he tracks my face with those brown eyes.

"If you were, I'd probably have that drink all over me right now." I move to lift my cup up as if to do just that. He holds up a finger. "I'm sorry." His gaze softens as he gets this almost pouty look on his face.

Well if he's going to be adorable... Sighing, I place my cup back on the counter. "Don't call me that again."

He returns to making his drink. "Did you like the show?" I can't stop staring at his lips and eyes.

I'm not sure which part of him is most appealing. All I know is that I wouldn't be disappointed to have either of them on me. I nod, tucking a stray strand of hair behind my ear, trying not to appear desperate because if he makes a move I won't stop him. He pours a little of each liquor into the cup before bringing it up to his lips, tasting it. Maybe his throat is the most appealing part of him.

"You guys sound really great. I especially liked the last song." A faint smile touches his lips as he adds some soda to the drink.

"I wrote that." He says before turning to grab ice from the freezer.

"You did?" The lyrics are about feeling invisible. It reminds me of my own life. How I hide from most people because I feel different than them. "It's amazing."

"Thanks. It's one of my favorites too." I smile at that. "How old are you?"

"Eighteen." I slide onto the bar stool he vacated, taking another sip of my drink. My birthday was last week and while the

SELF-INFLICTED

only celebration was a dinner Ali took me to and a gift card to a store my mom loves from the woman herself, I found myself enjoying the newfound adulthood.

"You're drinking." He points out with a slight scowl.

I frown. "Are *you* twenty one?"

He glances down at the cup in his hand before closing the freezer door, then gazes back at me. "No, I just didn't expect that from you."

My shoulders tighten. "What's that supposed to mean?"

His lips tilt up on one side. "No offense, but you seem like the good girl type."

I scoff in irritation. "Because I'm quiet?" Honestly, I don't really drink. It has more to do with the fact my mother has plenty enough for the both of us than it is about me being under age. The last thing I want is to be like her.

He takes a drink before setting the cup on the counter. "That and your appearance." He crosses his arms.

I narrow my gaze at him. "What's wrong with the way I look?" my anger is evident in my tone. I don't care. Remington is kind of an asshole.

"Nothing." He says quickly, shaking his head. "It's not a bad thing. You've got these big hazel eyes and pouty lips that make you look…innocent." He plants his hands on the countertop, leaning forward across the counter. His voice drops low. "You're not though, are you?"

I'm lost in his eyes, trying not to freak out at the fact that he's looked at me enough to notice my eyes and mouth. "I can be when I want to be." I say quietly.

He catches me off guard by sliding his palm along my cheek. I shiver beneath his touch, finding myself angling my body closer to his.

"Do you want to be tonight?" he asks in a soft voice that makes my heart race. He leans in closer to me. I can smell cinnamon and the fruit from the drink, creating an intoxicating aroma between us. He scans my face before focusing on my lips.

"No." I whisper.

He runs his thumb along my lower lip. "Good."

The kiss is apprehensive at first, as if he's testing to ensure I'm down. My lips part enough to feel his tongue brush against mine, alerting me that he has a piercing. The cool steel does little to ease the fire building inside me. He slides his hand down to my neck before tangling his fingers in the ends of my hair. I whimper against his mouth as he releases a groan, licking my bottom lip before drawing it between his teeth. My eyes open slowly against the dizzying effect from him when he pulls away.

I release a trembling breath as he straightens suddenly. I hear voices in the distance, turning when his gaze shifts past me to see Aly, Tyler and some guy I don't recognize come into the kitchen.

"Hey!" Aly throws her arms around my shoulders in a sloppy hug. "I wondered where you went."

Still reeling from the kiss, I lift my cup, shaking it slightly in her direction.

She sets her empty cup on the counter, smiling up at Remington. "I'll have what she's having."

Remington grabs the cup in front of me, passing it to her. "Here," he winks at me. "Do you want to go somewhere a little more private?"

Hell yes I do!

I peek at Aly who narrows her eyes at Remington for a moment before turning to me. A slow smile forms on her lips. "Don't let me stop you." I slide off the bar stool before she draws me in for another hug, whispering, "Be safe."

Remington grabs my hand as I round the island, leading me through the foyer and up the stairs. With each step, my heart pounds in my chest. Am I really going upstairs with him? Maybe it's the alcohol or my subconscious forcing me to rebel. Or maybe, I just want to let loose. Be young and dumb before I'm forced to go to college for a career I don't want in the Fall.

I hear Aly cat calling obnoxiously as we ascend the stairs along with Tyler's laughter. Rem chuckles when we get to the small landing at the top.

"That's not awkward," he mutters sarcastically.

We head for a closed door to the right and he releases my hand to open it before closing it behind us. When he flicks on the light I notice we're in a bedroom. There's a futon style couch, a wide dresser, and a double bed. He heads for the futon, sitting down. When I move to pass him so that I can sit too, he lightly grips my wrist, tugging me down on his lap.

"Who's room is this?" I ask, glancing around at the dark gray walls and blue bedspread, trying to ignore the way my stomach dips when I feel the warmth of him against my side.

"Connor's. This," he pats the cushion beside his thigh. "is my bed when I stay."

"Do you stay here a lot?" I shift in his lap so that I can see his face. He slides his left arm around my waist while his right hand glides absently along my upper thigh. My brain short circuits when he applies a slight pressure.

"Sometimes I come here and stay for a few days."

"Do you live with your parents?"

He begins moving his fingers along the skin on my thigh again. "For now."

Being this close, I notice golden flecks swirled within the russet color of his eyes. His square jaw is smooth yet I notice a faint scar above the dip in his upper lip, like it may have been split open at some point. His naturally tan skin is flawless apart from the scar and a mark on his left eyebrow as if he'd had it pierced at some point. Carefully I lift my hand, smoothing my finger along the spot.

"Did you have your eyebrow pierced?"

His lips lift slightly. "Got it done when I was sixteen. I still wear it sometimes."

"Do you have any other piercings?" I ask, glancing at his ears which have small black gauges in them.

His smile grows. "This," He sticks his tongue out to show the metal ball.

"I feel like it would hurt too much."

"It did at first but it heals quick."

"Yeah?"

I place my hand on his shoulder, sliding my index finger alongside his neck. His thumb swirls against my skin, creating a spark through my veins. Adam wasn't very affectionate other than going through the motions that led to my pants coming off. I'm enjoying the slow buildup of whatever comes next.

His voice drops low, his gaze falling to my lips. "I want to kiss you again."

A small smile forms on my face. "Are you asking permission?" He bites down on his bottom lip with a small nod. I lean forward until my lips are hovering over his. "Kiss me."

Unlike earlier, this kiss is more intense, more urgent. He grips my thigh as he slides his tongue over my bottom lip. This time I can feel the metal bar more intently. I angle my body closer to him, turning until both hands are on his shoulders. He removes his hand from my thigh, placing his palm against my cheek as he shifts, causing me to slide closer.

Electricity sparks in my veins when I feel his erection against my ass. He pulls back slightly, locking eyes with me. "Straddle me." He orders in a soft voice.

I pivot, placing my knees on either side of his legs. With his hands on my hips, he guides me down on his lap. I release a throaty moan when he rocks his hard length against my aching center. Our lips collide again and soon his fingers are slipping under my shirt, creating a path of fire while he inches his way up my ribcage to my bra. His lips travel to my jaw, then my neck before he shifts my hair to one side, trailing kisses against the sensitive skin there. I shudder against him when I feel the barbell. When he bites down, I whimper, grinding against him.

"Fuck, you feel good like this." He growls.

"So do you." I say in a voice that sounds foreign to me. I move my lips to his ear, letting out another moan. His hands still.

"Baby, don't do that." He begs in a broken whisper. He removes the hand from beneath my shirt, clasping my chin between his thumb and forefinger. There's a hunger in his eyes that melts me when our gazes lock. "You've got me so hard right now. If you keep doing that, I'll blow in my jeans."

Hearing him admit that does two things to me. One, it turns me on more to know how much I'm turning him on, and two, it seems like a challenge I might be up for. A slow smile forms as I lower his hand from my chin. I raise up a little on my knees before coming back down on him, bouncing slightly. His head falls back as he watches me through dark lashes.

"Damn. You're not innocent at all." He smirks. I place his hand against my breast, encouraging him to keep touching me. "Layla..." He breathes my name like a prayer as I lower my lips to his ear, letting out another moan.

We begin moving against each other faster, creating a glorious friction that makes my heart race. He works each breast with both hands, scraping his thumbs against my nipples through the fabric of my bra. I tangle my fingers in the hair at the back of his head, continuing making noises in his ear. He turns his head suddenly, kissing me again. Within seconds I feel myself climbing toward release. My ears ring as the pressure begins to build. He clutches my hips, spurring me on faster.

The moment I fall over the edge, I cry out, the sound muffled with our mouths locked together. His shoulders tighten, his eyes penetrating mine as he lets out a low groan.

"Holy...*fuck*." He grounds out. I smile down at him as his head falls back against the futon and he closes his eyes. I can feel his heart pounding when I lower my hand from his shoulder. He opens his eyes slowly. "That's never happened before."

"Really?" I ask in a far way voice, still coming down from the high.

His brows draw together as he shakes his head in disbelief. "I think I love you."

A laugh bubbles up my throat. "In all fairness, you made me do the same."

His lips tip up. "Yeah, that was hot."

I stand, glancing down at his jeans. "How are you going to fix that?" I ask, straightening my clothing. I low-key pat at my shorts, making sure they're not damaged. Thankfully, they're fine.

"I've got spare clothes here." He stands, gripping my chin to place a gentle kiss on my lips before he moves to grab a duffel bag near the futon, pulling out a clean pair of jeans. "Do you want to go back to the party or stay up here for a while?"

I want to get to know him more, but heavy footsteps outside the door along with a sharp knock gives me my answer.

"Rem! If you're fucking on my bed..." Connor's voice sounds.

"Not anymore." Remington hollers, shooting me a mischievous smirk.

I smile at him. "I'll go back to the party."

Pulling the door open, I glide past Connor who barely looks in my direction as he barrels into his room. I hear a loud thwack that sounds like someone getting punched before Remington laughs loudly. I smile to myself while making my way back downstairs. With any luck, I can find a way to disappear with him again. I have no desire to involve my heart, but my body is all for exploring Remington further. Maybe I'll start coming to Connor's parties more often.

Melissa K. Morgan

CHAPTER TWO

Rem and I end up exchanging numbers before I leave Connor's in the early morning with Aly. On the ride home I tell her all about what happened because of course she wants every last juicy detail. What are best friends for if you can't share your trysts with them?

The weekend at my dad's is pretty much spent hanging out in the spare room they let me use and watching television. Bridget is a good cook though so at least I had the opportunity to eat something more substantial than the mac and cheese I usually whip up at mom's or frozen chicken nuggets. I didn't get to meet Elijah unfortunately. I learned that he does as he pleases which sparks a bit of jealousy if I'm being honest. Not because I can't do the same at my moms, but because Bridget gushes about how responsible he is. My mom has no idea whether I'm a strung out junkie or at the mall most days. My dad makes it a point to coordinate a dinner next weekend so that we can finally meet each other.

Between running her salon and socializing, mom isn't home much. The home I've grown up in isn't as big as the one my dad now has, even if it's plenty spacious with three bedrooms and two bathrooms, nestled between other houses that look similar. Now that it's only the two of us, it feels darker somehow. I haven't seen her since I returned home Sunday night. She left me a note on the kitchen counter this morning saying she'll be late tonight because she's going on a date after work.

SELF-INFLICTED

As each day of my final summer break passes, I keep thinking more about the future I didn't have a say in. While my mom is disappointed in my father's behavior, she still wants me to follow in his footsteps by going to law school eventually. Not one to make waves, I let them control my life. Now that I'm an adult, I'm afraid I'll be stuck forever. The only solace I have is my part time job at Happy's, a small music venue and bar. My mother cringed at the thought of me waitressing at what she deemed '*a hole in the wall with bad music,*' but I love it there. Honestly, I'd be perfectly content to work there full time instead of going to law school. I'd be even happier to make music myself while performing on stage one day.

I feel like I'm falling down the rabbit hole of self-pity. I need to get out of this funk I so easily put myself in when I'm left alone. I usually have work or Aly to hang out with, however I'm not scheduled until Thursday and Aly is spending the day with Tyler. To try keeping myself from the intrusive thoughts that plague my mind, I decide to grab a notebook along with my favorite pen before going to sit outside. Plopping down in the oversized outdoor chair out on the back patio, I begin scrawling my thoughts down as they come to me.

I've always been introspective. I find it easier to work through my emotions when I can sort it all out by writing them. I have stacks of notebooks as well as my trusty guitar that I bought for myself with allowance money at twelve. Maybe one day, I can actually do something with them. That is if I can get out of my own head and away from the strict scrutiny of my parents.

Before long, I've got a full poem on the page. I wish things were different. That I had the opportunity to go to school for something I actually care about. I can't go to college to hone my skills because Happy's doesn't pay that well and neither of my parents would allow me to go to school for something so unpredictable. They were gracious enough to give me a car when I turned sixteen, but paying for insurance, gas and whatever else I may need leaves me low on funds most times. It's not like I can move out on my own or start college somewhere else.

One time when I was about thirteen, I expressed to them my desire to work in music one day. I quickly decided never to share a passion of mine again when my dad said I'd never make it while my mom wrinkled her nose, basically implying that I'm not good enough. She did that a lot growing up. I was expected to be like everyone else's kid, including the ones on television. Once I started high school, I tried to change who I was to please her. Despite getting good grades and being active in choir, I still wasn't good enough.

Then Adam happened and mom was all too eager to sing his praises. She would constantly tell me how proud she was that I'd found someone like him. When I explained why we broke up, she blamed me. Said I must have done something that made him want to cheat. That I threw the opportunity out the window by standing up for myself instead of fighting for him. The truth is, I didn't want to fight for him. I never wanted to be with anyone who disrespected me. Unlike her, I had no interest in having a man at my side just to say that I did.

My phone vibrates with a text on the side table near the chair, pulling me from my thoughts. I see Remington's name flash on the screen and a smile forms.

Rem: *What's up?*
Me: *Chillin like a villain*
Rem: *I doubt that very much.*
You're too cute to be a villain.

I smile even wider. I hate that I'm a gooey mess of a girl with him.

SELF-INFLICTED

Me: *I could be evil. Maybe I'm currently plotting a crime.*
Rem: *We should hang out this weekend. Unless you're in jail for the crime you're planning.*
Me: *I have to rob a bank Friday, Saturday I'm free.*

Friday night I'll actually be going to dinner with my dad to meet Elijah. My stomach swarms with butterflies at the prospect of Rem asking me out. We make plans to meet up on Saturday at Connor's house before I spend the rest of the afternoon enjoying the warm sun outside while scribbling random lyrics on the pages of my notebook.

✲

Friday morning, mom decides to take me out for breakfast which surprises me until I realize she has an ulterior motive. Turns out she wants to grill me about seeing my dad this weekend.

"Remember, you don't have to do things just because he's your father." She says, sprinkling her fourth raw sugar packet into her coffee.

She wasn't happy to learn that I plan on staying the night there tonight.

"I don't mind."

If sitting down to a meal will make my dad happy, I'll do it. Partially because I want to get it over with and also because I'm a little petty. Mom has been keeping late hours at work all week. The few times I've seen her, she only wants to talk about what she's been doing with her new boyfriend, Chad. My dad offered to have me stay with them tonight, so I agreed. It's not like I'm missing anything at home anyway.

The conversation ends when she seems to understand I'm not budging on my decision. The rest of breakfast is awkwardly quiet while I eat and my mother furiously scrolls through her phone, taking small bites of the fruit she ordered. Once we get home, I retreat to my room.

I'm jotting down lyrics while strumming a tune on my guitar when my phone vibrates atop the comforter on my bed.

> **Rem:** *I think it's only fair you let me hear you sing since you've heard me.*

Thanks to Aly, Remington discovered that I enjoy singing. He's been pestering me to sing for him ever since. I smile before shooting a quick text back.

> **Me:** *Yeah, right. My voice pales in comparison to yours.*
> **Rem:** *Doubtful. I've never won a trophy for my voice.*

I roll my eyes.

> **Me:** *I didn't win. My choir group did. I'm going to harm Aly for telling you that.*
> **Rem:** *I bet I can get you to sing for me after I make you scream for me...*

Chuckling to myself, I shake my head at the butterflies that take flight. I'm enjoying the ease of our flirty conversations more than I should, but it helps quiet my mind. My phone vibrates again and I see dad's name flash across the screen.

"Hello?"

"Hey kiddo, it looks like our reservation at Petrey's was changed. Can you be here in an hour?"

SELF-INFLICTED

Having nothing else going on at the moment, I reply, "Sure. I'll just get ready and be on my way."

"Great. See you soon, Layla Bug."

I toss my phone aside before changing into the dress I was planning on wearing to dinner. It's nothing too fancy, just a summer dress in a pretty canary color with a sweetheart neckline and short, flowy skirt. I try to make myself look decent when I'm going out even though I'd prefer a pair of comfy shorts, flip flops, and an oversized hoodie any day. After I slide into my sandals, I grab the overnight bag I packed, along with my phone before heading downstairs.

Mom is sitting at the kitchen island, thumbing through a gossip magazine while picking at a salad. A stemmed glass full of wine sits next to the plate.

"I'm heading out now."

Her shoulder's tense. "I thought you were leaving at five." She's been extra prickly since breakfast.

"The reservation was moved, so I'm going now." She shakes her head, muttering something rude under her breath. "Is that okay?" I ask in a hesitant voice.

"Fine." She says snidely, flicking a glare at me.

I roll my eyes. "Would it kill you to be nice?" my frustration is evident.

She stands abruptly, marching toward the refrigerator. "You know what? I think you enjoy hurting me."

I grip the strap of my bag as I turn away. "Whatever," I'm not engaging with her bullshit. She always accuses me of being the bad guy.

"Yeah, whatever," she snaps. "I'm sure he planned this on purpose. That man has no consideration for anyone except himself. Typical of him to change the time at the last minute as if I might not already have plans with you."

"You don't have plans with me!" I holler as I head for the door. She continues muttering about how shitty of a person he is. I hear the contents of the refrigerator door shelves rattle when she closes it. "I love you, mom."
"Whatever."
When I step out into the warm air, my stomach sours. If she's upset, she's likely to drink more. I've spent the better part of my teenage years taking care of her because my dad was always busy at the office, so it's ingrained in me to be concerned. I'm afraid of what might happen to her without me. Hopefully by the time I come back, she'll have cooled down some.

I open the back door of my car, tossing my bag in before sliding into the driver's seat. Blowing out a breath, I turn the engine, giving one more glance to the front door of my house. She's not sorry for what she's said. I don't know why I still hold such high expectations when time and time again I'm proved wrong.

Halfway to my dad's I'm stopped at a red light when my phone alerts me to a new text.

Rem: *What's your last name?*

I type out a quick reply before the light turns green.

Me: *Barlow. Why? Are you going to start stalking me?*

I don't want to say anything to dad about the fight with mom because I know he doesn't want to hear it. I'm also embarrassed. I feel like a disappointment for reacting angrily toward her all the time and for having a broken fucked up family when it seems like everyone around me is content with their life. I'm dreading this dinner more, the closer I get to his house. Faking

SELF-INFLICTED

pleasantries through dinner sounds worse now than it did when I agreed to it. I'm two blocks from my destination when my phone vibrates again. I reluctantly check the text.

Rem: *What the hell?!*

I know he didn't find anything incriminating against me online. I'm one of the only people I know that refuses to use social media. I don't like people in my business after years of my mom forcing me to smile for pictures and play pretend so she could post to the internet. I prefer to steer clear of it when I can. I certainly don't need to be accosted by him right now when my mom already hates me. Deciding to brush him off, I toss my phone into my purse. I'll text him later tonight.

When I pull into the driveway I stare at the expansive front lawn with full bushes along the front fence line. There's a basket of beautiful purple flowers hanging from the awning of the front porch. Everything is so perfect and pretty here which only sinks my mood further. The front door swings open as I kill the engine. Dad comes out to greet me, followed by Bridget.

"Let me carry that for you." Dad says, taking my bag after I grab it out of the back seat.

"Thanks."

My gaze shifts to Bridget who smiles warmly at me. I give her a short smile back, trying to keep a brave face.

"I'm so glad you could make it, Layla." She says.

"Me too."

I follow them toward the door, greeted by the smell of fresh cookies when we enter the tall foyer. It smelled similar the last time I was here. I think Bridget likes to bake.

My knees nearly buckle when dad says, "Elijah - er Remington is just in the living room."

Wait, what?

Bile rises in my throat. It's an odd coincidence, nothing more. Right?

"He's been going by his middle name since...well for the last year." Bridget explains. "You can call him whatever you'd like. I don't think I'll ever get used to it."

God can't hate me this much! There is no way this Elijah Remington is the same as my - no. He's not *mine*. My heart rattles against my ribcage, praying to anyone who will listen that I'm mistaken. This isn't happening. This cannot be happening!

Bridget turns right to go into the living room. I follow, keeping my eyes trained to the floor because I'm not ready to face this disaster yet.

"Elijah, meet your soon to be stepsister, Layla." She says.

Swallowing the lump that forms in my throat, I begin to lift my eyes. The first thing that comes into view is his black boots. Boots that look eerily similar to ones I've seen before. Tucked inside the boots are faded black jeans. As I move up his narrow hips, past the black button down shirt, my heart falls to my stomach. The familiar square jaw, the full lips and straight nose. His purposely disheveled black hair that's soft between my fingers. Those altogether unique and magnificent eyes.

This is a nightmare.

He's standing near the couch, his hands tucked into the front pockets of his jeans, watching me cautiously as if he's afraid I might turn around to run. Which honestly isn't an unlikely scenario at this point. His throat rolls in a swallow as I somehow find the ability to give him a smile despite the nausea and horror whirling within me. Probably from years of being fake for the sake of appearance.

He clears his throat. "Nice to meet you."

With clenched teeth, I say, "Yeah. You too, *Elijah*."

"I'm going to go finish getting ready. Why don't you two get to know each other." Bridget announces.

SELF-INFLICTED

I reluctantly shift my gaze to hers. "Okay," I can't say we already know each other. I can't tell anyone about this ever.

My dad nudges my shoulder. "I'll put your bag upstairs." His smile is tight when he glances between us before backing away toward the hall where the staircase is.

This can't be real. "What the fuck?" I whisper, squeezing my eyes shut.

Rem mutters something and I open my eyes, pinning him with a glare.

"I'm wondering the same thing." He bites out.

Anger bubbles up, overtaking the shock. "Why didn't you say anything?"

His nostrils flare as he steps closer to me, talking in a low voice. Probably to keep our parents from overhearing, which is fair, but I'm struggling to keep my rage at bay. "You think I knew?" he sounds incredulous, yet I'm not sure I believe it. There's no way he didn't know who I was.

Crossing my arms over my chest, I scoff, "How could you not?"

His lips turn down as he peers into my eyes. "I didn't know. I *swear*." His voice is softer, his gaze earnest. I want to believe him, but trust isn't something I give on a whim.

"I set your bag on your bed. We'll head out as soon as Bridget is ready." Dad announces, coming into the living room.

Exhaling soundly, Remington sits down on the couch, dragging a hand through his hair. I'm in no mood to break bread with these people now. It's bad enough that dad and Bridget lied about their affair. For her son to be a liar too really pisses me off. Why would he pursue me the way he did when he knew who I was? What kind of sick, twisted game is he playing? This is too much to process right now. How am I supposed to pretend like everything is fine when the guy I like and have heavily made out with, is soon to be family?

36

My dad sits in one of the arm chairs. "Eli - Remington is deeply into music. You two have that in common."

Remington scowls up at me.

"I wouldn't say my interest is deep." I reply quietly with a shrug.

"No?" dad chuckles. "When she was thirteen, she bought a guitar and started playing everything she heard without lessons. She's incredibly talented."

I bite back on my molars. I was twelve, not thirteen. I'm not sure why he's suddenly acting like the proud dad in front of Remington when he's never cared before. In fact, two years ago when I started working at Happy's, he balked at the idea right alongside mom.

Something in Remington's eyes shift, making me uncomfortable. He almost looks as if he's impressed by me. So we have music in common, big deal. It doesn't matter anyway because everything is different now. All of my fearing the worst through life should have prepared me for something like this. I shouldn't have let my guard fall so easily with him.

I excuse myself to the bathroom to avoid any more personal topics. Luckily once I'm coming back out, Bridget is heading down the stairs.

We take one car because it's just the four of us. My dad is driving with Bridget up front while I'm forced to sit near Rem in the back seat of the luxury sedan that I wish had more space. I spend the ride gazing out the window, maintaining just enough basic conversation with dad so that I don't come off as completely depressed.

Once we arrive at the restaurant, dad goes through the valet entrance where we all exit the vehicle. I wish I'd brought a sweater to wear over my dress. Either the temperature dropped considerably since we're near the water now, or my body is still in shock from realizing who Remington actually is. When we're seated at our table overlooking the bay, he sits across from me. I do my best to not so much as glance in his direction. I'm next to Bridget which is less awkward yet still uncomfortable. Too bad it's not hurricane season. I'd really love a fierce storm to roll through and put an end to my misery.

Bridget begins speaking after the waiter takes our drink order. "I'm really glad we could all get together finally. I've been wanting you two to meet since you're so close in age."

"You expect us to be *friends* because you two are getting married." Rem snaps. I nearly choke on the water I've just taken a sip of.

She glares across the table at her son. "You can never have too many friends, Elijah."

"You sure?" he raises a brow.

She gives him a look that only a mother can give their child. You know the one where they stare intently, daring with their eyes for the kid to act up just one more time before unleashing their fury. He backs down almost immediately, making me wonder if we have something else in common. He's not any happier about this arrangement than I am.

"It would mean a lot to us if you two would at least get to know each other. Layla doesn't have any other siblings." My dad says, looking at me. "An older brother looking out for you would be nice." I resist the urge to roll my eyes.

No more important than a father who might actually spend quality time with his kid, but that topic will never be on the table. The word *"brother"* makes me want to vomit. He's not my brother. He never will be. I take another sip of my water, staying silent.

"Your dad says you've been working at Happy's. Are you planning to continue that now that you're graduated?" Bridget asks.

"As long as I can." I say with a shrug. "Once classes start in the Fall, I'm not sure how much time I'll have."

She smiles. "Michael is so proud of you for following in his footsteps."

Remington scoffs. I glance up at him. "You're going to law school?"

My eyes narrow to slits. "That's the plan."

"Lame plan." He says. "So you *are* an overachieving good girl."

"Too dumb for college?" I shoot back.

His jaw clenches. "Too talented to waste my time."

"Elijah is in a band. They already have some small gigs lined up this Summer." Bridget says. I don't miss the proud smile on her face.

"Good for him." I mutter when the waiter comes back to take our order.

"Layla will excel at being a lawyer." Dad says after the waiter leaves. "She sure has the spirit for it." He chuckles. "She's always been great at arguing."

"There's a difference when it's standing up for yourself." I say to him. "It's difficult to not want something your parents forced you into."

He shoots me a look. I bite my tongue. "It is true. I've always wanted you to be successful."

I happen to glance at Remington again, half expecting him to make another snide comment. Thankfully, he doesn't. "Apparently success is measured only by the bar your parents set." I say with a tight smile. "So lame or not, the choice is obvious." He frowns.

"There is nothing lame about the law." Bridget says, giving her son another disapproving look. "I think it's a great career."

Sensing the tension of the conversation, dad steers to another topic. Soon after, our food arrives. I absently slice bite size pieces of my filet mignon until it's completely cut up while dad and Bridget talk about their upcoming wedding. I hate how quickly

SELF-INFLICTED

everything changes. Not even half a year in and they're going to be spouses. It's like the last eighteen years meant nothing to him. They each reiterate how great it is for us to all be together. I spend my time avoiding eye contact with Remington because every time I look at him I'm reminded of what we did. It makes me feel things I shouldn't. By the time dinner is over and we get back to the house, I excuse myself to the room I'm staying in, feigning tiredness. In reality, I can't stomach any more fake kindness when my world is a dumpster fire.

*

The one positive to being at my dad's is the bedroom I've been given. It's a lot more spacious than the one I have at home. There's a double bed on the far wall adorned with a black and white floral comforter as well as a purple throw blanket draped over the end that's softer than anything I've ever touched. I slide my bare feet under it as I sit on the bed, replaying the atrocity of newfound information.

I've been wracking my brain, trying to figure out if I'd somehow missed the signs of Remington being Elijah. Nothing comes to mind. There isn't a single thing that has let me know his identity prior. For starters, I thought his name was Elijah. I never asked or was told about his hobbies or interests. I'd only met Bridget recently, so it's not like I had much of an opportunity to find out who he is. Even his bedroom had minimal clues. Which makes a lot more sense now considering he doesn't stay here that often.

I'm not sure I believe that he hadn't known all along though. He seemed just as shocked as I was, but I don't know him well enough in the first place to determine whether or not he was lying about it. Although, if he had known who I was, why would he want to make out with me?

Part of me wants to talk through it with Aly. To ask her if she had any idea who he was to me. I feel like she would have told me if she'd known. Another part of me is mortified to tell her about this situation because I feel so dumb. It feels weird even if we're not related by blood or anything. Battling all kinds of confusion, I decide to take a shower since dad told me that the bathroom upstairs is stocked with toiletries. I'm not sure if Remington is still home or if he left. His bedroom door, which is down the hall from mine, is closed when I brave leaving my room.

Upon opening the glass door of the shower, I see an array of body washes on the small shelf and my stomach tightens. For some reason, the realization that he uses this shower too frustrates me further. I don't know why exactly. Maybe because this is more his house than mine. I feel like such an outsider. Turning on the water, I quickly undress before stepping into the warm spray. My shoulders relax as I let the water fall over my body, soaking my hair. I wash myself mechanically, my gaze stalling on the body wash that I know is his. Unable to help myself, I flip the cap open, inhaling the spicy soap. This is why he smells like cinnamon. Closing my eyes, I replay the memory of our time together at Connor's. Heat pools low in my belly followed by a wave of guilt. I hate that I let myself like Remington, that I considered the possibility of spending more time with him this summer. More than that, I hate how disappointed I am that it all has to stop. I place the bottle back on the shelf to finish rinsing.

After changing into a pair of sleep shorts with an oversized sweater, I timidly make my way down the stairs to grab a bottle of water. Dad and Bridget are watching a show in the living room, snuggled up on the couch together. He shoots me a brief smile when he sees me heading to the kitchen.

"Help yourself to whatever you want, Layla bug."

"Thanks."

SELF-INFLICTED

    I have the sudden sense of being watched once my fingers wrap around the bottle in the refrigerator. I straighten, closing my eyes. The familiar scent of cinnamon invades my nostrils just as I feel Remington brush his arm against my back. He steps around me to grab a sugar cookie from a plate on the counter. I open my eyes slowly, turning away from him to head back up to my room. It's better if we don't talk to each other, especially with our parents present.
    Before I take a step I swear I hear him mutter, "Lock your door."
    Ignoring what I may or may not have heard, I call out a goodnight before I climb the stairs to my room.
    Despite the comfortable bed and the plush comforter enveloping me, I'm finding it difficult to fall asleep. I can't stop thinking about Remington. Even though I know it's wrong now, I still want him. You can't erase attraction so easily. All of my thoughts are keeping me from relaxing enough to close my eyes. I stare up at the white, textured ceiling above my bed, continuing the mind fuck as I look for shapes and words in the swirls.
    "I think I love you."
    He had to be joking when he'd said that to me. However, the rush of gratification that came over me in the moment, left me reeling. Not because I hoped he loved me, but because it was nice to feel desired by someone. My only other experience was Adam. He was a douchebag that never complimented me. With him, I didn't really care because I was more interested in pleasing my mother. There's something about Remington that seems genuine. While I'm anti-love, I do want to be liked. Now everything is tainted.
    After another hour of not being able to shut my brain off, I pull a notebook out of the bag I brought, turning on the lamp atop the nightstand. I prop my pillow against the headboard to lean against it, bending my knees while balancing the notebook atop my

thighs. Clicking the pen, I stare at the faint blue lines against the white and release a heavy breath.

> Drowning in a sea of other's emotions
> No thoughts or feelings of my own.
> You make me want to forget for a while.
> I like the way you say my name and the piercing in your tongue.
> A kiss can get me drunk on you and I'm flying toward the sun.
> Just as I take flight, I'm already too high – the flares scald my skin.
> Before I had all of you, we committed the deepest sin.

I wish I would have brought my guitar with me. It's missing a string but still sounds decent. I start humming a slow tune to myself while tapping the pen against the page. A series of short knocks startles me from my creativity. I glance up at my door, seeing the handle turn before it swings open. Remington slides in quickly, closing the door behind him. His black hair is damp as if he's just taken a shower. It's long enough that it curls slightly over his ears. He's also shirtless, which captures my attention for an embarrassing amount of time. The black sweat shorts he's wearing are hanging dangerously low on his hips, highlighting his well-toned abs and another tattoo up his ribcage that reads, *c'est la vie.*

I'm about to ask what he thinks he's doing when he lifts a finger to his lips, motioning for me to be quiet. Scowling at him, I tense as he slowly approaches the bed before sitting down on the edge.

"It's after midnight," he says in a low voice. "why are you still up?"

SELF-INFLICTED

I close the notebook, placing it on top of the nightstand along with the pen. "Couldn't sleep. Why are you entering my room when you thought I might be sleeping?"

I keep my voice quiet because dad and Bridget's room is on the other side of my wall, but there's an annoyed edge to it that I can't help. He hasn't said a damn thing to me the last several hours and in the middle of the night he wants to talk? To be fair, I didn't say anything either. However, that's because I don't want to have this conversation.

He drags a hand through his hair. "I saw the light on through the bottom of the door." His gaze narrows at me. "We need to talk."

"Right now?" I glance at the clock beside my bed to enunciate the ridiculousness of his request. "I should be sleeping."

His lips kick up on one side. "You can't, remember?"

Rolling my eyes, I say, "Whatever. What do you want to talk about?"

He shifts, bending his knee to angle his body to face me better. "Seriously? I think there's a lot we need to talk about. Like why you allowed me to touch you the way I did when we're going to be siblings."

Bile rises in my throat as my heart skips a beat. "We're *not* related." I argue, my voice rising slightly.

"So, you knew." He states. I immediately interrupt whatever he's about to say next.

"I had no idea who you were. If you genuinely believe I did, then you don't know me at all. What about you? How did you not know who I was?"

His jaw ticks while he shifts his gaze to the floor. "Clearly I'm not that fucking observant either. All I knew about you was your name and that you lived with your mom."

"You didn't see any photos of me?" I ask, trying not to stare at the way his fingers curl against the blanket. Damn his sexy and capable hands. At least I assume they're capable based on what little I've experienced.

He looks at me again. "Why the fuck would I want to see pictures of you?" he growls. "I didn't give a shit about you. I'm hardly here." His words are a punch to my gut. I recoil as if he's struck me. His nostrils flare slightly as he shakes his head. "*Didn't* being the operative word, *Bug*."

I glare at him. What's with the sudden nickname? "You didn't care that the man your mother is marrying has kids of his own? Had a different family?" A simmering anger swirls in my belly. I inhale a deep breath, trying to tamp it down.

He scoffs. "I don't need or want a new fucking dad." There's a spark of pain in his eyes when he says that making some of my anger dissipate. This entire situation is no more his fault than it is mine. "While I may live here temporarily, I plan on leaving as soon as possible. Who my mom decides to be with is no concern of mine."

Envy begins to sprout. Everything is so easy for him when his mom probably didn't leave his dad for mine and obviously adores him more than my parents do me. "Lucky you." I snap snidely.

He chuckles darkly while he stands. "Yeah, I'm so fucking lucky." He bites out. "A dead dad and the girl of my dreams is my fucking sister." His nose wrinkles in disgust. I frown. "You're one to talk. Traipsing around town with no responsibility. You're the lucky one."

Was he really trying to compare scars right now? Pissed beyond belief at the nerve of him berating me in my own room in the middle of the night, I spring from the bed, marching toward him until we're toe to toe.

"I don't know who the fuck you think I am, but let me give you a word of advice," His shoulders tighten as he stares me down, locking his equally furious eyes on mine. "You don't know me.

SELF-INFLICTED

For your information, I am meticulously responsible. I liked you up until you marched in here and started acting like a prick. I still thought we could at least be friends." His jaw tightens. "I shouldn't have said you were lucky, I'm sorry for that. I don't know you either, but if you're going to treat me like shit all over a stupid mistake then you can go fuck yourself."

His brows inch up his forehead as he gapes at me. I cross my arms over my chest, standing my ground. I won't allow him to think he can walk all over me. I refuse to cower to his shitty behavior. My eyes drift to his lips as he runs his tongue along the bottom one. The sight of the barbell makes my stomach erupt in butterflies. Lowering my arms to my sides, I release a heavy sigh.

"This is stup-" before I can finish the sentence, Remington grabs my face, kissing me fiercely.

My lips part in a gasp and he uses the moment to brush his tongue against my upper lip, immediately washing away the anger and transforming it into a different kind of fire. Flames ignite my veins when he draws my bottom lip between his teeth, forcing me back until I run into the wall by the nightstand. His hands move to my hips before tugging me against him. I wrap my arms around his shoulders, whimpering when I feel his hard length as he grips my ass roughly, pressing into me. All too soon, he withdraws just as quickly as he started. I'm left with a racing heart and empty lungs.

He loosens a shaky breath before heading for the door. Before he leaves, he glances at me over his shoulder with a sly smirk forming on his lips. "Thanks for giving me something to think about while I go fuck myself."

I blink at the now closed door, wishing like hell that I never met Remington Paulson.

CHAPTER THREE

The following morning, I find myself in a terrible mood. I don't get enough sleep and wake up later than I planned. I have this constant urge to impress my father. To prove that I'm okay despite staying with my mom. I feel like he'll think I'm lazy or something if I'm not up with the sun like he typically is. I value what he thinks of me even if I am mad at him. After getting dressed, I brush my teeth and toss my hair up in a ponytail before heading downstairs. I really hope Remington isn't around. I don't want to face him yet. Not when the lingering feelings from last night are still warring in my mind. I'm contemplating whether I want to slap him for kissing me or convince him to sneak away. I hate that my mind isn't on the same page as my body when it comes to him.

I hear his voice when I step off the bottom stair, turning to enter the living room. He's sitting on the couch in those same shorts as last night, although this time he's wearing a shirt which I'm grateful for. The less I see of his nice body, the better. Being distracted by his tan stomach and tattoos is the last thing I need right now.

"You're going and that's final. You can hang out at Connor's after Layla leaves." Bridget says. She's standing near the kitchen island with a mug of coffee in her hands.

"This is fucking stupid." His eyes lock onto me as I approach the island. I quickly glance away.

SELF-INFLICTED

"Good morning, Layla." Bridget greets in a warm voice. "There's coffee in the pot if you're interested."

"Thank you." After his behavior last night, I decide Rem needs to be knocked down a peg. He had no right to kiss me the way he did then leave me hanging. "I do hope you'll join us, *Elijah*. I'm looking forward to getting to know you better." I say in my sweetest voice as I flick my gaze to his.

I have no idea what Bridget has planned for the day but I'll side with her over him if it irritates him. He glares at me from the couch, folding his arms over his chest. Bridget pats my shoulder as I pass by her toward the coffee.

"See? Go get dressed." Rem groans in frustration. I don't even try to hide my victorious smile. "I'm sorry about that." Bridget says after he heads up to his room.

Grabbing a mug hanging under the cabinet, I say, "It's okay. I'm sure no nineteen year old guy wants to spend the day with family." No eighteen year old girl does either, but I'm not going to tell her that.

"I thought it would be good for him to meet you. He has a friend from music camp and seems to be adjusting well, yet I still worry about him." My chest tightens.

He'd mentioned his father was dead last night. Had that happened recently? After pouring my coffee, I turn around to face her. Bridget must be hurting too if she lost her husband. I feel sorry for both of them.

"He's in a new town which I imagine is probably uncomfortable after years of growing up somewhere else." I'm just being nice but selfishly I would like to understand him more. Even if he is kind of an asshole. "I'm sure he'll be fine."

"Yeah, you're right. It's just that since his father passed away he's been different." She releases a sigh. "I'm sorry. I shouldn't be laying my problems at your feet. Not when you have your own." My shoulders tense. "It can't be easy living with your mother when she's rarely home for you."

I'm sure my dad told Bridget all about what a trainwreck my mom is. Hearing her admit to it though is a slap in the face. "I'm barely home anymore anyway." I lie. "Do you have creamer?"

She grabs some from the refrigerator for me before excusing herself while taking her coffee upstairs. Frustration and sadness creep in as I stare out the kitchen window at the abundance of lush flowers surrounding the pool in the backyard. To know others are aware of my mother's crappy behavior toward me hurts. I don't want people to think I'm some broken doll that needs fixing.

Remington's voice startles me. "You okay?" he asks, sliding past me to the coffee maker.

I tamp down the emotions before turning to face him. "Never better." I say in a cheery voice.

"Thanks for screwing me over by the way." He pours his coffee, pinning me with a dark look. "You don't want to do this shit any more than I do."

I take a sip of my coffee. "Exactly. Which is why you're suffering alongside me, pal."

His brows raise. "You're feisty."

My lips tip up in a smile. "You have no idea."

"I think I have some idea." He takes a drink of his own coffee.

My skin flushes as he eyes me over the rim of the mug, tracking from my head to my bare feet. He sets the mug down before moving closer to me. My pulse races in anticipation. God, it's like I can't control myself around him.

He lowers his head, placing his lips at my ear. A shiver snakes down my spine. "I'm going to make you pay for fucking with me." He whispers before backing up.

SELF-INFLICTED

I shoot him a glare, crossing my arms over my chest. "Are you going to be pissed off the entire time I'm here?" His shoulder lifts in a slight shrug, irritating me. "God, you're such a dick, *Elijah*."

Fuck him and his rude behavior. He's hot one minute then cold the next. I hate it. I don't need to deal with this. As I move to walk away, he grabs my wrist, stopping me. I glare up at him.

"Don't. Fucking. Call. Me. That." He seethes. A flash of pain shows for the briefest moment in his eyes before they narrow down at me. "This is your only warning."

"Why not?"

He releases my wrist, stepping closer to me until his bare feet brush against mine. "Because I said so." His eyes dart across my face.

"You're not the boss of me."

He chuckles as a slow smirk spreads across his lips causing butterflies to swarm in my belly. *Damn him.* His voice drops lower, "Stop lying to yourself, Bug. I own you now."

My shoulder's tighten as I immediately step back. His arms dart out, grabbing me by my hips, forcing me closer to him. His right hand slides up my body until it rests against my cheek, a thrilling heat consuming me. My gaze frantically searches the living room, fearing Bridget will come back.

"Coward." Remington murmurs before releasing me and taking his coffee upstairs.

What the hell is he thinking by touching me that way when our parents are inside the house? We could have been caught. How dare he insinuate that he owns me. I might be distracted by my attraction to him, but there's no way he'll ever control me. In fact, I'll go out of my way to prove just how wrong he is. When Remington comes back downstairs, followed by Bridget, he's wearing a pair of hot pink swim trunks. My father comes down a moment later, stopping just inside the living room. He gazes at each of us with a disappointed look on his face.

For a brief moment, I wonder if Rem and I have been caught, but then he says, "I have some bad news. One of my client's needs council. It's an emergency. We'll have to reschedule the lake day." Lake day? Thank God it was canceled.

I try to sound disappointed when I respond with a "Bummer."

"I'm sorry, Layla bug. You're welcome to spend the day here if you'd like."

"She was just mentioning how much she's looking forward to getting to know me." Rem says.

Dad smiles. "That's great!"

"Yeah, great," I mutter, flipping off Rem covertly. He chuckles. "I should probably head home to prepare for my week though. I have to work tomorrow."

"Okay. Well maybe we can do something next weekend." There's hope in dad's voice.

"Maybe. I might be busy." I'm not hanging out with Remington anymore if I can help it. Besides, I don't feel like I fit in here. Bridget is nice to me, but clearly has a poor opinion of my mother which is kind of a reflection of me. "I'll text you this week to let you know."

I quickly make my way to my room, tossing my clothes from yesterday back in my duffle bag. I give dad a quick hug and say goodbye to Bridget before sprinting to my car and getting the hell out of there.

SELF-INFLICTED

After I get off work on Monday afternoon, I meet Aly at the food court in the mall so we can each grab a coffee before shopping. I tell her about staying at my dad's and what went down with my mom. I'd go crazy without her endless insight. I leave Remington out of the conversation intentionally because I have no idea if I'm ready to share about it yet. I haven't heard from him since I left their house on Sunday morning, which is probably for the best. Then she springs a question on me that nearly makes me choke on my coconut, caramel cold brew.

"Care to tell me why Remington hates your guts now?"

"Where did you hear that?" I try to lie. She lifts a brow as realization smacks me in the face. "Tyler tells you *everything*, doesn't he?"

She shrugs, taking a drink of her vanilla latte. "Yes, he does. Rem was in a tizzy at practice yesterday according to Ty. He said he was bitching about you."

Huffing out a breath, I roll my eyes. Well there goes keeping things under wraps. We enter a shop and I head for the shirts. I'd like to get a few more plain ones to wear to work.

"Does Tyler know why he's mad at me?" I start browsing through the rack, not wanting to fuel anything until I know what she knows.

"I don't think so. He said something must have happened between you two because Rem was in a foul mood. When Ty asked him what his problem was, he said, 'Layla fucking Barlow'."

How sweet. I head for a row of shelves that have an array of different colored denim shorts. I hold up a pair of faded blue ones to my body, scowling. "Jesus, everything is so short." Putting them back, I grab a pair of black ones, doing the same. "Seriously, it's like the fashion industry wants a wardrobe malfunction."

"You're deflecting." Aly says, snatching the shorts from me, tossing them back on the shelf.

I refold the shorts, ensuring they're stacked properly. "Listen, it's not something I really want to talk about." I admit, shifting my gaze to her. Lowering my voice, I say, "Something *did* happen."

"What?" she taps her black polished finger against her chin in thought. "Come to think of it, I haven't heard from you since you went to your dad's and at that point you hadn't seen Rem." Her mouth pops open. "You hooked up again, didn't you?" she squeals. I shoot her a glare when I notice a guy walking by us stop to stare. Aly circles her finger in the air. "Mind your business." He raises a brow at her before walking away.

"Can you keep your voice down?" I snarl. "We didn't hook up."

She pouts. "Well, that sucks."

I snort. "No. It doesn't."

She searches my face for a few seconds, cocking her head to the side in thought. "I don't get it, Lay. You were all about Rem that night at Connor's house. We heard how good of a time you two had together." She waggles her eyebrows while a wave of nausea rolls through me.

"You listened?"

"Hey, I was curious."

I really regret agreeing to go to Connor's that night. I should have stayed at my dad's like a good girl, but no – I had to lead with my clit instead of my head. I take another sip of my coffee, trying to decide how to explain things to her.

"Tell me." She demands in a groan.

Inhaling a deep breath, I let the truth come out. "I met Elijah this past weekend. As it turns out, we've already met before. Although I knew him by a different name."

"I don't understand what that has to do with…" she inhales a sharp breath, her eyes widening in shock. "No!"

I nod solemnly. "I had the honor and horror of discovering who *Elijah* really is."

"Layla, please don't tell me what I think you're telling me."

"Unfortunately, I am."

"Ugh!"

My sentiments exactly. While a part of me is glad to share with Aly about this messed up situation, another part of me wishes I could find a way to pretend none of it is true. Now, I'm trapped in a drama bubble that will be a complete mess when it bursts.

I end up trying on a pair of shorts that fit properly, deciding to purchase a few pairs in different colors. We leave the store to head for another because while I enjoy music and writing, I find retail therapy helps too.

"This sucks, Layla. I feel so terrible." Aly says while we browse.

"Why do you feel bad about it?" I don't want her blaming herself for something beyond her control.

"I'm the one who introduced you to him and pushed you to talk to him. It's not like I was quiet about encouraging you to take a ride on his disco stick." I giggle at her choice of words. "I'm serious. This is just awful."

"I'd be able to move past it a lot easier if he wasn't being such an asshole to me now. I stupidly thought maybe we could still be friends."

"What did he say when you guys found out?"

"Nothing really," I reply. "He kissed me," Her eyes widen. "then he said he was going to go fuck himself."

"What in the hell does that mean?"

"I guess he's choosing to treat me like crap for something beyond my control."

"That's ridiculous!" she snaps angrily. "It's not your fault."

"I know that, but I can't really blame him either. Neither of us knew who we were when we hooked up initially. Maybe he's just as frustrated as I am about it, or maybe the good looks are all a façade and he really is a jerk."

"I'm sorry, Layla."

"I've been doing my best to avoid him as much as possible. Which is relatively easy right now."

Although Hank did mention the new hire starting this weekend. Bridget also brought up Happy's at dinner more than once. I swear if Remington is working with me now, I'm going to rob a bank before boarding a plane and leaving the country.

We end up spending another few hours shopping which helps elevate my mood. By the time we're done I have several new articles of clothing to add to my wardrobe along with a new pair of purple combat boots that I know mom will hate. Which is precisely why I had to have them.

I give Aly a hug before we part ways. "Are you going to be okay?" she asks as we step away from each other.

"I'll be fine." I think I sound confident in my response.

"Do you think he's told the guys?"

"I don't know." I'm hoping not because this is as mortifying as it is frustrating. Panic blooms as I ask, "Are you going to tell Tyler?"

"Not if you don't want me to." She says. "I swear your secret is safe with me. I can't even imagine what you're going through."

"It could be worse." I shrug. It really could be. We could have had sex or fallen in love. It's not like we were dating or anything before finding out. "For now, this stays between us. Unless you hear it from Tyler, don't say anything to him."

"I won't." she assures. "Text me later, okay?"

"You know I will." I say with a smile before heading to my car.

I text my mom to see if she's home because I really want to clear the air between us. For some reason there's always this

SELF-INFLICTED

festering guilt that eats at me after we fight. A part of me worries that I'll lose her for good. It makes me want to keep trying, even though I know she'll never bend.

    Mom is in the kitchen when I get home. She doesn't say anything except, "Hey," while pulling a tray of cookies out of the oven. Setting it on the counter, she picks up a glass of Rosé, taking a sip. I wish our relationship wasn't so one-sided all the time. For once I would love it if she offered an apology. She's never been openly affectionate toward me, so I shouldn't be surprised. Though would it kill her to at least ask about my day or where I've been? I set my bags down on the dining table, heading for the refrigerator to grab a can of soda.

    "What's the occasion?" I ask, glancing at the pile of already baked chocolate chip cookies on a plate.

    She smiles. "Book club. I'm hosting tonight."

    It's my understanding that book club is code for a weeknight get together that involves briefly talking about a book while drinking wine and eating sweets. I'm glad mom has friends to spend time with, even though they usually go until midnight. During the school year it made it difficult for me to sleep. Thankfully, I don't have to work until tomorrow afternoon.

    "That's cool." I tap the top of the soda can.

    "What's with the shopping bags?"

    I lean back against the island countertop, popping the tab. I take a quick sip before setting it down. "Just a little retail therapy with Aly."

    Her brow creases as those pale blue eyes focus on me. "Did your dad give you money?"

    "No. I got paid on Friday."

    She purses her lips before taking another sip of her drink. "Right. Shouldn't you be looking for something a little more…permanent?"

    "I like my job."

Mom gives me a slow once over. "I bet the customers like you there too."

My nose wrinkles. "What's that supposed to mean?"

She glances down at her hand, inspecting her manicure. "I know how men are, Layla. Flaunt a little cleavage and you're rolling in the tips. I think it's time you find something less trashy."

My mouth pops open as I blink at her, stunned. "For your information, I only waitress on occasion." I seethe. "Besides, I'm an adult now."

She shrugs, turning away toward the stove to add the fresh cookies to another plate. "Maybe I should start charging you rent. Tiffany's daughter is attending Summer classes to prep for the Fall. You could do the same."

I made a promise to myself to let the next two months be for me since the rest of my life will be over when September comes. I'm not backing down on that.

"I've been working my ass off the last year and stepping up when others wouldn't. Excuse me for wanting a few months of freedom before throwing myself into your stupid dreams." I clench my hands into fists at my side. "God! Why can't you just be happy for me for once?"

"Working part time at a shabby bar isn't that great of an accomplishment." She mutters, giving me a tight smile. "How was your weekend by the way?"

I roll my eyes. "It was fine." This obviously isn't her first glass since she can't seem to stay on topic.

"Is she fat? Ugly?" she quickly asks.

The rage that's been festering within suddenly explodes. "What is your problem?!" I demand. "Every time we talk, the conversation somehow turns into being about dad. I'm sick of it!"

"Don't yell at me, Layla!" she shouts. "You know what? I'm getting sick and tired of dealing with your shitty attitude in this

SELF-INFLICTED

house. Maybe you should go live with *him* if you think it's so terrible here."

Tears sting my eyes. "For your information," I say around the lump in my throat. "I want to be with you."

She scoffs. "Well I don't need you." The words sting. "Chad wants to move in anyway."

My heart falls to my stomach. "What?"

"My boyfriend. I told him he could move in."

Was she serious right now?

"This is bullshit!"

She crosses her arms over the pink cashmere sweater she's wearing. "I'm sorry you feel that way. However, it is *my* house. I want him here."

"What if I'm not comfortable with that?"

She rolls her eyes. "That's not my problem."

I can no longer speak through the anger roiling inside me. Grabbing my bags from the table, I stalk off to my room. Why does she have to be so mean to me? Can't she see that she's hurting me? Part of me is tempted to reach out to my dad to see if I can stay with him, but I'd just be acting out of anger. Besides, the last person I want to know about my fucked up relationship with my mother is Remington. Knowing how much of a jerk he can be, I'm worried he'll somehow use that against me to make my life even more miserable.

Instead, I put away my new clothes while blaring my favorite playlist. I spend the night in my room while drowning out the sounds of forced laughter and conversation that's phonier than the fake tits on my mom's chest.

CHAPTER FOUR

My life couldn't be going more off the rails at the moment. I can't stop thinking about the argument with my mom earlier this week. Add that to seeing Remington Paulson's stupid face tonight at work and I'm ready to skip town, change my name and start a new life. He's currently training for a part-time position with our lead bartender, Patrick. I'm doing my best to ignore him while I wait tables tonight which isn't easy. Unfortunately, taking orders for drinks from patrons puts me directly in his path.

"I need two IPA's and a whisky seven." I tell Patrick across the bar.

He beckons Rem, who's holding a glass in his hand, half filled with orange juice to come over. "Take her order and get her the drinks. It's an easy one." He says, taking the glass from him.

Rem glances at me expectantly, his brown eyes sparkling under the dim bar lights. I wish the butterflies in my stomach would wither and die already. "What can I do for you, Bug?"

I hate that he calls me that. I don't know if it's a play on the nickname my dad calls me or something else entirely. It frustrates the hell out of me. "Stop calling me that." I snap.

He quirks a brow. "No."

Groaning, I sigh. "I hate you."

His lips tilt up in a slow grin. "I doubt that very much." I'm about to argue when he cuts me off. "You should probably tell me what your customers need or they won't tip you."

SELF-INFLICTED

I narrow my eyes at him. "Give me two IPA's and a whiskey seven."

He shakes his head. "Are you going to say please?"

I blink at him slowly. Is he really testing my patience right now? "Give me. Two IPA's. And a whiskey seven." I ground out.

He chuckles. "Come on Bug, ask me nicely."

"You're pissing me off."

His face turns serious, eyes darkening as he gives me a slow perusal from my hair, which is tied up in a ponytail, to my chest which happens to be accentuated nicely tonight with my waitressing t-shirt. "Same."

I feel my cheeks warm under his scrutiny. I don't have time for his games tonight so I do my best to pivot my attitude. Smiling sweetly, I lean forward until our faces are inches apart. His throat rolls in a swallow.

"Remington?" I ask nicely. "Will you please make me a whiskey seven and get me two IPA's?"

My heart squeezes in my chest when he leans in, the scent of cinnamon permeating. His scent is a fucking drug. "Sure thing, gorgeous."

My eyes drift close, lost in him. I hear him inhale soundly, my eyes opening to see him backing away from the bar to begin making the drinks. I clutch the edge of the granite bar top, releasing a shaky breath. I don't know which bothers me more, when he's being a jerk or being incredibly nice to me.

For the next few hours I do my best to be cordial to Remington so he doesn't pester me for kindness when he takes my orders. The fact that everyone, including Hank, the boss, seems to like him annoys me. He'll probably be working here for a while. By the end of the night, I'm exhausted from being on my feet though fifty dollars richer thanks to some generous tips. After wiping down tables and putting chairs up, I make my way down the narrow hall behind the bar to the employee room.

"You're still here," I say, finding Remington standing near the lockers. He doesn't respond. Instead, he grabs me by the waist, guiding me further into the room before kicking the door closed with his booted foot. "What are you doing?" I gasp.

"Shut up." He growls before smashing his lips to mine.

My body instantly reacts to his kiss. Before I know it, I'm winding my arms around his shoulders, giving in to the instincts he elicits when that barbell contacts my tongue. I grip his hair, letting my head fall back as he devours my throat, nibbling on the skin. He backs me into the door, gripping my thigh to force my leg up until it curves over his hip. The moment I feel his hard length against my center, a moan escapes. He captures my lips once again, grinding into me.

Thankfully, common sense creeps its way to the forefront of my mind. I shove him back as he pins me with a harsh look, his chest heaving. I press my hand to my mouth, my fingers trembling against the swollen skin. Placing his hands on his hips, he shakes his head.

"God dammit, I can't stop wanting you." He admits in a gruff voice.

I lower my hand. "You have a strange way of showing it." I snap. His face falls. "One minute you're being a complete asshole and the next you're making out with me."

His jaw muscle ticks. I'm not the one unable to control myself. Even if there are times it feels like trying not to breathe. I reach behind me, grabbing the door handle.

"You can't do this here." I say. "Or at all. This has to stop. I don't care anymore if you treat me like shit because you're mad at yourself."

Shoving a hand through his hair, his chest rumbles in a low growl. "I hate you for making me feel things I'm not supposed to." My brow crumples as a sharp pain slices through my chest.

He has feelings?

He steps forward toward the door. "Move. I've got to get out of here."

I don't know what comes over me then. Maybe I'm tired of him building me up just to let me fall. We can't keep going rounds like this. It's bad enough that we've been forced together during work now too. That mixed with the conflicting emotions he has along with my morbid curiosity is a recipe for disaster.

"This hot and cold shit needs to end."

He huffs out a short laugh. "You tell me when you find a solution for that." His gaze sharpens. "Move."

"No." I say. "What do you want, *Elijah*?"

He groans in frustration, angling his face closer to mine. "I told you not to call me that."

"What are you going to do about it?"

His jaw ticks. "Do not press me, *Bug*."

I scoff. "Do you want to hit me? Call me names?" I don't know why I'm goading him. I've just had enough of his shit and if we don't nip this in the bud now, I'll spend the rest of my days walking on eggshells.

He lifts his hand suddenly, wrapping his long fingers around the base of my throat. A current sweeps through me when he glides his thumb along the skin of my neck. The pressure he's applying is minimal, yet that doesn't stop my heart from racing frantically or the ache that settles between my legs. Something is wrong with me to be turned on by this. His lips hover over mine. I can feel his breath against my lips.

"I want to fuck your mouth to shut you up." He whispers in a gruff voice. His tongue flicks against my upper lip, making me whimper. "You want this dance to stop?" He releases my neck before taking a step back. "Get on your knees."

The fact that I'm equal parts offended and aroused makes my legs tremble as I gape at him. At a loss for words, I reach for the door handle again, stepping forward to yank it open before he brushes out of the room. My head spins when I hear him chuckling as he departs. What the holy hell was that all about?

I head for my locker on still unsteady legs, my fingers fumbling along the combination lock. It takes me several tries before I get the damn thing open and grab my bag, slinging it over my shoulder. The nerve of Remington thinking he can continue toying with me. What's worse is the way I can't seem to control myself in his presence. Every time he looks at me, I'm lost in his mysterious brown eyes with the urge to run my fingers through his messy dark hair.

SELF-INFLICTED

The following day at work is easier thanks to Hank taking me under his wing for the day, allowing me to help him prepare the venue for a show that night. Rem stays busy in the bar. Other than a quick glance at him when grabbing a soda from Patrick, we don't engage with each other. My shift ends earlier than his so I can leave without incident. That's how the rest of the week plays out to my delight. Me working in areas at Happy's that don't put me near the man that irritates me.

I should have known my optimism would be shattered eventually when I walk into the house on Thursday night. It isn't so much what mom says, but the sight of her new boyfriend, Chad sitting comfortably on our sofa while drinking a beer with her. I'm not in the mood to argue even though the urge to explode on her is strong. I know I'll lose.

"He's staying." Her tone is blunt, her face a mask of annoyance when I roll my eyes.

I silently march to my room instead of screaming. I need to get out of this damn house desperately! The thought occurs to me again that maybe I should go live with dad. I don't want to exist under the same roof as Remington, but at this point, he may be the least destructive poison to pick. Not ready to commit with moving out, I send a text to see what Aly's got going on. I could use a night of venting to my best friend with some junk food. Unfortunately for me, she's hanging out with Tyler at Connor's house. I'd rather not risk being around Remington, so I decline the invite.

I scribble in my notebook for a while then strum on my guitar. When everything else in my life is falling apart, at least I have music.

*

Aly: *Rem's drunk.*
Can you come to Connor's?

I stare at the text on my phone before checking the time. It's nearly two in the morning and up until five minutes ago, I was blissfully lost in a dreamless sleep. Clearly I wasn't sleeping that soundly though because the vibration of my phone woke me immediately. My phone begins shaking in my hand as Aly's name flashes on the screen. Reluctantly, I answer the call.

"He's threatening to leave. We've all been drinking so we can't get him home." She says in a somewhat slurred voice.

I can hear his voice in the background along with Tyler's. "I want to go!"

I release a heavy sigh. "Can't he call an Uber or something?"

"We tried. There's no one available in the area right now."

Rolling my eyes, I grip the phone tightly. "Why me?" I mutter.

Aly chuckles. "Listen, you're the last person I want to call for this, but there's no one else the guys trust."

"That's sad."

"Please, Lay? You know where he lives. Tyler has been trying to convince him to stay and Rem is being stubborn as hell."

That doesn't surprise me. While I don't want to deal with him, I also hate to be the reason he might try driving intoxicated and potentially hurt himself, or worse, someone else.

"I'll come over on one condition."

"What's that?" she asks before I hear her muffled voice say, "Hey. What the hell?"

"Bug, you have to come get me." Remington's voice is gruff.

"Why should I?" I taunt. "You're a dick."

"Yeah, I know. I'm sorry about that."

It would mean a lot more if he was sober. "Are you going to be nice to me?"

"Promise." He vows. "Cross my heart."

SELF-INFLICTED

"Fine. But if you talk to me like you did the other day, I'll punch you in the face."

He chuckles. "Deal."

The line disconnects.

I change into a pair of jeans with a loose tank top with one of my favorite band's logos on it. Leaving in the middle of the night isn't difficult. My mom has always been a heavy sleeper. While it's sad to say, I don't think she cares if I'm home or not. The house is quiet when I leave my room and shoot Aly a quick text to let her know I'm on my way. She sends me the coordinates for Connor's house so I won't get lost. Although I've been there before, she'd been driving and he lives far enough outside town that I have little knowledge of the side streets or turn offs. I'm grateful for the directions because the dark roads in the country are a lot less visible at night. I nearly miss the turn to Connor's house. As I pull into the driveway, I see the garage door open, stunned by the full setup inside.

When I get out of the car I'm met by Aly who has a plastic cup in her hand. I can smell the fruity alcohol when she gives me a one-armed hug. My eyes dart around the garage as we enter. There's two mic stands, sound proof padding on the walls, a keyboard, a drum kit, and a beat up couch where Tyler is sitting next to Remington who is half laying against the armrest with his head tilted back.

"Hey, Layla." Tyler says.

"Hey."

Remington's gaze collides with mine. He grunts softly as he rises from the couch, heading in my direction. Despite his slightly glazed eyes, he seems to be standing upright on his own. Hopefully, he doesn't puke in my car. Surprising me, he wraps his arms around my waist drawing me into a hug that makes my heart skip a beat. I glance around the room at the others. Aly is smiling softly at Remington while both Tyler and Connor look between us curiously.

"Catch you later." Remington mumbles before heading toward the driveway.

"How much did he drink?" I ask, watching him stop in front of the car and tilt his head up to the starry sky.

"I lost count after the seventh beer." Connor says.

"Don't forget the shots of Jaeger." Tyler adds, wrinkling his nose.

I let out a heavy sigh. "Perfect."

Aly gives me another hug. "Call me tomorrow. Maybe we can grab lunch or something."

"Sure."

As I head to the car, I see Remington opening the back door. His shoulders sag before he crawls onto the back seat, laying on his side. I close the door before settling in the driver's seat.

"You better not vomit." I warn as I back out, heading down the dark gravel road.

"You better not…" he inhales a sharp breath. "*Fuck*. Pull over."

I immediately veer to the side of the road, slamming the car in Park. He groans as he sits up, opening the back driver's side door. He manages to hobble to the trunk before spilling whatever he drank all over the overgrown weeds off the road. Grabbing the bottled water I thought to bring, I exit the car to join him.

He braces himself on the lid of the trunk, his head hanging. "Here," I say, shoving the water at him. He drags a hand through his hair before taking it from me. "Sip slowly."

We stand there for a solid ten minutes. Him hydrating while I wonder why I'm doing him a solid when it will probably bite me in the ass later. I gaze out at a field beyond a barbed wire fence. The moon is bright in the sky tonight so I can make out an old barn in the distance and what looks like the silhouettes of cows.

SELF-INFLICTED

Remington inhales a deep breath. I glance over at him to see him standing taller now, the bottle of water nearly empty.

"Better?"

"My head is fucking killing me."

"That's what happens when you drink too much. Oh, I almost forgot..." I open the driver's door to grab the aspirin I'd thought to bring. "Take this." I dump three of the tablets into my palm, holding it out to him.

He lifts a dark brow at me. "Are you a girl scout?" he quickly grabs the aspirin, swallowing it all at once before guzzling the rest of the water.

"What?" I cap the bottle of aspirin, crossing my arms.

"You're so prepared." He walks back around the car, opening the passenger door.

I look at him over the hood. "That's boy scouts." I correct before sliding into my seat. He gets in too. "I wasn't in scouts. My mom drinks a lot."

I toss the aspirin into my purse before grabbing a pack of gum, handing him a piece. He takes it then grabs the pack from me, taking another. He pops two pieces in his mouth, chewing vigorously.

"That sucks." He says as I pull back onto the road. "About your mom, I mean." His voice is sincere.

I stare out at the road, not wanting to see whatever look is on his face. I don't want pity from him. "Yeah."

"Do you take care of her?"

I don't really want to dive into everything with him tonight, maybe not ever. It's bad enough we've shared a level of physical intimacy. Opening up to him about my trauma is a whole other level that won't help our current situation.

"Sometimes." I say simply.

"Is that why you don't live with your dad?"

I reach for the stereo, turning up the volume, letting some alternative rock song fill the cab. Risking a glance at Remington I find him studying my face. After a moment he gives a short nod before staring out the passenger window. The rest of the drive is silent other than the music. I turn off the headlights before pulling into dad's driveway and killing the engine. I stare at the house, looking for any signs of movement. I don't want to risk anything by leaving the car running nor do I want them knowing I'm here.

Remington unbuckles his seatbelt. I rest my hands in my lap, fidgeting with my keyring.

"Did you tell them?" he asks in a low voice.

I turn to meet his eyes. "No." I probably could have called Bridget to pick her son up, but the thought honestly didn't occur to me.

Remington looks genuinely stunned. "Really?"

I lift my shoulder in a slight shrug. "I didn't think you'd want our parents knowing you're wasted. You're not even legal to drink yet."

He rolls his eyes. "I'm not wasted."

"Whatever."

"Thank you. My mom would kick my ass if she knew I was drinking again."

My brow crumples. "Again?"

He's silent for a few beats. "I had a problem a while back. After my dad died I kind of went off the deep end. Drinking, drugs, staying out late and skipping school."

My heart squeezes in my chest. I want to ask him how his father passed away but if I'm not giving up my secrets, I doubt he will either. Besides, the less I know about him the better. The last thing I need is another reason to like Remington Paulson. Knowing there's a heart and soul beneath that inked skin and crass personality won't do me any favors. I decide to ask what I hope is a safer question instead.

SELF-INFLICTED

"Why did you get drunk tonight?"

His eyes fall to the center console before flicking back up to mine. "I was angry."

My heart drops to my stomach. I don't want to be the reason he drinks. "At me?"

"No. Shit, Bug, not you." He answers quickly, running a hand through his hair. "I was mad at myself. I shouldn't have said what I did to you. About getting on your knees. That was fucked up."

I snort. "Yeah it was." While I didn't appreciate his remarks, I wasn't all that offended by them. In fact, the more I thought about what he'd said, the more I fantasized about what it might be like to do that with him. I want to know what he tastes like, what kinds of noises he makes and whether he'd hold my face or grip my hair. Shaking my head, I release a sigh. "I wasn't upset about it. There's no need for you to be either."

His eyes narrow slightly, latching onto mine. We stare at each other for several minutes, the air thickening around us. Suddenly, his nostrils flare as he sits back, resting against the passenger door.

"Still. I'm sorry for being a dick." He glances out toward the house. "I'll try to be better." His gaze slides back to mine. "Friends?"

"Sure." I agree. Even though I don't think it can be that simple.

He sticks his hand out toward me. "I promise I'll try not to think about you in any way other than a sister." I don't want him thinking of me that way. "With any luck whatever is between us will subside."

I nod disjointedly, sliding my palm against his. He clasps his fingers around my hand, warmth spreading up my arm. "Sounds good."

"Great." He mumbles before opening his door. "Sweet dreams, Bug."

The passenger door closes quietly and I stare after him as he unlocks the front door, entering the house. I want more than anything for him to be right. That whatever is between us will go away on its own. The logical part of my brain accepts that it will happen. The reckless part still questions everything.

SELF-INFLICTED

CHAPTER FIVE

I've spent the last two weeks trying to avoid Remington at all costs during work hours while lying to Aly about being busy when she invites me to hang out at Connor's. I like Ty a lot and Connor too, but watching the band practice, which is every free chance they get, goes against my trying to stave off wanting Remington. The only time Aly and Ty don't go to Connor's is when they go out on dates. I'm not about to tag along to those. When I'm not working, I'm spending more time than I want to at home.

"Hey, Layla," Bryant, Hank's nephew, says.

I glance up from the stack of notes I've been typing out, smiling up at him. I'm in Hank's office upstairs doing some administrative work he asked for help with.

"Hey. What's up?"

"Just got done helping with a food delivery. Got any plans for the weekend?"

Bryant's cute with clean cut blond hair and pale blue eyes. "Not so far."

He grins down at me, showing off a set of perfect teeth. "Me either. I'll probably spend the night eating food alone in my apartment while watching Netflix."

"Sounds like my kind of fun."

"Yeah?"

"My life is pretty boring at the moment." I confess.

He grins. "Maybe we should grab dinner together. Tomorrow night?"

My heart beats faster. "You mean a date?" I ask then automatically scold myself. Of course he means a date.

He chuckles again. "Yes. Would you like to go on a date with me?"

"I don't really date." I say. "I mean, I'm not looking for anything serious."

Before I can explain further, Bryant tugs a sticky note off the desk, scribbling on it before passing it to me.

"No worries. That's my cell. Text me later."

I nod lamely as he walks away. Even if I'm not interested in any sort of true relationship, I like the idea of broadening my social horizons. By the end of the day, I'm looking forward to my date with Bryant enough that I text him before driving home to say as much. The best way to get over the irrational emotions I have for my future stepbrother is to focus my sights on someone more attainable anyway.

"This is your first grown up date." Aly says, lounging on my bed while I sit on the floor in front of my full length mirror, applying makeup. "Are you nervous?"

"A little." As if on cue, my stomach twists into knots. "Let's stop calling it a date though. It's a casual dinner." I know I'm kidding myself, however it sounds better in my head. Takes the pressure off a bit.

"Where is he taking you?"

I glide on a translucent lip gloss. "Bella Kitchen."

"Oh, swanky." I glance at her through the mirror, narrowing my eyes as she begins thumbing through my notebook. "Is he picking you up?"

"No." That would make the event seem more serious than I want it to be. I also don't like the idea of being at the mercy of someone else. Setting the lip gloss tube down, I turn to face her. "Quit reading my stuff."

Rolling her eyes, Aly closes the notebook, tossing it to the side. "You've been writing more." A small smile graces her lips.

"I've had a lot on my mind."

"Rem?" she questions. I glare at her. "What's his deal lately, anyway?"

"How should I know? I avoid him as much as possible."

"Tyler said they're thinking of renting a place together."

"I wouldn't know." I smooth the emerald colored sundress I'm wearing, glancing at the clock.

"They might find somewhere with spare room. Ty thinks we should move in."

I frown at her. "You want to move in with him?"

She shrugs, glancing down at the comforter while picking at invisible lint. "My mom would probably freak out even though I'm eighteen."

"That's serious commitment shit." I say, shaking my head in disbelief. I understand that people are entitled to their own judgement, but it seems they're moving too fast. "Are you still planning to go to cosmetology school in the Fall?"

"Of course. I'm already registered."

"Trust me, I know what it's like to want to get out from under your parents." I say. "I support you no matter what, but Aly that's intense." Not that I have any knowledge on what it might be like to live with a different sex.

"Not everyone is predisposed to antitrust like you, Lay." She says. "Listen, I know you have issues with falling in love and all that, but I really like Ty. Even if we don't live together, I believe there's a future with him."

Sighing, I sit next to her, placing a hand on her shoulder. "I love that for you. Honest. I'm sorry for projecting."

She smiles. "Thanks. I don't know if I'm ready to live with him yet because we're still so new. Although, I like that he mentioned it. I also thought it was sweet that he considered you."

"Yeah, there's no way I'd live under the same roof as Remington."

"Man, you really have it bad for him don't you?" Her hands shoot up defensively when I groan in frustration. She lets out a short laugh. "I don't even know if Ty has ran it by Rem yet. It was just a thought."

"I have to leave in twenty minutes." I don't want to talk about Rem anymore.

Aly pops up off the bed before squeezing me tight. "I should get going anyway. You look gorgeous, Layla. Call me later with details." She waggles her eyebrows as I usher her out of my room.

I don't plan on doing anything more than having dinner with Bryant. I'm going to see how the evening goes and let whatever happens organically flow. I'm too nervous to think about more than putting one foot in front of the other right now anyway. I take in my appearance in the full length mirror behind my bedroom door one last time before grabbing the small clutch purse off my dresser. Mom is with Chad in the living room. He's wearing a sharp suit and she's done up with a dress that's way too short in my opinion.

"Where are you off to?" Mom asks as I make my way to the door.

"I'm going out with a friend."

"Don't do anything I wouldn't do." she says with a snicker. *Yeah, right.*

I give her a quick salute before closing the door behind me. Keeping our interactions short has been a lot easier with Chad around.

SELF-INFLICTED

I park my car in the packed parking lot at the restaurant before meeting Bryant at the entrance. He looks good in a pair of dark slacks with a cobalt button down that brings out his eyes. He's cute in a boy-next-door sort of way.

"Looking good, Layla." He smiles down at me, leaning in for a hug.

I wish his arms around me made butterflies spring to life the way they do when someone else holds me. I tamp down the thoughts of comparison immediately. I refuse to think about *him*. Forcing a smile, he tucks my hand in the crook of his arm to lead me into the restaurant.

He's the perfect gentleman, pulling out my chair and allowing me to order first. As our meal progresses though, doubts begin to surface. Dinner with Bryant is nice, albeit a bit dull. The conversation flows easily, yet it's filled with a lot of surface level questions that quickly turn to nothing except his love of sports and old films. Don't get me wrong, I love cinema as much as the next person, however I couldn't care less about the lighting tricks directors use or the secrets and rumors on sets of cult classics. He grew up here with his parents who are still together. He went to a private high school and is attending college in the fall for business in hopes of taking over for his uncle at Happy's.

When he asks me about my plans for the future, I tell him the practiced response. That I'm going to college in hopes of pursuing a law degree. My eyes don't light up the way his do when talking. My voice is almost monotone when chatting about working at my father's practice one day. Once we leave the restaurant, I'm less motivated to keep the date going thanks to hurting my own feelings. So when he offers to take me to a movie, I decline, saying I'm tired. He walks me to my car.

"I had a great time." He says after hugging me again.

I smile because I'm nothing if not polite. Most of the time. "Yeah. Thanks for dinner, it was great."

"Would you want to go out again sometime?"

I swallow, unsure how to respond. I don't want to outright say no or be rude, but there's no chemistry with him. "Maybe. Like I said before, I'm not really looking for anything serious right now."

His lips tip up in a half smile. "That's okay," he slides his palm against my cheek, leaning closer to me. His voice drops lower. "I'm always down for something casual." Before I can stop him, he smashes his lips into mine. Stunned, I pull back, shoving at his chest. He chuckles. "See you around, Layla."

I shake my head as he walks toward his car. "Tool."

Clearly Bryant has the wrong idea about me. While I could easily waste my time with him or any other guy, I'm not sure it's worth the hassle.

I shoot Aly a text.

Me: *Date is over. Lame.*
Aly: *The date or the guy?*
Me: *Both*
Aly: *Do you want to come over?*

It's only eight o'clock and the idea of going home to an empty house sounds miserable. I should be hanging out with my friends instead of sitting in my bedroom, boring myself.

Me: *No Ty tonight?*
Aly: *It's kind of a party*

My heart sinks when I realize she didn't mention it to me earlier. Of course if she invited her boyfriend, the chances of his friends showing up are high. She probably didn't think I'd be interested if Rem was there too. Fuck that, she's my best friend. I'm not competing with him. I'm entitled more than he is to be there anyway since I've known Aly longer. Plus, I had a crappy date, so I want to relax with her. If he doesn't like it, *he* can leave.

Me: *I'll be there soon.*

I can't keep avoiding enjoying myself on account of whatever it is between me and Rem. If he realizes I'm going out of my way to avoid him, he'll know I'm not over him. God! Why can't I get over him?

When I get to Aly's, I let myself into the house, making my way to the living room where I hear voices. Aly is sitting next to Ty on the couch along with a girl from our high school, Jesse, and a guy, Marcus who I think is her boyfriend. Connor and Aly's cousin, Danny, are sitting in folding chairs. They're all around the coffee table playing some sort of card game. When I enter, I see Remington standing in the open concept kitchen. His gaze lands on me, scanning slowly from head to toe.

"Christ." He mutters before making his way back to the living room, taking a seat in the empty armchair.

I frown. That's rude.

"Hottie alert!" Aly calls when she sees me. I laugh as she springs up from the couch to give me a hug. "Want something to drink?"

"Sure." I follow her into the kitchen.

"I'm so glad you came. I wasn't sure if you would want to..." she trails off, glancing toward the living room.

"It's fine." I assure her. "I'm not going to live a life of solitude just because we don't get along."

She hands me a fruity seltzer from the refrigerator before tugging me back toward the coffee table. "My mom is at a conference and won't be back until tomorrow night. We're playing this card game Jesse brought. Want to join?"

"Yeah." I slide in next to her on the couch at the end. Rem is sitting across from me, still staring with those intense eyes.

"Sorry the date was lame." Aly says.

"What date?" Rem asks, his gaze narrowing. I watch his jaw muscle tick.

I roll my eyes. Does he really care?

"She went out with Bryant...something." Aly replies.

He scoffs. "That pretty boy from Happy's?" He cocks his head to the side, peering at me. "Didn't think that was your type, *Bug*."

I scowl at him. "My type is none of your business."

He shrugs slightly, taking a drink of his beer. "Just looking out for you. *Sis*."

My blood warms in anger. "You're being an asshole."

"Come on, be nice." Tyler says before turning his attention to me. "Don't listen to him. You look nice by the way." He shoots me a wink.

I smile. "Thanks."

"She's a stunner." Aly chimes in. "Say something nice, Rem."

He lifts a brow at her while she smiles sweetly. "Fine." He grumbles, focusing his attention on me. "You look amazing." His eyes flick over my body again, that heated gaze comes back full force.

Butterflies spring to life as I take a small sip of the seltzer. "Thanks." I mumble.

We all play the card game which is actually really fun. We each get a certain set of cards to create statements with whatever answer card is drawn. After a few hours, as the game comes to an end, Jesse and Marcus head home. Thankfully, the night stays drama free because Rem doesn't act like a total douche.

"What have you been up to, Layla?" Danny asks, taking a spot on the couch at the other end.

SELF-INFLICTED

"Not a lot." I say. "I've been trying to get more hours at Happy's since it's summer break."

Danny's is a year older than us. I've known him since we were kids. "Are you still writing?"

I smile fondly. "All the time."

"Writing?" Connor asks.

"I write songs and poems and stuff."

"She has notebooks full of them. Do you still have that broken guitar?" Danny chuckles.

"It's just missing a string. It's not broken." I argue through a smile.

That leads to a conversation about music that has the guys telling Danny about the band which they've decided to name Hemingway's Rejects. We all end up watching old music videos on some music channel. As it gets later, Danny decides to head home along with Connor. I only had two of the seltzers, so I'm probably fine to drive, but I'm not so sure I want to go back to an empty house or worse, one where Chad is.

Aly must see the indecision on my face. "You can stay in the guest room tonight if you want, Lay." She knows I haven't been happy with my mom's new boyfriend hanging around.

"Thanks."

She pins Rem with a warning look. "You're not driving home."

He scowls. "I'm not drunk."

"You're not risking it." She says sternly. I can't help giggling at the way she's scolding him.

He sighs. "Whatever."

Tyler releases a loud yawn. "Let's call it a night. We have practice in the morning." He reaches for her hand as they head toward the staircase.

"Where the fuck am I going to sleep?" Rem asks.

"Couch is free." Aly hollers as they make their way upstairs.

Groaning, he sits down on the couch as I'm getting up. I make my way toward the small hall where the downstairs guest bedroom is. "I wasn't joking." He says. I stop.

Glancing at him over my shoulder, I frown. "What are you talking about?"

The barbell in his tongue peeks out before he chews on his bottom lip, pinning me with a sultry stare. "You look really pretty tonight."

My stomach muscles clench from the look he's giving me. One that conveys everything he shouldn't be feeling for me. Swallowing roughly, I shake my head. I can't seem to get enough air in my lungs when he stands, stalking closer to me. His booted feet echo on the hardwood floor. I tense when he lifts his hand, tracing his finger over the thin strap on my shoulder.

"I like this dress." He whispers.

I'm immediately enveloped in the warmth his body emanates and that signature cinnamon smell of his. Lightheaded, I whisper back, "Do you?"

His lips brush my ear. "Definitely."

I should tell him to stop touching me before retreating to the safety of the guestroom. Instead, I follow his line of sight, transfixed by his long fingers trailing along the strap of my dress to the low neckline, forming goosebumps on my skin.

"Remington." My voice is breathy. I'm not sure if I'm asking him to stop or keep going.

He releases a heavy breath, his fingers skimming down the center of my chest before settling on my waist. Everything happens quickly after that. One minute we're standing face to face and the next our eyes are locking while my arms wind around his shoulders as he grips my hips, tugging me against him. My lips crash into his when he lifts me up in his arms, pinning me against the living room

SELF-INFLICTED

wall. The hem of my dress rides up my thighs when I wrap my legs around his waist. The moment I feel his hard length against my center, I'm lost in the way his tongue sweeps against mine, igniting a fire. One of his hands lifts to my face, palming my cheek while the other tentatively slides upward toward my chest, stroking just below my left breast. I feel the prelude to release building as I grind against him. Tearing his lips away from mine, Remington tilts his head back to look me in the eyes.

"You're fucking magic." He whispers, holding me still. I try to move against him again but he stops me. I groan in frustration as a wolfish grin forms on his full lips. "What's the matter, Bug?" He nips at my bottom lip, tugging it between his teeth.

Releasing a shaky breath, I ask, "Why are you stopping?"

He rests his forehead against mine. "Because I know this is wrong." He lowers the hand near my chest to my thigh, inching his fingers under my dress. When his thumb rests against the tight nub, I inhale a sharp breath. He strokes up and down leisurely, teasing me. "You're soaking wet for me when you shouldn't be."

"Yes." I breathe.

"Does it feel good?" he whispers, stroking me through the lace fabric so gently that I feel like I might combust.

"Yes."

He stills suddenly, leaning back. I lift my eyes to his. "Better than whatever that ken doll does?"

My veins turn to ice, stunned by his words. Tears prick my eyes when he chuckles before releasing me. My knees nearly buckle when my feet hit the floor.

"You're an asshole." I choke out. Frustration and anger consuming me. "I hate you!" I cry before cocking my fist back and projecting it forward, landing a blow to his left eye.

I don't stick around to see what kind of damage I inflicted to his pretty face.

CHAPTER SIX

I do my best to keep things professional with Bryant at work when I see him on Monday. Though, I'd kind of like to punch him too after catching me off guard with that kiss on our date. He'd texted me a couple times about getting together again which I politely declined, explaining that I had other plans. Okay, so instead of womaning up and telling the truth, I may have lied a little. I was hoping if I ghosted him enough or evaded his advances, he'd get bored and set his sights elsewhere. By Tuesday afternoon, I knew that plan wouldn't work. He cornered me here in the small break room where I'm trying to enjoy a cold brew and pen some random lyrics in my travel notebook on my break.

"If you're looking for something to do this weekend, I've got tickets to the local baseball game." Bryant sinks into the chair next to me.

I flinch when he attempts to grab my notebook.

Slamming my hand on his, I tug it away, immediately closing it. "Where are your manners?"

His jaw tightens. "What are you writing?"

I cradle the notebook against my chest. "Nothing."

"Okay..." he replies. "So, baseball game on Saturday?"

I shake my head. "I don't think so."

His brow crumples, the rejection evident on his perfectly symmetrical face. I stare at his handsome features and pale blue

SELF-INFLICTED

eyes. Even his dirty blond hair is perfectly styled. He kind of does look like a ken doll.

"I'm sorry." I say quickly. "I'm just not…interested."

He leans into me, uncomfortably close. His lips graze my ear, my stomach turns in an unpleasant way. I pull back from him. "I told you I'm fine with casual." He whispers conspiratorially.

I immediately begin shaking my head, standing. "That's not my style."

He shrugs. "Your loss," tilting his head, he smiles at me. "If you ever change your mind, you have my number."

"Not likely."

"Your uncle's looking for you." I look up to see Rem leaning against the doorframe.

Bryant stands, glancing down at me for a moment before heading out of the break room. I collect my stuff, standing as well. Without saying anything, I place my notebook in my locker and shove past Remington. I don't need him fighting my battles for me. If he's looking for an apology for his eye, he can keep on waiting. I have to admit I feel a little bad about the bruised eye he's rocking on the left side of his face. If I'm being honest though, he looks kind of cool with it. I overheard a few people asking him about it earlier and he played it off as if he didn't get decked by a girl.

A while later, I approach the bar to order a pitcher of beer for a table, seeing Rem free. "I need a pitcher and three glasses, please." I holler over the loud music.

He gives a single nod before moving away to get my order. I place my hands against the edge of the cool granite, waiting patiently. It's warm here tonight with the crowd. I'm grateful I decided to wear a pair of black jean shorts and my Happy's tank top. Suddenly I feel a hand curve around my ass. I stiffen, whirling around.

A clearly drunk guy that looks to be barely legal grins sloppily at me. "What's up, baby? Come here often." He slurs as bile rises in my throat at the stench of too much liquor on his breath.

"Walk away." I demand in a strong voice.

His head tips back as he laughs. "Oh, come on. You here alone?"

"Back off." I say when he steps closer, invading all kinds of personal space.

"Hey!" Remington shouts from behind me capturing the guy's attention. "Step back."

"Fuck you, man. Mind your own business." He scoffs, leaning closer to me until his face is inches from mine.

There's nowhere to run with the bar counter pressing into my back. He reaches up to grab my face when I hear glass shatter behind me and something, no, *someone* jumps over the counter from behind the bar, grabbing a handful of the guy's throat. I gape at Rem holding the man steady while squeezing his fingers into his windpipe, getting in his face.

"I'll break your fucking fingers if you touch her again." He warns in a deadly snarl. Everyone in our vicinity turns to watch the drama unfold. "Do you want that?"

"N-No." the guy chokes out, trying to shake his head, yet failing to do it very well with the death grip on his neck.

"Good. Now, get the fuck out of here. If I see your face again, I'll destroy it. Understand?"

"Y-yes."

Rem shoves him away before facing me. I blink up at him, stunned at what I've just witnessed. "You okay?" he asks, gently placing his hand under my chin and tilting my head side to side.

"I'm fine."

"Damn man, you can fly!" Patrick says in a laugh as he approaches us. "That was amazing."

Rem releases my chin. "He was being a dick."

"I caught that." Patrick says, shifting his gaze to me. "Are you alright, Layla?"

"Yeah." I'm shaken up, but not from the interaction with a drunk patron. I had no idea Rem could be that protective.

Patrick angles his head toward the back. "You two take a ten. I'll get your tables, Layla."

I head for the break area with Rem following behind me. He closes the door after we enter and I sit down in one of the chairs at the small table while he grabs two bottles of water from the mini fridge that Hank keeps stocked. He slides one to me before sitting as well. I unscrew the cap from my water, taking a sip.

"Are you sure you're okay?" Rem asks in a low voice. I glance up to find him studying me closely with concern in his eyes.

"Totally fine." I say. "He grabbed my ass, that was it."

His jaw tightens as a murderous rage fills his eyes. "What?"

I raise a brow at him. "It's not a big deal. He was drunk."

"He touched you without consent." He argues.

"Again, he was drunk."

It pissed me off too, believe me. However, other than feeling violated for a brief moment and entirely angry, there's nothing I can do about it now. He got his threat. With any luck, he'll never show his face here again. I'm not going to hunt him down.

He frowns. "You're sure you're okay?"

My eyes narrow at him. "Why are you so concerned about me?"

"I don't like people that take advantage of others." He says. "You don't deserve that shit. If I wasn't worried about getting fired, I'd probably go outside and bash his head in."

My eyes widen. "Damn. Violent much?"

He scoffs. "When you fuck with my-," he shakes his head. "Never mind." He takes a long tug off his water.

I lean my elbow on the tabletop, propping my head on my hand. "I don't understand you."

"What do you mean?"

"One minute you're making me hate you and the next you're coming to my defense."

His lips tip up slightly. "You don't hate me, Bug."

Rolling my eyes, I say, "Don't be so sure about that."

He chuckles. "You're a good girl. Hate isn't your nature."

If I'm such a good girl, then why do I want to do unbelievably bad things to his body? I point to his face. "Really?"

"You mean, punching me in the face?" he lightly swipes his finger under his eye, wincing. "That fucking hurt by the way."

"Good." I say with a small smile. "I'm not apologizing for that by the way."

His eyes narrow as he scans my face. After a few moments he releases a heavy sigh. "I wish I could promise that I won't piss you off again, but if our short history has taught us anything, it's that we can't get along."

"We could if you didn't mess with me."

He leans toward me, catching me off guard. His breath coasts along my lips as his eyes pin mine. "But it's so much fun."

My breath catches in my throat. "Why?"

His throat rolls in a swallow. "Because you're under my skin and when I saw you with that preppy motherfucker earlier, I wanted to do bad things."

Curiosity gets the best of me. "What kind of bad things?"

His lips slide into a mischievous grin. "The bashing faces kind."

"I'm not yours." I say before taking another sip of my water.

He stands. "Don't make promises you can't keep."

SELF-INFLICTED

He winks at me before walking out of the room. Once again I'm left staring after him, wondering why all common sense goes out the window when he's near.

*

"We're selling the house." It feels as if someone sucker punches me in the stomach.

She's all smiles, gazing up at Chad adoringly. He's looking at me, his arms crossed in a defensive way. There's no kindness in his eyes, no emotion at all. It's obvious he doesn't care for me in any capacity. Neither does my mother if she's pulling the rug out from under me like this.

"Why?" I ask, trying to keep my tone even.

I'm too exhausted to yell at her. I worked a double yesterday to help cover one of the server's shifts and spent the morning helping Hank set up the venue for an anniversary party he'd rented out to for the day.

"It's time to move on." Mom says simply.

"From what?"

She scoffs, shaking her head. "The memories of this place are too much for me, Layla. Besides, Chad has a job offer in Seattle."

"You want to uproot your entire life because of *him*?" I point my finger at Chad. That's when the yelling starts.

"Whatever issues you have, you need to get over!" she screams. "This is *my* house which I don't want anymore."

"You're leaving me!" I shout back, tossing my arms in the air. "Your daughter."

She blinks at me. "Leaving you? You don't care about me and you never did! Chad loves me. He is there for me!"

Dumbstruck, my throat clogs with emotion. "What am I supposed to do?" my voice cracks as a wave of nausea rolls through me.

Mom shrugs. "Stay with your dad for the rest of the summer or come with us."

"I have school here in the Fall!"

"Well the house goes on the market next week."

Tears form as I wrap my arms around my waist, trying to keep myself together in their presence. Sniffling, I turn away from them. I can't move to another state across the country. Why am I always forgotten when my parents make decisions? Inhaling a shaky breath, I swallow the lump in my throat before facing my mother again.

"Do you even care that you're hurting me?"

She rolls her eyes. She might as well have shoved a steak knife in my heart. "What about *my* pain? I will not live in this house any longer."

"You can happily move out if you don't like the rules." Chad interjects.

A murderous rage slips over me.

"Oh, shut up, Chad!" I yell before sprinting off toward my room, slamming the door so hard the walls shake. Maybe I'll do some damage so she doesn't get the most out of the sale.

Before I can lock the door, a force behind it pushes it open and I step back in surprise, raising my hands in front of me as Chad appears. His gray eyes are angry, his face a shade of red. For the first time in my life I feel genuine terror.

"Get out!" he bellows. I flinch when he takes a step toward me. "All you do is sit in this room, eat the food your mother pays for, and socialize with your friends."

"I have a job." I manage to squeak out meekly.

Mom comes in behind him. "A disappointing one." She says, kicking me when I'm down. "Sylvia's daughter is in Europe. Donna's daughter is already engaged to a man who is in Med school. Why can't you be like them?"

SELF-INFLICTED

Pain slices through my chest as my heart breaks into pieces. Is that what she really thinks of me? I'll never be good enough no matter how hard I try. Chad huffs out a breath before walking away. I can't control my tears any longer.

"Why don't you go stay with your dad for the night. I'm sick of this." Mom says before leaving as well, closing the door behind her.

I crumple to the floor, pulling my knees to my chest while burying my head as I sob uncontrollably. I didn't ask to be born to her or my father. Am I really such a bad daughter for wanting to pave my own way? Life isn't about the best colleges or what sounds good on social media. It's about the moments you feel alive, the time you spend doing what you love. Here I am breaking myself for the sake of pleasing her, pleasing *them*, and I'm still failing. What's the point anymore?

After my tears dry, I take myself up off the floor to start packing my duffle bag with every piece of clothing I can fit in it. I heave it over my shoulder, grabbing my phone and keys before making my way down the hall toward the front door. I have no idea where I'm going yet. All I know is that I can't stay here. I'll drown if I do.

"It's just so hard. He's poisoned her, I know it." Mom cries into Chad's chest in the living room. I roll my eyes as I slip past them, not bothering to look back before closing the door.

When I start my car, my brain goes on autopilot. I'm not sure what I'm doing until I turn down the familiar suburban street with large, impeccable houses and manicured lawns. I would have gone to Aly's if she hadn't already told me she'd be out of town this week with her mom. I didn't call or text beforehand which I'm regretting now because it's nearly dinner time. I hope I'm not interrupting their evening. I didn't know where else to go.

Grabbing my bag, I walk up to the front porch, standing in front of the door, staring at the doorbell. Do I ring it or walk on in?

As my anger and sorrow dissipate, embarrassment floods me. I shouldn't be here. I start to turn away when the door suddenly swings open. Remington stands before me with his eyes narrowed.

Great. I get to deal with his shit now too?

He catches me off guard when he steps forward, bending his head to look me in the eye. "Who did this?" his voice is soft yet there's a hint of fury in his tone.

Another lump forms in my throat. I can't tell him about my mom. What if he agrees that I'm a disappointment?

"Elijah, what are you…Layla?" Bridget steps around him. "What's wrong, honey?"

That's when the waterworks come back full force. I break down right there on their front porch, my duffle bag slipping form my shoulder to the ground. Bridget wraps her arms around me in a hug that does nothing to quell the pain running through me. She smells like berries. I hate that her comforting me feels like taking a long drink of water after being in a drought. I hate that she soothes me with soft whispers, telling me it's okay and that she's here for me. I hate that I cling to her desperately, wishing my mother had ever hugged me or told me she loved me. Wishing I could remember the last time she had.

"I'm sorry." I choke out in a sob. "I'm s-s-sorry." I don't know what I'm apologizing for, but it's all I can think to say right now.

"You're okay, Layla. Come here," she says softly, keeping an arm wrapped around my shoulder as she guides me into the house.

We sit on the couch in the living room while I wipe my watery eyes, wishing I could make the tears stop. Bridget leans sideways to the end table by the couch, producing a handful of tissues that she passes to me.

"Thanks." I mumble, dabbing at my eyes.

SELF-INFLICTED

I probably look like a giant snot monster right now. This will surely change Remington's mind about me though I don't care. At the moment I want comfort that surprisingly, I'm finding in my soon to be stepmom. She rubs my back as she sits with me until I begin to calm down. Little by little, my eyes dry out, my breath becoming less labored.

I glance up to see Remington watching me near the edge of the living room. His face is unreadable, his eyes glued on me. When I meet his gaze his brow crumples and he looks away quickly, stalking off toward the stairs.

"Would you like something to drink?" Bridget asks.

I swallow, my throat raw. Nodding, I say, "Please."

She gives me a small smile before making her way to the kitchen. "I can make some tea."

I smile back. "Sure. Thank you."

She fills a tea kettle then places it on the stove, before grabbing two mugs from the cupboard and adding a teabag to each one. "I'm sure whatever happened caused you a great deal of pain." She says, turning to look at me over the kitchen island. "Would you like to talk about it?"

I'm not certain she's someone I should confide in about this. "Where's dad?"

"He's working late tonight." She glances at the clock. "He should be home in an hour."

What could I even say to dad that wouldn't turn into him complaining about mom and further upsetting me? Releasing a heavy breath, I decide it doesn't much matter who I talk to. I just need someone.

"My mom is selling the house to move with her boyfriend to Seattle." I close my eyes, trying to keep my composure. I don't want to cry anymore. "We got into a fight and they told me to get out."

Bridget's lips turn down, her eyes full of pity that makes me feel shittier. "I'm so sorry."

"She said I was a disappointment."

"You know that's not true, right? You're a good kid from what Elijah tells me." Has he really said that? "Your father said you averaged a three point nine GPA this last year. I know it's none of my business, but can I offer you a piece of advice?"

I'll take any help I can get at this point. "Yes."

"When Elijah's father and I separated, it wasn't easy. Granted it was under different circumstances. Your mother has an addiction, Layla. I know you know that."

"I do."

"She's lost your father. She's hurting and probably worried about a future she didn't plan along with a life she didn't expect. You're the closest thing to her which unfortunately makes her frustration and anger misplaced."

"That doesn't give her the right to treat me the way she does." I say defensively.

Bridget smiles. "I didn't say it did. What I'm saying is that you're forced to bear the weight of your parents' decisions which aren't fair to you. She has no right to treat you poorly regardless of the situation. My advice is to not let her words or actions get the best of you."

That seems easier said than done in the moment. "She's my *mother*." I say. "If she doesn't love me, who else will?"

"Me and your father do." She answers automatically. My shoulders tense. The tea kettle begins whistling so she turns away to tend to it. "You're welcome to stay here as long as you need." She says while pouring the steaming water into each mug.

Getting up from the couch, I slide onto one of the barstools at the island. She sets a mug in front of me. "Thank you. Not just for the tea, but for being here."

SELF-INFLICTED

"Of course," she sips her tea. "You know, Elijah had a rough relationship with his father when we first divorced. Maybe you can talk to him about it."

"He did?"

She nods, glancing toward the entryway of the living room briefly. I almost look back myself. However, if he's standing there again I'm not sure what I'll do. I hate to think he's listening to me complain about my life.

"He blamed him for the divorce and harbored a lot of animosity for several months."

"Why did you two separate?" I ask, unsure if the question is appropriate.

"He was a dreamer with a million goals. A nomad at heart. I loved the man, but I'm more of a realist." She chuckles, shaking her head. "Eli had a way of convincing me to follow him around the country. When we landed in California, I just couldn't handle the lifestyle anymore."

"Lifestyle?" Wait. Did she say Remington's dad was named *Eli*?

Bridget sighs. "He was the manager for a relatively famous band so his job required him to travel frequently. Once Elijah entered middle school, I decided he needed roots. I didn't want him getting an education on the road or moving around to different schools."

I wonder if that's where Rem's desire to make music comes from. If he'd grown up around musicians his whole life, he probably got a taste of the rockstar lifestyle.

"How did he pass?" I ask, suddenly curious for more information.

Her face falls slightly before taking another sip of tea. "His busy lifestyle got the best of him. Managing a band can be hectic. He died of a heart attack just over a year ago."

Melissa K. Morgan

    I can't imagine losing a parent or dealing with the emotions that come with it. Talking with Bridget is less difficult than I thought it would be. As the minutes pass, I discover she's actually a genuine and thoughtful person. She doesn't have to comfort me or listen to my problems, yet she does, seeming happy to do so. How vastly different from what I've been used to my whole life.

    By the time my father comes home, I'm doing better. He offers, as Bridget did, to let me stay as long as I'd like. I decide to take them up on it. Perhaps I need some space from mom for a while. I can't help thinking about Remington's father and what Bridget told me. I would hate for something to happen to her before we can repair our relationship. I'm glad he was able to find a way to be close with his dad before he passed, but I'm not sure at the moment where me and my mom stand. With any luck, she'll come to her senses and realize I'm not a bad daughter. Although lately, It seems to be proven that luck isn't on my side.

CHAPTER SEVEN

With each step I take along the concrete path toward the front door, my stomach twists tighter. Three days ago I left my childhood home, deciding to stay at dad's for good. Yesterday, I called mom to break the news. After her blasé reaction, I know I'm making the correct choice, even if it's breaking my heart. The more I go over it in my head, the more I realize that I'm simply not strong enough to deal with her right now. Not when she's hurting me by her actions and refusing to acknowledge how I might be affected.

Anxiety simmers inside me as I approach the porch. As soon as I place my hand on the knob, the door swings open, my mother standing before us as if she's been watching out the window. I would have preferred to come alone, but after the incident with Chad forcing into my room, which I let slip to Bridget, they felt more comfortable having someone with me. My father would have come himself if he wasn't busy with a case at work. Plus, Remington happens to have a truck so it's easier for me to load everything in one trip.

Mom's hair is styled perfectly straight, her lip gloss fresh and her lashes as fake as the gold bracelet I ordered off some third-party website last year. She barely gives me eye contact before her gaze settles on Remington beside me.

"Well, hello there." She beams at him. "I wasn't aware Layla made a new friend."

"This is Remington. Bridget's son." I say, sliding past her into the house.

"Oh." Her voice drops. "What a shame." I roll my eyes as I head for my room while he follows behind me. "I probably should have told you..." my mom begins when I reach the end of the hall, opening my bedroom door.

The air ceases in my lungs. My room is nothing at all how I last left it. All of my notebooks are haphazardly strewn across the bare mattress of my bed along with my guitar. My closet door is open to reveal an empty space. Three boxes are stacked up and sealed against the wall with the words "Layla Clothes" scrawled across the sides. Anger replaces the anxiety. I screw my eyes shut tightly, praying I don't lose my shit in front of Remington. It's bad enough he knows the cliff notes of what transpired the other night.

Turning around slowly, I avoid looking at him, zeroing in on my mother. "What did you do to my room?" I ask in the calmest voice I can muster.

She gives me a tight-lipped smile. "We figured we'd get a head start on clearing things out. Chad and I-"

My spine stiffens. "You let him go through my things?!"

"Please," she rolls her eyes. If we didn't have company, I'd probably throw a full on tantrum. "We just started packing you. Nobody read your notebooks or raided your panty drawer. I also cleared the junk from your desk."

"For your information, everything in my desk was meant to be saved. I had notes in there with lyrics and-"

My mom starts laughing. It takes everything in me not to slap the smug look off her face when she turns her attention to Remington. "My Layla is a bit of a dreamer. Instead of striving for a *real* job, she thinks she'll make money creatively."

Remington's brow creases. There's a tightness in his jaw that I recognize as annoyance. *Great*. She's managed to offend him within our first few minutes here. I wouldn't be surprised if he left me to figure out how to move my stuff on my own.

"You had no right to go through my room. I told you I was coming to get everything." I say.

She shrugs. "Well, we want to get the house on the market as soon as possible. I wasn't going to sit around waiting for you." There's a spiteful tone in her words which I know has everything to do with the fact that I'm choosing dad.

Releasing a sigh, I decide not to argue further. There's no use trying to out snark the snark expert that is my own mother. Shifting my gaze to Remington, I say, "This should be quicker than I thought." Before grabbing one of the boxes of clothes.

He picks one up too, mom stepping aside to let us pass before disappearing to another part of the house. I hear her talking to Chad when we come back in to grab more of my stuff. He better not say a damn thing to me or I'll punch him too. Once the boxes of clothes are loaded, I place my guitar in the truck, then begin sorting what my mom left of the contents of my desk while Remington stacks my notebooks neatly on the bed.

"You write a lot?" he asks as I unfold random napkins and paper scraps I'd saved from moments when inspiration struck out of nowhere. At least she didn't toss everything in the trash.

"Yeah."

"These are pretty good, Bug." I glance over my shoulder to see him thumbing through one of my notebooks.

Marching toward him, I rip it from his hands. "Don't read my stuff."

He frowns. "Why not? Isn't the point of writing lyrics to have them heard one day."

"Yes, though in order to do that, you have to have a presence in the industry. You have to know someone who knows someone in order to gain any interest in what you can offer. I don't have that."

He lifts a brow. "You could find that if you tried."

Simmering with annoyance, I toss the notebook on the stack. "Let me ask you something. Does your mom believe in you? Would she move the earth to ensure you have every opportunity available and allow you to chase your dreams like nothing else matters?"

The venom is evident in my voice and when his jaw muscle ticks, I know I've pissed him off. I don't care. The truth is you can't get anywhere in life without the support of those who love you. When it feels as if no one does, you can easily become trapped, even if you think you're good enough.

"You seem to be doing well for yourself at Happy's." He snaps, standing from the bed.

I laugh at the fact that he has no idea what it's like to feel more like a prisoner than a child to your parents. "At the cost of disappointing my parents." I say. "I don't want to be an Ivy league recruit or an Instagram model."

He tilts his head to the side, confusion flashing on his face. "They don't support you?"

"No." Releasing a sigh, I shake my head, running a hand through my hair. "I don't know what my dad thinks anymore." I'm sure he expects me to stick to his plan.

"Maybe you should talk to him about it."

"Listen, I'm sure in your world where there's unconditional love and support, that seems easy. However, that's not the case for me."

He crosses his arms over his chest. "I never said things were easy."

"Anyway," I roll my eyes. "God, everything is an argument with you."

I turn away from him to continue going through the stuff from my desk. I don't care what my dad thinks anyway. I'm not talking to him about it. It's easier to avoid the crushing disappointment I'll surely feel when he rejects my ideas to pursue something other than law.

Remington grabs the stack of notebooks, leaving to put them in the truck. I find an empty shoe box, putting all of my notes and random keepsakes in it. As I'm doing one more final check to ensure I have everything, he comes back into the room, marching toward me. He grabs my wrist, forcing me to look at him while staring down at me for several seconds, not speaking, simply searching my face. I'm so stunned by the sudden behavior that I don't know what to say.

"Nobody will give you what you want." He says in a gruff voice. "Despite your best efforts, there will always be obstacles and excuses keeping you from following your dreams. Don't let them win." He releases me before grabbing the shoe box sitting on my desk.

I stare after him, trying to wrap my mind around the unsolicited pep talk.

Mom enters the room with her arms crossed, eyes scanning what's left which isn't much. "The posters?" I can't tell if it's a genuine question or a dig at the myriad of random rock bands and inspirational quotes.

Sighing heavily, I walk to the wall opposite my bed and carefully peel the tape off the only thing I care to take with me. It's a posterboard with photos of me and Aly through the years with glittery stickers on it. She made it for me for my seventeenth birthday, filling it with our favorite song lyrics and silly quotes about being best friends. Pressing the tape to the back side of the poster, I roll it up.

"You can toss the rest." I say, slipping past her toward the hall.

"So that's it? You're just leaving now?" her tone is snide.

Stopping, I look at her over my shoulder. "Did you need me for something else?" I ask. "Because you made it abundantly clear that you wanted my room clear so you can run off into the sunset with your boyfriend."

Her piercing green eyes narrow at me. "Careful, Layla. Too much time around those people and you'll turn into a snotty bitch like your father's fiancée."

"Nope," Remington growls from the mouth of the hallway. I bite down on my bottom lip as he crosses his arms, pinning my mom with a dark glare. "You can talk shit about people all you want when you're alone in the safety of your stark white walls and bullshit fake succulents," She gasps audibly as I press my lips together to hide a smile. "but in the presence of her son, I'd watch what you say about my mother. *She* didn't choose herself over her child."

Mom gapes at him for a moment before turning a murderous glare at me, her cheeks red with anger.

"How dare you!" she marches up to me, raising her hand. For a moment I think she's going to slap me. She must think better of it, because she lowers her hand, straightening her designer tank top instead. "Your father already has his claws so far in you." She shakes her head. "I said it to him before he left and I'll say it to you too," she leans toward me, dropping her voice filled with bitterness low. "Get the fuck out and don't ever come back."

It's too difficult to think straight with a steady stream of tears and the sharp knife of heartbreak from being rejected by my own mother. I can't bring myself to respond, so I walk away instead. Away from her hostility, away from the house I grew up in, away from the man who I made the mistake of liking before I realized he was off limits. Embarrassment floods me as I leave down the concrete path, to the passenger side of Remington's truck. My fingers tremble as I buckle the seatbelt before resting my head back against the seat, closing my eyes. I don't care that my skin feels like it's on fire from the mid-day sun and rolled up windows. It doesn't matter. Nothing does because Remington is

SELF-INFLICTED

right. Nobody will give me what I want. Not even a mother whose daughter has only craved one thing from her. Love.

When he comes out to the truck, Remington remains silent. After starting the engine, he cranks the stereo before shifting into gear. I keep my eyes trained out the passenger window, facing away from him. I hate that I'm still crying when he parks in the driveway at dad's. I hate that he witnessed the monster that is my mother. That he heard what she said about his mom. He probably thinks I'm weak, that I'm a coward for not standing up to her the way he did. I wish I had the same courage that he does to say something. I always bottle in my retorts, keep my head down, and allow her to walk all over me.

When he opens his door, I don't move. I'm just *exhausted*. Emotionally, physically, and spiritually. Perhaps I made some grave mistake in a past life that I'm now being punished for. Why is everything always so heavy?

"Hey," Remington says, standing outside his truck now. I swipe my hand across my cheek, refusing to look at him. I'm not a pretty crier. "Bug…"

The nickname snaps the last thread I'm holding onto. Whirling my head in his direction, I scream, "Why do you call me that?!" He recoils as if I punched him again. "Seriously, why?" I demand. "Is it because I'm annoying to you? Or maybe you think I look like one? Or is it that you think I'm immature because my dad still calls me that stupid nickname from childhood?" I cut him off before he has a chance to respond. "You know what? I'm sick of everyone picking me apart all the time. If I don't fall in line with their beliefs, their wants, I'm nothing. Well fuck that and fuck them. And especially, fuck you!"

Shoving my door open, I take off sprinting into the house. I hear my dad call out my name as I race upstairs, ignoring him. I'm just as angry at him as I am at my mother. The last thing I want to do is start another fight I can't win. He could have forced me to come with him when he left. He could have stood up to my mother when she treated me like shit. He could have left her a long time ago instead of selfishly waiting until I turned eighteen. I hate him for not once thinking about how the situation would affect me, for not having the decency to ask me.

After closing my bedroom door, I fall face down on the bed. I'm not sure how long it takes before the crying subsides, but I eventually stop. When I do, my mind clears enough to realize that I let my emotions get the best of me. *Again.* I'm ashamed for lashing out at Remington the way I did. For not even having the courtesy to thank him for helping me out. It isn't his fault I'm the product of two people that clearly care more about themselves than their kid. Why am I such a moody bitch?

I scan my face in the mirror behind my door, wiping away the mascara that ran down my cheeks. The end of my nose is still a little red and there's splotchy marks near my mouth from sobbing like a baby. I've been crying entirely too much this week. I'm so fucking over it. Inhaling a deep breath I move away from the mirror to peer out the window when I hear a door close. Remington just shut the passenger door of his truck, before making his way into the house. He'd cleared out all of my things by himself, making me feel like the worst person ever. I owe him an apology.

A knock on my bedroom door makes my chest tighten. I really hope my dad doesn't want to talk about what happened at mom's. I pad to the door, reluctantly opening it with an excuse ready so that he'll leave me alone. The words die on my tongue when I see Remington standing there with his arms full of my notebooks and my guitar.

"Figured you'd want these up here." He says quietly.

I swallow down the new set of tears that threaten to surface. I think it's sweet that he brings me my most prized possessions even if I don't deserve it.

"Thank you."

SELF-INFLICTED

I take the guitar, setting it against the wall near the closet. I grab the notebooks from him next, placing them on the floor at the end of the bed.

"That thing is missing a string." He mutters.

I roll my eyes. "Thanks, Captain Obvious."

He smiles. "Do you want to get out of here for a while?" he scratches the back of his neck, staring at my comforter. "I thought maybe we could take a drive or something."

My brow crumples. "You want to hang out with me?"

He stalks toward me slowly, pinning me with a heated stare that makes my stomach dip. "Shut up," his hands coast along my waist, drawing me into a hug. His lips graze my neck, creating goosebumps as a shiver trickles down my spine. "Beautiful. Unique. Girl."

What?

My breath snags in my throat. It's an acronym. B.U.G.

"I'm sorry," I say quietly. "I shouldn't have exploded like that."

"No, I get it." He says, pulling away from me. The loss of his warm body wrapped around me causes me to wrap my arms around myself. He raises a brow. "Can I be honest with you?"

I snort. "Aren't you always?"

"Fair point." Dragging a hand through his hair, he sighs. "Your mom is a fucking bitch."

Maybe I'm losing my mind or I'm still hysterical from earlier. A laugh bubbles up my throat and before I know it, I'm shaking in a fit of giggles. Remington laughs too.

"It's not funny." He says through a smile.

"No, of course not," I chuckle again. "but she kind of is."

"Is she always like that with you?"

"I always thought it was because of the alcohol. Maybe she doesn't need inhibiters to hate me."

"It's her loss." He says, pinning me with a serious look. "You're amazing. Anyone who doesn't see that isn't worth your time."

My lips tip up in a small smile. "Thanks."

"So, do you want to get out of here?"

"What about our parents?" I say, lowering my voice.

"We can hang out. It's not like they think I'm going to drive you out to the country and ravish you in my truck." My stomach tumbles when his eyes darken. "Not that it doesn't sound like a great plan."

"Stop." I scold, swatting his arm playfully. He flashes me a grin. While I don't like the idea of being mixed up in our spicy chaos, the thought of getting out for a while sounds amazing. "You sure I'm not taking you away from more important things?"

"Nah," He says, heading for the door. "I'm sure the guys would love a night off. We've been busting our asses with practice."

"Okay."

"Meet me downstairs in ten minutes."

After Remington leaves, I slide my notebooks under my bed then grab a light jacket from my closet. I go to the bathroom to freshen up as well, making sure I no longer look like I've been bawling my eyes out. As I descend the stairs, I hear my dad's voice.

"Be home by midnight. No drinking and driving. If there's so much as a hair out of place…"

"Michael, they'll be fine." Bridget says when I enter the living room. She offers me a soft smile. "It's nice to hear you two are giving each other a chance."

My brows raise as I glance between her and my dad. He smiles tightly. "Be safe, Layla bug."

"We're just going for a drive then maybe grabbing a bite." Remington says. "She owes me for helping move her stuff today."

SELF-INFLICTED

"Have fun." Bridget says.

I follow Remington to the front door. As soon as he closes it behind us, I shoot him a questioning look. "What did you say to them?"

He twirls his keyring on his finger as we walk to his truck. "I told them we were going out for a while. Your dad looked like he wanted to chop my dick off." I snort. "I figure it's better to be transparent. Keeps me accountable." He opens my door for me.

"Accountable?" I ask, climbing into the passenger seat. He shoots me a wicked grin before closing my door. I watch him walk around the front of his truck. "Where are we going anyway?"

He starts the engine before backing out of the driveway. "Well you're definitely buying me dinner." It's the least I can do. "I actually know of a spot just outside town."

"So you are taking me to the country?" I say jokingly.

"Yeah." He comes to a stop at a traffic light.

I instantly sober. "Rem…"

He turns to look at me, his eyes darting across my face. There's a glimpse in his eyes that I can't quite place. "You called me Rem." He says sounding almost in disbelief. Any other time I've addressed him it's either Elijah or Remington. He smiles before focusing on the road again. "I like that."

"Okay, weirdo." he chuckles.

I actually understand what he means. He rarely calls me Layla so when he does, it sounds better than anyone else saying it. Yeah, this is a bad idea.

As we eventually end up on the highway, I pray that the evening stays platonic. It's so easy to fall into him despite my best efforts at keeping my hormones at bay. I can't help observing his full lips as he sings along to a song on the stereo or the way his long fingers flex on the steering wheel. Don't get me started on the sound of his voice either. An old Three Days Grace song comes on and when it gets to the part with a low growl, he mimics it perfectly. I'm sure my panties are soaked by the time we pull into the parking lot of a quaint looking roadside restaurant and lounge.

"This place has the best cheeseburgers." Rem says as we head for the door.

"I didn't even know this place was here." I admit in a soft voice, disappointed in myself for having lived so close my entire life.

Between my mother's affinity for her social life and my father's ability to disassociate with work, we never traveled much. The furthest I've been from home is the two times we went to New York when I was almost too little to remember. If not for a worn photo in an old frame on the mantle above the fireplace, I'd have no memory of Times Square.

He holds the door for me allowing me into the quiet restaurant first. I'm greeted by the smell of fried food and decadent desserts that I can see behind a glass case near the hosting booth. The inside of this place matches the exterior with rustic exposed wood adorned with iron fixtures. Faint rock music plays over the speakers. To the left of the entryway is a small hall where I see a long bar top with gold accents and black stools. To the right, over a short wall is a classic diner set up with bright red booths and white tables.

"Hello!" a middle-aged woman with short, brown hair in a bob style greets us as she rounds the counter. She offers me a warm smile before glancing up at Rem. "Where's the other boys?"

I turn to glance at him in confusion, watching as he smiles at the woman. "Hey, Patty. Just me tonight." He tosses an arm over my shoulder casually. "This is Layla."

Patty smiles at me again. "Nice to meet you, Layla." She grabs two menus from a bin.

We follow her to the furthest end of the diner area, my heart hammering in my throat while Rem continues keeping his arm around me. We pass a booth with a group of people I recognize from my high school. Am I the only one who has never been here before? Patty stops at the last booth with a window that overlooks the parking lot. I slide into the seat that faces the rest of the restaurant when Rem releases me. I prefer to keep my wits about me, especially in foreign places. Having my back to a wall gives me comfort. Rem sits across from me while Patty hands us each a menu.

"What can I get you to drink?" she asks.

Rem glances at me for a moment before turning his attention to her. "Double chocolate shake." He says with a wry grin.

"So, the usual." She says. "Cheeseburger with extra crispy fries too?"

He nods. "Please."

"I'll have the same." I say when Patty glances down at me. After the terrible afternoon I've had, nothing sounds better than a greasy cheeseburger with a shake.

She walks away to put in our order as I shrug out of my jacket, laying it beside me in the booth. Rem rests his forearms on the table top, clasping his hands together. "I can't believe you've never been here before." He says. "Connor tells me all the kids from Hancock High spent their free time here."

"I've never been the poster child for school spirit or large groups of friends." I admit, glancing around at the funny signs adorned on the wood walls. One says, '*Our service depends on YOUR attitude.*'

"Do you do anything besides work and go to school?"

"I hang out with Aly a lot."

He squints slightly. "And write."

I hate that he's read parts of what I've written. My cheeks heat. I glance away from him. "It's therapeutic." I reply quietly. "I'm not the type that craves social interaction. It gets exhausting pretending to be perfect."

Risking another look at him, I notice he cocks his head. "You care about being perfect?"

"No," I place my hands on the table in front of me, interlacing my fingers. "*I* don't care at all. However, my parents..." I shake my head.

I don't want to get into all the details of my life with him right now. Especially when we're going to be living together for the foreseeable future.

Drawing his arms back, he crosses them against his chest, leaning against the booth. Just then, Patty brings us each our shakes. I grab the paper straw she set next to the tall glass and shove it into the thick liquid, drinking up the fudgy treat. It tastes amazing. Like a liquified brownie or something.

"This is really good." I say, taking another sip.

Rem lifts his lips in a small smile. "Right?"

"How often do you come here?" I ask. "Patty seems pretty familiar with you."

He dips his index finger in the whip cream atop the shake before slowly sucking it off. *Jesus, Mary, and Joseph.*

His gaze flicks to mine. "We're here at least once a week before practice. Last week, they let us play a small set in the bar."

"Really? That's so cool!"

"It wasn't that busy considering we played on a Wednesday night. They offered to let us come back again though. We're thinking of playing next weekend."

Jealousy springs to life in my gut at how simple it seems for them to find a gig. If I wasn't such an introverted downer, maybe one day I could summon the courage to perform somewhere. Although, I doubt anyone would want to hear me. Hemingway's Rejects has only been an official band for a little over a month and are already growing a presence in town. Although, it makes sense for them. They have the looks with the talent to back it up.

"That's awesome."

SELF-INFLICTED

"You should come." He says.

I nearly choke on the milkshake.

"You...want me to see you play?"

He plucks the cherry off the whip cream. I stare at the juicy, red fruit as he brings it to his lips. "Why not? We need all the support we can get."

He bites the cherry off the stem. I can't help being captivated by the way his throat rolls when he swallows it. He then places the stem on his tongue before closing his mouth.

"What are you doing?"

He doesn't reply as he shoots me a wink. His mouth moves side to side for several seconds before his lips part, tongue poking out slightly as he grabs the stem that's now twisted into a knot. Why does that give me butterflies?

Placing it on the table between our two glasses, he says, "Just because you're off limits to me, doesn't mean I don't want you as a friend." I blink down at the cherry stem as he leans forward, dropping his voice. "I like you Layla. It would really mean a lot to me if you came to support the band."

When our eyes lock, I can see in his piercing gaze something more, something dangerous that I don't want to uncover. Can we really be friends after what's transpired between us? Is it that easy for him to shut down whatever feelings he's had or still has and act like there's nothing there? More importantly, is that something I can do? I want to. Truly I do. More than anything, I want to pretend that I don't know what his hands feel like on my body, that I have no idea what he sounds like when he's kissing me. Or what his body feels like against mine. Heat threatens to engulf me so I look away quickly, shuddering out a breath.

Luckily, Patty shows up with our food. I change the topic of conversation, asking him when he first began loving music and as I'd suspected, he told me his dad was in the industry. I didn't pry too much about his father, though he did tell me that up until his father passed, he'd spent time with him on the road during breaks from school.

"It's in my veins." He says. "I can't imagine myself doing anything else." I nod in agreement because I feel the same way, even if I don't have the same opportunities.

"Did you want to move here?" I ask in between bites of the delicious cheeseburger.

He dips a fry in ketchup, chewing it slowly before responding. "I had the option to stay in California."

"What made you change your mind?"

"Even though my parents split years ago, it felt too raw back home. It didn't help that I hung out with a crowd of bad characters. I told you before that I used to drink a lot and miss school." I nod. "I'm the type of person who needs grounding. Something to keep me from getting lost in dark thoughts. It's so easy for me to fall down the rabbit hole of demise." He admits. "I also hurt my mom a great deal and still feel guilty about it. So, I made the choice to come with her."

If it wasn't for writing my thoughts out or having Aly to talk to, I probably would have ended up quite similar to him. "I know what you mean."

"I thought you might." He says quietly. "Layla, what happened at your house with your mom…" My chest tightens when he looks me in the eye. "There is absolutely nothing wrong with you."

I place my hand up, palm out. "Rem-"

"No." he interjects. "You're beautiful, smart, and talented. You're incredible despite the fact that your mom can't see that, that you might feel like your father can't either. It doesn't mean that you're not capable of more."

Tears threaten to pool up again. I quickly swallow the lump in my throat, breaking his gaze.

"I yell at her." I say softly. "We fight and sometimes I slam my door or scream at the top of my lungs." Closing my eyes, I release a breath. "Before that dinner a few weeks ago, I told her that I loved her and she didn't say it back. She never says it back."

"There is nothing-"

"Everyone leaves me." I choke out, looking at him again. "My mom chooses friends, drinking and men. My dad chose his career, chose your mom." I shake my head. "Adam," I sniffle, "he chose half the cheerleading squad."

"Who the fuck is Adam?" he grimaces.

"My ex-boyfriend. We dated for a whole year before I found out he cheated on me and not just once either. Apparently I was the last to know about how fascinated he'd been with other girls."

Seems the apple didn't fall far from the tree in some ways. I bristle at the comparison to my mother.

"That's fucked up, Bug."

I laugh without humor. "Give it time." I quip. "I'm sure before long, you'll discover just how unlovable I am."

He pushes his plate to the side, leaning over the table, startling me when he swipes his thumb under my left eye. I inhale a sharp breath.

"I've spent the better part of the last few weeks trying to find one thing wrong with you. Believe me, I've searched for the most miniscule shit I could when it came to you." Was he trying to make me feel better because this tactic wasn't resonating. "Do you want to know what I've discovered?" I swallow, unable to respond. "You wear your heart on your sleeve. You fucking lead with it in everything you do whether you're conscious about it or not."

I sit back. "Thanks?" irritation springs to life. I'm admitting my biggest weakness while he's picking me apart.

Releasing a heavy sigh, he sits back as well. "What I'm saying is that of all the things I tried to find wrong with you, to get myself to stop…wanting you…" His brow crumples. "The only fatal flaw I found was that your heart is too damn big. That's not a bad thing, Bug. I know this probably sounds redundant, but you shouldn't worry about what everyone else thinks."

"It's kind of hard to retrain your brain to think you might be worth a damn when history proves otherwise."

"Do you want to spend your entire life crying over what shitty people think of you?" he asks.

I glare at him across the table, crossing my arms. "No."

He shrugs. "Then stop. Quit apologizing for being who you are, for enjoying what you do. You don't owe your parents a damn thing, or some fucking tool who used you."

What he's saying makes sense. It isn't any different than what I've tried to tell myself a thousand times before. The problem is putting the words into action. Allowing myself the grace to be true to myself without worrying about other people's opinions. Without fear of them poking fun at me or judging me. It's terrifying to put yourself in the spotlight, no matter how badly you crave it, when you're shy as hell and afraid of people.

He pops another fry into his mouth. "I moved here because being stuck in the same cycle of using wasn't appealing. Throwing your life away for the sake of a false comfort, isn't worth it."

Throughout the rest of our meal, his words keep playing in my mind. Am I throwing my life away by being too afraid of disappointing my parents? Instead of wallowing in self-pity, I push the what ifs to the back of my mind so that I can enjoy this moment of freedom. While I'm still not sure if we can ever be friends, I'm appreciating Rem's company. By the time we're done eating I'm grateful that he offered to take me out for a while. Before Patty comes back with the check, I excuse myself to use the restroom and when I come back out, Rem is waiting for me at the doors.

I find out he already paid the bill which annoys me. As we step out into the dark, warm evening air, I say, "I was supposed to buy your dinner."

Remington shrugs. "Don't worry about it." He walks to the passenger side of his truck, opening the door for me again. His chivalry is refreshing as well as a little unsettling. "Or you can pay me back in another way," he mutters suggestively. I frown at him before climbing into the cab. He chuckles as he shuts my door. When he settles into the driver's seat, he says, "God, Bug get your mind out of the gutter. I meant a platonic, wholesome way."

I narrow my eyes. "Really?"

"Yes, really." He turns the ignition over. "You could sing for me."

"I don't sing for anyone." Other than messing around with Aly in the privacy of our bedrooms on occasion, I've never sung in front of an audience.

He puts the truck in gear before backing out of the space. "I want to hear you sing one of my songs."

Like I'd do a Hemingway's Rejects song justice. I shake my head. "That'll never happen."

"You should come to one of our practices at Connor's."

"Why?"

I notice a smile form on his lips. "To learn."

Oh. "Does it freak you out at all to perform in front of people?"

"No. I've never been the shy type." *Lucky*. "Ty gets stage fright though. The social aspect of being a musician terrifies him even though he loves performing. He's more reserved and introverted."

I had no idea. "I don't see it."

"That's because you're only around him when Aly is by his side. She's good for him."

I smile. "The thought of performing one of my songs in front of people makes me want to break out in hives." I confess.

He shoots me a quick glance. "The only way to get over that is to gain more confidence. It's less scary each time."

He drives through the small town before exiting back onto the highway, heading back toward the city. Between the faint music playing over the stereo, the warmth of the cab and a full belly, I'm finding it difficult to keep my eyes open. It probably doesn't help that I've spilled more tears today than anyone should. Despite that, I'm content for the moment. Something so rare for me most days. I relax against the headrest of my seat, closing my eyes.

When I open them again, I'm staring out the windshield of Rem's truck with the side of my head resting against the passenger window. I blink a few times as I sit upright, releasing a yawn. We're back at my dad's place in the driveway. All the lights are off in the house except for the porch light. I turn my head, noticing that the truck is no longer running. I see Remington staring at me. My blood pounds in my ears when that barbell in his tongue peeks out before he slides it over his bottom lip. Has he been watching me sleep?

"What if we pretend," he says in a gruff whisper. "you're not you and I'm not me."

Am I dreaming?

"Rem..."

He shifts, leaning over the center console, sliding his hand over my jaw. Warmth surges in my chest. "I don't care."

My breath hitches. Where is this coming from?

"You might after." He strokes my bottom lip with his thumb.

"Tomorrow is full of broken promises." His gaze falls to my mouth as I hold my breath. When his eyes flick up to mine he adds, "I can't shut it off, Bug. Not when I want you so fucking bad. I know it's wrong now that we're..." he releases a shaky breath. "I can't even say it. It's fucked up, right?" He sits back, dragging a hand through his hair.

"We didn't know."

"We do now and I still don't care."

"You're thinking with your dick." I state. His eyes narrow. "It's easy to get mixed emotions after what we did. We never...sealed the deal." At least that's what I've been telling myself the last several weeks.

A slow smirk forms on his face making my stomach dip. "Is that how you feel?"

Rolling my eyes because there's no way I'll tell him, I say, "It's like when you want something you can't have. It's ingrained in us as humans to wonder. We never had sex."

"Do you wish we had?"

"Don't ask me that."

"I'll take that as a yes."

Releasing a sigh, I say, "Fine. Yes. I've been dying to know what you're like and it crushed my fucking spirit to discover I'll never have the opportunity." How's that for being honest? Maybe it's the clarity of what he said earlier about false comforts and being myself. There's no point in trying to hold it back after already sharing with him some of the darkest parts of me today.

He blinks at me in stunned silence. After a few minutes his lips curve up in a smile. "Your spirit is crushed?"

Rolling my eyes, I shove his shoulder, knocking him back slightly. "Shut up."

He tilts his head to the side, studying me. I begin to grow uncomfortable under his scrutiny so I move to open my door. He stops me with a hand on my forearm.

"How good do you think I am?" he asks. There's a seriousness to his tone that gives me pause.

"What do you mean?"

"You said you've been dying to know what I'm like. Why?"

I gape at him. "Um...you're hot." He raises a questioning brow. "Plus, after we...well, I just feel that if you're that good with clothes on, you're probably even better..." I shake my head.

"Naked?" he smirks at me.

Releasing a frustrated sigh, I say, "This is not a conversation we should be having."

"I know." He sits back fully. "I know. I'm sorry."

"As much as I appreciate tonight, we shouldn't do things alone anymore. The temptation is too much. With others around, it will be easier to distract ourselves."

"Yeah," he says. "I'm sure in time we'll get over it. I mean once our parents are officially married, that might help."

"We just need time."

"Time." He agrees.

The air lightens some as the question that I've wanted to ask for weeks now, finally spills out. "You didn't mean it, right?"

He cocks his head to the side. "What?"

"When you said you thought you were in love with me." I chuckle lightly. "I mean, I'm fairly sure you were kidding after what we did, but it's kind of been gnawing at me this whole time. You didn't mean it, did you?"

His eyes fall to the center console, his head slowly shaking. "No." he says quietly. "No, I didn't mean it."

"I have to admit that kind of freaked me out." I say. "I mean, love isn't really my thing."

His gaze snaps back up to mine. "What do you mean?"

"Love sucks, Rem. I have yet to see it work out amongst anyone I know. I'd rather not have my heart broken any more than it has been."

His shoulders become rigid in the dim light of the cab which makes me wonder if I've upset him somehow. "We should probably get inside." He says after a few moments. "Your dad mentioned a midnight curfew and it's late."

He opens his door and I do the same, unable to shake the air of tension emanating from him as we walk to the porch where he unlocks the front door. I head for the stairs once we're inside, thinking he's right behind me but when I glance back, I watch him stalk off into the living room.

"Thanks again for tonight." I say, unsure if he'll respond.

He stops without turning around. "No problem. Goodnight, Bug."

There's an edge to his voice that I want to question even though I know that I shouldn't. Not when we just agreed to remain amicable. The last thing we need is another fight that leads to either a catastrophic division or a massive mistake. So, I take his words at face value and carry myself up the stairs to my room, telling myself that I'm imagining things.

CHAPTER EIGHT

The first few weeks of living at my dad's is an adjustment. Being in a house that's not only more spacious, yet also exponentially quieter, feels odd. The biggest change is the lack of negativity in the house. Bridget is happy all the time. Like more than anyone I've ever met which is kind of weird to me. She's positive and warm and she bakes as if she's vying to enter a competition despite working full time at my dad's firm. She's a completely different person than my own mother. I'm finding it difficult not to like her. Even in a short time, I feel comfortable in the house which has a lot to do with the way she treats me. She's always asking how I'm doing, how work is going, and if I'm okay with whatever she's cooking for dinner. Her thoughtfulness is more endearing than it is annoying.

Another learning curve of my new home is Remington. I remember him telling me he spends a lot of his time at Connor's and I know they've got a gig coming up, so I'm trying not to blame myself for his lack of being home. He did invite me to go to their practice earlier in the week. I went, though I refused to sing or even bring my guitar. Me and Aly ended up watching them for a while then left to catch a movie. I haven't really seen much of him since which is probably for the best because the more I think about him, the more I'm riddled with guilt and confusion.

SELF-INFLICTED

"So, I was thinking maybe we can go dress shopping this afternoon if you're free?" Bridget sets her bowl of oatmeal on the table before sitting down across from me.

I nod, as I glance up from my half eaten bagel. "Sure, that sounds nice."

The wedding is three weeks away now. The closer it gets, the less enthused I've become. Most of that has to do with the affair her and my father had. It barely has anything to do with the fact that I'm about to become family with a guy I can't stop wanting. Barely. Honest. Yeah, right.

"Okay, great." She smiles at me. "It will really mean a lot to me if you walk with your dad down the aisle."

I quell the urge to roll my eyes. If they want to get married, I'll accept it. However, being a part of the actual ceremony is incredibly uncomfortable for me. I set my bagel down on the plate, no longer hungry. Just then, dad comes downstairs in a suit and sets his briefcase on the table.

"This trial will be the death of me." He mutters, readjusting his tie.

Bridget stands from her seat, automatically approaching him to ensure the tie is straight. She smiles up at him and for a moment, I see the look of pure adoration in each of their gazes as they stare longingly at each other. Bile rises in my throat.

"Just a few more weeks to get through then we'll be sunning on a beach in Bermuda with cocktails." She says.

He bends to kiss her lips. "Can't wait."

I think I've fully lost my appetite, so I get up to take my plate to the sink after tossing the bagel in the trash.

"Layla agreed to go dress shopping this afternoon." Bridget announces.

Dad steps over to me, wrapping an arm around my shoulder. "That'll be fun!" he kisses the top of my head which startles me. I haven't had that sort of affection from him in a long

120

time. He releases me to pour coffee into a travel mug. "Are you working today?"

"I'm working tomorrow. They need someone to manage ticket sales for a show."

"Don't spread yourself too thin, kiddo. Your courses will keep you plenty busy."

I bristle at the statement. This isn't the first time he's mentioned me quitting my job in a roundabout way. "I like staying busy." I say. "Plus, I love the work. It doesn't even feel like a job most of the time."

Dad frowns. What he doesn't understand is that I would be perfectly satisfied to work at Happy's while pursuing more creative courses to study music instead.

"I still think you should come to my firm if you want a part-time job. We could use another secretary."

My chest tightens. "No way. I don't want to be somebody's personal assistant."

"Are you not already doing something similar?" he argues.

I glare at him from across the kitchen. "I'm more of a jack of all trades at Happy's."

"That's not a career, Layla. Your future should be as important, if not more so, than your present."

"I don't even want to be a lawyer." I mutter.

Bridget cuts him off before he continues arguing. "You don't?" she shoots him a cursory look of annoyance.

He sighs. "I'm not having this dispute again. Dreams don't pay bills."

Frustration takes root. I cross my arms, tilting my chin in indignation. "Rem gets to follow his dreams of being a musician." I say, glancing between him and Bridget.

Bridget frowns while dad angrily grabs his briefcase. "He is also nineteen and already on his way to succeeding with his vision."

SELF-INFLICTED

"I'm an adult!" I state, even though I stamp my foot like a petulant child.

Dad lifts a brow at me, noticing the tantrum. He shakes his head. "We already set aside money for your tuition and filled out the forms to enroll you."

"So?" I toss my arms up before letting them fall back to my hips. "I can resign. I can go for writing instead and minor in music." I've looked into it. Months ago before graduation, I wanted to see what my options might be if I ever decided to stand up for myself.

He's silent for so long, I'm worried about what he'll say next. "I don't have time for this." He eventually says. My heart sinks.

He never has time.

"Right." I reply before heading up to my room.

My irritation is at an all-time high as I ascend the stairs. I hear the faint sound of an acoustic guitar being strummed, noticing that Rem's bedroom door is narrowly open. I stop just before it, listening as he strums out a haunting melody. He usually plays an electric guitar the few times I've seen Hemingway's Rejects perform. I continue standing there until the music fades to an end before forcing myself to retreat into my room. Part of me wants to tell him how good whatever he's playing sounds, but I know better. We agreed to not put ourselves in a position where we might slip up. As much as it bothers me to be avoiding each other on purpose, I'm also glad for the space. It's hard not to notice what he's wearing or the way his hair is styled. Every time I see him, my stomach floods with butterflies and the memory of what we shared still remains.

Dress shopping with Bridget doesn't turn out to be so bad. After trying on a few styles, I discover pink is not my color and an empire-waist is not my friend. However, I do learn that royal blue accentuates my hazel eyes and an A-line looks good on my body type. After I say yes to a dress, Bridget takes me to dinner, asking me all kinds of questions to get to know me better. Including some hard hitters about what I want my future to look like.

"You don't want to go to law school." It isn't a question.

"No, I don't."

Her brow crumples. "Michael has always made it seem like that's your dream."

Setting my fork down, I sit back. "No offense, but I'm not sure dad is always forthcoming or truthful." Her frown deepens making me immediately feel like a bitch. "I'm sorry."

She shakes her head, clasping her hands together atop the table. "I know you think that he left your mother for me. That we had some sordid affair or acted on impulse without a care in the world."

My brows raise. "Didn't you?"

"No." she says simply. I roll my eyes.

"Why should I believe you?"

She shrugs, a soft smile forming. She's always smiling at me. There's no way anyone can always be so nice.

"Layla, it isn't my place to share with you the circumstances that led to your father and I being together. That's his story to tell because he is the one responsible for you feeling the way you do. Perhaps you should speak with him about it."

"From my perspective, he left within a week of me turning eighteen, ran off with you and now you're getting married a few months later. It all happened so fast, it's weird."

Bridget nods before taking a sip of her iced tea. "I understand it seems fast to you. Please be assured, I am in no way a home wrecker. Elijah has always come first. I raised him mostly by myself and while he's had his fair share of issues, I have always been there for him. Just as I would like to be there for you. Michael has been transparent about you and despite what you might think, I care about you as if you're my own."

"You don't know me."

"You're right, I don't know you. While in time, I hope we can get to know each other better, I want you to recognize that what I do know, I like. You're a smart girl and from what I've seen, you are strong-willed. I can appreciate that, which is why I'm planning to talk to your dad."

I squint across the table at her. "About what?"

There she goes smiling again. "About his expectations of you and how he may mean well, but you have a right to find your own path."

My mouth drops open as I blink at her. "What?"

"You need to talk to him. Alone. Tell him what you want. Clear the air about our relationship as well. I honestly think both of you need that. I would prefer we enter this marriage with no secrets or confusion."

I scoff. "You're new to him, Bridg." I say, picking up my fork again. "There's no arguing with Michael Barlow when he has his mind made up."

She chuckles lightly. "Oh, trust me, I know that. However, I've seen firsthand his ability to sympathize with people. While he has high expectations of you, I'm certain he would prefer to see you happy."

While I appreciate her concern for me, I'm also skeptical. There have only been a handful of times in the last five years that I've tried to argue what I did and didn't want as far as college goes with my parents. Mainly because I always end up thinking I'm breaking dad's heart when all I've ever wanted is to make them proud in my own way. Can talking with dad now be any different than what I've experienced before?

Something Remington said to me when we were at dinner, surfaces. *'Quit apologizing for being who you are.'* Perhaps it's time to take control of my own life. Now that my mom is leaving me behind, she shouldn't get a say in my future anymore. Plus dad's moving on too. I'm the one who will be left to deal with the repercussions of my actions, not them.

※

When we get home Rem is in the driveway, loading his guitar into his truck.

"What time is your band playing tonight?" Bridget asks him while I grab my dress from the back seat of her car.

"Eight." He frowns at the garment bag I'm holding up. "What's that?"

I glance at the white, nylon bag. "My dress for the wedding."

"You and Michael are going tux shopping next weekend. Don't forget." Bridget says.

"Right." He mutters, shutting the back door of his truck. "I've got to meet Connor at his place. Are you coming to our show tonight, Bug?"

Shit. He invited me to come after missing their gig last week due to work and I totally spaced it. Supporting the band is a nice gesture that doesn't mean anything. Although, watching them perform might lead to us hanging out after, so I'm not so sure that's a good idea. Besides, I really want to talk to dad tonight when he gets home before I lose my nerve on demanding some freedom with my future.

Tucking a strand of hair behind my ear, I shake my head. "I think I'll stay in. I need to talk to my dad and I have to work tomorrow."

SELF-INFLICTED

I don't miss the look of disappointment in his dark eyes. Pressure clamps my chest. "Cool." He says before rounding the front of his truck to the driver's side.

"Are you coming home tonight?" Bridget asks.

Opening his door, he gives me another look, narrowing his eyes slightly. "I'll stay at Connors."

A knot forms in the pit of my stomach that I try to ignore as I carry my dress into the house. Rem is obviously upset that I'm not going, which doesn't make sense. It's not like it matters that I'm there. I'm sure they have a ton of people supporting the show tonight.

When my dad comes home, I mentally brace myself for our talk before finding him downstairs in his home office. He's still wearing the suit he left in, yet that tie he was so worried about is completely undone now. His brown hair, like mine, is graying at the temples. I've never noticed that before. With dark framed glasses, he stares at the laptop screen on his desk, his hand tucked under his chin. He glances up at me with tired eyes. I almost chicken out, concerned that I'm bothering him when he's obviously busy.

"Layla bug, come in." he says with a brief smile.

I plant myself in one of the high back chairs in front of his desk, pulling my feet up to the cushion before wrapping my arms around my knees.

"Are you busy?" My gaze shifts to the two framed pictures on the corner of his desk. One is of us when I was ten, the other of him and Bridget.

"Just finishing up some notes." He says, typing on the keyboard before closing the laptop. "What's up?"

I inhale a deep breath, holding it for several moments. I'm not sure where to start. "I had dinner with Bridget after dress shopping today. She's nice."

A slow smile forms on his face as he removes his glasses. "I think so too."

"I can't believe you two are getting married so soon." I say quietly. "Are you sure you're ready?"

He releases a heavy sigh and leans back in his desk chair, folding his hands over his flat stomach. "We haven't talked much since I've moved out."

I lift a shoulder in a brief shrug. "We never really talked much."

He frowns. "I'm sorry, Layla." Something swells in my chest at his words. He's never apologized to me. "I want you to understand that me and your mother's relationship has never had anything to do with you. When I left I wanted you to come with me, though I knew I couldn't force you."

He's right. I had the option to decide where I wanted to stay. I chose mom because…well because I worry about her. I know my dad can take care of himself.

"I know that your relationship wasn't perfect. I witnessed the arguments and noticed you gone a lot…" tears I wasn't expecting begin to surface. I take a cleansing breath before continuing. "I feel abandoned by you both. Mom is never home. In the last few years you've been distant too. Did you ever wonder where I was or who I was with, or what I was doing?"

Dad chews on his bottom lip while thinking. "Honestly, honey I didn't worry about you. You've always been a good kid. You obeyed our rules, focused on school, and never gave us reason to think you'd get into trouble."

"Because I'm so compliant." I say, lowering my feet to the floor. "Do you even know why I don't make waves?" I don't give him time to reply. "You have all these expectations of me. Get good grades, go to college, then law school. Mom wants me fit, pretty, and sweet to all her friends and their kids. I'm a puppet for you two."

SELF-INFLICTED

He leans forward, a look of concern on his face. "Layla, I never want you to feel that way."

"Yet I do." I say. "You've been forcing me to follow in your footsteps. You spent years pestering me about good grades and SAT scores. Yes, you let me play that beat up guitar, however you never bought me another one when I asked. You never encouraged me when I'd sit in my room, singing my lungs out to lyrics I'd written."

"I'm glad that you enjoy music. Truly, I am. Layla, musicians are a dime a dozen though. I'd feel more comfortable if you were in a stable career."

I stand to my feet. "I'd feel more comfortable if I had the freedom to be me! Not you, not mom with her myriad of fake friends. *Me*. You said yourself that you think I'm responsible. Why can't you trust me to pave my own future?"

I notice a faint trace of tears lacing his eyes. "You've grown up so quickly." He murmurs in a shaky voice. "Please," he stretches his hand out, motioning for me to sit once again. I obey, folding my arms against my waist. I can't give in this time. I have to stay firm. "All I've ever wanted for you is to be happy. To not struggle the way your mother and I did growing up. I think a part of me has always feared you would end up like her."

There it is. He's finally admitted something I myself have feared for a while now.

"I don't want to be like her, dad." I say. "I know what her lifestyle involves. It's miserable. It's so disingenuous which I hate."

Except when it comes to me. How many times do I paint on a mask of something entirely different than who I am or what I feel. All for the sake of keeping the peace. I'm a fraud too.

"I know, kiddo. Believe me, I notice more than you realize. You've always been independent. A trait you and I both share." He smiles briefly. "I suppose I've planned your whole future out according to what would make *me* happy, instead of thinking of what *you* want. I'm sorry for that."

Another apology? This is unexpected. Maybe Bridget does know him better than I thought. She might even know him better than I do. "I don't want to go to law school." I admit. "I wouldn't mind going to college in the Fall or furthering my education. I just want to study music and writing."

"Remington mentioned you writing."

My heart drops to my stomach.

"You spoke about me?"

"Yeah," he scratches at the stubble on his chin. "he said you have a lot of notebooks full of lyrics. I always knew you were into music. I guess I never fully understood how deep that went."

"I play my guitar constantly."

He nods. "Yeah, I've heard. You've improved a lot over the years."

I can't help the small smile that forms. "Thanks."

"Listen, Layla, if you want to pursue a different career, that's fine with me. We can change your courses. However, I want you to be realistic about this, okay?"

"Okay." My voice is hoarse. I'm stunned that he's bending to me right now. Dad never compromises.

"Good." He stands from his chair, rounding his desk. "Come here," he says, reaching for my hand to pull me up from the chair. He wraps his arms around me in a tight hug. I inhale a deep breath, squeezing him back. I'm not sure if we'll ever be super close, but it feels good to have this moment with him right now. He tucks his chin atop my head. "I'm sorry for keeping you in the dark." He says softly. "You need to know that Bridget and I have been together longer than a few months."

My spine stiffens. "What?" I pull out of his embrace.

"Your mother and I made the decision to divorce two years ago. She sought comfort in the arms of another man. With her drinking on top of that, I couldn't do it anymore. We were legally separated a year and a half ago. The divorce was finalized this past May."

What?! "So you didn't leave her for another woman?" I ask incredulously.

"No. The divorce was rather amicable actually. We both agreed that we would continue to live together for your sake until you were closer to eighteen."

She made me believe that he was the one who chose to abandon us. That he chose another woman over us. Sorrow punches me in the chest, stealing my lungs.

"Why did she lie?"

His brow furrows. "I don't know, Layla. Maybe she wanted to blame me for whatever negative feelings you might have about me. The woman has never been the type to admit her own faults." Yeah, I know that all too well. "I don't want you to hate her. I would never expect you to take sides."

It's a relief to hear those words. All this time I've felt pitted between them. "Thank you."

"I feel complete with Bridget. Something I never felt with your mom if I'm being honest. I know it's important to her that we marry with your blessing."

I shake my head, blowing out a breath. It's wild that we think we know the truth based on those we trust telling us what they want to. My mother treated me as if I was a terrible person for wanting any kind of relationship with my father. She aided in me disliking Bridget who has only ever been kind to me. The realization that she's the guilty party in this is a hard pill to swallow. It's going to take some time for me to recover from that.

I gaze up at my dad, swiping at the last of the tears I want to cry in this situation. "You have my blessing." I say and I mean it with all my heart.

Later that night, I'm curled up on the couch in the living room, binge-watching a reality show about people who marry strangers. I need to know whether or not they'll choose to stay with each other after eight weeks even if it seems a bit ridiculous. While I have to work in the morning, I keep telling myself 'one more episode.' After the finale, I decide to call it a night. I'm folding the throw blanket I was using when the front door opens, startling me.

Rem's boots sound on the hardwood floor before he appears in the entryway. "Weren't you staying at Connor's?" I ask, tossing the blanket on the back of the couch and shutting off the television.

He shrugs, stalking toward the open kitchen to the refrigerator. I watch him grab a bottle of water before turning around, using his hip to close the door. He unscrews the cap, taking a long tug off the bottle before noisily setting it on the island counter.

"Changed my mind." He says, sliding his gaze over me from messy bun to bare feet.

I wrap my arms around myself, feeling exposed even though I'm wearing a loose sweater over my sleep shorts. He cocks his head to the side when our eyes meet again. Heat radiates in my chest as I zero in on the bright mark along the side of his neck. White hot anger replaces the discomfort of his stare as my hands fall to my sides. I have no right to be jealous at the sight of a hickey on his neck, no place to be upset that he might have hooked up with someone. In theory, I know that. Though it doesn't stop my emotions from scattering my brain.

"What's that?" I ask, my voice icy.

Rem's brow crumples in confusion for a moment before he slides his finger against the red mark. A slow smile forms as he says, "Oh, just a souvenir from some girl. Think her name was Mara or Maria?" he shrugs. "Aly knew her from school."

My stomach rolls violently. "Marla Higgins?"

"Yeah! That's her name. Cute blond with blue eyes?"

"Yep." I reply, popping the p.

That's just fucking great. Not only did she steal Adam from me, but now she's gone and stolen - Wait. Rem isn't *mine* to steal. The frustration whirling within me shifts gears to myself. I shouldn't be mad about this. It isn't my business who Remington spends time with. I hate how jealous I am that she got to spend time with him tonight. Maybe I should have gone. No. No, I was right to stay home. I wouldn't have had my breakthrough with dad if I did. I needed seeing this to remind myself how volatile it is for us to keep toeing a thin line.

He chuckles, pulling me from my thoughts. My gaze snaps to his.

"What's the matter, Bug? Are you jealous?"

Snorting, I roll my eyes. "Please, you can do whatever you want."

"Yeah, right." I hear him mutter when I leave the room.

"We sold the house." Bile rises in my throat the moment my mom utters those words. "We're heading to Seattle this weekend to sign paperwork on a condo."

I quickly shut down the tears that form. I'm not going to cry about this now. Not while I'm currently sitting in the break room at work. I can hear the din of a large crowd beyond the doors. If I didn't promise Hank I'd wait tables during the battle of the bands set tonight, I'd skip out early.

"Great." I say quietly.

Mom sighs, "Oh, come on, Layla. Where's your enthusiasm?"

I bite down on my bottom lip to keep from making a smartass comment. I have zero excitement about my childhood home being sold off so she can start a new life with Chad. Especially now that I know the truth about why her and my father divorced.

"I'm happy for you." I try to sound sincere. I don't think it's convincing.

"Well, you should be. You're welcome to come visit sometime, although it's a small place so you can't stay with us. Unless you're fine with a blowup mattress on the floor." She giggles at the condescending joke.

"Yeah, maybe some time soon."

"You can come with us this weekend. Oh, wait. Your dad's wedding is happening isn't it?"

As if she doesn't stalk social media and already know that. The amount of times she's brought up what he's doing in conversations is proof that she thrives off drama. Before it was my dad, it would be random co-workers or family members. Yet another reason I steer clear of the internet.

"Yeah it's this weekend."

"Well, that will be fun for you." I can hear the sarcasm in her voice.

SELF-INFLICTED

The only positive to dad and Bridget getting married this weekend is having a few days off from work. Something I've desperately needed since I've been taking on more hours.

"Sure." I mutter. "Listen, my break is almost over. I have to get back to work."

"Okay. I'll text you pictures of the condo."

"Can't wait to see it." Yes I can. "Talk to you later."

"Bye." She hangs up before I can pull the phone away from my ear.

Releasing a sigh, I slip my cell into my back pocket, finishing off the last of my iced coffee that Aly so thoughtfully brought me before tossing the cup in the trash. Hemingway's Rejects are here tonight to participate in the band competition. Apart from talking to my best friend a bit, I keep my distance from their table. I head for the bar area, slipping behind the counter to clock back in at the register.

"Table ten ordered these fries," Patrick says, setting a tray on the bar counter. "Can you run it to them?"

"Sure thing." I grab the tray before navigating through the crowded room to the tables that have been placed on the normally open dance floor. As I approach the table, my stomach twists into knots when I see Marla Higgins with her little clique.

She makes eye contact with me as I place the basket of fries on their table. "Layla Barlow," she says. "I didn't know you worked here."

I plaster a fake smile on my face. "Yeah."

Me and Marla never got along before the Adam incident. Since then, It's only become worse. She went out of her way to destroy me before graduation with cruel rumors. If ever I had an archenemy, it would be her. I was the quiet, brooding girl in the corner while she sparkled in the limelight, capturing everyone's attention.

She runs a perfectly manicured hand through her thick, blond locks. "Wow, how great for you. Buckling up your bootstraps to earn a living while the rest of us relax before college." Her friends giggle as I roll my eyes.

"I don't need mommy or daddy to pay for me." I shoot back.

Her blue eyes widen for a moment before narrowing on me. "Well, how can they when your home is broken? Adam said your mom drinks her earnings away."

I bite back on my molars, gripping the tray tightly. How I'd love to bash her perfect little face in with it. The lights lower in the room then, the crowd applauding. I turn toward the stage, seeing Connor, Ty, and Rem walking out to take their positions. Not wanting to engage with bitchy Marla anymore, I slip back through the crowd toward the tables I'm responsible for.

"Lay, are you going to watch?" Aly shouts over the sound of the guys warming up on stage when I pass by her table.

"Yeah, just let me check in with my customers."

I go around to check in and take a few orders as the band starts playing, listening to them while continuing to work. They start with a song I've heard before that's upbeat which the crowd seems to love. The harmony Rem and Ty have together when singing is impressive. I just know they're going to have a successful future. Despite whatever animosity I have with Rem, I'm happy to see them performing. I serve a few more tables before sliding into a seat next to Aly.

"I'm so proud of them!" She says.

I smile because I am too. "They sound awesome tonight."

When the song ends, Ty begins speaking to the crowd.

"We're Hemingway's Rejects. We want to thank you guys for coming out tonight and allowing us to play a couple songs for you." The audience cheers. Ty smiles. "My name is Tyler Sitter, this is Remington Paulson, and that is Connor Waits." He introduces each of them, earning more cheers from the crowd. "This next song is a new one called, "Quicksand"."

Rem starts strumming the opening. I immediately recognize the haunting melody from when he was in his room the other morning. He steps up to his microphone while he plays solo, keeping his gaze trained on the strings of his electric guitar. He stops suddenly, his head lifting as he stares out to the crowd, his eyes slamming into mine.

"I keep on sinking. Sinking in the quicksand." His voice echoes through the room, silencing everyone.

Connor breaks into drumming as Rem plays again, the melody faster yet equally captivating. Turning his attention to the audience, he continues singing.

"I'm a loner and a freak, in the streets and in the sheets.

But you bring me to my knees, make me weak with a disease.

You're a liar and a cheat, giving me hope to believe that there's more to you and me than a moment we can't keep. So I sink."

Ty joins him now as they belt out a chorus.

Hanging on for dear life to a hand that's not dry.
Cuz there's blood on your skin and poison within
Your heart's full of ice yet you claim to be nice.
And release me to die while you laugh.
I'm sinking in the quicksand.

I sit in stunned silence, listening to the range of emotion as Rem sings another verse about feeling used. The powerful lyrics snag at something inside me when his eyes collide with mine again. He's singing about me.

"You're a menace in my brain and I'll never be the same.

Melissa K. Morgan

bay.
      Got these shackles on my thoughts, that I have to keep at
      If the truth of us is known and we spend more time alone, I'll be heavy as a stone and I'll sink."

      A lump forms in my throat as I listen to the chorus again, realizing if he wrote this, he thinks I'm toxic. That I'm trying to hurt him somehow by wanting space to avoid falling for him. Not wanting to hear anymore, I tell Aly that I have to get back to work. The sting of dismissal in the song burns through me even after it ends and the band leaves the stage.

      All this time, I thought we were on the same page. What bothers me the most is that he never said anything to me about what exactly he feels or even attempted to speak with me. Now he's singing about us in front of a crowd of people, in front of me. If his goal is to hurt me, he's succeeded. Now I'm left wondering if the person I wanted to consider a friend is actually an enemy.

SELF-INFLICTED

CHAPTER NINE

Hemingway's Rejects wins the battle of the bands which earns them a trophy and prize money. I'm happy for the guys as a whole for winning, but as far as Remington Paulson is concerned, I couldn't care less. I convey my pride to both Ty and Connor, hugging each of them when the announcement happens. I ignore Rem before heading home for the night.

I spend the next week consuming myself in work, jotting down lyrics in my notebook, all while trying to forget about him and that stupid song he sang, which is difficult when everything I write seems to revolve around him.

I'm surprised to find my guitar laying on my bed Thursday afternoon, freshly strung and tuned with a folded piece of paper lying next to it. A part of my armor cracks when I read the quick note left by Rem, telling me that I'll have an easier time practicing with a full set of strings. Despite the radio silence, he took time to do something nice for me. I don't know if it's his way of apologizing for the song or if he's trying to make me feel worse. Not sure how to convey my appreciation without risking vulnerability, I slip my own note under his bedroom door, thanking him.

Saturday, I do my best to push all confusing emotions aside. The only thing I'm focused on at the moment is not tripping in the heels Bridget insisted on me wearing with my dress. I walked with my father down the aisle while Remington gave

Bridget away. The ceremony was short, which I appreciated. Now we're an hour into the reception at this fancy winery on the outskirts of town while I'm wishing someone would sneak me a glass of champagne. I move my fork around the plate of salmon, my stomach in knots. I'm happy for the newlyweds, yet sick about the fact that I have a new stepbrother who I hate with every fiber of my being and find far too attractive. I'm a certified mess.

"Layla, you've grown up so much." My aunt Steph says as she sits down in the chair next to mine.

I smile at her. My dad's sister is just as successful in law as he is. I haven't seen her since I was ten when she visited us for Christmas the year after my grandma passed away.

"I'm officially an adult now." I say.

She rubs my shoulder. "I can't believe it. How have you been?"

I stab the fish on my plate. Something about the sharp point of my fork jamming into the soft flesh is satisfying. "Good. I've been working a lot."

"I hear you live with your father now and your mom moved."

"Yeah," I sigh wistfully. "I'm powering through."

"Are you getting along fine with that boy?" she asks.

I frown. "Who?"

Her gaze slides toward where Rem is standing, talking to some man that I think is a relative of his. She smirks. "He's a cutie. Is he nice to you?"

I have three options - tell the truth that he's kind of a dick and I hate him right now, tell a lie and say he's completely cordial, or evade the question. I choose to evade.

"Hey, how's Caleb? Why didn't he come to the wedding?" Caleb is my twelve year old cousin.

SELF-INFLICTED

"He's at Soccer camp this weekend. He's good. We were talking about getting together for the holidays this year. It's been too long since we've all spent time with each other."

I force another smile. "That'd be nice."

Her eyes drift behind me before she stands. "Looks like you're needed. We'll catch up later, Layla."

I turn to see my dad and Bridget coming my way with Rem trailing behind them looking moody.

"What's up?" I ask my dad.

He wraps an arm around Bridget's waist. I have to admit her cream colored, strapless gown is beautiful on her. The small sequence placed throughout the tool skirt shimmers in the soft light of the room.

"Since this isn't our first wedding, we want to do a different kind of first dance."

I rest my fork against the porcelain plate slowly, "Okay…"

Bridget smiles at me. "We thought we'd skip formalities. You and Elijah can dance together when we do and we'll encourage others to dance as well."

I bite down on the inside of my cheek to keep from screaming. Is she serious? It's bad enough that I have to be at this event with him. That I was forced to sit next to him during the ceremony. Now they want us to freaking dance together?

"It's one dance." Dad says, giving me a stern look. "Can you two manage that for us?"

I glance at Rem who rolls his eyes. "I'm fine with it."

"Fine." I mumble as I stand. I swear if I roll an ankle in these heels, I'm going to hire someone to prosecute my father.

"Thank you, it means so much to us." Bridget says, pulling me into a quick hug before leading dad toward the DJ near the far wall.

"You could at least have the decency to pretend you're happy." Rem mutters.

"Sorry, I can't be fake like you." I retort.

He scoffs. "That's bullshit."

"Maybe," I shrug, "though so is putting someone on blast in a room full of people." I glare up at him, crossing my arms over my chest. He gives me a sidelong glance. "Seriously, *Elijah*. What the fuck?"

A low growl rumbles in his chest as he steps forward before stopping himself. "You want to fight right now, Bug? At our parents' wedding?"

I release a breath. "I want to punch you in the eye again." I say. His lips twitch as if hiding a smile. "Or maybe knee you in the dick."

His brows raise. "Ouch." He bends his head, dropping his voice low. "I'd prefer it if you were nice to my dick." My face flames as he straightens. I hate the way my stomach flips in excitement.

The DJ announces the first dance before a slow, piano heavy melody echoes through the room. Sighing, I cautiously walk around the table to the dance floor where dad and Bridget embrace each other to start dancing. I turn to face Rem who grabs my hand easily, drawing me into him before placing his other hand on my hip. He folds his fingers over the back of my hand, guiding me closer.

"Put your hand on my shoulder." He says softly, staring into my eyes.

I obey reluctantly, shivering when he places our joined hands against his chest.

As we sway to the music, every joint of mine is locked tight. I hate being this close to him. I hate that he didn't deny his song is about me. I hate that I can smell his distinct cinnamon scent and it gives me butterflies. Instead of looking at him, I scan the room, watching as other people begin to join us on the dance floor. My heart pounds in my throat when Rem places his lips at my ear.

SELF-INFLICTED

"You're beautiful." He murmurs.

"Stop." I say breathlessly, my eyes darting around to make sure no one can hear us.

His shoulders tighten, matching the sudden set of his jaw. I know it's wrong to want him and even worse to lead him on. I'm just as much to blame on this tightrope we've been walking. I don't want to encourage it any longer.

The moment the song ends, I sprint away from him back to the table. I'm ready for this reception to be over so I can go back home. However, there's more than just tonight to deal with. Dad and Bridget are leaving for their honeymoon tomorrow for an entire week. Seven days and nights of us being alone at the house. The only thing keeping me from having a full blown panic attack is the hope that Rem will be with the band and we'll both be busy at work so that we don't have to engage much.

Melissa K. Morgan

    The first day dad and Bridget are gone, I end up working longer than my scheduled shift to keep my mind busy. Thankfully, I'm too exhausted to care when I see Remington's truck parked in the driveway when I get home. A hot shower is the only thing on my mind as I enter the house. He's lounging on the couch, watching some movie. I choose to ignore him as I grab a soda from the refrigerator in the kitchen before heading up to my room.

    The toilet flushes from the half-bath downstairs when I step on the first stair, halting me. Moments later, the door swings open, revealing a smug looking Marla Higgins. What the hell is she doing here?

    She smirks at me, flipping her immaculate blond hair behind her shoulder.

    "Hey, *Bar*flow." She sneers.

    The bitter taste of irritation settles in the back of my throat as I narrow my eyes. Her and her stupid group of friends loved throwing around that nickname before the school year ended. I don't have time to respond before she walks into the living room.

    It's bad enough Rem has already fooled around with her. Now she's spending time in our house when our parents are out of town? As the awareness of my jealousy hits, it breeds a form of anger I've never felt before. I will not be walked on by someone as cruel as her or Rem. There's no way I'm staying under the same roof with a girl who already took one boyfriend from me. After years of being the bigger person and cowering to those louder than me, I've had enough.

    There's a good chance Rem doesn't know about my resentment of the girl. Regardless, he's parading her around in front of me intentionally which is a low blow. Instead of simmering in the sting of his blatant rejection, I decide to fight back. I think I saw his phone on the charging base in the kitchen. Setting my purse and soda on the stair, I head back for the kitchen, barely passing a glance in their direction.

SELF-INFLICTED

"You forget something, Bug?" Remington asks as I look in the pantry for a snack.

Marla giggles, capturing my attention. She's lying beside him on the couch, her arm on his torso, her finger swirling against his bare chest. Ugh!

"*Bug?*" She giggles again.

Swallowing the bile that rises in my throat, I plaster a fake smile on my face. "Just looking for a snack," I say sweetly, grabbing a bag of potato chips. I set the bag on the island, shifting my attention to the phone sitting near the outlet. "Do you want something?"

His eyes narrow slightly. "No."

I shrug before turning to grab a bowl from the cabinet. I peer into the living room, monitoring them so I'm not caught. Rem goes back to watching the movie while Marla kisses the side of his face. The thought occurs to me to throw his phone in the garbage disposal and turn it on, but I don't want to pay for that.

Using one hand to pour the chips, I slide my other over the granite countertop toward his phone. Pulling it toward me, I thank the good Lord he doesn't have a passcode on it. A fun fact about me is that I've been learning French since freshman year. I click on the settings icon then the language tab. It takes less than a minute to put his cell in another language. I take my bowl of chips, grabbing my purse and soda before heading to my room.

Game on, Paulson.

An hour later, I hear the sound of Rem's truck firing up. I peek out my bedroom curtains to see him leaving with Marla. If he's noticed the change on his phone, I haven't heard about it yet. I'm proud of myself for not laying down and taking the pain he's inflicting as I settle back under my covers to fall asleep.

I awake the next morning to the roar of heavy metal music blaring from Remington's room. Groaning, I sit up in bed and check the digital clock on my nightstand.

"Seriously?!" I snarl, seeing that it's barely seven. I was planning on sleeping in today.

Springing from the bed I fling my door open, ready to raise hell. I stop short, seeing his bedroom door wide open. He isn't even in there! Groaning in frustration, I continue down the hall to the stairs. Upon inspection, he's not in the kitchen or living room either. I head for the sliding door, finding him sitting in a lounge chair near the pool on the back deck.

Pulling the door open with more force than necessary, I march toward him, contemplating pushing him into the pool. He lifts his head toward me, a devilish grin forming on his face. I hate that he's shirtless, wearing a pair of hot pink swim trunks that accentuate his naturally tan skin. I hate that despite the dark sunglasses, I can feel his eyes on me.

"Morning." He murmurs.

Crossing my arms, I roll my eyes. "What's with the loud music?"

He interlaces his fingers, resting his hands against his lower stomach. "Oh, I'm sorry," he says in a way that conveys the opposite, "did it wake you?"

I glare down at him. "Duh. Why are you such an asshole?"

One dark brow lifts. "Me?" he shifts, reaching to pull his phone out of his pocket. "You switched my phone to French."

I scoff. "I have no idea what you're talking about."

He cocks his head to the side, his jaw ticking. "Really, Bug? You're going to lie to me?"

Shrugging, I say, "Maybe your girlfriend did it."

Rem's nostrils flare in irritation as he stands. "She's not my fucking girlfriend. Though I'm sure you'd assume that, wouldn't you?"

My nose wrinkles. "What's that supposed to mean?"

SELF-INFLICTED

He chuckles darkly. "Your lack of faith is obvious. It's so easy for you to think the worst of everyone. Far easier than having hope they might actually have a heart."

"Whatever." I snap.

"Yeah, *whatever*, Layla." He places his phone in his pocket. "Don't touch my shit."

Unfolding my arms I flip him off with one hand. "Don't invite sleazy bitches into my house."

He huffs out a laugh, placing his hands on his hips. "What are you going to do about it? Call our parents and tattle like a child?"

A wicked grin forms on my own face. I move closer to him, stopping close enough that I have to lift my chin to meet his gaze. "I'll touch whatever I want, *Elijah*."

Before he can respond, I pivot on my heel, rushing back into the house. Upstairs I enter his room, slamming the power button on his stereo. Then, I grab the power cord from the wall, rolling it up before marching back into my room to hide it.

I'm not proud of myself for being petty, but I don't know what else to do. I have all these feelings whirling around inside me when it comes to him with no way to release them. It's not like I can talk to anyone about this. No one needs to know that I'm crushing hard on my stepbrother. That despite the fact our parents are now married, nothing has changed for me even though it definitely should. Or that the thought of him with someone else makes me want to rage like I'm She-Hulk. God, I need to get over this.

After a while, I go downstairs to make some breakfast. I pop a couple pieces of bread in the toaster then brew some coffee. As I sit at the island to eat, Remington comes in from the back. Without a word, he sprints upstairs, slamming his bedroom door shut. I finish my breakfast and decide to text Aly to see if she wants to go shopping with me. We agree to meet up later this afternoon. I'm glad to be getting out of the house and as far away from Rem as possible.

*

"How are things going at your dad's?" Aly asks.

We decided to have dinner together at a new café after shopping.

"It's going okay for the most part. Dad and Bridget are in Bermuda for their honeymoon." She takes a bite of her turkey club sandwich, chewing slowly. I can tell there's something on her mind. "Just spill it." I say, rolling my eyes.

Swallowing, she shakes her head. "It's just that I heard a rumor. If it's true, I know you're probably mad."

"Why would I be mad?" I pop a salt and vinegar chip into my mouth.

Aly takes a sip of her iced latte. "Rem is seeing Marla. I heard it's casual, but still I thought you'd want to know."

While I'm well aware, I don't expect her words to cut so deep. "I already know." I say, taking a bite of my own sandwich to avoid speaking further.

Aly frowns. "Layla, she slept with Adam while you two were together. Now she's spending time with Rem and you-" I lift a hand to stop her.

"There's nothing between us." I interject. "It's dead, Aly. Don't bring it up again."

"You liked him though. You guys have this connection…"

"The only connection we have is our parents." I say. "Apart from that, we're nothing. We'll never be anything. Let it go." I'm talking more to myself than her even though I'll never admit that.

A look of uncertainty crosses her face. "It doesn't bother you?"

Whether it bothers me or not doesn't matter. The fact is, there is nothing I can do about it. Besides, hating him is easier.

SELF-INFLICTED

Remington doesn't belong to me. I have no control over his life and as much as it hurts to see him involved with my worst enemy, my words hold no meaning.

"It sucks." I admit with a shrug. "Yet what can I do? I'm not his keeper."

She nods slowly in agreement before a smile forms on her pink lips. Leaning over the table she says, "Kyle Fuller keeps looking at you."

My stomach muscles clench. Kyle was in my English Lit class last year and is totally hot. His dad works for a well-known indie record label in New York. I glance over my shoulder to see him wiping down a table. Our gazes lock for the briefest moment before I turn away.

"He's cute." Aly whispers.

I smile. "He is."

She looks past me, her eyes widening. "Oh my god, he's coming over here."

"Hey, Layla." Kyle says softly as I glance up at him.

His black hair is buzzed close to his scalp, his light hazel eyes sparkle under the fluorescent lights of the café.

"Hey, Kyle." I say. "I didn't know you worked here."

He smiles. "My mom owns the place. We opened two weeks ago."

"That's cool."

"How's your summer been?"

Pretty fucking horrible actually. "Not too bad."

"Nice. We should catch up sometime. Are you free tomorrow night?"

I feel my cheeks warm. "Sure."

He drags his teeth over his bottom lip. "Cool, can I give you my number?" I pull my phone from my back pocket, handing it to him so that he can enter the number then I text him so he has mine. "I'll call you later." He says before going back to work.

"That was awesome!" Aly beams as we continue eating. "I'm so proud of you."

I scoff. "I'm not a nun. I've been on dates."

She rolls her eyes. "You've been off the market since Adam, other than you know who."

I scowl. Yeah, Rem's the only person I've paid attention to this summer. There was Bryant but that fizzled before it even started. At least with Kyle, I might have more in common.

"I'm glad you're getting back in the saddle." She waggles her eyebrows.

I laugh. I'm glad to be giving a Kyle a shot too. If anything, I'll have something else to occupy my time to keep my distance from my stepbrother.

SELF-INFLICTED

CHAPTER TEN

Kyle is really sweet. I allow him to pick me up from my house on Tuesday night. He takes me to a fun restaurant for dinner that also has an arcade. I discover that we have more in common than our English Lit class which is nice. I even have the courage to tell him that I'm planning to study music. At the end of the night when he drops me off, I let him kiss me and while it isn't reckless and passionate like what I've shared with Rem, it's still nice.

I've been doing my best the last few days to stay away from Rem. However, his pettiness is on the same level as mine. He found the power cord I stole from his stereo, so he pulled down all the clothes that were hanging in my closet. It took me an hour to rehang everything while organizing it according to the type I preferred. So, I swapped out his shampoo for dish soap. That resulted in him swapping the sugar for salt which made me gag on my first sip of coffee Thursday morning. I threw his truck keys in the pool as retaliation, forcing him to frantically search for them. Not only did he have to change his clothes, but it also made him late for work last night. Unfortunately, my prank went wrong though because he tossed his wet clothes on my bed which resulted in me having to do laundry late last night.

Now, I'm busy getting ready for another date with Kyle. This time, he's picking me up to see a movie. I haven't decided how to get back at Rem yet, though I don't really care at the moment. I'm applying my lip gloss when I hear noise outside in the driveway. I glance out my bedroom window to see Connor unloading a drum kit from the back of Rem's truck. I continue to get myself ready, deciding to wear a pair of black denim shorts and a t-shirt that I got from a concert last year. As I'm sliding on my sneakers, I hear them coming into the house. Grabbing a small wallet and my phone, I place them in the back pocket of my shorts before heading downstairs.

"Hey, Layla. How's it going?" Ty greets, lugging an amp into the living room.

"Living the dream." I say. "What are you doing?" I follow him, narrowing my eyes at Connor setting up his drums. They've pushed the couch toward the wall, making room.

"We're practicing here tonight." Ty replies.

"My mom is having people over." Connor adds.

Thankful to be leaving, I nod in response.

"Is that a problem?" Remington asks from behind me.

I turn to face him. He's holding his electric guitar with a smug grin on his face that makes me want to punch him again.

"Fine with me." I shrug. "I'll be leaving shortly."

His face falls. "Where are you going?"

"Not that it's any of your business, but I have a date."

His jaw muscle ticks. Maybe this is how I get back at him for the wet bedding.

"Aly told me that you and Kyle Fuller are hanging out." Ty says.

Rem's gaze shifts to his friend.

"Who the fuck is Kyle Fuller?" he asks in a gravelly voice.

"A friend," rolling my eyes, I head to the foyer to grab my keys off the hook. I hope he's as jealous as I am about Marla Higgins. "He's picking me up in a few minutes."

I grab my phone when it vibrates, seeing Kyle's text that he's here.

SELF-INFLICTED

"Remember your curfew." Rem hollers from the living room.

"Bite me." I holler back before leaving the house.

I head for Kyle's car which is parked behind Rem's truck, smiling to myself.

The movie date is at the drive-in outside of town. My nerves are keeping me from allowing myself to fully relax with Kyle even though he's being a total gentleman. I love that he's so easy to talk to, but I'm afraid of getting attached. By the time we pull into a spot, I feel like my heart is going to leap out of my chest. Kyle turns the car off after activating the radio he's parked beside for sound. He unbuckles as I do the same, my fingers trembling against the seatbelt. Why am I so nervous?

"Have you ever been to a drive-in movie?" he asks, leaning back against his seat.

"Not that I remember." I glance out at the other cars pulling into spaces.

"It's pretty fun." His hand moves over the center console, folding over mine on my lap. I swallow the lump in my throat as I turn my head to meet his eyes. "You okay? You look nervous."

I form a tight smile. "Honestly, I am a little bit."

He chuckles. "The movie is supposed to be good. I didn't bring you hear to show you my backseat." He assures. The ball of stress in my gut lessens. "Unless you want to see it."

I laugh uncomfortably. "Not likely." I say. "I mean, not tonight." I blow out a breath. "Man, I'm rambling. I like you." I flip my hand over, squeezing his. "I'm just not ready for something serious."

"Neither am I." he uses his free hand to tuck my hair behind my ear, leaning closer.

The gesture makes me shiver and not in a good way. It reminds me of when Remington's done that. Kyle leans toward me, pressing his mouth to mine. I close my eyes, trying to get my stepbrother off my mind. Kyle slides his hand in my hair, tangling his fingers in the ends. Bile rises in my throat. Rem's done that too. Hating myself for comparing the two of them, I push past the intrusive thoughts, kissing him back. Within minutes, his hands are on my waist in an attempt to pull me closer to him. With the console in the way, I'm stuck on my side which I prefer.

I pull back suddenly, gasping for air. "Kyle, we should watch the movie."

He swallows roughly. "Right."

He holds my hand again and before long, I'm finding myself more relaxed thanks to the comedy on the screen. He doesn't try to paw at me or initiate another kiss.

"Are you hungry?" Kyle asks, exiting the drive-in lot.

"Yeah."

"There's this great place just a few miles from here." He says, pulling onto the main road. "Do you want to grab food?"

"Sure."

I regret my answer minutes later when he pulls into a familiar parking lot. It's the same restaurant Rem took me to last month after the rough day with my mom. Grateful to not see a familiar vehicle, I let Kyle hold my hand as he opens the door for me. Part of me wants to ask him if we can go somewhere else, but I feel like that would be difficult to explain.

A hostess seats us quickly in a booth near the front. I catch myself peeking out the window leading out to the parking lot every once in a while, hating myself for not being able to relax. I make it a point to order a soda with a salad instead of the cheeseburger and shake that Rem recommended. As good as it was, I feel weird about ordering the same thing. Kyle and I talk about our plans for the future.

"I'm going to stay with my dad for the summer. The record label has an internship they offer."

"That's really cool." I say, sipping on my soda. "Do you want to work for them eventually?"

"For sure. My dad scouts talent and attends shows for a living. Who wouldn't love that?"

I smile. "That'd be awesome."

We eat while continuing our conversation when our food is brought to the table. We talk about school coming up. He's planning on attending some of the same classes as me which helps me chill out a bit more, thinking our friendship has the potential to grow. I like Kyle a lot despite the questionable feelings regarding Rem.

A set of headlights shines against the window, capturing my attention. As I peer out at the familiar truck, my heart sinks to my stomach. Damn it. Things were going so well. Loosening a breath, I do my best to keep my head down, focusing on our conversation. Maybe they won't see us. Kyle continues talking while I do my best to listen, working on my salad until a shadow casts on our table.

"Hey, *sis!*" Rem says with the fakest smile I've ever witnessed.

I glare up at him as he focuses on Kyle who looks confused. "I thought you had practice." I grit out before turning to Kyle. "This is my *stepbrother*."

"We finished and got hungry." Rem says, sliding into the booth beside me. My face flames in mortification. What the hell is he doing? "You know we come here when we practice."

"I'll grab us a couple menus." Connor says.

I blink at his back as he walks away. Are they going to join us?

Rem leans against the back of the booth seat, crossing his arms. "You Kyle?" he asks my date who looks annoyed at the intrusion.

"Yep. So, you two are stepsiblings?"

"Our parents got married last weekend." I say, kicking myself for not mentioning Rem at all until now. Honestly, I didn't think it mattered.

"That's cool." Kyle replies. "What are you guys practicing?"

Connor comes back to the table, handing Rem a menu before grabbing a chair to sit at the end of the table. *Fuck my life.* Why are they doing this to me?

"We're a band." Connor says absently, scanning the menu. "Hemingway's Rejects."

Kyle's eyes light up as I bite down on the inside of my cheek. I feel Rem's boot tap against my sneaker. I shoot him a sidelong glance.

"I hate you." I say quietly.

He winks at me, setting his menu on the table.

"You guys won the battle of the bands at Happy's a few weeks back. You were amazing!" Kyle says.

I roll my eyes. So much for hoping he'd tell them to leave us alone.

"We're playing a gig next weekend at The Starlight. You should come." Connor says.

Rem grabs my soda, taking a sip. "Not as good as the milkshake. Right, Bug?"

I pull my glass back from him. "Go away."

He chuckles as the waitress comes over to take their order. Kyle is a total fanboy with Connor and Rem, who orders his usual. I barely touch my salad, unable to stomach much more. I hate that Rem inserted himself into our date. He's ruining my evening.

I excuse myself to the restroom, seriously debating calling an Uber to come pick me up. As I apprehensively make my way back to the table, I'm grateful to see that Connor and Rem are seated at the counter now. I don't miss the arrogant smirk on

Rem's face when I pass them. I glare at him before sliding into the booth.

Kyle glances at me briefly before looking away. "You ready to get out of here?"

"Yes, please." I say, grateful that he doesn't want to stick around.

The drive back to my place is quieter than usual, forcing dread to take over. When we pull into the driveway, Kyle leaves his car running, not even placing it in Park. Irritation springs to life.

"I had fun tonight." He says with a small smile.

I smile genuinely, trying to keep my temper from flaring. I don't want Kyle to know how angry I am at Rem.

"Me too. Sorry about the intrusion."

Kyle chuckles lightly. "No worries. I did think for a moment that he was going to bash my face in."

"When I saw you with that preppy motherfucker earlier, I wanted to do bad things."

"What kind of bad things?"

"The bashing faces kind."

Unease settles in my stomach. "Did Remington say anything to you?"

"Not really," Kyle says. "just that it would be in my best interest to call it a night."

"Why?" I grit out, the simmering rage threatening to spill over.

He releases a sigh, running a hand over his buzzed hair. "Something about a curfew and that your dad doesn't allow you to date." He shakes his head. "Which I thought was weird considering you were with Adam Danvers for a year."

I inhale a sharp breath. "That motherfu-"

Kyle lifts a hand. "Look, I don't want to be the reason you fight with your brother."

"He is *not* my brother."

"Still. He obviously cares about you. Plus, if your dad doesn't want you dating…"

"My dad doesn't care!" I shout, instantly regretting it. Great. Now Kyle is looking at me like I'm hysterical. Which I am, just not at him. "I'm allowed to date, Kyle. Rem shouldn't have said that."

Kyle nods slowly. "We were just having fun right? Maybe we can meet up again some other time."

Quelling the urge to roll my eyes, I nod. "Sure. When?"

"I'll call you." My heart deflates.

No he won't.

He doesn't make a move to kiss or even hug me to my disappointment. I walk to the porch, unlocking the front door. Slamming it closed behind me, I trek into the living room, flicking on the light. I spot Remington's guitar sitting in its stand next to Connor's drums. He sabotaged me tonight. Usually, I'm the one doing that to myself yet here he is helping me along.

The resentment is palpable, reverberating in each step that I take toward the instrument. How dare he threaten Kyle! How dare he hook up with that skank Marla! Desperately wanting to get him back, I do something that will likely end bad for me later. It'll probably cost me my savings too, though I don't really care right now. Grabbing the guitar from the stand, I march with purpose to the back slider, pulling it open before stepping out onto the deck.

"Fuck you, Remington Paulson!" I scream at the top of my lungs, smashing the guitar against the ground.

The head cracks and chips, small fragments flying off in every direction as I keep going. I don't stop until all that's left is four snapped strings, a small chunk of the head and a bit of the neck. Then I toss the remainder of the damn thing into the pool, drowning it along with the fiery pain of regret.

SELF-INFLICTED

"What the fuck did you do?!" Rem demands in a frightening growl that forces me upright in bed. Blinking wildly at the sudden burst of light in my room when he flips the switch, I slowly take in his appearance. His dark eyes are narrowed to slits as he stalks toward my bed, hands clenched into fists at his side. "God dammit, Layla! What is your fucking problem?"

I am not a morning person. I sure as shit am not a middle of the night person when I've been awoken by an asshole with disrespectful behavior. Yanking off my covers, I spring from the bed, matching his stance.

"My problem?!" I scream right back. "As if I'm the one with the problem, *Elijah*."

He shakes his head, his shoulders tight. "Fuck. *You*."

I glare at him. "No. Fuck you." I snap. "How dare you lie to Kyle! You sabotaged my date like some sort of jealous ex." I eye him head to toe. "I should have known you'd stoop so low."

He quirks a brow, crossing his arms over his chest. "Says the one who started shit with me because I was paying attention to another girl."

I scoff. "It's not *any* girl, jackass." I lift my fisted hands, groaning in frustration. "God! You're such a dick."

"You're a bitch," he growls. "I don't know what your fucking problem is because you don't talk to me."

"I'm not going to either." I seethe. "Get out of my room."

He stands his ground. "No."

My entire body trembles in exasperation as I step closer to him. "Go away!" I move to push him but his hands dart out, capturing my wrists. "Let me go."

"Why? So you can punch me again? Or better yet, destroy more of my shit?" he bends his head, locking his gaze to mine. "Do you understand the value of that guitar?"

My nostrils flare. "I don't care. Buy another one when you're rich and famous."

He laughs without humor. "Right. Is that what this is? You're jealous of me because I might have a future, that I've fought for by the way, while you sit here and rot. Too afraid to move forward because of self-consciousness."

I tug my wrists from his grasp. "Get the fuck out of my room."

Rem rolls his eyes. "Sure thing," he heads for the door, stopping at the threshold to glance back at me. "One way or another, you're going to pay for what you've done."

"Doubtful." I snap.

He leaves, closing the door behind him. I sit on the edge of my bed, running a hand through my hair. I deserve his anger for destroying something that means so much to him. I don't deserve his malicious behavior though. I shouldn't have smashed his guitar even if I was furious at him for scaring off Kyle and for dating Marla.

The next day, I stay in my room except to shower or grab food. Luckily, I have to work tonight which helps me take my mind off Rem's anger. Before I leave the house, I notice the music equipment is gone. My shift breezes by thanks to a busy night with a local band playing. Rem's shift ended a few hours before mine so I'm trying to stay optimistic that he won't be around tonight.

I crank the stereo on my way home, letting Kellin Quinn's voice drown out the bullshit in my head. Sometimes a girl needs loud, screamo music to calm down. As I turn onto our street, the frustration that's been festering all day spews out. There's a line of cars in front of our house with the driveway full, so I have to park nearly a block away. After locking my car, I make the trek to the house, figuring out how I want to handle the situation.

The closer I get, the more I hear the sounds of a full-blown party taking place with music blaring. Apparently my stepbrother has a death wish. Pushing the front door open, I'm greeted by a group of bodies belonging to people I don't recognize. I squeeze through the foyer, making my way up the stairs, grateful nobody is lingering here. I drop my purse on the bed, toeing my shoes off before heading back down the stairs. There's no way I'm letting Remington chase me out of my own house tonight. I don't even care if I make a scene at this point.

I navigate through the crowd in the living room, searching for him with no luck, then notice another group of people out on the deck through the open back slider. Wandering outside, I find Rem sitting in a patio chair at the outdoor table with Marla Higgins on his lap. He hasn't noticed me yet because he's talking to Connor across from him. Good, I'll blindside him and ruin his evening.

When I approach, Marla's the first to notice. "*Barf*low, you're here." She says, eyeing me with annoyance. "Did you work hard tonight?"

Rem's gaze snags on mine. I shoot him a glare.

"So hard." I say with a dark smile, flicking my eyes to Marla. "Though you wouldn't know what that's like, being a spoiled brat your whole life."

She snorts. "Good comeback. At least my mom isn't a raging alcoholic."

My shoulders tighten. "I bet you wish she was." I reply snidely. "It seems to me you want to live my life." I look back to Remington. "What with enjoying *all* my sloppy seconds."

He pins me with a glare. Crossing my arms, I tilt my head to the side, matching his intent look. I hope he feels like shit for hurting me. I also hope this party crashes and burns.

Marla shakes her head, giggling. "Still bitter about Adam? He never even loved you."

I ignore her, keeping my gaze trained on Rem who appears to be clenching his jaw hard enough to break his teeth. "Call off the party."

"No." he bites out.

"Do it. *Now.*"

"What are you going to do if I don't?" he counters, pushing Marla off his lap to stand. She huffs before storming off into the house.

"Do you really want to fight me on this?"

He scoffs. "It's a fight you'll lose."

Instead of responding, I go back into the house to make my way upstairs. Once I'm in my room, I pull my cell phone out of my purse.

"What are you doing?" Rem demands, marching into my room.

I dial the emergency number on my phone before holding the screen up with my thumb hovering on the call button. "Do you want to do this the hard way or the easy way?"

"You'll call the cops? Is that all you've got?" he rolls his eyes, making my rage increase. "God, you really are a good girl, aren't you?"

Tossing my phone to the bed, I step toward him until we're toe to toe. He breathes deep, glowering down at me.

"You like it when I'm good." I say, dropping my voice low. I lift a hand, running my finger over his chest against his thin t-shirt. "Would you rather I be bad, Rem?" I bat my lashes at him.

A low growl rumbles as he grabs my upper arms, shoving me into the wall by my door. His breath falls against my lips when he leans into me, his eyes frantically searching mine. My lungs restrict when heat circles low in my belly, pooling between my legs. Why am I still attracted to him after all this?

"God, I fucking hate you." He breathes, resting his forehead against mine.

My eyes close, inhaling his distinct smell.

"Same." The word comes out breathy, doing little to hide my lie.

Lifting his head, he smirks down at me, pinning me with those dark eyes. "It was purely physical, Bug. No *love* lost. Right?"

SELF-INFLICTED

My stomach dips as I swallow down the longing that's trying to surface. "Fuck you."

He chuckles, lifting his head. "Ah, yes. Fuck me, right? That's what you wanted to do until fate had other plans for us. What's the matter? Still want what you can't have?"

"I don't want you." I seethe, shoving against him so that he backs up. He barely moves.

His brows raise. "No?" bending his head, he lowers his lips to my ear, releasing a groan that ignites a fire in my belly. His hand slides down my jaw to rest against my throat, applying a slight pressure. I whimper, pressing my thighs together. "Are you wet for me?"

I loosen a shaky breath. "Yes." *No!*

He leans back to look me in the eye. "Of course you are." Releasing me suddenly, he steps back with a sinister smile before leaving.

My lungs tighten as I attempt to draw oxygen back in while tears threaten to surface. Why does he insist on playing games with me? I'm so tired of this! For once I want to make him suffer the way I do every time we get into an argument. I want him to be the one left breathless and riled up.

"Hey!" I shout, marching out of my room. I see Rem's shoulders tense before he glances back at me near the top of the stairs. "You want this dance to stop?" I ask, throwing his own words from months ago back in his face.

He turns fully to face me, his hands clenched at his sides. There's a darkness that creeps into his features as his lashes lower slightly.

"Careful…" He warns in a gravelly voice that gives me the motivation to keep going.

I take one step, then another, pushing the rejection to the furthest parts of my mind. My brows lift, giving him the most arrogant look I can muster as I stop in front of him. "Get on your knees."

I think he's going to retort with something hurtful, yet he doesn't. Instead, he rushes toward me, gripping my hips and forcing me back into my room. His booted foot kicks the door closed before he lowers to the floor, gazing up at me with a look that's sinful. Heat pools between my legs as his hands slowly glide to my bare thighs. Rem licks his lips, angling his head toward the fly of my shorts. His tongue darts out, licking across the most sensitive part of me through the material. Drawing back, his lashes lift and I'm paralyzed by how deliciously handsome he looks right now. His dark eyes searching my face while on his knees before me.

"Is this what you want?" There's no teasing in his tone, no anger.

He touches me between my legs, my body jolting when his finger slides over my center. My brain short circuits as I nod. With steady fingers, he unbuttons my shorts before lowering the zipper. I watch him grab the hem, tugging them down my legs until they fall to my feet.

His eyes flick up to mine. "Blue is my favorite color." He says, referencing the lacy underwear I'm wearing.

"Is it?" I ask, breathless. My heart is pounding in my throat making it difficult to speak.

His lips kick up in a wicked smirk. "Fuck yeah."

He positions his head, running his tongue along me again. I cry out, my knees nearly buckling. He works me through the thin lace fabric, his tongue deliberately moving like a skilled expert. His hand coasts down the back of my thigh, forcing my left knee to bend while he continues his glorious assault with his mouth. My fingers tangle in his hair, urging him to keep going as a low grunt rumbles against me. Rem hooks my left leg over his shoulder while the other hand steadies my hip, keeping me from falling. My breath quickens and I bite down on my bottom lip, stifling a moan when my lower stomach muscles clench.

"Oh…god…" I pant as tension builds within.

He tugs at the fabric between my legs, moving it to the side. I gape down at him as he runs his tongue over my bare skin before pulling back with a sexy smile. I nearly topple over when he releases me, standing to his full height. My ears ring as the haze of euphoria fades and the reality of what I've done slams into me. I quickly pull my shorts back up, fastening them.

Rem leans against my bedroom wall still wearing that satisfied smile, his dark eyes searching my face. As much as I enjoyed the moment with him, I can't shake the betrayal I feel for him hooking up with Marla and throwing a party here. More than that, the anger comes back full force when I realize just how much I want him to touch me again. How desperately I want to kiss him, convincing him to end this party and spend the night in my room. The line we've been walking is almost completely crossed now. I let this go too far.

On shaky legs, I step closer to him, lifting my chin until our lips almost touch. "Good boy." I whisper before darting for my door and tugging it open.

CHAPTER ELEVEN

I retreat into the bathroom to shower, attempting to wash away the dirty aura of using him for pleasure. I'm not built the same way. I can't fake it the way he can. It's too difficult to turn myself on and off, knowing the agony of being denied. By the time I'm clean, I notice that the house is eerily quiet. After putting on a pair of leggings with a baggy t-shirt, I make my way downstairs.

Rem is standing in the kitchen, leaning back against the island counter with his arms crossed over his exposed chest. As I round the island, I notice he's wearing a pair of black sweats hanging low on his hips, his feet bare. Apparently the party is over. I have no clue what to say, so I stay silent as I open the refrigerator to grab a bottle of water.

"I'm sorry." He says in a thick voice, catching me by surprise.

I glance up at him, watching his jaw muscle tick as he stares out the kitchen window.

"For…?" I unscrew the cap to the water bottle, taking a sip. I feel like I should be the one apologizing right now.

He turns his head to look at me. "I didn't know you had history with Marla."

I shrug, setting the bottle on the counter. "You can hang out with whoever you want."

"No, I can't." Uncrossing his arms, he drags a hand through his hair. "If I knew who she was to you, I never would have paraded her around here."

"But you'd bring someone else around." I'm going to hate knowing he's with anyone else regardless of who it is. "It doesn't matter."

He glares down at me. "I disagree."

"Whatever, Rem. Be with whoever you want."

"So that you can date Kyle or some other idiot that doesn't deserve you?" he snaps.

Is he seriously trying to shame me for that. "It is none of your business."

He shakes his head, eyes rolling to the ceiling before landing on me again. "You see, Bug, I don't think you believe that when you say it. Everything you do is my business."

I match his glare, lifting my chin. "Why?"

His chest deflates, shoulders sagging. "Because I can't fucking shake you. Seeing you with other guys pisses me off."

I scrub a hand over my face. "What do you want me to do?" I ask, glancing back up at him, motioning my hand between us. "This will never happen."

"You're the one who said love sucks."

"What?" I can't keep up with this conversation right now.

He releases a low growl. "Why are you dating if you don't want more?"

I frown when I grasp what he's saying. What he'd said earlier about no love being lost. He emphasized the word love. Oh god, he can't really be considering that we're in love with each other, can he?

"Is that what all this bullshit has been about?" I ask quietly. "Just because I don't want to be in a relationship, doesn't mean I can't make friends."

He squints. "*Friends.*"

"You have a hickey visible." I glare at the faint mark on the side of his neck, venom coursing through my veins.

His throat rolls in a swallow before he closes his eyes. "I hate you for making me feel shit. I'm fucking drowning in you every day while you go out with others and wear a mask of strength even though you're a coward."

My shoulders tighten. "So, it's okay for you to treat me like shit?" I scoff. "Is that how you justify your behavior, Remington? Does that make you sleep better at night?"

He pushes away from the counter, shouldering past me. "I was wrong about you. Your heart is fucking poison." He storms off, taking the stairs two at a time before slamming his bedroom door closed.

What the fuck ever. Clutching my bottle of water, I go to turn off the lights then remember my car is parked down the street thanks to Remington's stupid party. When I go up to my room to grab my keys, I realize they're not in my purse. Cursing him for probably hiding them from me as one last immature slap in the face, I go back downstairs to find them hanging on the hook near the front door. When I open it, my heart sinks as the bitter taste of shame coats my tongue. He moved my car into the driveway for me. He also told everyone to leave after I used him despite me being at fault too. He's right. I am a coward. My existence is miserable living this way, yet I don't know any other form of self-preservation. I started this by instigating fights, by initiating the prank war when Marla was over. It doesn't excuse his behavior, but it's not fair to accuse him of the same stuff that I do. He was apologizing and instead of accepting it, I swatted it away with mean words and accusations.

Releasing a sigh, I lock the door before making my way up to his room. I don't know what's going on in his head or what type of emotions he's having. All I know is that I don't want to hurt him. I don't want to hate him either because deep down, I know that I don't. I actually like him a lot. Even when we fight he makes me feel something I've rarely felt. *Alive.*

Knocking lightly on his door, I don't expect him to answer. I can hear the faint sound of his stereo playing within and am about to turn away when he cracks the door open. There's only a small light on atop his nightstand, casting a dark shadow against the side of his face.

"Thank you for moving my car." I say in a quiet voice.

"Yeah." He murmurs, staring past me.

"Thanks for ending the party too."

He lifts a brow. "What do you want, Bug?" His gaze drifts down to my fingers, tangled together in front of me.

Licking my lips, I lift my chin. "I want to apologize for hurting you. I don't know what feelings I gave you, but I'm sorry for them. I don't want to hate you, it's just…"

"Easier." He answers. I nod as he opens the door further. "Do you want to come in?" My gaze lands on the queen sized bed, my chest tightening. "No pressure, just offering." He says, turning away to sit on the end of the bed. I watch as he drags a hand through his hair, displaying the muscles in his abdomen and arm. "I'm moving out next week."

My lips part in a gasp. "Rem-"

"We found a place to rent." He smiles slightly. "That's why I threw the party here. I figured I'd take advantage of one last moment of irresponsibility." He shrugs. "I guess I also wanted to piss you off one last time too."

I frown. "You make it sound like we'll never see each other again."

His eyes fall to the floor. "We won't. The place is in New York."

My feet are moving before I realize it. I sit down on the bed next to him. "You're leaving?"

He nods, lifting his gaze to mine, his lips turned down in the corners. "There's more opportunity for our band there, plus I never planned on staying here long anyway."

I remember Bridget mentioning that he was moving out at some point. I guess I didn't expect it to happen so soon. Everyone leaves. That's what I'd told him at one point and here he is proving me right.

"Can I tell you something?" he asks, his voice low.

I swallow the lump in my throat. "Yes."

He inhales deeply, his left hand slowly coming up to cup my jaw. "I'm going to miss you."

The conviction in his voice makes my eyes sting as my heart squeezes tightly in my chest. I close them, my brow crumpling at the heavy emotions swirling inside me. Even through all the turmoil we've caused each other and the fact we've only known each other a short time, there's a deep connection with Remington that I can't shake. Defeat swirls in my stomach, stealing the breath from my lungs. This isn't fair. That's been at the root of it all since the beginning. My anger and frustration was never directed toward him but because of him. He brought out something in me I was only just beginning to understand and he's the one person I can't be around.

"I'll miss you, too." I confess. "Of all of the terrible luck in the world, why does it feel like meeting you is the worst?"

He chuckles lightly. "I ask myself that every day, Bug." My heart races when his hand lowers from my jaw to graze along my neck before his forehead touches mine. "It's the purest form of torture to want something you can't have. To know that it could be the best damn thing you've ever experienced while also being scared shitless of the repercussions."

I do something I know I'll live to regret later. I place my hands against his ribs on either side of his body, tilting my chin up until his lips hover above mine. "Part of me wants to not suffer now and deal with the consequences later." I admit in a soft voice.

He'd mentioned pretending before. What if we could really do that for one selfish moment?

"We're not us right now. Just two people, living in a daydream." His voice is smooth as honey, dripping with desire and promise.

"Okay,"

Remington's lips collide with mine, effectively silencing me. Creeping thoughts begin to take hold because I know this is wrong on so many levels, yet I push them away to the furthest corners. I'll have all the time in the world to reflect on the brutality of this moment later. A low growl rumbles in his chest as he kisses me fiercely, wrapping his other arm around my waist, forcing me closer. My fingertips sink into the skin of his torso, holding on for dear life because my head is clouded, my body weightless from being caught up in what only he can elicit. I feel the steel barbell from his tongue against the roof of my mouth, making my body tremble with need. He rips his lips away from mine, his breath coming out hard and fast.

"Lay down." He whispers. I scoot back to obey. He hovers over me, kissing a path from my temple to my chin. "Good girl." He whispers.

His voice is intoxicating. I love that he praises me. He continues exploring my skin with his lips, trailing down my neck while tugging the neckline of my t-shirt to the side to kiss a path to the upper swell of my breast. I breathe out a moan, my head angling up toward the ceiling as he cups that same breast with his hand, gliding his thumb over my nipple. I let my legs fall to either side, aching for him to settle between them. He maintains his position with one hand holding himself up while the other coasts down to my hip.

His eyes flick up to mine. "You have no idea how badly I've wanted to touch you, to hear you moan while I worship your body." His gaze slowly rakes down and back up. "For tonight," he lowers his head, brushing my lips with his. "you are mine." He kisses me passionately before straightening again. His hand cups between my legs. "This is *mine*."

"Yes." I hiss when he strokes his thumb over the tight nub.

He applies more pressure, swirling his thumb and pressing a finger against my wet center over the fabric, not taking his eyes off me. My lungs tighten as the orgasm rocks through me intensely. Before I can come up for air, he begins sliding the leggings down my legs along with my underwear until I'm fully bared.

Biting down on his bottom lip, he gently spreads my knees apart. "Fuck, you're stunning."

His hands slide up my thighs as he bends at the waist. I hold my breath when he angles his mouth directly over my clit. I swear my heart stops beating for a second. He did this earlier except I wasn't exposed like this, so it didn't feel nearly as intimate. He keeps his eyes on mine as his tongue darts out, tasting me. I smash my lips together, stifling the cry that erupts.

He stops abruptly.

"Don't you dare keep quiet." He demands. "I want to hear how good I make you feel. I don't give a fuck if the whole world knows what I'm doing to you right now." He goes back to his task, pressing a palm flat on my lower belly while cupping my ass with the other, feasting on me.

I can feel the barbell on his tongue when it slips inside me, creating a glorious friction. "Oh, god, Rem..."

He groans, the vibration of his mouth my undoing. Another earth shattering release takes hold. Remington sits up slowly, licking his lips with a devilish grin. His hands fall to the hem of my t-shirt and I sit up to help him remove it. Raising to my knees in front of him, my fingers tremble when they reach the waistband of his sweats, eyeing the bulge of his hard length. I rotate my palm, flattening it against him. He lets out something between a groan and a whimper. My pulse pounds in my throat.

"That feels good." He rasps as I continue stroking him through the fabric.

His body is trembling when I remove my hand to pull his pants further down. My eyes widen when I realize he's not wearing anything underneath. More than that, the lamp light glints off a piercing at his tip.

My gaze flicks up to his. "Did that hurt?" I ask because my curiosity gets the best of me in the moment. He doesn't seem fazed by the question.

Lifting a brow he says, "Would you think less of me if I said no?"

I gasp. "Really?"

He chuckles. "I don't mind the pain."

There's a look in his eyes that makes me believe there's more to what he's saying, but now isn't the time to get into it. I wrap my hand around his shaft, stroking him while gliding my thumb across the damp tip, making him moan. As my movements become faster, he halts me with a hand on mine.

"Wait," he pants. "I want to be inside you."

I release him before he gracefully stands from the bed to fully remove his sweats. It's difficult not to stare while he walks to the nightstand, opening that top drawer. I glance down at the still unopened box of condoms. He tears a packet open with his teeth, captivating me as he rolls it onto his hard length, watching himself in the process. He lowers himself to the bed again, resting his head against a pillow before reaching for me, guiding my hips until I'm hovering over him, my knees on either side of his thighs.

He tilts his head back, meeting my eyes. "I'm giving you full control."

My throat tightens. I've never tried in this position before. With Adam everything was so...vanilla.

Rem must sense my apprehension because he cups my chin, stroking my bottom lip with his thumb. "Are you okay?" he asks in a soft voice that tugs at my heart.

"I'm not that experienced." I confess in a whisper.

His lips tilt up on one side. "You're a virgin?"

"No." I respond quickly, my cheeks heating. "I've just never done *this* before."

He chuckles, releasing my chin and gripping the base of his cock. "Go slow."

I lower myself carefully, feeling the pressure of him against my opening. He sucks in air through his teeth, his shoulders flex against my palms where I'm bracing myself. Releasing himself, his fingers curl around my waist to help ease me down until I'm taking every last inch of him. Rem lifts his hips, forcing a moan from the back of my throat. All coherent thought quickly leaves then. I begin moving against him, swirling my hips while his head falls back, observing me. I can already feel myself close to release as I slide up and down his length. I grab one of his hands, placing it against me over my breast. He squeezes gently before sitting up to suck on my nipple. In seconds I'm crying out, bucking my hips into him as I ride him faster.

"God, you're hot." He groans, cupping my ass roughly. "Keep going. I want you to cum again."

Lowering my lips to his, I curl my arm around his neck, kissing him while building myself up all over again. He bites down on my lower lip and I return the favor earning a moan from him that makes my toes curl. The sound of our bodies connecting rings in my ears as pressure builds between my legs.

"Fuck, I can't hold it anymore." He grits out.

The next orgasm comes quick when I feel his body stiffen as he presses his fingers into the skin of my thigh, hard enough to bruise. Suddenly, I'm on my back with him hovering over me, kissing me intensely. I can feel him moving inside me still, each throb sending ripples of heat through my body. Eventually, his mouth slows and he lifts his head. The hunger in those brown eyes is still evident, yet mixed with something else, something that looks too much like an emotion I don't want to name. My throat tightens when he trails his index finger down my temple to my cheek, cupping it before drawing my lips back to his in a simmering kiss that leaves me breathless.

He lifts himself away, inhaling a deep breath through his nose before sitting up. A blast of cold air falls over me with us separated. I sit up as well, wrapping my arms around my knees, pulling them to my chest. Remington is quiet as he stares up at the ceiling. I quietly examine the squareness of his jaw that flexes sporadically, the length of his lashes that fan his cheeks, and the way his throat rolls in a swallow.

It's funny how life works. Minutes ago, I was cursing fate for allowing us to meet, only to sweep the rug out from under us. Now, I'm weightless. I thought I'd feel guilty afterward or dirty for acting on impulse. Yet I don't. Not at all.

My stomach tightens. *That's the problem.*

Releasing a sigh, Rem lifts off the bed, grabbing his sweats to put them on. My heart drops to my stomach as disappointment rushes through me. Apparently pretending is over. Time to go back to hiding and forgetting anything that happened between us. I'm quiet as I collect my clothing to dress myself. Running a hand through my hair, I close my eyes against the hollow pain seeping into my chest. When I open them, Rem is watching me from across the room. He mutters a curse before placing his hands on my waist and pulling me into him until our hips are aligned.

"I'm not trying to hurt you, Bug. Believe me, that's the last thing I want to do." He confesses in a soft voice. "It's just that I want you. Again. Forever."

My breath snags. "Forever?"

He frowns, releasing me. "I don't know. My head is fucked right now. I thought..." he trails off, shifting his gaze to the floor.

"You thought it would go away." I whisper. That has to be what he wanted to say. I feel the exact same way.

His head bobs in a nod. "I've never met a girl like you before." his eyes flash to mine. "Don't get me wrong, I want your body," he scans the length of me, my blood heating all over again. "but I want everything else too."

I struggle to breathe as what he's saying sinks in. While a part of me really likes the idea of pursuing more, the more rational part knows that we're young, that he's got dreams to follow and so do I. More than that, the ugly truth of our roundabout relation is something that could seriously disrupt both our lives as well as those around us.

"So, this is it." I say aloud even though I'm desperately trying to reassure myself of the same thing.

"Yeah, Bug. This is all we'll ever have." He reaches out, placing his warm palm against my cheek as he tilts his head down, gently kissing my lips.

Overwhelming dread builds inside me when he moves to pull away. I wrap my arms around his shoulders, lifting up on my toes. He instantly envelopes me in his arms as I kiss him back, pouring every ounce of what I feel for him into the action while silently praying that somehow things can be different, that we can continue to see where this leads. A nagging voice resonates in my head, bringing on a wave of nausea as we separate.

Stupid girl.

SELF-INFLICTED

CHAPTER TWELVE

Five days after our night together, Remington moves out. Focusing on the future of Hemingway's Rejects is priority number one, which I can't blame him for. There's no use lying to myself by thinking that a future with him is possible. Not when he's destined for greatness with his band while I have no clue where I'm headed.

The night the guys officially leave, I lie to Aly when she invites me to send them off, saying I'm not feeling well. I can't stomach the thought of saying goodbye to Remington officially even though I do support their move. Now that he's gone, I spend most of my time working at Happy's or focusing on my first courses in college. I've decided to stay living with dad for the time being to continue saving up money for my own apartment eventually. Aly says she'll happily be my roommate since she's staying in town until she graduates from cosmetology school. When I'm not working or in class, I hang out with my best friend as much as possible. After finally confessing the full story to Aly, because I couldn't hold it in any longer, I'm beginning to do my best to move on.

Things with Kyle probably won't ever be what they could have been, but in the past few months he's become a good friend. It helps to know someone in my classes. I'm actually grateful that we're just friends anyway. It's pointless to date when I have no interest in something more. It wouldn't be fair to either of us. One of the main things I took away from Rem and his somewhat infinite wisdom, is forcing myself to be more positive. While I still have a long way to go, I know I can't continue living a life that makes me miserable. Even dad seems more encouraging with me pursuing music. I'm sure I have Bridget to thank for that.

"You should bring your guitar and sing." Aly says. "Close your eyes." She's standing in front of me while I sit in her vanity chair, letting her practice a smoky eye. I've been enlisted as her guinea pig which I don't really mind. I'll do anything to help support her dreams.

Kyle mentioned an open mic night at the café his mom owns. Aly hasn't stopped pestering me for days.

"I don't know…" she cuts me off.

"Layla, I love you. Truly, I do."

I open my eyes to look at her. "But…?"

"You need to branch out. I'm so proud of you for standing up to your dad and pursuing what you want. However, I know you. You second guess every move you make even when it's right."

"I hate being judged." I whine.

She lightly grips my chin. "Close your eyes." I obey as she continues talking. "Judgement is a part of life. Whether we're aware of it or not, someone is always going to form an opinion about us. You know, Ty used to be terrified of performing." I remember Rem mentioning that. "He still gets nervous, but he's gotten a lot better. Do you know why?"

"Why?" I try not to squeeze my eyelids too tightly against the tickling of the brush.

"Lots of practice. That and his determination. You have to face your fears." She's right. Although, that doesn't make me any less terrified. "You're the only one who has to live your life. Don't you want to be happy?" My best friend smiles down at me when I open my eyes again. "Singing makes you happy. Writing makes you happy."

SELF-INFLICTED

"It does, but-"

"But nothing!" she shouts, her tone stern. "Stop finding excuses, Lay. Do you think anyone who's ever chased a dream let fear get the best of them?"

No. If they had, then they would have given up. There's a million people in the world who would be nowhere because of that. No matter how big or small, dreams are what makes the world go round. Innovators, scientists, doctors, lawyers, musicians and more have to want it bad enough to make it happen. Either that or they just get lucky, which is probably true for a lot of people, though it doesn't lessen how rewarding it might feel to accomplish something.

She works on finishing my makeup as I mull over the possibility of finally spreading my antisocial wings. While the thought of performing for complete strangers terrifies me, I know I'll never get anywhere by not trying. The only sure way to fail is to not try at all. I've always been a good girl – reasonable and subservient. Maybe it's time to rebel a little. To prove to myself that I'm so much more than a daughter worried about her mother or pleasing her father, and a woman afraid of following her heart.

*

Inhaling a deep breath, I grab my guitar, making my way to the stage. Aly let's out a loud whistle that pierces my ears before shouting encouragement. A small smile forms on my face as my cheeks heat. This is completely nerve-wracking. Even as I take the steps up onto the stage and plant myself on the bar stool in front of the mic, doubt clouds my head.

Releasing the breath, I flick my gaze out to the small crowd of maybe fifteen people, not including the employees at the café. Most of them are here to perform too, which helps me feel a little less queasy about the whole thing. We're all trying to put ourselves out there, sharing our passions with each other whether it be through song, poetry, or musical instruments.

    Ty is next to Aly. He shoots me a wide smile that helps calm me. Knowing I have supportive friends makes this easier. I slide my right hand along the neck of my guitar, positioning my fingers on the strings. Taking another deep, cleansing breath, I begin strumming the intro to a song I wrote just a few weeks ago. I close my eyes as the lyrics pour out of me.

> *Stupid girl, dreaming big.*
> *Wishing you could get a hit.*
> *Of the freedom they all know*
> *Catching whiffs as the winds blow*
> *From the chaos of the storm*
> *Swirling around you, stealing warmth*
> *She's an addict, he's a god.*
> *They'll never break from the façade.*
> *Hold your head high, keep that smile.*
> *Pretend you're perfect for a while.*
> *I'm going down the rabbit hole.*
> *Of everything I've ever known*
> *Wondering why I'm so alone.*
> *And they don't want me anymore.*
> *Is this all inside my head.*
> *Or do they really wish me dead?*
> *I'm a mess and it's your fault.*
> *In breaking cycles, I got lost.*

    I open my eyes after the chorus, gaining the courage to scan the room. A few people are chatting quietly at their tables while others are looking at me, some even bobbing their head to the tune I play on my old guitar. Something inside me blooms, causing me to sit up straighter, projecting my voice further as I sing into the microphone, glancing at Aly who's smiling like a proud mother at her toddler's dance recital.

> *Stupid woman, now she's grown.*
> *And dreaming of a place called home.*
> *Something she has never known.*
> *Being content to not roam*
> *Living with the sordid ghosts*
> *Sleeping without other's close*
> *Will I be enough for you?*
> *Or just one of the lucky few?*
> *I'm going down the rabbit hole.*
> *Of everything I've ever known*
> *Wondering why I'm so alone.*
> *And they don't want me anymore.*
> *Is this all inside my head.*
> *Or do they really wish me dead?*
> *I'm a mess and it's your fault.*
> *In breaking cycles, I got lost.*
> *In breaking cycles, I got lost.*

As the music drifts to an end, several cheers ring out with the applause. Both Aly and Ty give me a standing ovation which makes me chuckle nervously. I hold my guitar tightly as I hop down from the stage, making my way over to them.

"That was incredible!" Aly beams, wrapping her arms around me in a tight hug.

"Thanks," I say as we separate. "not at all terrifying." I set my guitar back in the dinged up case on the table.

Ty drapes an arm over my shoulder. "It gets easier. You're amazing, Layla. I'm impressed." He squeezes gently before releasing me.

A swell of pride sweeps through me. That means a lot coming from him. "Thank you."

"You killed it, Bug." Turning slowly, a lump forms in my throat. Remington stands before me, his messy dark hair covered with a baseball cap. Those full lips of his tip up in the corners, displaying a sexy smile that reminds me of his hand between my legs. "I knew you would." He wraps his arms around my waist, drawing me in for a hug that makes my throat tighten as his signature scent invades. "I'm proud of you."

I'm completely dumb struck. "What are you doing here?" I ask in a breathless whisper. His face falls.

"Ty said you were performing. Figured I'd check it out." He says in a shrug as he steps back from me.

"That's kind of you." Why did that come out so condescendingly? "I mean you didn't need to."

His eyes narrow beneath the brim of the baseball cap. What does he expect me to do? Jump in his arms while gushing about how sweet I think it is for him to see me? Because that's what I'd love to do if it wasn't for the fact that I'd probably never let go of him. It's too difficult to be around him after everything.

Rem's jaw clenches as he glances at Ty, then Aly. "Give us a minute." he says in a gruff voice before grabbing my hand. Pulling me toward the glass doors then outside.

"What are you doing?" I demand as he takes a left, guiding me to the side of the building.

Remington releases my hand reluctantly, placing both hands in the pockets of his jeans. "This isn't going to work if you're going to be a bitch to me."

I scoff, crossing my arms. "So now I'm a bitch?"

His jaw muscle ticks, his eyes scanning my face under the fluorescent light above us. "When we last talked, I thought we had an understanding. That we could pretend nothing ever happened."

SELF-INFLICTED

"I'm tired of pretending all the time." I bite out. "It's better if we don't see each other ever again."

He recoils as if I've slapped him. "You don't want that."

Huffing out a sigh, I lower my arms. "No, I don't. But what choice do we have? I haven't seen you in two months. Honestly, it's better this way."

He takes a step closer to me. "I hate that we can't pursue something we both want." He says in a low voice. There's a sincerity in his eyes, a sadness that makes my chest tighten. "I was hoping the feelings would go away after some time apart. They haven't."

"Don't say that!" I snap. It hurts more knowing he feels the same.

"I'm being honest." He argues. "It kills me not talking to you, not seeing you."

"It doesn't matter, Rem. We can't run the risk of something happening again. What if we get caught? What if someone finds out we're stepsiblings?" I run a hand through my hair, blowing out an exasperated breath. "I appreciate you coming even though you shouldn't have."

"I want to support you."

"You don't need to." I say. While I know it will break me in a way I may never repair, the next words I choose are for the best. To ensure that our relationship never goes further. "What we have is fleeting. You only want me because you can't have me and one day, you'll wake up to realize I'm not for you."

"You don't mean that." He grits out. "You're everything-"

"I'm nothing!" I shout, my resolve slowly crumbling while frustration and bitterness sink into my skin. Remington Paulson is sunshine and passion, a beating heart full of promise and light. I'm a girl who doesn't fit into that mold. We'd never work because I'm a broken mess figuring life out while he's on a trajectory to excellence. "You deserve better than me. Better than this town and what it has to offer. I'll only hold you back." Tears well in my eyes as I speak my truth. "This is a blip on the radar compared to all that your future holds." I inhale a sharp breath as a tear slips down my cheek.

He steps back from me, his beautiful brown eyes glazing over. "No." he whispers hoarsely.

A sob breaks from my chest. "Yes. You have to move on. *I* have to move-"

"I meant it." He interjects. My heart sinks to the pit of my stomach. He cups my face in his hands, resting his forehead against mine. I tremble from the warmth of his touch. "I meant what I said that first night."

He may have thought he loved me, he may even think it now, but admitting to it will only hurt me worse. It will hurt him too, which I don't want.

"You didn't mean it." I say, partly to myself to help soothe the sting of breaking his heart. "Rem, you can't love me."

His gaze meets mine. "I did. I do."

As much as it breaks my heart to put my foot down, I know it's for the best. There's no further the two of us can go without a lifetime of guilt and disappointment. I've already had enough of that for the both of us without adding our relationship to the mix. If he finds stardom, makes a name for himself with his band, I'll be a black cloud threatening to rain on his parade. I refuse to be the reason his opportunities are held back. I refuse to be the reason why people might cast judgement on him. There is no happy ending for us if we choose each other.

More tears form in my eyes as I grasp his hands, lowering them to his side before releasing him. "This isn't meant to be."

He lifts his head toward the sky, blowing out a heavy breath of defeat. "I hate you for this." He whispers. I'm not sure I hear him correctly until he levels his head at me with a look of disdain that steals my breath. His words are like venom, seeping into my soul, making me sick. "Fuck your excuses."

Stunned, a stabbing pain shoots through my chest. He turns abruptly, stalking back toward the front of the building. Banging my back against the exterior wall, I slide down to the cracked asphalt with tears pouring down my face while my heart collapses to the deepest pits of darkness before shattering to a million pieces.

I hate me too.

PART TWO

FIVE YEARS LATER...

"One need not be a chamber to be haunted."

Emily Dickinson

CHAPTER ONE
Layla

What do you do when you find out something you thought was real, rapidly becomes an illusion? If you're me, you drink away the pain while continuing to truck on. I may have changed a bit over the last five years, yet some things have become so predictable that I'm beginning to wonder if I'm clairvoyant. Either that or just really poor with my decision making skills when it comes to men. Probably the latter.

Max Tate isn't really what I would call husband material. He's been a decent boyfriend over the last two years though, up until I found out he slept with someone else. I thought what we had was exclusive. Maybe it isn't fair of me to assume he'd remain faithful while we dated constantly and slept over at each other's places more often than not. After all, I made it clear I wasn't the commitment kind. With each of us on our own career paths in the music industry, time or distance would eventually break things anyway. I'm just grateful I chose to leave him before I looked like a fool in front of millions of people.

He was everything I thought I wanted in a man. Attractive, funny, charismatic, talented, and one of the most dedicated people I know. If you would have asked me a year ago if I thought he was the one, I'd probably consider it. If you asked me even a month ago, I would have been surprisingly optimistic about our future.

SELF-INFLICTED

Now it's a completely different story. Instead of a fairytale, I'm in the middle of some sort of nightmare. Maybe the universe is still conspiring against me after all these years. Or perhaps Max wore me down over time in hopes that I'd chase him around the world, becoming his life-long groupie.

I'm beginning to wonder if I'm being punished for the trail of broken hearts I left in my wake before I'd met him. I guess I don't fit his vibe anymore. He doesn't want to be with someone who can't be near him every second of the day. Honestly, I've felt a bit controlled by him for a while now. Even though it stings to be rejected after two years, I feel like I can finally breathe again. I'm the one who can't be tamed. At least that's what my mother says. She's always reminding me of my shortcomings. Like I said, some things never change.

I dumped Max less than twenty-four hours ago. While it was my clear and conscious decision, I still feel terrible about it. I hadn't anticipated him being apologetic about sleeping with some random girl at a friend's bachelor party last weekend. A fact I found out through the goddamn hellfire that is the internet. It doesn't matter if he lapsed in judgement and was what he says, "High on Molly." That is a shit excuse for completely upending a relationship that seemed to be working so well. I made plans with the idiot, a future. Then he threw it all away because the rockstar lifestyle is apparently an aesthetic that despite being troubling, is widely accepted. Fuck that and fuck him.

I grieved the only way I know how too anymore, by drinking my troubles away. My appearance seems to match the theme of a horror story. Day old makeup caked onto my eyelids from crying myself to sleep – hair matted and tangled. I look like I've been through hell or am still trekking through it. I guess it depends on whether I'm having a glass half-full kind of day or not. No, the glass is definitely empty, just like the bottle of whisky on my nightstand. I pluck it up, sniffing it. The moment the scent hits my nose, my stomach rolls.

"Ugh!"

I set the bottle back on the nightstand. I'm an idiot for drowning my sorrows last night when I know better.

It isn't the heartbreak that caused me to drink last night. Well, it isn't exactly the entire reason. Part of it also has to do with who I'm going to see today. Remington Paulson. After five years of short conversations during the holidays and avoiding each other like the plague, we're going to be all up in each other's business for three months.

Yay.

In the two and a half years I've been legal to drink, I can count on one hand how many times I've been drunk. I hate myself for turning to a bottle the way my mom does when things get too unbearable. I don't want to be anything like her, yet here I am following in her footsteps by masking my pain with brain damage while ruining my liver. The consequences of my actions slam into me full force when I realize I'm stuck slapping on a smile today while pretending like I'm the happiest bitch you ever met. Not that I'm unhappy to be going on my very first tour as a solo artist. I just wish I hadn't tied one on so heavily last night because I'll be miserable all day today.

It turns out music gets to be more than merely a dream for me now. Writing and recording my own songs is amazing. I'm grateful for the opportunity after spending time in college taking writing courses while honing my performance skills. I still get nervous in front of people, but I've learned to push that fear to the back of my mind. It helps to pretend I'm playing a roll. Theater class helped bring me out of my shell a lot more than I thought it would when I first started. I'm indebted to my father for allowing me to follow my passion. Career wise, everything is looking promising. My personal life though? Not so much.

SELF-INFLICTED

It makes everything that's recently happened with Max sting that much more because I know Remington will be all too happy to see me miserable. The last thing I want to do is tour with Hemingway's Rejects when I've just been dumped. His ability to piss me off hasn't changed. In fact, most of our interactions over the years have been bitter and toxic. I understand it in a way, I guess. I did apparently break his heart after all. Though, sometimes I feel like he only said he loved me because he wanted to hurt me. Make me feel guilty for being strong enough to walk away from something that never would have worked in the long run anyway.

Sighing, I pick up my phone when it vibrates to see a text from my manager, Billy. The record company assigned him to me when I signed my contract two short months ago. I like to think of him as the older brother I never had. A positive, friendly, supportive brother unlike the son of the woman my father married.

"Morning, sunshine!" I hear Aly cheer as she enters my small, studio apartment.

The smell of fresh arabica beans permeates instantly when she holds a cup to my face. I inhale soundly, my lips tilting up in a brief smile.

"Coffee, my savior, my solace." I say, greedily taking the cup from her. This should help me feel better – albeit temporarily. "Thanks, bestie."

She smiles before heading for my closet. "Billy says he's coming at ten. You have a couple of radio interviews to do before soundcheck at the venue."

There's no way I can kick off a tour or be interviewed looking like I do in my current state. Thankfully, I have Aly who is officially my tour stylist and makeup artist for the road. I have Billy to thank for making that happen. There's no one else I'd trust to make me look my best on stage than my best friend.

"I'll grab a shower." I say, taking my coffee with me to the bathroom.

I'm out of the shower within ten minutes. I wrap my hair in a towel, taking bigger gulps of the coffee now that it's cooled down some. The caffeine is already helping with the pounding headache. When I come out of the bathroom, Aly is standing next to the small vanity I have tucked in the corner near my bed.

She's been staying with me the last few weeks while we've prepared to head out on tour. I'm grateful that she agreed to camping out in my tiny apartment when she could be staying with Tyler. I'd be utterly lost without her. Even if she is engaged to my enemy's bandmate. I take a seat on the stool, still wrapped in my towel, squinting at the array of different beauty products. I have no idea what half of them are, but if they make me look more human, I'll take it.

"We're doing the natural look today. Highlight and concealer to get those dark circles to disappear with neutral colors." I nod, closing my eyes as she begins brushing whatever products onto my face. "So, I take it it's officially over?"

"Yep. Funny how my confidence nearly faded the second he showed up here last night. I almost took him back." She stops brushing. I risk opening my eyes. "What?"

"Lay, that would have been the dumbest thing you could ever do."

My stomach twists into knots, remembering Max coming by last night. I invited him over to break things off in person, though I think he had a different idea. He was more upset than I thought he would be when I told him it was over. We talked for three hours about how our relationship wouldn't work anymore for a multitude of reasons, including him being unfaithful.

I need time to clear my head away from him. When I explained that, he got angry. He said I was nothing without him. I chalked it up to his feelings being hurt, yet a part of me is afraid he might retaliate in some way. He's always been a very headstrong and cutthroat person. Looking back now, I'm disappointed in myself for being with someone like him. The thought of taking him back crossed my mind because I don't want to deal with what he may be capable of. However, I know staying together to keep peace is a dumb reason. I've seen first-hand how that can negatively affect people.

"I'm not going to do it." I say.

"Was he even sorry? Did he show any remorse at all?" Aly removes the towel from my hair, brushing the long multi-colored strands out.

"Yes, though it might have all been an act. He shifted from heartbroken to angry pretty quickly. After he left I decided to drink whisky. From the bottle." My stomach rolls again, proving just how ridiculous my pity party was.

Aly frowns. She knows that isn't normal behavior for me. "At least you have something to distract you for a while. I can't wait for you to perform on a real life tour."

"I'm a fill in opener." I remind her.

The only reason I have this opportunity is because another band had to bow out. When Kyle and Billy brought it up, I immediately said yes. Despite Kyle and I briefly dating years ago, we've become great friends. Without him, I wouldn't be nearly as far along in my music career as I am.

"You'll be amazing. Ty is so excited to have you on tour with them."

"That's because you're coming too."

He proposed to her on Valentine's day and they're getting married this fall after the tour ends. When she asked me to be her maid of honor, I happily agreed. Though I'd be lying if I said a part of me is afraid for her that things might not work out. I know Ty is different than most guys. I also know that he loves her, but I'm a cynical person when it comes to love. I'm not sure that will ever change.

She smiles wider this time. "He's also incredibly happy for you. Who would have thought five years ago that you'd be signed to the same record label as them."

"Not me." I mutter as she adds product to my hair before blow drying it.

I never thought I'd have a chance at this if I'm being honest. I like to think I have some skill and talent, but I can't help worrying that people might not like me or my music.

Once I look more human than hibernating bear, I step into the bathroom to change quickly. Glancing in the mirror, I see the magic that Aly has performed on me. The dark circles under my eyes are basically gone and my hair looks a lot tamer than it was when I woke up. Nerves tighten in my stomach after I dress when I realize I'm hours away from seeing Remington. Not only has he added more ink to his skin, but he's grown up a lot in his looks. His once sinewy arms have bulked up, showing off more muscle definition that only adds to his appeal. He changed his messy dark hair to something more alternative. It's now shorter on the sides with a faux mohawk. He's still hot, still makes my heart race, and I still wish things could have been different between us.

Pulling on some black boots, I grab my cell from the nightstand before following Aly out to the hallway. Our bags are already packed for the tour, ready to go near the door. Billy said he'd make sure they get to the tour bus for us while I'm doing my interviews. We meet him outside my apartment building where he's parked in a black town car.

"You ready for this, Layla?" He gives me a quick side-hug before motioning for us to get in the backseat.

I'm incredibly nervous to speak to people, but I'm excited to have the opportunity to share the music I've been working on. I've since discovered that my thoughts really aren't that different from others. When I was starting out, doing open mic nights or playing at bars, people would tell me how grateful they are for my lyrics. It makes me feel good to know that I can offer them a moment of comfort in my creativity.

An hour later, I'm finishing my last interview with radio deejays. All of them have been incredibly welcoming. They take the time to let me play an acoustic version of my very first radio single that began airing a month ago. Luckily, no one asked about Max, though they did mention Hemingway's Rejects. The one question I hadn't anticipated threw me off guard for a moment but I recovered quickly.

"I'm sure it helps knowing the band you're touring with. You and Rem Paulson are related, right?"

"My dad married his mom."

To this day, I loathe referring to him as my stepbrother. Knowing the public is aware of our relationship doesn't help the emotions I've tried to push down. We're tied together whether we want to be or not. While I've come to accept that, I'm still bothered by our connection.

Once the interview concludes, they ask me to take some photos before Billy whisks us off to the venue where I'll perform tonight to kick off the tour. Immediately after that, we'll set off for more cities across the country to promote Hemingway's Rejects sophomore album along with my first. We arrive at the back entrance of the venue where I see a large tour bus parked. Different crew members are standing around, some of them taking in equipment through a door. Seeing the bus in person has me second guessing the other part of what I agreed to. The label wouldn't spring for my own since it's quite expensive. I had the option of riding in a van with my equipment or bunking with the guys. Ty wants Aly with him anyway, so he made sure to get the label to agree with us sharing.

Following Billy, I make my way into the venue, staring at the stage where I'll be performing in just a few hours. It's surreal to know that I'll be singing at a location twice the size of what I'm used to. I scan the stage, watching as a member of the crew sets up the kit my drummer will be using. I play both acoustic and electric guitar while singing so the label hired a drummer and bassist for my album that are now joining me on tour. Seeing Layla Barlow stamped across the face of the bass drum fills me with a sense of pride.

"They'll be here in twenty minutes." Aly murmurs.

Just like that, my mood deflates. I begin chewing on my bottom lip. Whether I like it or not, I'm stuck back in the mess I left five years ago. Aly has supported me no matter what, even if she disagrees with my decision to cut ties completely. That's mainly because Aly is a hopeless romantic who isn't in the situation. I don't want to deal with the negativity that might surround us. I especially don't want to go down in history as a problematic musician or the one who ruined Remington's promising career. Because let's face it, at the end of the day, most of the general population will blame me over him. I am a woman after all. Plus, he's been around longer than I have in this industry.

Moving forward. That's the plan now. If I look ahead, I won't be hurt by my past or all the choices I made that led me to where I am today. It hasn't all been bad. In fact, thanks to Remington, I learned how to be stronger, to take what I want without apology. That made it easier for me to voice my interests with my father. If it hadn't been for Bridget, I don't think I would have ever gained the courage to talk to dad either. She's a huge support, even now. I've grown to love her more than I thought I ever would.

Inhaling a deep, cleansing breath, I nod. "Can't wait."

"Miss Barlow?" I turn to the sound of a woman's voice. "My name is Rose. I can show you to your dressing room."

"Thank you." I follow her along with Aly toward a door near the back of the stage.

SELF-INFLICTED

"There's refreshments in here," Rose says as she leads us down a narrow hall to a black door. "If I can get you anything else, please let me know." I gape at the little room when we enter. There's a small sofa, a coffee table with a basket of cookies, and a cute little hand painted welcome sign with my logo on it. I smile at the thoughtfulness. "You have a bathroom in here as well." She adds, pointing to another door.

"This is amazing." I say, beaming at Aly who is smiling as wide as I am.

Rose chuckles lightly. "I'm so glad you approve. I'm your girl if you want anything special tonight. We're happy to have you playing here. My daughter loves your music."

"Thank you. I appreciate that."

"You're welcome. I'll check in with you later." She says before leaving.

Aly spins in a small circle, taking in the room. "You're big time now, kid." She says, pulling me in for a hug. "I'm so proud of you Lay."

Tears spring to the surface as I squeeze her back. Despite me being stuck in my own head most of the time, I can't help getting lost in this moment. A sense of rightness washes over me, as if this is what I'm meant to be doing or at least where I'm meant to be.

Rem

"You're going to wear a fucking hole in the floor." Connor says as I pace in front of the bar. "Sit down and drink your beer or something."

I stop in front of the stool he's sitting at alongside Ty to shoot him a menacing glare. "Bite me."

"Told you he was high strung." Ty says.

Connor rolls his eyes as I go back to my pacing.

It has been six months since I last saw Layla Barlow. Five years since I kissed her luscious lips and held her body against mine. Over one thousand, eight hundred, twenty five days since I enjoyed the incredible pleasure of being inside her while she moaned in my ear, screaming my name. A shiver rolls down my spine that I immediately shake off. Fuck. I hate thinking about her.

When I saw her at our parents' house over the holidays, I kept to myself like I always do, barely saying hello to her. She was fucking gorgeous as usual in a pair of black leggings with an oversized hoodie. Her now colorful hair was in a messy bun. Every time I'm near her, my heart beats faster. I curse fate for bringing her into my life. Max Tate doesn't deserve her. I don't care if he just got nominated for a Grammy. In fact, I almost punched his lights out when I caught him kissing her at our Christmas dinner. However, the last thing I wanted to do was upset my mother. I also didn't want to deal with the inevitable lawsuit I'd likely have on my hands. Max is a fuckboy but a good musician who pisses excellence while turning everything he touches into gold. Apart from Layla. She's been a fucking diamond forever. I hate the guy for selfish reasons and can't let my emotions ruin me or my band's own trajectory to greatness.

I'd be lying if I didn't admit I was tempted to mess everything up though when I saw her last. I wanted to drag her away to my old room to fuck her until her eyes crossed. I wanted to slit my wrists and bleed out in front of her while begging her to love me. Dramatic I know, but it's the damn truth. From the moment she let me kiss her the first time to this very moment, I've loved her. It has always been her face in my head, her voice in my ears when I'm with someone else. She's ruined me for life without any idea the extent of her actions.

Fuck my life.

I'm happy she followed her dreams instead of wasting them away with what her parents wanted. I like to think I helped her gain the strength to stand up for herself. Though I'm not sure I can forgive that jackass, Kyle Fuller for offering to bring her on tour with us when the other band had to cancel due to a death in the family. I still low key hate him for dating Layla years ago, but that's become water under the bridge since we started working together.

"You're going to play nice, right?" Ty asks when I plop down on the stool beside him. I take a swig off the beer I'd left sitting.

"I'm not an asshole."

Connor snorts. "That's a lie." I narrow my eyes at him.

Shrugging, I rest the beer bottle on my thigh, picking at the label. "I can be nice for the sake of our tour. It's not like we have to hang out."

"You liked her back in the day. A hell of a lot if I remember correctly, then suddenly you couldn't stand her. Aly won't tell me what happened between you two."

I flick my gaze to his. "Good."

I prefer to keep it that way. Not because I'm ashamed like Layla is though. It's because she stabbed me in the heart. Every time I so much as think about that moment, it feels like it's happening all over again. She's the only woman that's made me cry. The only woman who brought out feelings that I worked so hard to keep buried away after my dad died. Feelings that I wish I could repress now.

The double doors from the back room swing open, my shoulders tensing when I gaze at the trio entering. I recognize Billy immediately, her manager. My focus slides to Aly who is smiling wide as she sprints toward my bandmate. Ty sweeps her up in a hug before full on making out with her. I still can't believe they're going to get married. We're young and it seems like they should wait, but what the fuck do I know? I'm sprung on my stepsister so I'm not a great moral compass for relationships.

I risk a glance at Layla, my chest tightening painfully. My beautiful, unique girl is just as pretty as ever. Her hair falls in loose waves over her chest that's developed more since we were younger. The cropped blue shirt she's wearing accentuates the curves of her hips. I bite down on the inside of my cheek. Now is not the time to get a hard-on. That's probably why I hate her the most. She still fucking turns me on. I stop scanning her body to meet her eyes. For the briefest moment when we lock onto each other, time stands still. Too quickly though, she looks away with her jaw clenched.

She hasn't looked me in the eye since that night when we were last together. When I watched in the shadows as she strummed her guitar like a pro while singing with that voice that still haunts me. She has no business acting guilty for breaking my heart. I hope she's happy with her choices. Maybe Max Tate will die in a fiery fucking crash so she can be miserable like me. Harsh? Yes. Valid? Probably not. Although for once I'd love to see her suffer the way I have.

"Hey guys. How's it going?" Connor asks, standing to hug Layla and shake Billy's hand.

She smiles for him, keeping her attention anywhere except on me.

Look at me!

"Good to see you." Billy says, shaking my hand.

"Yeah."

"You know Layla." He glances at her as she crosses her arms, looking so uncomfortable that it brings a small smile to my lips.

"Hey, Bug. Good to see you."

She hates the nickname even more now which only makes me use it as much as possible. Two years ago she told me to stop addressing her that way. I told her to fuck off. Getting under her skin is my favorite hobby, apart from playing music.

"Yeah," she says quietly, tucking a strand of hair behind her ear. "you too, Rem."

Riley, our manager, enters the room then, introducing himself to Layla and Aly who finally separates from Ty. "Now that introductions are out of the way, we should get to work."

"We have three hours before we open doors." Billy says, checking his phone.

I hear that we're expected to have a big turnout. We're not selling out arenas yet but we've headlined a few shows for bigger bands in them. We've now worked our way to concert venues with higher capacities. It's been a dream really. I couldn't have asked for a better career so far.

"You excited to play tonight?" Connor asks Layla.

"So excited!" she says with a smile. "The greenroom reminds me of something out of a movie. I can't believe this is real life."

"You're going to do great. Enjoy it." Ty adds.

"I hope so."

Look at me. Damn.

"We should get you ready for soundcheck." Billy says to Layla who gives my bandmates and Aly a brief wave before following him toward the stage.

I kick the back of Ty's leg. "You can suck your girl's face later." I growl as I follow Connor toward the door behind the stage.

SELF-INFLICTED

CHAPTER TWO
Layla

    I think my soundcheck goes well. I sang a few songs while my drummer, Aaron and the bassist, Jackson, tuned their instruments. I was strumming a few chords on my guitar when I caught Rem walking across the floor, heading toward their manager Riley. He didn't look in my direction, but I could see the tension on his shoulders. I did my best to ignore him while we finished. It was difficult not to fall into old habits when we greeted each other earlier. He looked good in faded jeans with a tight t-shirt, his hair styled perfectly. I had to force myself to look away from him so that he didn't catch me staring. After soundcheck, me and Aly decide to hang out in the greenroom until showtime. A part of me wants to watch Hemingway's Rejects do their soundcheck because I haven't seen them live in years, but the less I'm around Rem the better.

    Billy enters the room a while later. "We've got to discuss the tour arrangements."

    "Okay." I say with a mouthful of sugar cookie.

    I don't know where the cookies came from. I've already eaten four. Rose told me they were sent by a local bakery, so I had her give me their info so I can visit them when tour is over.

    He angles his head toward the hall. "With the other band. We'll chat in their room."

Inhaling a cleansing breath, I follow him out into the hall to the room across from mine. Riley opens the door after Billy knocks.

"We leave tonight following the show." Riley says as we enter the small room, getting down to business. "First stop is Pennsylvania, then North Carolina. There's enough room on the bus for everyone including extra bunks."

"What?" Rem grounds out.

Riley slides his gaze to him. "You're sharing the bus."

Rem glares at his manager. "This is news to me."

"Dude, we talked about it." Ty says.

"Yeah. You said it was cool." Connor adds, clapping him on the back.

"Did I?" he asks, flashing his glare at me.

I place my hands up, palms out. "I knew about it."

"This is bullshit."

"Fuck you, Remington." His eyes widen as I pin him with my own glare.

I will raise hell if he's trying to start something already. There's no reason for him to be so angry.

He chuckles darkly. "You'd love that."

My nose wrinkles. "You wish."

"Hey!" Connor captures our attention, clapping his hands together once. "You two are going to get along. I'm not putting up with this shit for the next three months." He looks between me and Rem, focusing on the latter. "It's fine, right?"

Rem's jaw muscle ticks. "Fine."

"Are we going to have a problem?" Riley questions, annoyance evident in his tone.

"No." Rem and I both say at the same time.

"Great." I mutter.

"Isn't it though?" he bites out sarcastically with a wicked smirk.

SELF-INFLICTED

"Can I go now?" I ask Billy.

"Sure. You're on in thirty minutes."

I promptly march across the hall to my room where Aly is laying out the makeup she's going to put on me.

"Everything okay?" she asks as I plop down in the chair she set up.

"He's already being a jerk."

Aly frowns. "Are you sure-"

"I'm fine." Rem can be mad all he wants about sharing a tour bus with me. "If he wants to be miserable, that's on him. I'm not going to let it bring me down."

Aly smiles. "Good."

Within a few minutes my eyes are smoky and my lips are painted purple. Aly picks out a black tank top to pair with these killer purple pants that match the lipstick almost exactly. I put on my stage outfit, adding a pair of black ankle boots as well as a few accessories to complete the ensemble. I smile at myself in the mirror, ready to rock.

I'm surprised by the warm reception the audience gives me when I step on stage to begin my set. Learning from my time spent in theater class, I work the stage, pretending to be someone other than the fragile, self-conscious person I normally am. While scanning the crowd I even see a handful of people singing along to my song, "Poison Ivy," which is the single I just released. By the time my set ends, I'm full of energy, buzzing from the high of performing. I can't help watching Hemingway's Rejects from the side of the stage when it's their turn, making sure to stay in the shadows where Rem won't see me. Despite our issues, I admire the band and am a huge fan. He plays the guitar with an intensity that's addictive to watch while Ty belts out the lyrics to a new song. Connor definitely brings the energy on the drums, doing a solo that keeps everyone's attention for ten minutes straight. Aly and I join the band in their greenroom after their set ends.

"You want a drink?" Connor offers, holding up a can of beer from the mini fridge in their room.

"Not happening." I say, shaking my head.

Aly quirks a brow. "Still feeling the hangover?"

I rub my forehead, nodding.

"So where's your man?" Connor asks.

Sighing, I pick at the label of the empty water bottle I'm holding. "Couldn't make it." I lie. I'm not talking about Max right now. It will only bring my high down along with everyone else's.

He frowns. "For your first big show?"

I shrug, glancing at Aly to help change the topic, which she gracefully does.

"Since we're all together," she says. "I figure we can discuss the wedding. We have four months before the big day. I know my two cousins aren't here, but I want to go over some details."

Rem sits back in the chair beside the couch, crossing his arms. "Fun."

"Did Jane and Rena get their dresses?" I ask, tossing the empty water bottle onto the coffee table.

"Jane's coming to the wedding?" a look of concern flashes in Connor's eyes.

Rem chuckles. "Maybe there'll be two weddings."

"Fuck off, Paulson." He snaps.

Rem laughs loudly, causing my stomach to dip. I missed his laugh and that small dimple that forms in his left cheek when he smiles big.

"Yes," Ty hisses. "Jesus, you guys are out of control. We literally went over this last month."

"I wasn't paying attention to that part." Connor says.

"Because you were chasing pussy." Rem jokes.

Connor flies out of his seat, lunging for a fistful of Rem's black t-shirt. Rem stands, stepping back while holding his hands up in surrender.

"At least I'm not sprung on a fucking illusion."

Rem's eyes darken. "Fuck off."

"Enough!" Ty barks. They both sit back down. I blink at him, stunned because I've never heard him snap like this before. Ty's gaze slides to mine. "Are you prepared to deal with this shit for the next several weeks?" He smiles at me.

I smile back. "I can manage."

"Yes, Jane is coming. She's in the wedding." Aly says, rolling her eyes. "She's walking with Rem."

"Who am I walking with?" Connor asks, giving Rem a death glare.

"Rena," Aly replies. "Layla is walking with Ty's brother, Gavin. He's the best man and she's the maid of honor. Do you guys ever pay attention?"

"Are you honestly surprised?" I ask.

Connor gets up, "I've got a call to make." He mumbles before leaving.

"Told you he'd fuck it up by sleeping with her." Rem says to Ty.

"I still hate her for hooking up with him before you guys moved." Aly complains.

Everyone knows Connor likes to play the field. Jane is a sweet girl that lives by the same rules, so honestly, they're kind of perfect for each other. I don't know all the details, but I wonder if one of them got a little too attached after the hookup.

"Never sleep with someone from your home town if you're moving away." Ty says.

"They might follow you." Rem says, flicking his gaze to me.

I glare at him. "Hate me all you want, just be sure to do it quietly."

He cocks his head to the side, studying me. I hate that my heart beats unevenly under his scrutiny. His eyes fall to my lips, causing a flood of heat to rush between my legs. How can a single look affect me so much? After all this time, he still has the capability to make me desire him. He licks his lips, the barbell in his tongue glinting from the overhead light. I briefly wonder if he has the other piercing still, until I'm smacked out of my ridiculous thoughts when a slow grin forms on his face. God! I shouldn't be thinking about him. I squeeze my eyes shut, trying to rid the inappropriate thoughts.

"We should grab our stuff to get on the bus." Ty announces.

I open my eyes once again, avoiding Remington.

"Catch you later, Bug." He says before following Ty.

"Well that was fun." Aly mutters.

Releasing a sigh, I sweep my hand through my hair. "Yeah."

Crossing her arms, she pins me with a knowing look. "Are you sure you can handle this?"

I really wish people would quit asking me that. "It's fine." I say more to myself than her.

It will be fine. He can't stay mad at me forever, can he?

*

A large plate of cheesy fries along with a chocolate milkshake does wonders for the soul. Taking my mind off Remington and the anxiety of us touring, Aly and I discuss my breakup with Max over lunch the next day in Philadelphia. My first night on the bus went pretty smoothly. My bunk is tucked in the back, away from Remington who is closer to the front. I'm not sure if he intentionally picked something far away from me or not. Not that I care. It's best we keep our distance as much as humanly possible based on his attitude yesterday.

"At least you two weren't living together or sharing a dog." Aly says, swirling a fry in ranch.

"I feel like such a chump though. This is the second time I've been blindsided in a relationship. I'm so naïve."

"Don't beat yourself up over it. It's not your fault." She says before popping the fry into her mouth.

I stare at my phone on the table, glowering at the five missed texts from Max.

"He said the same thing. That he feels terrible for his moment of weakness. Why don't I believe him?" I ask, flicking my gaze up to hers.

She frowns. "Lay, you have to trust your instincts. If they're telling you to let him go, then do it."

I nod, picking up a fry. "Do you think he would actually do something though?"

Aly's hand slides over the table, tipping my phone screen toward her to read the texts. "Does he really think anyone will believe that you left him for someone else?"

After trying the polite route and not getting a response from me, Max resorted to nastier texts that threatened to paint me in a bad light. I think he's worried that I'll tell people he's a cheater, which maybe if I was more scorned or devastated about the breakup, I would. I'm not though, so I don't know what that says about me as a person. Shouldn't I be more upset about our relationship ending? Or at least, as upset as he is?

"I mean seriously, space is good for you two right now." Aly adds, reading the single text I finally sent him this morning, telling him to let me breathe for a bit.

I've dreamed of having a career in music for so long. Now that it's finally happening, I don't want anything to taint that. Even if I'm risking a toxic ex-boyfriend. Although, I am concerned about what Max might say about me. I've always been faithful, always transparent about my belief in that. Him dragging my name through the mud or accusing me of leaving him for someone else when he's the one that made the mistake is outrageous. If anyone believes him, I'll end up looking like a terrible person. More than the stress of being judged, I worry it could destroy my career.

"What if he ruins me?" I ask, my voice snagging in the back of my throat. "I don't want to have made it this far for it all to go away."

Aly sets my phone down, reaching across to pick my hand up, squeezing it. "Let him do whatever he wants. Keep your head down, work hard, and kick ass. Your actions will speak for you."

Inhaling a deep breath, I square my shoulders. "Do you really think that will work?"

She smiles, releasing my hand. "He has no proof of you doing anything wrong in your relationship. I wouldn't sweat it too much."

Grabbing another fry, I force a small smile. "I don't know what I'd do without your pep talks."

She smiles back. "He just lost the best damn woman on the planet. I'm sure he probably regrets it. You're a rockstar both literally and figuratively. Be your authentic, badass self and forget about him."

I'm not sure my authentic self is a badass, but I appreciate her support just the same.

"Maybe this is karma for being a bitch to Remington all those years ago."

Aly takes a sip of her vanilla milkshake. "He's really laying it on thick, isn't he? I mean, what does he expect from you?"

"Right?" I say, popping the cherry covered in melted ice cream into my mouth. The memory of Rem tying the stem of a cherry with his tongue all those years ago threatens to invade as my stomach clenches. "He went to New York while I stayed behind to go through school. It never would have worked to be together for a myriad of reasons. It still can't work. He has to know that."

She purses her lips in thought. "Do you think he's in love with you?"

My shoulders tense. "Are you insane?"

I seriously doubt he loves me. How can he after I dropped him like a bad habit when he came to see me perform at that café back home? I wasn't nice to him then and I sure as hell haven't been all that cordial since. Who could love me through all that?

She shrugs. "You said he told you he loved you once."

"We didn't know each other long enough to be in love. Besides, with all the other issues, we were doomed before we started."

She props her hand on the side of her head, resting her elbow on the table. "You didn't love him?"

Butterflies spring to life in my belly. I care about Rem a lot. I think I always will because he's been such an integral part of who I am now whether he knows it or not. I'm a logical thinker though. While I admit it's hard not to love Rem, I know I can't entertain that emotion when it comes to him. The pain is too much, so I shut myself down before going down a road that will only end in heartache.

"No." She rolls her eyes as if she doesn't believe me. Maybe I'm lying to myself, however admitting the truth of what I feel for Rem isn't necessary.

After our lunch, we head out to do some shopping. One of the perks of my career is visiting new places I only ever knew from pictures or television. Despite the drama with Max and the conversation about Rem, I'm happy. With any luck, I'll stay busy enough during my free time to not think about what my ex may do or what underlying issues might come to a head with me and my tour mate.

Rem

Connor enters the greenroom backstage where I'm tuning my guitar, tossing his phone on the table.

"Trouble in paradise?" I tease when he smooths a hand over his shaved head.

"She's not mad, just disappointed." He says. I bite my lip to stifle my laughter. He pins me with a glare. "Fuck you."

"I'm sorry," I say in sincerity. "in fairness, I did tell you not to hook up with Aly's cousin. Is she cute? Yeah. Is it worth the potential drama though?"

Connor groans. "I know. I shouldn't have sent her flowers."

"You sent her flowers?!"

He sighs, glaring at the floor. "Shut up. I messed up and now shit is going to be awkward at the wedding."

I shrug it off because telling him he's obviously in love with the girl isn't going to make him feel better. "What can you do? Just be nice. Don't flaunt other girls in her face or anything."

He raises his brow. "I'm not like you, Rem. I can't be fucking celibate."

"I'm just not a man whore like you, dude," I say, setting my guitar against the arm of the couch. "and I'm not celibate."

He scoffs. "You haven't hooked up with anyone since that girl in Denver. That was over a year ago."

"I can hold out longer. Unlike you, I use this head." I say, pointing to my face.

Tyler comes in the room with Aly under his arm, Layla following behind them. She looks like a rock and roll princess with her hair done up in a high ponytail. The black liner makes her hazel eyes brighter. That purple stain on her lips reminds me of succulent grapes. Jesus, she's breathtaking. The black thigh-highs beneath the long t-shirt dress isn't doing me any favors either. I miss those fucking thighs.

"Shouldn't you be heading to the stage?" I ask, not even bothering to hide the fact I'm checking her out. We've been touring for a week now. Every day is torture.

"I wanted to talk to you." Her voice is quiet, apprehensive.

My brow crumples. "About what?"

Her eyes dart to Tyler who responds for her. "About our song."

"Waterfall," she adds. "It's my favorite."

"Okay..." I say, looking back at her.

It's my favorite too. It's the one I wrote with Connor after my dad passed. The one she said she liked that first night we met. The one fucking song I don't enjoy playing anymore because of her.

Her delicate throat rolls in a swallow. She looks directly at me, piercing my soul in the process.

"I'd um...like to cover it." She bites down on that purple lip and my eyes falls to it.

"You want to add it to your set? Why?"

What am I going to do, tell her no? When have I ever been good at doing that?

She smiles at me. My fucking heart squeezes in my chest. *Don't smile at me, sweetheart.*

"I know it's an older song of yours and isn't on an album, but I love it." She replies. "I thought it would be cool to play one of your songs since I'm opening up for you. I plan on going acoustic with it."

I nod. "Okay, Bug."

"You're really okay with this?" Layla asks, moving to sit on the arm of the couch. She crosses one leg over the other causing that dress to ride further up her thighs.

"Yeah," I mutter, trying to look anywhere except at that delicious, exposed skin. "Why wouldn't I be?"

She shrugs. "I thought for sure you'd say no. Connor said that one is retired."

"It is, for us. You're welcome to play it." There's no way in hell I'm going to reject her playing my song.

"Because I'll probably botch it?" she asks, the hint of a smile forming on her face.

My heart drops to my stomach at the teasing tone. I wink at her. "Exactly."

That's definitely not going to be the case.

The fans seem to enjoy hearing "Waterfall" sung by Layla. I watch her from the side of the stage while she strums the guitar perfectly, her sultry voice making the song sound like an ethereal version of what it used to be. Another piece of my fragile fucking heart fuses together when she smiles the final line before bowing her head graciously. I smile. God, she's incredible. I wish she saw the same light that I did in her. Commotion behind me captures my attention as Layla begins talking to the crowd to wrap up her set.

"What are you doing here?" I hear Aly ask when I enter the hall, catching sight of Max fucking Tate.

"Wanted to see my girl."

"You shouldn't be here." She says, glancing over her shoulder at me as I approach them.

"Is there a problem?" I ask, noting Aly's panic stricken face.

"No problem, man." Max says.

"I think you'd better leave." Billy adds.

"She doesn't want to see you." Aly grounds out.

Riley waltzes over to us, looking at me. "Checked with security. Someone let him in."

"He's not supposed to be back here." Billy seethes, pinning Max with a glare. "You need to leave now."

"Not without seeing Layla."

"Max?" Layla's soft voice sounds behind me. Aly immediately goes to her friend, placing a hand on her shoulder. "What are you doing here?" she folds her arms around her waist, shaking her head. "Leave."

"I thought I'd catch your show since I'm in town. Everyone is talking about how great you are."

Her throat rolls in a swallow. "Please, go."

"Oh, come on." He says, stepping closer to her. I instinctively straighten my posture, scanning the two of them. I don't know why she doesn't want him here, but I'll happily remove him if needed. "I texted and you never answered. I wanted to check in to see if you're doing okay."

What the fuck?

"If she doesn't want to see you, you need to go." Riley says.

Max glares at him. "Fuck you. Do you know who I am?"

"You're not welcome here right now."

"You can't keep doing this shit to me." Layla says, the pain in her voice evident.

My jaw clenches as I look between them. If he fucking hurt her I might kill him.

"Layla..." he takes another step so I block his path.

"Get out of here, Max." She says in a broken voice as Aly wraps an arm around her.

They head for the greenroom as Max let's out a frustrated growl. I pin him with a dark look. "Sorry man. Maybe call first next time." I clap his shoulder.

He glowers at me. "No surprise you're here guarding her."

"We're on tour." I glance over at Billy and Riley who are now talking to a security guard. "She's working."

"Thanks to you…"

"What?" I ask through gritted teeth, meeting his eyes again.

He angles his chin toward the direction Layla left. "Come on, man. You say jump and she obeys, am I right? That's how it has always been with you two. Do you think I never noticed the way she followed you with her eyes when you were around? That I didn't catch you staring at her like a fucking creep? You know as well as I do that she isn't made for this shit." He says, stepping closer to me. My spine stiffens.

I laugh it off. "I don't know what you're talking about."

His jaw tenses. "Is she sucking your dick as payment or does she make you finger her too?"

I'm in his face before he finishes the sentence. My hands clench into fists at my side. "Say it again!" I ground out, bumping my chest into his.

"Woah! Rem, man back off!" Billy grabs me around the waist, attempting to pull me back. I stand firm.

Max chuckles darkly, before the security guard grabs his shoulder. "Watch yourself, Paulson." He taunts before being escorted away.

"What was that about?" Riley demands as I shrug out of Billy's hold.

"He's a fucking clown." I march down the hallway, hollering over my shoulder, "If he shows up again, make sure he's handled. If not, I'll do it myself."

The last thing anyone wants is bad press when we're only one week into a three month tour. Unfortunately, I don't give a damn about any of it right now. Not when that piece of shit is saying nasty things about Layla. Tour or not, I'm not joking. If I see him again, I'll break his fucking jaw.

SELF-INFLICTED

CHAPTER THREE
Layla

I splash some cool water on my cheeks, trying to calm down after seeing Max. Over the last several days he's tried calling and texting after I told him I needed space. When he mentioned coming to see me, I begged him not too. I even told Billy about it so we could ensure Max didn't have a way to sneak backstage, which obviously still happened. His messages have gotten more aggressive and he's still threatening to sully my name. At this point, I'd rather him do that than have to listen to him claim he gives a shit about me in person.

I can't believe he showed up! Part of me wonders if he did it to try getting into my head. Either way, with each passing day, I realize that I never loved him. Honestly, I think the sting of him cheating was more about my pride than actual hurt feelings which is really sad. I'm mad as hell that he had the nerve to show up here. I'm humiliated at the spectacle this likely caused. That he thought I'd be naïve enough to let him in after the shit he's been saying. I walked away from Max the same way I walked away from Adam after his infidelity back in high school. Like I walked away from Remington before it got to a point that he'd hurt me. Because at the end of the day, I know he would have.

I break down when I step out of the bathroom to see Aly there waiting for me. I sit down in the chair closest to me, beginning to cry, wishing that for once in my life, I could be wrong about my fate with relationships. I'm also frustrated with the embarrassment Max has now caused. If people didn't know we were broken up already, they certainly do now. I cry on Aly's shoulder, effectively ruining the baby pink t-shirt she's wearing. She doesn't seem to care though.

"Shh, it's okay, Lay. He's a dick for showing up here. You did the right thing." She says, consoling me.

Pulling back from her, I swipe my index fingers under my eyes. "Why doesn't it hurt as bad as it should?" I ask with a tight throat.

She uses her left hand to tip my chin up until I meet her eyes. A line draws between her brows. "What do you mean?"

Inhaling a shaky breath, I release it slowly, willing the tears to stop. "I knew eventually something would happen, Aly. I didn't really love him. I stayed with him out of convenience, nothing more. I knew it would end." I shake my head. "What is wrong with me?"

A look of sadness creeps into her expression as she releases my chin, using her thumb to wipe away the dampness on my cheeks.

"Nothing is wrong with you." She assures. I don't agree.

I straighten, tugging out the too tight ponytail in my hair before running my fingers through it. "I didn't love him the way I should have." We'd never really said those words to each other, come to think of it. "Maybe it is my fault that he cheated. Maybe I should take him back."

"You don't want *him*. Honey, I think it's time for me to be real with you." Aly says, placing a hand on my knee, squeezing gently. "Remember when we were thirteen and you talked about one day being a singer and falling in love with a rockstar in California?"

A fond smile forms on my face. "I was such an idiot back then." I say with a chuckle.

She nudges my shoulder with hers. "That's not true. You used to be open to the idea of love, but then you discovered that life can be brutal. After what happened with your parents, with your mom…" She sighs. "Your perfect world took a nose dive. You don't know what you really want so you keep chasing things that are unhealthy out of fear."

I scoff. "I'm not afraid."

She pins me with a look that expresses she's on to my lie. "Layla, you are. What happens if you find someone who doesn't cheat, doesn't ruffle your idea of what you actually want? Would you give them a chance?"

She knows the answer to that question as well as I do. My best friend is right as usual. Adam was the type of guy my mom wanted for me. Everyone else that came along after was the opposite. Fame had a way of changing her tune with Max. She sure enjoyed gloating about him to her friends. When she invited us to visit Seattle last year, that's when I began distancing myself from him. Remington was…well he wasn't exactly her or my father's idea of a proper suitor which might be why I fell so hard for him in the first place. It's like I purposely sought someone that might break the mold they'd built for me while damaging myself in the process. Jesus, I am so messed up.

Suddenly the greenroom door swings open. Remington marches in, his eyes colliding with mine before shifting to Aly. "Get out." He orders in a gruff voice.

I blink at him in stunned silence. Aly on the other hand, isn't fazed. "Excuse *you*, king shit."

"My apologies, Aly." He plasters the fakest smile on his face. "*Please*, get out. Now."

She pins him with a vicious glare for several seconds before standing to her feet.

"Be nice or I'll kick you in the dick." She says as she passes him, closing the door behind her.

I scrub my hand over my face, groaning inwardly. Rem takes a seat at the end of the couch, angling his body toward me in the chair. I curl my arms around my knees, bringing my booted feet up on the cushion. He smooths his hands over his dark denim clad thighs, searching my face. I don't like the way he's studying me when it's obvious that I've been crying. I'm sure my face looks like a freaking abstract painting with all the makeup I was wearing. He looks concerned and pissed off at the same time.

Inhaling a deep breath, he releases it slowly. "If you don't distract me right now, I'm going to climb the stairwell to the roof and flying elbow drop that motherfucker outside."

SELF-INFLICTED

Rem

Thankfully, I get the reaction I was hoping for from Layla when I threaten to pull a WWE move on her bastard boyfriend. Her lips twitch for a split second before she's laughing which makes my heart beat like a kick drum.

I hate it when she cries. Knowing she's crying over *him* pisses me off more than words can express. Being the one to make her smile is satisfying enough to let it go. For the moment. I don't want her night ruined by some asshole, so I thought it better to try shifting the mood. If I don't do that then I'll end up making things worse by asking what happened between the two of them. Even if I am dying to know. Even if it isn't my fucking place.

I grab a tissue from the box sitting on the coffee table, handing it to her. "Your face is a mess." I say with a wink.

She rolls her eyes. "Thanks." She says, dabbing the tissue under each of them. "Better?"

I squint my eyes pretending to inspect her face again. Truth is, she'd be the most beautiful thing on the planet with a face smeared in elephant dung.

"You're a knockout, Bug." The words slip free before I can reign them in. I bite down on my bottom lip to shut myself up.

"Why are you here?"

I clasp my hands together between my knees. "Thought I'd cheer you up."

"Don't you have anything better to do?"

I shrug. "I was going to challenge Connor to a dance off, but that can wait." She giggles. "He thinks he'll outshine me on the dancefloor at the wedding. I need to school him."

"Liar." She says with an unconvincing glare.

I smile. "Our set doesn't start for another twenty minutes." Her eyes track over my face, up to my hair before she frowns. "What?"

Pursing her lips, she glances away from me. "Nothing." She says eventually.

I'm not buying it. "That most definitely means *something*."

"Well, your hair is-"

"What's wrong with my hair?" I smooth a hand over the longer hair on top of my head. It feels fine.

"I miss it." She says in a quiet voice.

I scrape the barbell in my tongue against my teeth. "My hair?"

She nods timidly and in that moment, I wish I could magically grow my hair back out like a fucking chia pet. A faint pink colors her cheeks.

"It was always...soft." She mumbles.

I reach out, grabbing her hand, the one closest to me. Bending forward, I slide her fingers along the side of my head above my ear where it's shorter. Then I move her hand to the back where it's longer. Her breath snags, her eyes drifting closed.

"Still soft?" I whisper, watching the way her long, dark lashes fan her high cheekbones as she curls her fingers into my hair.

"Yeah." She says just as quietly.

A shiver snakes down my spine when she lowers her feet to the floor, leaning closer to me. My entire body trembles, eager to pull her into my arms. I'm an addict for her. Always craving more without ever getting high enough to be satisfied. I remove my hand from hers, stunned that she keeps it there. I know I'm not supposed to touch her, that it will likely break the spell she's currently under, but I can't help myself. I slide my hand along her knee, curving it around her thigh, squeezing gently. I glide my fingers up the outside of her thigh-highs until they contact her bare skin. Her lips part, giving me the urge to run my tongue along that bottom lip before sucking it between my teeth.

SELF-INFLICTED

Layla's lashes lift slowly, those hazel eyes full of desire mixed with apprehension. "Rem…" she breathes my name like an angel.

God, I love her voice.

I lift my free hand up until its cupping her cheek. Running the pad of my thumb over her bottom lip, I say something I wasn't expecting. Something that has been weighing on me heavily the last five years. The one question that's been tormenting me since she shattered everything.

"Why did you let me go?"

In a blink, whatever was simmering between us dissipates. She releases my hair, dropping her hand as if I'm made of fire before standing abruptly. All that's left in her gaze is anger.

"You should go."

Biting back on my molars, I stand as well, placing my hands on my hips. "Just tell me." My voice comes out harsher than I anticipated. She might be annoyed with the question even though it's valid. I'm mad too and deserve to know the truth. When she doesn't respond, I release a sigh. "You always do this."

She crosses her arms defensively. "What are you talking about?"

"Run. That's your thing, Layla. You get lost in your own goddamn head all the time and talk yourself out of shit. That's why you stayed with your mom so long. Hell, it's probably why you ended things with that dickhead."

She recoils as a darkness creeps into her features. For a moment I think she might punch me in the face again like she did years ago. Right now, I'd probably fucking welcome it. It's better than nothing with her.

"You have no idea what you're talking about!" she seethes. "Don't act like you know me."

My eyes narrow at her. "Oh, I don't know you?" her shoulders tighten. "I was there that day your mom packed all your shit up without your consent. I heard the conversation about the way she treated you despite all you'd done for her. I know you withhold emotions, acting tough to keep yourself from breaking. You dig your own grave to keep from feeling."

"So?" she lifts her arms, slapping them against her thighs. "What's the harm in that?"

"You harm yourself!" I roar. She freezes in place. Releasing an exasperated breath, I try to quell my anger. God, I hate watching her self-destruct. "You like the pain, don't you?" I might be projecting my own shit on her, yet a part of me hopes that what I'm saying resonates. "You're not happy unless you're drowning."

"I don't like it." She argues. "It's just the way it is, *Elijah*. It's none of your business."

My nostrils flare as a sharp pain slices through my chest. I shift toward her as she backs up against the wall. Dipping my chin, I get within an inch of her face.

"Don't fucking call me that. Especially now."

She lifts her chin in indignation. Our lips are so close that I can feel her breath on mine. She smells like vanilla, making some of my frustration fade. All these years gone without her knowing why it bothers me to hear my first name. Fuck if I'll tell her though. Not when she won't tell me why she's so damn scared to be with me.

A knock sounds on the door before swinging open. Billy glances between the two of us looking frantic before apologizing when he sees the state of Layla's face. He probably thinks I'm the one who made her cry. *Great*.

"Riley is looking for you. Your set is about to start." he says to me before shifting his gaze to Layla. "Everything okay in here?"

"Yes," she says, shoving past me. "I'm tired and ready to get on the bus."

SELF-INFLICTED

*

Layla and I are like a match to dry tinder. Put us together too long, we'll eventually start a fucking wildfire. I'm a pro at deflection though, so instead of wallowing in my argument with her, I brush it off to do my job with my band as if nothing ever happened. We chat with some fans after the show then unwind in the greenroom while the crew packs our stuff. I'm irritated yet I'm letting it go. That is until I see Riley with a scowl on his face, entering the room and heading straight for me.

"I'm telling you right now, whatever shit happened between you two needs to be nipped. I'm not risking the drama here."

"Okay..." I say slowly, lifting my hands defensively.

Typically Riley is a pretty laid back dude. I've never been confronted by him this way.

"That shit you pulled earlier? Trying to fight Max, is liable to get you a lawsuit. Worse, it makes the band look bad. It makes *her* look bad."

"Uh, no shit sherlock. It's not like I intentionally started something. He's the one that mouthed off first when he appeared out of nowhere. Why he did it is beyond me."

His lips form a thin line. "Doesn't matter, Rem. If her being here is an issue, we can stop this now. Say the word and you guys get a new opening act."

I bite down on the inside of my cheek. That's not what I want at all. Layla deserves to be on this tour. I will not take the opportunity away from her.

"It's no problem." I assure him.

He seems to relax a little. "What is it between you two anyway?"

My brows raise. "Excuse me?"

"Max made a suggestive comment. Did you two have a fling or something?"

My throat tightens and I swallow roughly. *Something*. That doesn't matter now. At least according to her.

"No," I lie. "it's family shit, man. It's squashed. I'll behave."

He nods once, seeming to believe my response. "Good, because if there's more I need to know, you have to tell me. This tour will either hurt or benefit your guys' career."

Irritation sprouts in my gut when I watch him leave. I'm a musician because I want to be, because it brings me closer to the man I lost that I love. If this shit doesn't work out with the label, it won't stop me. Layla though, she lives for worrying about other's opinions. Does whatever she can to keep herself under the radar to not make waves. If it means protecting her, I'll do my best to keep my cool. Although, I'm not quite sure my best is going to be good enough because the second I'm within a few feet of her, I lose control of most cognitive thinking skills.

SELF-INFLICTED

CHAPTER FOUR
Layla

    Today is the first day in two weeks that I have zero plans. Having interviews with local radio stations, performing nearly every night, and dealing with seeing Rem daily is exhausting. I've been enjoying the performance part a lot more than I anticipated. It's exciting traveling to different cities and meeting new fans, however living on a bus with several people is not for the faint of heart. Between the noise of the guys practicing new songs, and Aly with her boyfriend constantly showing public displays of affection, I'm grateful for the alone time in a hotel room. I need to be able to clear my head in a quiet space.
    Max has tried texting me a few times since he was escorted out of the venue back in North Carolina. I refuse to respond. As much as I want to hope that he's over the breakup, I'm not holding my breath. Especially when I was scrolling on my phone last night before bed. I saw a newly posted photo of him with some mystery girl on social media. He was flipping the camera off in the photo while his tongue was shoved down the poor woman's throat. If he's trying to make me jealous, it's not working. I'm more repulsed actually and hoping that instead of focusing on bringing my reputation down, he'll move on with his life. According to his last text, my "days are numbered." Whatever that means.
    I've been heeding Aly's advice by staying in my own lane, minding my own business. I refuse to add fuel to whatever fire he's

planning on igniting. Though that doesn't mean I'm not in a foul mood because of Max. The anger is more prevalent than anything which makes me upset with myself for even feeling it at all because I know he isn't worth my time. I can't help it. I'm a brooding little bitch at times. I'm just hoping it runs its course soon. Until then, I plan to veg out in my room like a proper cave troll to relax.

I spend the day doing only the bare necessities. Aly offers to hang out with me and possibly go to dinner, but I decline. I curl up in the super soft hotel bed instead to binge-watch some reality show about dating a rock star. For someone who isn't all that keen on love in real life, I sure am a sucker for drama and romance. Maybe it's the hope in the story that warms my frigid soul, or maybe I'm a glutton for punishment knowing I'll probably never experience a meet cute or a man that serenades me with a love song. Instead, I've had meet disasters and a man serenade me with a hate song.

I'm snuggled under my favorite purple throw blanket, the one I stole from my dad's guest bedroom. I decided to bring it with me on tour as a reminder of home. I'm blissfully watching the drama unfold after one woman finds out another woman got a kiss from the famous man, when a soft knock sounds on my door. I scowl at it before pausing the show. We aren't performing until tomorrow night, so I don't want to be bothered. Whatever this is, better be important.

Reluctantly tossing the blanket off, I pad to the door, glancing through the peephole. *Son of a bitch.* I'm not in the mood to deal with *him* right now. We haven't spoken much since North Carolina. I've been retreating to the bus after my sets or minimally joining into group conversations to avoid the inevitable fight bound to happen.

Remington coming into the greenroom to help cheer me up was too sweet of a gesture that I didn't deserve. Running my fingers through his hair sent me back to the past, reveling in memories of kissing him, being touched by his hands. I know what will happen if we're left alone together. I'm afraid of what that's going to do to me. Because if we revert back to that place we were, I know we'll fall into the same chaotic space of bickering and sexual tension.

Flipping the lock, I reluctantly open the door. Rem stands before me, hands in the pockets of his faded blue jeans. The t-shirt he's wearing is white, offering glimpses of the ink on his skin beneath it. He smiles at me, a small tilt of his lips. Cue those pesky butterflies. Stupid, attractive man.

Squaring my shoulders, I take a step back. "Hey."

"Hey, you busy?"

I glance back longingly at the paused show on the television. "Not really." I turn back toward him.

He plays with the piercing in his tongue, a nervous habit I picked up on years ago. "Can I come in?" his voice is hesitant when he asks the question which makes me lower my defenses a little.

I motion with my hand for him to enter before closing the door. He steps further into the room, standing beside the edge of my bed. When he faces me, his eyes slowly scan down my body before lifting to meet mine. I cross my arms over my chest, suddenly feeling exposed in the pajama shorts and tight tank top I'm wearing.

"So, what's up?"

Rem sits down on the bed, resting his elbows on his knees. "I wanted to see how you were doing. You've been quiet."

"A simple text would do." His eyes narrow. I roll mine. "Fine, but you're interrupting a solid television masterpiece." I say, plopping down at the head of my bed, curling a leg up.

"Oh, yeah?" He glances at the television, chuckling. "You watch reality dating shows?"

"Don't knock it. It's a great escape."

"Is this season two? You'd think after the first one, the love he was searching for would have stuck."

I laugh. "It's season four actually."

He shakes his head, clasping his hands together between his knees. "Aly said you found out about me confronting Max."

"Yeah, I did." Aly told me that Max said something – something that no one will share with me – and Rem wanted to fight. I'm glad it didn't lead to anything like that. This is yet another reason why Rem and I shouldn't be friends. Not if he's going to threaten every guy that says something negative about me. He's liable to ruin his career. My gaze falls to his long, capable fingers. I quickly meet his eyes again. "That shouldn't have happened."

"He provoked me." Rem says and there's a menacing edge to his tone.

No surprise there. Max is pretty hot headed at times.

"I don't doubt it." I frown. "Do you think I blame you?" I had also been told that Riley gave Rem a pretty strict talking to after the incident.

His shoulders lift in a shrug. "Maybe."

"Max shouldn't have been there. I'm glad he was kicked out. Whatever he said to you was probably just to piss you off. You shouldn't waste your time on him."

His jaw muscle ticks. "He said you were paying me with blow jobs."

My mouth pops open as rage fills me. "What the hell?!"

Rem's brown eyes flash to mine. "He also said you don't belong on tour."

"Oh," that punch straight to the heart deflates me. Max is part of the reason I gained momentum in recording my album. He said I was good. That I had loads of potential. It hurts knowing he might not have genuinely believed that. Releasing a heavy breath, I decide to address the first topic because I'm not talking to Rem about my relationship issues. "Listen, he doesn't know about our past. I didn't say anything."

"I don't give a shit if you did." Rem seethes. "What I care about, is that fucking asshole talking about you negatively. He's a prick, Layla. Why in the hell were you with him?"

Irritation sprouts. "I don't know, Remington. Clearly, I have poor decision making skills when it comes to men."

"Can you not drag yourself for one second?" he groans, scrubbing a hand over his face. "Jesus, it's like you can't handle things not being your fault."

I glare at him. "Don't analyze me."

He matches my glare with one of his own. "Don't change the subject. Why are you with him?"

Releasing a heavy sigh, I run a hand through my wavy hair. "I'm not *with* him. Not anymore. Maybe I liked him because he was different."

His brow lifts. "From what? *Nice* people?"

"We both know I don't do nice."

"Why did you break up with him?"

Irritation flares. "Who told you that?"

"Aly."

I sit back against the headboard, tucking my knees up to my chest. Damn her for spilling my tea.

"I broke up with him because I found out that he cheated on me." I explain. "Besides, I don't love him. I don't think he ever loved me either." The sting of rejection is evident in my voice but there are no tears. "Honestly, I can't even say I'm sad about it. Like it hurt, sure, yet I knew it was going to happen eventually."

He closes his eyes briefly, muttering a curse. "Always so pessimistic."

"I prefer to think of it as being a realist."

"*Realistically*, you can do better." He captures my gaze, his brown eyes holding me hostage. "You're killing it with "Waterfall," I don't think that song has ever sounded so good."

Warmth swells in my chest. "Thanks."

He continues searching my face, so intense like he's staring into my very soul. Something in the air shifts between us before Rem clears his throat, breaking the trance.

"I just wanted to apologize. You know, for almost kicking your exes ass." He speaks low. "I should go."

"Wait!" I say as he starts to get up. He turns to face me, now standing. He's staring at me expectantly causing me to almost lose my resolve. I have to be the bigger person here, for once. "I'm sorry."

He crosses his arms over his chest, cocking his head to the side. "What?"

"We're always fighting."

His shoulders lift in a slight shrug. "Yeah, it's our thing." He shakes his head. "After all this time, you're going to apologize for it *now*?"

Frustration blooms. Our *thing*?! We don't have a thing. We don't need a thing. I refuse to apologize for fighting with him. If anything, he should be the one to say sorry. He started it all those years ago by being a dick after we found out the truth. Okay, bigger person. Right. That's who I'm going to be now.

"I don't want this tour to be ruined because of it."

"I won't let that happen, Bug."

"Still. I don't want everyone thinking we can't get along." I say quietly. "So, I'm sorry that Riley got upset with you after the Max incident. Aly told me to ignore his threats, so I'm going to focus on the tour, nothing else. I won't let this ruin anything for you."

Anger washes over his features. "What threats?"

"It's nothing." I assure him. "I just want you to know that despite what you think, I truly want what's best for you guys as a band and for you personally."

His lips turn down, shoulders tightening. I hope he understands how sincere I'm being.

He glances down at the dark hardwood floor near his feet. "Maybe we should go back to playing pretend."

"We both know that's impossible." I say, studying his face as he stares at the floor.

He looks like he wants to say something else. I hate the way my stomach twists into knots when he lifts his head to look at me.

"Is it?" he asks in a soft voice. "We're awfully nice to each other when we pretend."

Yeah, we are. Which is why that's a dangerous road to travel down, now more than ever.

"Rem..."

He pins me with a look that's softer. Something I so rarely see when he looks at me. Usually there's a small ounce of hostility. "Layla, I can't promise you that we won't fight."

"I don't expect you to." I say. "We can try-"

"Trying is useless." He snaps. "Every fucking time we *try*, it ends up blowing up in our faces. Don't be naïve."

I bite back on my molars. "I'm not naïve."

"This!" he shouts, motioning with his hand between us. "We're already fighting."

I blow out an exasperated breath. "Well then why don't you leave?"

His eyes narrow at me. "There you go, pushing me away again."

I spring to my feet, standing toe to toe with him. "Stop narrating what you *think* I'm doing!"

"You're fucking impossible." He says, placing his hands on his hips.

"So are you. *Elijah.*"

Inhaling a deep breath through his nose, he shakes his head. "Do you know why I hate when you call me that?" he asks, his tone less edgy than before.

I cross my arms tightly against my chest. "I'm sure it's the same reason I hate when you call me Bug."

He laughs without humor. "Not even close." My brow crumples.

Rem closes his eyes, pinching the bridge of his nose with his thumb and forefinger. My heart beats an unsteady rhythm. He's silent for several moments before opening his eyes, leveling them on me. The anger that was once there is replaced by pain that brings to the surface a surge of compassion for him that almost knocks me off my feet. I don't like sad Remington.

"I was with him when he died. My father." He says quietly. "I thought he abandoned me when I was a kid, when he and my mom first separated. It turns out they were simply no longer compatible." A fond smile forms on his lips. "I had the opportunity to tour with him on school breaks. I'd hang out with bands, catch free shows. He's the reason I fell in love with music."

I smile too despite the sorrow lacing his voice. "I remember you sharing that with me." It felt like a lifetime ago when we went out for cheeseburgers and milkshakes, spilling our secrets to one another.

He nods. "I had just turned eighteen. It was the end of Spring Break. He was planning to fly me back home that morning." His gaze loses focus as if lost in thought. "We were in the hotel room, saying our goodbye before I went to the airport. One minute we're making plans for me to visit over Christmas, and the next he's dropping dead to the floor."

SELF-INFLICTED

A tear rolls down my cheek that I quickly swipe away. It's absolutely heartbreaking to imagine what must have been going through his head when that happened. "I'm sorry." I whisper.

"I was named after him." He confesses. My heart squeezes painfully in my chest.

Bridget called him Eli which was obviously short for Elijah. How had I forgotten that? The sudden urge to wrap him in comfort overwhelms me. Before I can stop myself, I'm moving toward him. I throw my arms around his waist in a crushing hug. His chest heaves a shaky breath as he folds his arms over my shoulders, squeezing me back. I feel his head rest against the top of mine as I inhale his distinct cinnamon scent, still the same after all this time.

"I'm so sorry, Rem. For how it happened, for what hearing his name does to you." I pull back to look up at him, seeing the unshed tears in his eyes. "I didn't mean to hurt you."

I don't just mean calling him by that name, but for five years ago as well. I pick fights when people get too close. I isolate myself to keep from giving too much away. I've never allowed myself to be vulnerable with anyone apart from my best friend. Even then, I find myself holding back sometimes.

"There's something else," he swallows roughly, lifting his hand to my cheek, swiping his thumb under my eye to clear the tears that fell. My body trembles at the contact. "I don't like when *you* call me…Elijah." His thumb moves to my lower lip, pressing against it. "These pretty lips saying my real name unravel me, Bug."

Electricity charges the air around us as I find myself melting against him when he slowly lowers his head, capturing my lips with his. Fire licks up my veins when it shifts from slow and tentative to fierce and hungry. His tongue slides along mine, making me whimper. I press my body against his as he devours me like a starved man at a feast. His hands find my hips, gripping them as he lifts me into his arms. I wrap my legs around him, tossing my arms over his shoulders. He grips my ass with one hand, cradling my head with the other to gently lower me to the bed. The nagging thought that what we're doing is wrong creeps into the back of my mind as his lips travel down to my neck. His teeth scrape against the soft flesh of my throat. Instead of begging him to stop, I moan.

We're bad for each other in so many ways, but when he's touching me this way – igniting my body with his fingertips – I don't care about the consequences.

SELF-INFLICTED

Rem

I shouldn't be kissing Layla. I *really* shouldn't be groping her tits while moaning softly in her ear, but she likes it and I refuse to deny her. Besides, I'm not the type of guy that asks permission first. I'm the type that hopes for forgiveness later.

It's true, I hate my given name because of the vicious reminder of painful memories. I hate it more when Layla says it though, because I fucking love it when she addresses me, the *real* me. It makes we want to drop to my knee and put a sparkly ass ring on her finger. That feeling hasn't gone away in five years.

Layla's head falls back against the mattress as I work her left breast before moving to the right. She swirls her curvy hips, grinding that hot pussy against my rock hard length. A groan erupts from my throat. I need her naked. I grip the hem of her tank top, rolling it up her torso.

"Off." I order, lifting slightly to give her room to move.

She doesn't even fucking hesitate which is one of the things I love most about her. She's always been an exceptionally good listener when it comes to these interactions. As soon as the tank top is over her head, I thank whoever I should be praying to that she isn't wearing anything underneath. I lower my lips to hers, biting down on her bottom lip before soothing it with my tongue.

"Good girl." I pull back, taking my time, inspecting every ounce of skin exposed to me. She's so sexy, so perfect to me. I raise up on a knee and she immediately opens her legs. I palm her breasts, kneeling between her thighs, admiring the way her hazel eyes struggle to stay open. "Fuck, I've missed these." I say before taking one into my mouth, sucking hard.

She bucks her hips, trying to get me to rub myself against her. I like teasing her. She curls her fingers in the hair at the back of my head, pressing my face into her chest. My self-control diminishes then. I sit up suddenly, tugging at her shorts. I'll admire her more later. I stand to remove my shoes, shirt, and jeans before grabbing a condom from my back pocket. I wasn't imagining this with her, but I always keep one handy just in case. Layla's lying completely naked now, her hair fanning around her head like a halo. My dark little angel. I roll the condom on before easing onto the bed to settle between her legs. She sucks in a sharp breath as I slide myself against her wet pussy. My throat tightens. She's always so wet for me, so ready. I prop myself up with one hand beside her head, fisting my dick with the other.

"I'd very much like to fuck you." Her eyes widen. I smirk down at her, easing in a little. "Hard," I slip further in. "Fast," my body quivers when I get halfway. "Rough." I sink in fully, stilling myself.

She bites down on her bottom lip and I swear her eyes roll back in her head for a moment. God damn, she drives me crazy. "Yes." She moans. "Fuck me, Rem."

I slide out of her before slamming back in, making her cry out. She drapes her legs around me, forcing me closer as I pump my hips, reveling in the tight heat that welcomes me. Damn, she feels good. Better than I remember. Bracing myself with one hand, I use the other to wrap around her throat, applying a small bit of pressure. She gasps as her eyes fly to mine.

At first, I'm worried I've scared her. Then she whispers, "I like that."

I thrust into her harder, pushing her into the mattress with my hips. "I want to hear it."

Her moans grow louder, bringing me closer to the edge. That fucking voice is like a siren's song. I'm powerless against it. Hearing how good I make her feel makes me believe I'm the king of the world or some shit. I need to make sure she goes before me, that she remembers she's all mine. Sliding my hand from her throat, I palm her breast as I lean forward, my lips hovering over hers. I flick my tongue against her upper lip, feeling her muscles clench around me.

Moving my mouth to her ear, I groan, "Tell me how good it feels."

"So…good." She cries.

I thrust harder. "I'm going to make sure you don't forget it."

Her hand flies to my back, sinking her nails into my flesh. I capture her chin in my hand, forcing her to turn her head before sinking my teeth into the side of her neck.

"Oh. My. God!" she screams as I suck the skin hard, marking her.

Her hips move faster, chasing the release before she stills for the briefest moment.

"*Mine.*" I grit out, sensing the rush of warmth against my cock.

I pump into her once, then twice before stars dance behind my eyes. I screw them shut, exploding so hard I think I might pass out. Breathing heavily, I force my eyes open, gazing down at my beautiful, unique girl. Her hands are resting on either side of her head as she stares up at the ceiling, her chest heaving while she tries to catch her breath. My eyes fall to the side of her neck and a surge of pride swells in my chest. I like seeing my bitemark on her.

Sliding my fingertip against it, I ask, "Does it hurt?"

Her eyes flick to mine. "Yeah," she breathes before huffing out a short laugh. "I can't believe you bit me." I frown. She swallows, shaking her head, seeming to see the look of disappointment on my face. "I think you were right." She shrugs. "I kind of like the pain."

That makes two of us. Maybe that's why we're so right and wrong for each other. Neither of us know how to cope without suffering. Which is probably why we can't shake this connection. I bend my head to kiss her swollen lips before easing out of her.

"Don't go anywhere." I murmur, glancing over my shoulder at her as I head for the bathroom.

The last time we'd done this, everything ended quickly. I'd been in a rush to get away from her so I could make the situation make sense in my head. I needed the quiet, the darkness of my room to work out in my mind why I hadn't felt more shame after what we did. Why I wanted more from her. This time, I know the reason. I won't let her keep pushing me away so easily. Not when I know without a shadow of a doubt that we belong together.

Layla is still on the bed when I exit the bathroom, only now she's nestled under that blanket of hers from our parent's house, with her head laying on a pillow. My heart jams in my throat at the sight of her looking blissfully content in bed. I'm not sure what moves me more at the moment. The fact she didn't kick me out or because she's comfortable enough with me to fall asleep.

I slip under the covers, behind her, wrapping an arm around her waist. I take a strand of the multi-colored hair between my index finger and thumb, testing the softness of it with the other hand. How long have I dreamt of sleeping next to this beautiful, broken woman? Inhaling a deep breath that smells like vanilla and cinnamon, I nuzzle in behind her. She stirs slightly, moaning something unintelligible as she backs into me, pressing her bare ass between my hips. If I wasn't tired as fuck, I'd wake her up with my dick inside her. I want her again already, but I'm not going to push too hard. Not yet.

I curl my arms around her loosely, burying my face in her hair while closing my eyes. The hand on her waist slides to the skin of her belly and I trail my fingers back and forth, committing this moment to memory. If I had my way, she'd never leave my side. She would want me as much as I want her and stop worrying about the consequences of us being together because fuck everyone else. As long as we're happy it shouldn't matter. I'll do whatever it takes to make sure she learns that.

CHAPTER FIVE
Layla

I wasn't planning on having sex with Remington. I thought I'd apologize for fighting with him then we'd go our separate ways. However, for the first time since I'd met him, there was a vulnerability about him that I'd never seen. One that made me want to be there for him the way he'd been there for me all those years ago by distracting him from the painful memories.

I can feel the weight of his arm draped over my hip. When I open my eyes, I see his other hand lying palm up near my head. I also hadn't anticipated falling asleep with him. Yet after the incredibly intense and passionate time last night, I'd been too exhausted to fight it.

The only other person I'd ever fallen asleep with was Max when I'd stay with him occasionally. Even though we'd been in a relationship, there was something more intimate to me about waking up next to Remington with his arms around me. Probably because I've wondered what this would feel like more times than I can count which means I need to end this as smoothly as possible. The heat emanating from him isn't stifling despite how close he's lying next to me. I can feel his erection pressed up against my ass, reminding me how good he felt. Wanting him again is dangerous. Yeah, I need to get up.

I carefully lift my hand, gliding my fingers over the tender skin alongside my neck. A shiver rolls through me. He'd fucked me, hard. I could still feel the pressure of it between my legs. Maybe I welcomed the pain he gave to punish myself for hurting him all those years ago or maybe he unlocked a carnal desire within me that I've been refusing to acknowledge. Either way, I wasn't afraid of him. Despite the guard on my heart, I trust Rem. Which is all the more reason to get him out of my room.

Holding my breath, I gingerly slip out from his arms before rolling to the floor, catching myself on my hands and knees. Not the most graceful way to slide out of bed, but I'm not sure how to broach waking him or telling him to leave. As I stand, I grab my clothes then make my way to the bathroom. I have no idea what time it is. Judging by the specks of light seeping through the dark curtain in the room, it must be late morning. I'm supposed to meet with Aly today for lunch. After managing to silently close the bathroom door, I flick on the bright fluorescent light. I use the toilet and wash my hands before getting dressed, then set about brushing my teeth.

When I look in the mirror, my eyes snag on my skin. "Holy shit." I wince at the purple and red mark near the base of my throat.

It looks more painful than it feels. Examining it closer, I find subtle teeth marks at the edge of the area. How am I supposed to hide this from view? Hopefully, Aly can work her makeup magic. A flood of heat curls in my belly as I smooth my finger over the mark. He's the only man I've ever allowed to take me in such a way. The only one who has seemed to care enough about getting me off first. I frown at the sudden realization of it all. As long as we're not speaking, we're in sync with each other, almost on a soul level. He gives me what I need and I like to think I do the same for him. Guilt is an icy reminder that chills me to the bone.

Releasing a sigh, I gain the resolve to face the music as it were. When I step back into the room, Remington is sitting up in bed with my blanket draped over his hips. My mouth dries at the sight of him shirtless, hands curled over his lap and that messy hair on top of his head. Heart hammering in my chest, I slowly approach the bed.

"Are you kicking me out, Bug." He asks in a husky voice that almost undoes me.

Why does he have to be so delicious and inviting? At least he knows me well enough to know I want him gone.

"I am." I sit down in the desk chair. I can't get too close or I'll cave.

"Why do you always do this?" he asks. "It's as if you're afraid of me."

"I am." I admit, curling my fingers against the metal arms.

He cocks his head to the side. "Why?"

Growing irritated, I sit up straight. "It doesn't matter."

He arches a brow as a wicked smirk forms on those earth shattering lips. "I think it does. Explain it to me."

Growling in frustration, I say, "Get out."

"No." he glares back at me, his jaw muscle clenching. "Tell me why you're afraid."

"You're a dick."

He snorts. "So you've told me, plenty of times."

"I don't want to get too close. I can't." It's not the only reason, but it's something.

"Maybe if you try it, you might like it."

I blink at him like he's speaking a foreign language. "No," I say. "relationships are cruel. It's a construct forced upon us as a society to give us a false sense of security. It's always conditional."

His eyes fall, a sadness creeps into his features. I feel bad for raining on his parade but he won't change my mind. He's a pain in my ass, just like I'm one in his.

His gaze flicks up to mine. "Do you really believe that?"

I shrug. "I haven't been proved wrong yet."

He chews on his bottom lip, seeming to be in thought for a few moments. "*If* I leave, can you promise me something?"

Yeah, right. I'm not putting myself in a position to be indebted to him. "You once told me that tomorrow is full of broken promises."

His lips tip up on one side. "I did say that didn't I?" he leans forward, locking his gaze on mine. "Be with me."

My heart drops to my stomach. There's no way I'll risk what weird friendship we have by pursuing something with him. He's relatively famous and I'm, well I'm not yet. Though I sure as shit would be if the truth of us ever came out. Not in a good way either. Being with him could damage us both.

"I can't do that." I whisper.

Rem is undeterred. He stands swiftly, marching toward me before dropping to a knee at my feet in all his naked glory. My mouth waters at the sight of him. The way he's kneeling before me does something funny to my heart. He slides his hand against my cheek, raising up enough to gently kiss my lips. When he pulls back, I want to follow him but I don't. We have chemistry for sure, and I like the way he makes me feel alive. Especially when we're having sex, however physical acts aren't everything. We'd get bored eventually.

"No strings, no expectations. Our little secret." He says, running the pad of his thumb against my lower lip, making me shiver.

"A secret?" I ask, spinning the idea around in my mind.

If no one knows, there would be no judgement. If all we did was sleep with each other, I wouldn't get hurt. He wouldn't get hurt. Was a scenario like that actually possible?

I shake my head, getting rid of the naïve thoughts. "That's a recipe for disaster and you know it."

SELF-INFLICTED

He nods, lowering his hand. "Yeah," he's silent for several seconds. "After last night though, I don't think I'll be able to stay away from you."

My brow creases as I stare down at the floor. I'm not so sure I'll be able to stay away from him either. I should have never agreed to this tour. Although... we're two consenting adults. We're more mature now, more experienced. Why am I talking myself into this when I shouldn't be?

"No one knows." I say firmly, meeting his eyes. "Me and you, we're nothing as far as anyone else is concerned."

"For the remainder of the tour." He agrees.

A deadline will keep me in check. I can prepare for it.

I raise a questioning brow. "What about after that?"

He swallows roughly. "We break for good."

Pressure clamps down on my chest. It would be nice to not fight for the next few months, though I'm not sure it's worth it. "You think that's possible?"

He sits back on his heels, glancing at the rumpled covers on the bed. I wait for him to respond, noticing the way he closes his eyes briefly before turning to look at me again.

"That's what you want, right?"

I want to say, no. I want to tell him that breaking at all is a shit plan. That this ridiculous pact will blow up in our faces. I don't. I can't. Because the selfish part of me that's been dying to be with him is quickly taking the reins. If I tell him anything other than yes, he'll have hope. Hope that I have no business giving because he deserves better than me. We've been down this road before and yet, this time feels different. This time, we both know it's brief.

Inhaling a breath, I stick my hand out for him to shake. His palm coasts along mine, causing a shiver to run down my spine. "It's for the best. Do you agree?"

Squeezing my hand gently, he nods once. "It's a deal."

Can we stick to this pact or will it destroy everything we've shared with each other? I'm not certain. However, this is one of those rare moments we're actually in agreement so I'm willing to test the theory. What else do I have to lose anyway?

"Deal." I say, sealing my fate.

*

"Holy shit, did you get attacked by a vampire?" Aly shrieks as I immediately slap my hand against the hickey on my neck. "Is that why you're wearing a hoodie when it's eighty degrees? It's been humid as hell and here I was afraid you were coming down with a flu or something and had the chills." She forces my hand away, inspecting the mark closer. "Who did this?"

There's been moments in our friendship that I've told little lies to Aly. Once was when she got a really bad haircut in the seventh grade and I told her it was cute. Another time, she'd asked for her berry lip balm back. I told her I lost it, when in truth, I wanted to keep it for myself. After that it was the hookup with Rem that I eventually admitted to. This time, I'd be lying worse than ever before. While it makes me feel like an unworthy friend, I can't tell her what actually happened. The deal is a secret and I already know that Aly will be totally against it if I admit that Rem is the one who marked me. Besides, I have to get ready for my set tonight.

"I met up with someone." I close my eyes so that she can place shadow on my lids. It's best I don't look at her. Although she's silent for so long, I open them again.

She frowns at me through the vanity mirror in front of her. "Who?"

"I think his name was Rob or Rich or something." I lie. "I had to get out for a while last night. I found this guy on a hookup app and one thing led to another…" I shrug.

SELF-INFLICTED

There's a glimmer of shock along with curiosity in her eyes. "You had a one night stand? Lay, that's…wow! Good for you."

I chuckle. "Thanks."

"So, what was he like?"

Lying to her further, I make up a story about meeting the guy at a bar that led to us going back to his place. I hate the fact that I'm being dishonest. However, if anyone knows about me and Rem, there will be questions I'm not prepared to answer.

"I want to do a red lip tonight." I say, distracting her from the topic.

Aly tucks her loosely waved hair behind her ear, picking up a makeup brush. "We're not done with this conversation."

"Thirty minutes to show time." Billy hollers from the doorway of the greenroom.

"Later." I promise her, though I have no intention of keeping that promise.

Although lying to Aly about the make-believe hookup leaves me feeling sort of gross and disappointed in myself, it subsides when Rem shows up in the greenroom after their set. The crew is busy loading up the tour bus. I think Aly disappeared into Hemingway's Rejects' room to hang out with Ty.

"Hey." I say, taking in his purposely disheveled hair and brown eyes that sparkle at me. A wicked grin forms on his lips as he quickly shuts the door behind him before grabbing my hips, tugging me into his body. "What are yo-" he cuts me off with a searing kiss.

His hand glides down to my ass, squeezing while that piercing scrapes against my tongue. A dull ache immediately forms between my legs as I wrap my arms around his shoulders, curling my fingers in his hair. He releases a shaky breath before stepping away from me, my arms falling to my sides.

"I miss you." He murmurs, reaching for my waist again, or at least that's what I think is happening until his fingers move to the front of my jeans. He flicks open the button before working the zipper down.

"Rem!" I whisper shout, glancing at the door.

Ignoring my protest, I'm lead to the small bathroom where he closes the door, turning the lock quickly. My jeans are lowered down my hips before he slips his hand inside my panties. His finger glides along my already wet slit and he growls low.

"Always so fucking wet for me." His eyes flick to mine. "Do you want me to stop?" he asks, inserting that finger inside me. I whimper. "Or do you want me to make you cum?"

I grab ahold of his shoulder as he pumps his finger in and out, then adds another. "Don't stop."

"Good girl." He leans down to kiss me again while slowly fucking me with his fingers. The moment his thumb swirls over my clit, I no longer care that he's barged in. "I fucking missed this pussy today."

With two fingers pumping steadily, his thumb circles my clit making my knees wobble. I hold tight to his shoulder to keep myself from collapsing. He's a magician, finding the sweet spot almost instantly and moving faster. Within a few seconds, my body goes rigid while the warm rush of release takes over. I exhale an unsteady breath, opening my eyes as he removes his hand. Winking at me, he sucks those same two fingers between his lips, groaning. I blink at him as he readjusts my jeans, fastening them again.

"Have a good night, Bug." He says before striding back to the door, leaving me standing there with my heart beating wildly in my chest.

SELF-INFLICTED

Rem

"Great job tonight, man!" Riley slaps my shoulder.

"Thanks." I say. "The fans seem to be enjoying that encore."

"Definitely. It was a good idea to start playing "Jackknife" again. I'm also glad you and Layla are getting along."

"We came to an agreement." I mutter, grabbing a bottled water from the mini fridge in the green room.

Five days ago, we made our pact. I'm eager to spend every ounce of my free time bringing her pleasure. I don't want to waste a single second of her now that I have a deadline. The truth is, I know this arrangement will likely end up hurting me in the end, but I'd rather have my beautiful, unique girl for a few months than not at all. I might also have an ulterior motive, though I'm biding my time to spring that on her. I need one last chance to prove how good we are together. I want her to miss me like I miss her and want me like I desperately need her. I have one shot to convince her that losing me is a mistake. If she rejects me again, I'll be a fucking disaster, but at least I'll know for sure that she doesn't feel the same.

That's why I caught her by surprise the other night after our set. To make sure she knows I'm all in with our deal. That I'll be there to take care of whatever she needs as long as she lets me.

"Well I'm happy to hear it." Riley says. "She's doing well for someone with so little experience. I've heard the label is pleasantly surprised with how many people enjoy her music."

It's really no surprise to me. Layla is awesome. "Yeah, that's great."

"If she keeps it up, maybe they'll offer her a full contract."

My brows crumple. "What do you mean?"

"She was offered up by Kyle Fuller. He vouched for her and begged his dad to give her an opportunity. This is kind of a trial run to see if she sticks."

I swallow down the anger threatening to surface. Why does no one believe that she's capable of this? I might be somewhat bias, but I genuinely feel like she has just as much merit to be out here with us every night as anyone else. Max made a similar comment that night he showed up. Not wanting to make waves, I half-ass a response before getting up to head to the bus. As I exit the greenroom, a few fans beg for photos and autographs. I'm exhausted after the show, yet I happily sign their merch and let them take a few selfies with me.

"You are so hot!" a woman with blond hair, who doesn't seem sober enough to walk, calls out.

I shoot her a smile. "Thanks, love."

"You want some company tonight?" she flirts while her friend beside her giggles.

It's flattering to be the object of someone's affection. In my years performing, I've heard my share of offers. I've even taken a few women up on them. However, it isn't in me to be someone's bucket list item. Besides, I have the girl of my dreams to spend time with already, even if it is temporary.

I chuckle. "Thanks for the offer," I say, stepping backward toward the bus, "I've got to get going." I slap Connor on the back who is currently signing some other girl's chest. "Ask him." *He's* the one she'd prefer anyway.

"Dick." I hear him mutter as I flip him off, walking away.

I step onto the bus to find everyone gone except for Layla who is scowling at her phone on one of the couches. It's quiet as I slide onto the couch next to her. I take a drink of my bottled water, noticing her gaze shift to my mouth. She has no idea what those expressive eyes do to me. How badly I want them on me at all times.

SELF-INFLICTED

"What are your plans tonight?" I ask, peeling at the label of the bottle.

She lifts her shoulder in a shrug, pocketing her phone. "Thought I'd take over the world."

I smile at her, leaning in close, catching a whiff of vanilla. She always smells amazing. "You want some company?" I trail a finger over the back of her hand that's resting in her lap, loving the way goosebumps rise on her skin.

Her eyes close, a faint smile tugging at her lips. When she opens them again, there's a burning desire that warms my blood.

"Come to my bunk?" she asks as she gets up, heading for the back.

I stare at her ass while she walks away, my dick straining against my jeans. She's wearing a black tank top that fits her like a glove with a pair of jeans that I'm jealous of. Yeah, I'm that fucking sprung on her that I envy the damn clothes that get to touch her body. I'm not sure what she's planning, but I'm totally willing to find out.

After waiting for a few minutes to ensure I'm not seen, I make my way to her bunk. Luckily, hers is toward the back so no one seems to be alerted to my destination. I climb in quickly, immediately closing the privacy curtain. Lying down next to her, I graze my hand over her hip. She lifts her hands, placing them on my shoulders.

"Is this okay?" she whispers.

I lean in, placing my lips against hers. "Perfect." I say quietly before kissing her.

She presses her thigh between my legs, moving against me as I bite down on her bottom lip to stifle a groan. It's like her body was made for mine. The way she slides her palm against my jaw, kissing me back just as fiercely, makes my heart beat faster. I help her remove my shirt while we continue making out for several minutes until she pulls back suddenly. Her hands move to the button on my jeans. I shift my hips up, helping her pull them down before she quickly grabs me, rubbing her thumb over my tip.

"Fuck." I murmur against her lips when she leans in to kiss me again.

She continues her touching for a while before pulling back to look at me. "I want to try something." She says in a low voice.

There's a slightly sheepish look on her face. I catch the faint pink of her cheeks in the dim light.

"What...*damn*." I shudder out a breath. A million ideas run through my head, but it's hard to concentrate when she's tugging on my dick like this. "What do you want to try?"

Instead of answering, she places her lips against my neck, slowly descending over my chest, forcing me to my back.

Oh, fuck.

I watch her through heavy lids as she carefully positions herself over me, working those luscious lips down my stomach to my hips, still fisting me. She slides down further, flicking her gaze to mine, her mouth hovering over me.

"I've never done this before." She admits quietly. My throat tightens.

Jesus, fuck!

"You seem to know what you're doing." I breathe out, enchanted as her tongue glides over her bottom lip. My brow crumples as her admission sinks in. "Never?"

She shakes her head. "Wasn't interested, except with you."

I can tell by the look in her eyes that she's being honest which makes my chest tighten. She'd never rode a guy until me either. I was her first in a lot of ways even if I wasn't the one to take her innocence. The thought of that makes me wonder what else she wants to experience. I'd love to teach her everything.

Despite the intensity of her still stroking me, I ask, "Why me?"

She opens her mouth, licking my tip casually. A smirk plays on her lips when I hiss, gripping the blanket beneath me. "You wanted me on my knees."

She doesn't say anything more. I clench my teeth as she swirls her tongue over the tip again. Her lips close over me while she lowers her hand to the base, sucking on me like I'm a goddamn lollipop. I watch her take me this way, burn it into my memory for the rest of my life. She begins sucking me off harder while moving her hand quickly, bobbing her head over my shaft.

Jesus, I'm going to fucking blow.

Something about this woman keeps me from controlling myself. My lips part and I fist my fingers tightly into her hair, encouraging her to keep going. She softly moans around me as I release a grunt when I feel the back of her throat. This feels too good. It's difficult to keep quiet. Her eyes lift to mine as she takes me all the way into her mouth.

"Fuck." I choke out harshly.

My spine stiffens, stomach muscles clenching as the release bursts through me like a fucking missile. Layla slaps my hand away when I try to grab my shaft, interlacing her fingers with mine as she drinks me in, taking every last drop.

I'm trembling when she slowly lifts her mouth away before repositioning herself to lay next to me. Shifting onto my side, the urge to speak overwhelms me. Before the words tumble out, I reel them back in. Instead, I place my lips against hers, communicating everything I'm dying to say into a kiss that I hope she'll never forget.

An hour later, my eyes keep drifting closed. We're snuggled together, her head on my chest with an arm draped over my waist while I absently play with her hair. I've been listening for any signs that someone might be awake on the bus. It's still quiet other than the steady hum of the engine. Lowering my hand from her hair, I press her against my side.

"I should go." I whisper softly.

Layla lifts her head, "Yeah, that's probably a good idea."

Leaning forward, I place a kiss on her forehead. I don't want to risk being caught even if it's killing me to leave her.

"Goodnight, Bug." I say before grabbing my shirt and exiting her bunk.

I head toward the front of the bus, startled when a hand darts out, grabbing my leg. I whip my head down to find Connor glaring up at me from his bunk.

"What the hell?" I demand in a soft voice.

His brows raise. "You sure this is smart, Rem?"

I narrow my eyes, ripping his hand off me. "What are you talking about?" I glance back toward Layla's bunk. Does he know?

"I'm your best friend, douche." He whispers. "You think I don't know what you two are doing?"

"Let it go." I say, continuing on toward my bunk.

"That's what I told you to do five years ago." He calls out.

Ignoring him, I slide into my bunk. I know Connor won't tell anyone about us. That doesn't mean he isn't going to give me shit for it every chance he gets. After our last fallout, he told me to give her up. To move on to someone more attainable. While I can understand his concern and appreciate it, he doesn't get it. I can't let go of her that easily. She's imbedded in my skin, a brand on my conscience, the keeper of my fucking heart.

SELF-INFLICTED

CHAPTER SIX
Layla

    Maybe I'm a masochist. I've spent the better part of my life dwelling so much on the negative when it comes to relationships that I'm certain the only thing I know is pain. Which is likely why I've decided to join into this purely physical relationship with Remington that deep down I know will end in catastrophe. Instead of reveling in him wanting me, I want to break him into pieces and find all the flaws I can in order to not get attached. I've been trying to think of *anything* about Rem that I don't like. So far, I've got nothing.
    I chew on the end of my pen as I stare out the side window of the tour bus, watching the trees pass by quickly. The driver said we're nearly to Colorado. I'm trying to focus my thoughts by writing. Though it's proving to be difficult when I keep thinking about Rem. It doesn't help that he's sitting on the couch across from me, working with Connor and Ty on a new song. I have my ear buds in, listening to a playlist I recently made. He shot me a wink a few minutes ago when I glanced over and those damn butterflies sprang to life. I smiled at him, feeling like a giddy teenager. I'm glad that we're not fighting anymore. That instead of denying ourselves of each other, we're giving in. Though I can't help the simmering disappointment that gnaws as each day passes.
    My phone vibrates next to me on the cushion.

Melissa K. Morgan

Mom: *Care to explain?*

Attached to the text is a link. This can't be good. I release a sigh as I click on it, taken to a social media page that covers news in the music industry. The article has a picture of Max with some beautiful woman. The headline reads,
Max Tate is Moving Up!
After a bitter breakup with Layla Barlow, the rocker says he's setting his sights on love again with someone better.
That's seriously degrading and hurtful, but I'm not surprised. The problem is that he's still threatening to ruin my reputation. He's in my head way too much which is driving me crazy. While it irritates me to no end having people assume they know anything, I won't fall down the rabbit hole of some stupid tabloid.

Me: *Stay off the internet mom.*
Mom: *She's really pretty.*
You should have held on to him.

I don't hear from mom very often since she moved to Seattle. While I weighed the thought of trying to mend things with her a few years ago, I quickly discovered she had no intention of ever apologizing for her behavior. The moment she found out about me not going to law school, she berated me over the phone. Then she somehow found a way to blame dad for coddling me because he felt guilty. I did my best to avoid her as much as possible for my own personal sanity.

Me: *Thanks for the unhelpful advice.*

She only cares about how I make her look to her friends and anyone else she might socialize with. I toss the phone beside me, not wanting to deal with her any longer. I used to feel rejected by her comments. Now it just annoys me. I hate that I feel anything toward her still. I wish I could be indifferent but I don't think that's possible. She is my mom after all.

I'm startled when I feel a hand land on my shoulder. I snap my gaze to the right, seeing Rem standing above me. He nods toward my phone as I pull out an earbud.

"You okay?"

Lifting my shoulder in a shrug, I say, "Yeah, my mom was texting me yet another article involving Max."

He frowns. "Does she do that a lot?"

"Almost daily." I pull out my earbuds.

I wish no one else was around. Maybe I could distract myself by disappearing with Rem for a bit. That seemed to help the other night when I invited him to my bunk after seeing a text from Max, telling me that it's only a matter of time before my fifteen minutes of fame is up.

"Why?"

"It's probably her version of tough love or something. You know her."

His lips tip down. "Try not to let it get to you. She's not worth it." He squeezes my shoulder gently.

"I know."

He moves to sit down beside my legs which are folded against the couch. "So, we had an idea." He begins, glancing toward the other two.

I follow his gaze, brows crumpled. "Okay…"

Ty smiles. "We were thinking it might be cool if Rem does "Waterfall" with you. You could have him join your set for the song. I bet the fans would enjoy it."

Me and Rem singing his song *together*?

"What do you say, Bug? I bet we can harmonize together easily." He gives me a knowing smirk. I roll my eyes. He chuckles.

"Okay. I'd be willing to try it."

"Nice." Ty says. "You two should start practicing now." He passes the acoustic guitar beside him to Rem who takes it easily. "We can squeeze it in tonight at the show."

Rem begins strumming out the melody to "Waterfall" on his guitar. "I think you should sing the intro," he says to me as he continues playing. "I'll join in the chorus and sing the second verse."

I smooth my hand through my hair, setting my notebook down with the pen. "Are you sure? It's your song."

"It sounds better when you sing it." He stops strumming, shifting in his seat. "Want to give it a try?"

I bob my head to the music as he begins playing the opening chords again. It's hard not to watch his fingers plucking the strings or sliding along the neck of the guitar. Closing my eyes, I begin singing. To my surprise, our voices do blend well together as we start the chorus. When the song ends, Connor is shaking his head in disbelief.

"Woah." He says in a stunned voice. "Yeah, you guys have to play that tonight."

"I agree." Riley says, coming out from the back area. "Damn, that sounded phenomenal."

I can't help the smile that spreads across my face.

Rem nudges his shoulder into my bent knee. "We make a good team."

We continue practicing the song a handful of times as the bus rolls on to Denver. By the time we arrive at the venue I've forgotten all about my mom and Max.

SELF-INFLICTED

"What are you going to wear tonight?" Aly asks, rummaging through my clothes in the greenroom of the venue.

I brought in a few different outfits because I wasn't sure what I wanted tonight. Being with Remington on stage for the first time is nerve-wracking.

"I'm not sure. Do I go more casual or dressy?"

"You can literally wear a garbage bag as a dress while looking good, Lay." She assures me.

I doubt that very much. Sighing, I twist my finger around a curled piece of hair. "It's weird singing a song with Rem. I know the fans seem to enjoy it when I do "Waterfall," but *with* him? What if my voice cracks or something?"

She lifts her brow. "You're overthinking it. You're going to be just as great as you have been." She sorts through the items I brought in before pulling out an off the shoulder, white crop with a pair of denim shorts. "This is cute."

"I trust your judgement."

As she's finishing my makeup, there's a knock on my door. I go to answer it while Aly places the cosmetics back in the travel bag she uses. My mouth goes dry at the sight of Rem standing before me, wearing a black t-shirt that hugs his body with a pair of light jeans with holes in the knees, tucked into black combat boots. His hair is styled in a spiky, disheveled way, highlighting the faux mohawk on top of his head. I blink at the tiny black hoop in his eyebrow. He'd told me once before that he wore it occasionally. This is the first time I've seen it. I'd be lying if I said I didn't find it sexy. His lips kick up on one side in a half smile.

"You busy?" he asks, raising a dark brow. His eyes rake down my body as he bites his bottom lip.

"Oh, hey Rem." Aly says, breaking my trance.

His gaze slides to hers. "Hey."

"Your outfit is laid out in the bathroom," she says to me. "I'll let you two prep for your performance."

I mumble an "okay," as she slips past us out into the hall.

"So..." Rem's voice drops low as he leans forward. I'm hit with the smell of cinnamon that makes my stomach flutter. "am I interrupting anything?"

I swallow roughly, my blood warming. "No."

A slow, wicked grin appears. I don't even hear the click of the door closing when he begins devouring my mouth with his. The barbell in his tongue grazes my bottom lip, making me moan. I slide my hands up his chest, shoving him back.

"I have to be on stage in less than an hour." I whisper breathlessly.

"I can be quick." He says, moving in to kiss me again, slipping his fingers to the back of my hair.

"Wait." I'm trying to sound firm, but it's challenging when I'm ready to rip his pants off and force him between my legs. Reluctantly, he steps back. "Aly already did my hair and makeup."

His eyes track over my face. "You look gorgeous, Bug."

Rolling my eyes, I say, "Thanks. My point is you can't mess all this up." I swirl my index finger in front of my face. I lick my lips, angling my head toward the couch. "Sit down."

Fire explodes in his eyes as he does what I say instantly. A wave of excitement rushes through me. Is that what it feels like for him when I obey? After checking to make sure the door is locked to the greenroom, I walk toward him to step between his legs.

Lowering my lips to his ear, I place my hands on his shoulders. He trembles beneath my touch. "Good boy."

"Jesus, you're perfect." He says, grabbing my hips.

Keeping my hands firmly on his shoulders so as not to mess up his hair either, I kiss him, whimpering when he nibbles on my bottom lip. He grips my ass, squeezing roughly as I reach for the waistband of the leggings I'm wearing. He helps me remove them along with my panties before undoing his jeans. When his cock springs free, showing off that piercing in the tip, my mouth waters.

SELF-INFLICTED

I thoroughly enjoyed sucking him off the other night almost as much as when he's fucking me. He pushes his jeans down to his knees while I kneel on either side of him. I sink down onto his shaft, letting him fill me completely. I love the way he feels inside me, the way he teases me by pulsing his cock.

Rem's hands move back to my hips, his gaze locking on mine as I move gradually at first, finding the rhythm that will get me off quickly. I don't look away from him as I pick up the pace. A moan creeps up my throat, escaping before I can stifle it. He releases a shaky breath.

"Fuck, I'm not going to last long."

"Don't cum yet." I beg, riding him faster. I'm so close to release, I can feel the wetness around his bare cock gathering. I lean back a little, using his shoulders as support while he palms my ass, forcing my body closer to his. My scalp prickles as the blissful orgasm rocks through me, forcing my eyes closed. "Oh, god. Fuck!"

He continues pumping into me, as a growl rumbles through his chest. My eyes open when his shoulders tighten. I stare into his pretty brown eyes, feeling him erupt inside me, his cock throbbing against my walls, drawing out another wave of release. My arms and legs are shaking when I lift myself off of him to stand.

Liquid slides down my inner thigh and Rem's eyes fall to the skin there. That blazing heat is still present as he flicks his gaze to mine. The realization of what just happened causes fear to sink in. He must read the emotion on my face because his brow crumples.

He stands as well, pulling his jeans back up and securing them before placing his palm against my cheek. "I'm sorry," he murmurs. "I got caught up. I wasn't thinking." He shakes his head, "That's not a good excuse."

"It's fine." I blurt, even though I don't really know if it is. I'm on birth control, but that's not always effective. I wasn't even thinking about protection at the moment which is incredibly stupid. Who knows how many women he's done that with. At risk of ruining the moment, I ask, "Do you do that regularly?"

A veil of anger seeps into his features, his jaw tightening. "Fuck, no." he snarls. "I've always worn a condom. I'm clean."

I scoff. "It was just a question." I pull my panties back on. "Can't be too careful."

"What about you?" he demands, irritation lacing his voice.

I have always made sure every partner I've been involved with wrapped their tools prior. Rem's the only one that brought out these irresponsible actions. Like him, I'm clean.

Plastering a sarcastic smile on my face, I say, "You're my first."

His eyes narrow. "Oh, yeah?" his gaze falls to my thighs again before shifting back to mine. A possessive heat creeps into his features.

Why is he looking at me like that?

"Yes, *caveman*." I snap. He actually smiles at that remark. Jerk! "I need to clean myself up and get dressed."

"You want some help?" his voice is dripping with promise.

I know if I cave, I'll never get on stage. "No." I say with a shaky breath that gets lodged in my throat when he bends to kiss me slowly.

"I promise that won't happen again." He says. "In my defense," he reaches into his pocket, flashing the condom packet. "I came prepared."

"If we're going to continue this, you need to make sure you're always prepared."

"That's fair." He says, shoving the condom back in his pocket. "I'll save this for later," he waltzes toward the door. "See you soon, Bug."

Once he's gone, I immediately rush to the bathroom to clean myself up. Thankfully, my hair and makeup look just as flawless as when Aly first did it. I dress myself in the outfit Aly picked out, double checking to make sure I look as perfect as possible. As silly as it sounds, I'm a lot less anxious since Rem showed up. He has a way of calming me down even when he's riling me up.

    I head for the steps of the stage, hearing Billy up there announcing me. Aly comes to stand beside me, giving my hand a squeeze. As he says my name, the crowd begins to cheer, making my chest swell. Just yesterday Billy said I'm doing well. I honestly hadn't anticipated such praise halfway through this tour. Giving Aly a smile, I make my way onto the stage.

Rem

    I don't normally watch Layla's full set, but tonight is different. As soon as the song she's currently singing is finished, I'll be joining her. A surge of pride sweeps through me as I watch her tackle the stage, singing to the crowd. Even with an electric guitar slung over her shoulder, she's working the stage like she owns it. I don't know what the fuck Max was talking about when he said she didn't belong. I hate that her own mother still treats her like shit too. She's got everything it takes to be up there. She looks happy which is something so rare for her most days. She always picks on herself, which is something I noticed early on when we were younger. I wish she could see what I see and understand just how incredible she is. I pull out my phone, quickly snapping a few pictures of her.
    As the song comes to an end, she places her mic back on the stand before removing the guitar and handing it to her bassist.
    "Thank you guys so much for all the love!" she says into the mic. "I have one more song for you tonight, and this one is really special." Jackson moves a stool from the corner of the stage next to her before placing a second mic.
    "When I was offered the chance to join Hemingway's Rejects on their tour, I knew I had to take the chance. This has been a dream come true." She says. She smiles out at the welcoming crowd. "They've been gracious enough to let me cover one of their songs while we've been touring. Tonight, we're going to try something a little different with it."
    I make my way up the steps, placing the acoustic guitar around me as I move across the stage to the stool. Instantly, the roar of the crowd increases. I lift my hand in a wave, my eyes on Layla. She's beaming at me as I approach her, her hazel eyes sparkling in the stage lights.
    I lean in with my lips at her ear. "You ready, Bug?"

SELF-INFLICTED

She nods before turning her attention back to the crowd as I sit.

I begin strumming out the melody for "Waterfall," closing my eyes and letting the music guide me. It's surreal to be playing this song with her, up here. My heart squeezes tightly in my chest when I think of my father. Of the emotions that created the lyrics for the song, the person I was before he left me, the person I didn't begin to find again until Layla entered my life.

As she begins singing the first verse, I open my eyes, caught between staring out at the dark crowd and watching her. I join her in the chorus, closing my eyes once more as I let the feelings I've kept down for so long, resurface. It's like stepping out of a blizzard into the sun for the first time. She's quiet as I sing the second verse. When I go into the chorus again, she joins me perfectly. We fit together so damn perfectly. After the song ends, the audience erupts in applause. I slide the guitar behind me as I stand.

Grabbing my mic I place my hand out in Layla's direction. "Give it up for Layla Barlow!" she gives a mock curtsy which is adorable as hell. "She's good, right?" They continue their praises.

She waves. "Thank you all, again! Have a kickass night. Next up is this guy," she hitches her thumb at me. "and the rest of Hemingway's Rejects!"

We place our mics back on the stands before I motion for her to go ahead of me off the stage.

Aly immediately squeals, hugging Layla as she steps off the stairs. "God, that was so incredible! You two should collaborate more often."

I chuckle. "That was fun for sure."

"That's staying in the set." Connor says as we make our way back down the hall. We'll go on in a half hour after the stage is reset. He tosses his arm over my shoulder, pulling me closer. "You two should just give it up and be together already."

I watch the girls disappear into her greenroom, my shoulders tensing. "Tell that to her." I mutter, shrugging away from him.

Reality is a swift kick to my balls while the reminder of our deadline flashes in my mind. I join the others in our greenroom, shifting the anxiety aside. I'm not going to think about what happens in the next month. I want to soak in as much of this as I can before the potential demise. Riley informs us that there's some reporter or person from a social media page wanting to interview us before our set so I push down the uncomfortable truths regarding Layla to do my job.

That is until the guy begins asking questions about her.

"Layla Barlow is gaining a lot of popularity thanks to this tour. Her songs are rising on the streaming charts. How does it feel to know you've had a hand in her success?" he asks.

"I can't say we've had a hand in her success. She does a good enough job speaking for herself." Ty replies.

The reporter nods, looking at me. "Rumor has it that you taught her everything you know. Did you guys practice a lot together growing up?"

She isn't musically talented because of me. "We didn't grow up together." I say. "She was already playing music when we met."

"There's a source that claims you two have a romantic history together. Care to comment on that?" Shock is a rapid punch to the gut.

Fury rolls through me at the question. "What the fu-"

"Sources aren't always accurate." Connor claps me on the back. "Where did you hear that?" he asks.

The reporter leans in, whispering he says, "Between us, Max Tate made a comment on the record two weeks ago."

I'm going to fucking kill that bastard! Clenching my jaw, I keep my mouth shut. Dispelling rumors is a waste of time when we

SELF-INFLICTED

all know those who are the loudest always win whether they're right or not. It doesn't piss me off that anyone has an opinion about us, it pisses me off that Layla will catch wind of the rumor which will probably eat her up for the rest of the tour.

"From what I've seen, he's moved on." Ty adds. "No need to embellish his comment when they aren't together anymore."

The reporter nods. "Thanks for your time tonight, guys." He shakes each of our hands. "Have a great show."

After he leaves, we head toward the stage. "That was fucking weird." Connor says.

"Why would Max Tate bring anything regarding you two up?" Ty asks.

"Fuck if I know." I shrug. "Sounds like he's jealous or something."

"Maybe he's pissed because Layla's outranking his band with her single right now."

A smile spreads as I glance at Connor. "Really?"

"Yep, Max is probably mad at himself for dumping her. We all know he only got to where he is because of his money."

"What money?" I ask.

Connor rolls his eyes. "Dude, read an article. You're so uninformed."

Ty chuckles. "You know he doesn't stay up to date on anything. He lives in his own world."

"I just don't believe everything I see. I'm cautious about shit." I argue.

"Anyway," Connor says. "I heard from Riley that five years ago, Max Tate used his father's power and influence to start a band. Do you know who his father is?" I stare at him expectantly. He knows I don't know. "Gary Evans. The CFO of the Diamond Label in California."

I stop, cocking my head to the side. "Seriously?" Connor nods. That's the parent company of our own label. "Why is his last name Tate then?"

"It's a stage name probably." He says with a shrug.

I wonder if Layla knew anything about this or if he'd kept her in the dark. He plays decent guitar, but he's no prodigy.

"Anyway, don't let the rumors get to you." Ty says as we approach the steps to the stage. "It's not like you two are actually together."

Connor shoots me a look that I ignore. Even if the public did find out we had a past relationship, it wouldn't make a difference. It's not like our careers would be on the line for something we did five years ago. Max Tate can't have that much pull in the industry. My stomach sours as I head up the stairs. The past isn't the part I'm worried about. If we're caught now, there's no way Layla will stay with me.

*

The whole party scene isn't really my thing. A lot of people associate rockstars with sex, drugs, and chaos. I've been there, done that and bought the fucking t-shirt. I spiraled a bit after my dad died by taking it upon myself to obliterate my brain cells as often as possible. The day I realized how badly I'd hurt my mom by abandoning her when she was grieving too, was the day I decided to grow the fuck up. I could have stayed in California with my friends, could have spent my nights at Hollywood Hills parties and snorting the good shit. Hell, I probably could have slept my way to a music career sooner, but that's not what I wanted. I earned my position. There's something about working hard and reinventing yourself that feels a hell of a lot more rewarding than having shit handed to you. Life isn't easy, it's real. My dad taught me that. I'm glad I can remember his little nuggets of wisdom even though he's been gone so long.

SELF-INFLICTED

This random bar is more my speed. They decided to give us a night off here in sunny Arizona before we play tomorrow night. It's hot as fuck, though I'd be lying if I said I wasn't enjoying the outfit Layla is wearing due to the heat. She's got a short plaid skirt on that has me thinking inappropriate thoughts, with a hot pink tank top that does little to hide the black bra underneath. Her multi-colored hair is done up in a high ponytail. It's taking every ounce of willpower I have to not drag her somewhere dark and private.

We're staying in a hotel tonight, so that means I'll have the chance to make her scream for me again. Something she already promised to do when I cornered her earlier on the bus, begging her to let me taste her. Yeah, I begged. She brings out the needy, greedy bastard in me.

When Riley and Billy told us we could have some freedom for an evening, Connor suggested we go out. He was the only one interested in a night club, so since the majority rules, we decided on this little bar that has karaoke and music that plays at a reasonable volume. It's still pretty crowded, though no one seems to be paying us much attention.

"Shots!" Connor announces as he sets a tray on the table of the round booth we're sitting at.

We all grab a small glass off the tray. Layla sniffs at the amber liquid, her lips turning down.

"No way." She says, sliding the glass to the side toward me since I'm sitting next to her.

I chuckle before taking my shot then slip hers to Connor. "You're up, slugger."

"Lame asses." He grumbles before knocking it back.

"She doesn't drink that shit."

"Actually, I have." Layla corrects. I quirk a curious brow at her. Because of her mom's alcoholism, I know she doesn't drink much. I'm surprised to find out she's tried whisky. She glances down at the table top. "Only once and I regret it."

I don't press further because I can tell by the look in her eyes that she doesn't seem keen on discussing the reasons. Instead, I casually place my hand on the bare skin of her thigh, sliding my index finger over it.

"I like you sober anyway." I whisper.

"So, who's up for some karaoke?" Aly asks excitedly from the other side of Layla.

I'm barely paying attention to the conversation as I continue moving my fingers against Layla's skin. She's so warm and soft. I know I shouldn't be touching her right now when we're in public, yet I can't help myself. She's like a magnet that won't release me. I inch my hand up further, slipping it under the skirt. Her hand lowers from the table, resting on my thigh where she squeezes tightly, pinning me with narrowed eyes.

"Stop." She says quietly, but there's desire in her eyes.

My lips kick up. "What's the matter, Bug?"

She licks her lips slowly, stealing my attention. "Someone will see."

"Then we should go somewhere private." I suggest in a low voice.

She bites down on her bottom lip. The look in her eye tells me she's contemplating acting on that. Straightening in the booth, she cups her hand over her mouth, whispering in my ear, "Meet me in the bathroom."

Before I can respond, she asks Aly to let her out before walking away.

Holy shit!

I play it cool, grabbing my bottle of beer off the table before taking a drink. Am I really going to follow her into the bathroom of this bar? Um…fuck yeah, I am! Aly grabs Ty's hand, dragging him over to the karaoke area to check out the song options while Connor texts on his phone. I guarantee he won't notice my absence. I get up from the booth, making my way across the near empty dance floor to head for the back hall where the bathrooms are. There are two doors, both are unisex and only one is closed. I reach for the handle of that one, pushing it open.

Layla is sitting on the small vanity, her hands resting behind her on the countertop. The way she's angled displays her perky tits. The skirt is so short that the creamy skin of her thighs beckon me. I quickly lock the door before marching toward her, wrapping my hand around her throat as I lean into her.

"Jesus, you're a fucking dream. You know that?" I immediately capture her lips with mine, tasting her sweet lip gloss before I slide my tongue against hers.

"Wait…" she pants. I release a frustrated growl that makes her giggle. "We have to be quick if we don't want to be caught."

Releasing a breath, I nod while stepping back. "Hands against the wall." I order in a gruff voice, angling my head toward the tile near the door.

Her hazel eyes widen for a moment, then she's sliding off the vanity before rushing to the spot I chose, planting her palms flat against the tile. I stare at her ass in that short skirt while I take my time approaching her, enjoying the way she looks from behind. I reach out when I'm close enough, running my right hand up the back of her thigh until I cup her ass. Leaning forward, I place my lips at her ear.

"Do you have any idea what you do to me?"

Reaching around, she palms me through my jeans. "Yeah," she breathes over her shoulder with a cute little smirk.

Groaning, I step closer to pin her hand between us. "I've dreamed of taking you this way." I growl when she squeezes my shaft.

Taking her wrist, I plant her hand back on the wall before crouching behind her. I reach up under her skirt, tugging the panties down those long, sexy legs until they're around her ankles.

Flipping the skirt up, I lift my chin, licking along her already soaking pussy from behind.

"God, Rem…" she moans.

I smile to myself as I fuck her with my tongue.

"You taste so good, Bug." I murmur against her, already feeling her legs shake. I palm her ass as I continue feasting between her legs. "Cum for me, baby. I want to fuck you badly."

A tremor rolls through her when I feel the liquid heat gather on my tongue. Knowing we're on borrowed time, I stand quickly, yanking open my jeans and pulling a condom from my back pocket. I slide it on in record time before wrapping my hands around Layla's hips.

"Tip toes, baby." I say, guiding her up higher. My head is spinning when she obeys my command. I enter her from behind, swift and hard. I bend my lips to her ear, "Good girl."

She keeps her palms flat while I hold her skirt up over her waist, fucking her from behind. I lift a hand, coasting it along the front of her throat to bring her head back to my shoulder.

"Holy…god!" she moans, the sound of her voice sending me over the edge.

Pumping into her two more times, I cum hard, pinning her to the wall with my body as I grasp at her hip. I lean my forehead against her shoulder, trying to take deep breaths while I calm my racing heart. She breathes heavily too, her hands slipping from the wall. I pull out of her, tossing the condom in the trash before doing my jeans up. Then I bend to help readjust her panties under her skirt.

Layla turns around to face me with a satisfied smile on her gorgeous face. I pull her close, cradling her in my arms. There are so many things I want to say to her. So much fucking emotion I wish I could express without scaring the shit out of her. It isn't time yet though. I hold her tight, resting my chin on her head until she wraps her hands around my waist, simultaneously warming me while filling the empty void in my chest.

"We should get back out there." She says quietly after a few moments.

Reluctantly, I release her. "Yeah, you go first." I say, unlocking the door.

She stands there for several seconds, her eyes searching mine as if she's contemplating something. I stare back, wishing things were different. That I could hold her hand in public or kiss her any time I want. A small smile forms on her lips before she leaves me.

I drag a hand through my hair, blowing out a heavy breath. "I fucking love you." I whisper to no one.

CHAPTER SEVEN
Layla

    It feels good to dance out my troubles with Aly on the dance floor. Not only after being with Rem who produces feelings I can't bring myself to speak of, but also because of the text I got earlier. Max sent me a photo of one of my notebooks. One that I'm not sure how he could have gotten unless he stole it a long time ago when I allowed him in my apartment. Along with the picture was a text that said, 'I know everything. You're going to fall from the top so fast.' There's no direct mention of Remington specifically in any of my notebooks, though the one Max is now in possession of was from when I was eighteen. The one with the poem describing how I felt about him. There are other lyrics peppered throughout that definitely elude to a forbidden romance. It wouldn't take a leap of logic for him to put it together. I texted him back, calling him a thief, demanding that he give it back. Of course, he refuses to respond now. I'm mad as hell that he would invade my privacy that way. Not knowing if he'll actually take the notebook public has me paranoid.
    In an interview yesterday I was asked if there was ever a romantic link with Rem. I was able to negate the rumor smoothly, yet I know it's only a matter of time before Max shares with the world what's written on those pages. He certainly knows how to play to one of my greatest fears. Perhaps he knows me better than I thought.

SELF-INFLICTED

Not wanting this to spoil the tour, I'm doing my best to tamp down the fear by distracting myself. Which is why I need Rem more than ever. It's also why I'm imbibing a little more than usual tonight. I've only had two cocktails, but I'm definitely catching a buzz. The atmosphere of this cozy bar and a successful tour so far, has me on a high. That and the release Rem gave me an hour ago.

Aly spins me on the dance floor. I giggle as she tries to dip me and fails. "Having fun?" she asks as we continue moving to the upbeat rock song.

"I actually am." I reply, shaking my hips.

"I like you like this."

I place my hands on her shoulders. "Me too."

It's nice to shut my brain off for a while.

"Nothing new from Max?" she asks as she tries to spin me again.

"No. I put my phone on 'do not disturb'."

Thankfully, the conversation is dropped when I feel a hand on the small of my back. I turn to see Connor behind me.

"Jell-o shot for milady." He winks, passing me a small plastic cup.

I happily take the shot from him before knocking it back. I think I've had at least three of these since he found out earlier that I didn't enjoy whisky. I like these though. They go down smooth. Aly and I continue dancing until my head gets cloudy. I feel like I'm floating when we wander back to the booth where Rem and Connor are talking. I slide in next to Rem who pushes a tall glass of ice water toward me.

"Drink up, Bug." He says before talking to Connor again.

I drink nearly the entire glass, which helps a bit.

Aly fills out a slip of paper on the table. "You're singing a song!" she says to me.

I giggle when I read the one she wrote down. "Isn't this kind of a duet?"

Rem picks it up, reading it. "Take me home tonight."

"It's her all-time favorite." Aly grabs the paper from him before walking off to the karaoke area.

He looks at me, a smile forming. "Is that true?"

I roll my eyes. "Eddie Money is fire. Don't try to change my mind."

He chuckles. "You're adorable."

"You are." I reply, trailing my finger over the dimple on his left cheek. His eyes darken as he captures my wrist, lowering my hand.

"Behave," He whispers, "or I'm going to kiss you."

Licking my lips, I lean in to him. "I dare you to."

"She's drunk." Connor announces and we both turn toward him across the table. He lifts a brow, leveling his gaze on me. "No more shots for you."

Eyes narrowing, I say, "You're not the boss of me."

His eyes flick to Rem. "Careful." He warns before leaving the table.

"What was that about?" I ask, taking another drink of my water.

"He's worried we'll be caught."

My shoulders tighten. "He knows?" Rem bites down on his lower lip, nodding his head. "What the hell?"

"It's fine. He isn't going to say anything. He's just worried about us with the rumors-"

"You know about that?"

"Yeah, I was asked about it a few nights back." His brow creases. "Were you hoping I didn't?"

"Ugh!" I groan, placing my spinning head in my hands. "This is just great."

"Hey," Rem gently lowers my hands, tilting my chin with his finger so I'll look at him. "It doesn't matter, Bug."

"You're wrong." I say. "If people think we dated, it will mess everything up."

He doesn't get it. I don't want to be tied to him romantically. Not when it could end our careers. Not when our parents might find out through some stupid article online. What happens down the road when we inevitably get into one of our epic fights in public? Nothing about this is okay.

"It's just a stupid rumor."

I pin him with a glare. "No." Exhaling soundly, I shake my head. "God, I didn't want to tell you this..." I trail off, closing my eyes as the room tilts.

"Tell me what?" he asks, forcing me to open my eyes.

His wary gaze makes my belly twist unpleasantly. I'm already hurting him by being in his life at all. I hate myself for not being strong enough to push him away for good.

"Max has my old notebook from five years ago. One where I wrote out some...feelings."

His lips tip up in a smile. "You wrote about me?"

Rolling my eyes, I lightly punch him in the shoulder. "That's not the point, dummy." He chuckles. "The point is, that while your name isn't mentioned, the...implication is there."

He begins nodding, his gaze tracking around the room.

"I assume he's taking it public." He says after a few minutes.

"Yeah, that's the plan I think."

He gives me a sidelong glance. "Then we do it first."

My mouth pops open. "No!" I shout, earning a few strange looks from other patrons.

He shrugs. "You keep saying "no," but it's the only way to get ahead of this." He must read the look of fear on my face because he dips his chin, leaning closer to me. "Bug, this isn't the end of the world."

Yes it is. "It could be the end of our careers." I say through gritted teeth, growing frustrated with his easygoing attitude about the situation. "If we admit to something going on between us, people might be repulsed."

His jaw tightens, eyes darkening. "Are you repulsed by me?" How could he even think that? Caught off guard, I can't form the words to respond. "Are you ashamed of me, Layla? Of us?"

Suddenly, my arm is being tugged. I turn to find Aly shouting excitedly. "It's your turn! Let's go rock!"

Before I can protest, she's pulling me up to the karaoke area, passing me a mic. The intro music begins blaring through the speakers, making my ears ring uncomfortably. I sing the opening lyrics to the song, my focus trained on the booth where Rem is still sitting alongside Connor who came back with two more large glasses of water. I'm not repulsed by him or ashamed. I hate that I've hurt him again by saying things I can't take back. Instead of going through with the second verse, I set the mic down.

"Sorry. I can't..." I say to Aly before sprinting to the bathroom.

Once I'm inside the small space, I splash water on my overheated cheeks, scowling at myself in the mirror. I'm scared. Scared of what others will think, of what our parents will say. Of what my mom will say. That fear is what's always held me back when it comes to him. It's like I told him when I broke his heart the first time, I'm not good for him. I'm nothing and will only hold him back.

"How you doing, Lay?" Aly asks as she enters the bathroom, leaning against the closed door.

"I'm good," I mumble.

There are moments I want so badly to tell her what we've been up to. To confide in her about all the mixed emotions, yet I can't bring myself to do it. Even if it's beginning to eat me alive. I begin washing my hands. Why? I don't know, maybe because I feel contaminated by bringing Rem down with me.

"You had a lot of Jell-o shots." She says with a smile, handing me a paper towel.

"Thanks." I take it from her. "You know I'm not much of a drinker. This place is fun, but I'm not the party type."

"If you want, I can go back to the hotel with you."

As much as I appreciate her support, she needs to have fun with her fiancé. I know exactly how little time they've spent together prior to the tour starting. It would be selfish of me to not let her soak it up. Besides, I kind of want to be alone.

"No, it's okay." I say, making my way for the door. "I'll see if Connor or someone else can take me."

"Maybe Rem?" she asks, grabbing my wrist, forcing me to face her. "Layla, are you two...?"

"No!" I reply immediately. Her eyes widen. "No."

Aly cocks her head to the side, peering at me with narrowed eyes. She doesn't believe me and honestly, I don't blame her. "Do you think I didn't notice the flirting that's been happening all night?" I knew going out would be a bad idea. "What are you doing?" she asks in a soft voice.

I swallow. "Nothing. It isn't...Listen, it's nothing. Okay?" I can't think straight right now.

She shakes her head, crossing her arms. "Layla, I don't want you to get hurt."

"I won't. Trust me, my heart isn't in it." *Liar!* My brain screams at me. I ignore it. "I promise, this isn't like last time." It's exactly like last time.

Her brows raise. "Why? Because you're older now? Or is he totally over you and completely fine with being used? Are you fine with that, with *him*?"

Irritation springs to life. This is why I didn't want her to know. She always acts as the voice of reason, pushing me into something that I can't be in. I don't care if she believes in soul mates and unbreakable bonds.

"We have three weeks left of this tour." I say, shrugging. "After that we'll walk away."

She rolls her eyes. "You know I love you, right?"

"But?" I ask and she huffs out a sigh.

"This will not end well, Layla. Not for him or for you."

"That isn't your problem."

"I am your best friend, of course it's my problem!" she shouts and I recoil. "You won't be happy. You'll continue throwing your life away to whoever is convenient, all the while wishing things were different so that you can be with Rem. It's a miserable road. Don't take it."

My nostrils flare as the sting of her words sink into my chest. "Not everything is a fucking love story and I'm not throwing my life away!" I shout back. "What do you care anyway? It isn't your life to worry about."

"I love y-"

"Then back off!" I turn for the door again. "I don't need any more people in my life telling me what to do."

"Layla!" she hollers after me.

I continue out the door toward the booth where the guys are sitting. "I need to go back to the hotel." I mutter to no one as I head for the exit.

Too many people for too long have told me how to live my life. I refuse to go back to being a doormat. I'm sure as hell not going to listen to Aly when her life is sunshine and rainbows all the time. Rem has always been my escape. The one place I feel comfortable and not judged. The one place I can truly be myself. I don't care if it's a few weeks and never again. For right now, I don't feel the nagging inner voices of my mom telling me I'll never be good enough. I don't feel the pain of Max's threats or the fear that my entire career could end at any moment because nothing lasts forever.

I. Don't. Care.

Standing on the sidewalk outside the bar, I pull my phone from the inside of my bra where I had it tucked. I immediately notice several missed texts from both my mother and Max. God! They both need to get a life outside of me. Ignoring those, I open up the rideshare app on my phone.

"I'll take you back." His deep voice doesn't bring me peace like it usually does. He sounds as exhausted as I feel.

Turning, I look at Remington, standing just behind me with his arms crossed. "You don't have to do that."

He shrugs. "I'm not feeling it anymore anyway." Just then, a black car pulls up to the curb. "Already ordered a car." He says, heading for the sedan.

I follow him, sliding into the back seat when he opens the door. He closes it softly before rounding the back then getting in next to me. After telling the driver where to go, we sit in silence all the way to the hotel. The lobby is empty apart from the man at the front desk who gives us a brief nod as we go to the elevators. I internally kick myself for letting Aly sour my mood. When we step off on our floor, Rem reaches for my hand, interlacing our fingers. He leads me to my room, taking my key card from me to open the door.

"How are you doing?" he asks as I sit on the edge of the bed, removing my platform boots.

"I'm fine." I peel off my socks, glancing up at him. His back is nearly against the door, his hands in his pockets. My brow crumples. "You're not staying?" I ask, making my way to the bathroom.

A shower sounds so good right now after sweating in that bar.

Disappointment creeps in when he says, "No."

I turn on the shower before stepping back into the room, unzipping my skirt on the side and letting it pool at my feet. His eyes track the movement.

"You sure?" I ask when his gaze flicks up to mine.

His jaw muscle pops. "Layla…"

Licking my lips, I tug at my hair, releasing the ponytail. He watches me with rapt attention. I slide my hands over the tank top I'm wearing, slowly lifting it up.

"I'm sweaty and I want to shower." I say before pulling it off me. I'm left standing in a black bra with matching panties.

He mutters a curse, taking a step toward me before stopping himself. "You're killing me." He groans.

My lips curve up slightly. "Why?" I ask, blinking up at him innocently.

"Because I want to talk to you and you're…"

I reach behind me, unclasping the bra. "What?" I ask as it falls to the floor.

He loosens a shaky breath. "You're distracting me."

I step into him, biting down on my lower lip as I grab his right hand, placing it over my breast. "We don't need to talk, *Elijah*." My voice is low. "I know *this* is what you want from me."

He palms my breast when I release his hand, running mine over his hard length in his jeans. I lift up on my tip toes, kissing him. He pulls away abruptly, taking several steps back.

"What the fuck is your problem?" I demand. I'm angry that he isn't giving me my distraction right now.

"You." He grounds out with a glare. "We need to talk."

"I don't want to talk." I say. "I'm drunk." I'm actually clearer headed since the drive. He doesn't need to know that though.

"Who's fault is that?"

Damn him! I pin him with an equally angry look. "I hate you."

He cocks his head, crossing his arms. An arrogant smirk spreads on his lips. "You are such a terrible liar, Bug."

Marching toward him, I lift my arms, pushing them against his chest. Rem doesn't budge or say anything. I hear a deep chuckle that only piques my frustration further.

His head tilts down, eyes leveling on me. "I'm not having sex with you if you're not fully in it," He says, his voice laced with anger. "I care about you too fucking much to not notice that."

My breath snags when he places a hand on my hip, the other curving around my cheek as he walks me backwards until my back hits the wall. He kisses me roughly, the barbell in his tongue scraping against the roof of my mouth before he draws my bottom lip between his teeth, biting down. Heat pools between my legs at the pleasure mixed with pain. I whimper when he pushes his hips into me. All too soon, he releases me again.

"Believe me, I would love to join you in that shower." His eyes sparkle in the light pouring out from the bathroom. "But not until we figure shit out."

"You don't get to do this." I seethe. "We agreed to be together for the tour. You don't need to know everything about me. You sure as hell don't need to comfort me or talk things out with me."

"Then we're done." My throat tightens at the sincerity in his voice. "If you think we're simply fuck buddies than you're blind. If you think after five years that I wouldn't still know the look on your face when your heart breaks, than you're dumber than I thought."

I glare up at him. "Don't call me dumb."

He quirks a brow. "Quit evading. What Max may or may not do is eating you up inside. Whatever happened between you and Aly was huge. We all heard it."

Sighing, I clench my hands into fists at my side. "Let me get this straight," I say. "you're mad at me for not crying on your shoulder?"

He pins me with a dark look. "I'm mad at you for shutting me out. For carrying a heavy weight without asking for help." He growls, dragging his hands through his hair. "Fuck, Layla, I'm tired of seeing you self-inflicted with pain."

"God, I hate how observant you are." I mutter, moving around him to snatch my tank top off the floor.

"I hate that you think you can lie to me."

"Fine." I grit out, pulling the top back on. "She knows about us. At least, I think she does." I make my way back to the bathroom, turning off the shower before planting myself on the vanity counter. I stare at the tiled floor as I continue, "She thinks we'll get hurt again. That I'm throwing my life away." God, I hate that she said that. My heart squeezes in my chest at the memory.

Rem joins me, leaning against the counter. "How are you throwing your life away?"

I slide my gaze to his. "Because I keep chasing something I'll never find. She knows me better than I know myself at times." I admit in a calm voice. "I know she loves me. I appreciate her more than words can explain. It's just that…" I blow out a breath, glancing back at the floor.

"You don't want to hear it." Rem answers. I nod slowly. "Is it because she's right or because you don't like being told what to do?"

I flick my gaze to his, my heart hammering in my chest. How could he possibly peg me so well? "Both."

"I know," he replies, angling his body toward me, lifting his hand to cup my cheek. "You also hate being told how to live because that drags up past emotions with your parents." His thumb slides over my jaw in a way that comforts me. His eyes lock on mine, solely focused as if I'm the most important thing in the world. He always makes me feel that way. "Can I tell you something?"

"Yes."

"Trying to get over you has been the hardest fucking thing I've ever had to do. Worse than grieving my dad's death. You're this poison in my system that won't leave. Connor saw what it did to me back then. I'm willing to bet that Aly saw it too."

Letting out a sigh, I say, "We were kids."

"It was five years ago." He disputes. "That's not that long ago."

"We're different now."

"Are we?" he asks, hand slipping from my face. "Layla, I can't forget you. I've tried countless times to ignore the feelings I have for you, to push away the urge to call you and check in. It never goes away."

Have? "You should go." I slide off the counter, brushing past him into the room.

The vulnerability is too fucking heavy.

"Layla, I-"

"No! This is why I don't want to talk to you. It's too intimate. I'm not doing this!"

"Five minutes ago you didn't want me to leave." He says, his voice low. "You use me, treat me like a drug to get high off of then toss me away."

Back facing him, I wrap my arms around my waist, biting down on my lower lip. Aly said something similar. It struck a nerve then just like it does now. I do use him. I hate myself for it. It kills me to hurt him this way. He's always been my distraction, the one constant that I can count on when I need escaping. That's why I fell in love with him. He's always seen beneath my thick, unpleasant façade.

"You make me feel like shit." He says, his voice strained.

"Then leave." I bite out, not daring to turn around to see the look on his face because I can't stomach being the one to cause him pain. "Go now before it gets worse, Remington. Before I cut you so deep you'll never recover."

I hear him release a breath, then it's silent apart from the pounding of my heart in my ears. His voice cuts into the room after several minutes, my throat tightening.

"It's too late for that."

The door whisks open and I know he's gone. The soft click of it latching back into place sounds similar to the final nail in my coffin.

CHAPTER EIGHT
Rem

"You have to at least act like you're having a good time." Riley says.

I want to rip that damn camera from the photographer's hand. The label wants a shot for their social media of us with Layla to promote what's left of the tour. Two weeks to go before she walks away from me for the last time. Fourteen days until my life goes back to being meaningless as fuck. I sling my arm over Layla's shoulder, careful not to place my hand anywhere that might cause people to speculate. Connor is on the other side of her while Ty leans in, giving a hand sign that looks like devil horns. This is cheesy as fuck. I'm over it. All I want to do is climb in my bunk and fall into a fucking coma.

"That better?" I ask.

Layla tenses under my touch.

I know I struck a brutal chord with my parting words to her the other night. The pain in her hazel eyes is evident even now. Riley reminds Layla to smile too. The moment she does, the photographer snaps a series of pictures before saying, "That'll work."

I release Layla quickly before picking up my beer. I've probably drank more than I should, though I really don't care right now. Whatever helps dull the pain of realizing I'm never going to hold onto her. I wander down the back hall of the venue toward the lot where the bus is. Layla made it perfectly clear that she doesn't belong to me. Just like she did all those years ago. She's a beautiful wildflower in a meadow that stands tall against all the others. I want to covet her and take her home so she can only be seen by me. Even though I know in doing that, she'll be miserable and fade away.

The problem with Layla has always been her inability to attach. She doesn't trust people. I don't blame her after learning how her mother treated her or how her parents' divorce influenced her. I want so badly to show her that there is more than the harsh reality of two people who weren't meant to be. Although that's difficult to do when she's been burned by every other guy she's fallen for. If she'd give me a chance, I feel like I could change her mind.

"You're quieter than normal, dude. You okay?" Connor asks, catching up to me.

"I'm good. Thinking I might crash soon though." My head hurts.

He grips my shoulder just before I reach the exit door. I stop to look at him.

"Still not over it, huh?"

I take a swig of my beer, shaking my head. "What the fuck is wrong with me?" He raises a brow so I punch him in the bicep. "Fuck off." I say, chuckling. "You know what I mean, man." I shift my gaze down the hall where I'd come from. "What's the big deal? Why does she have this hold on me?"

"Because she's off limits and that kills you." He states as if it's that easy.

I scoff. "There's a ton of women I can't have. Why *her*?"

"Maybe because she's different than the others. You used to always go for the pretty girls with the outgoing personalities. The ones who care more about the newest lipstick color in fashion than where they want to be in ten years. Layla isn't like that. She's deep, she's stubborn, and she's ambitious as hell."

If it were any other guy talking about her, I'd punch him, but Connor's right. One minute I was looking to hookup, then the next I was professing my love to her. All because of that captivating, siren voice when she moaned in my ear, making me blow in my jeans. It's like she's a fucking succubus or something with magic qualities that sunk in my skin and took hold before I ever realized what was happening.

"I thought being around her would be easier. That after enough time passing, we'd... I don't know, be friends or some shit." I confess. "Then the minute I saw her, all those feelings she brought out in me came back. Now I'm living in my own personal hell."

"Does she know how you feel?"

Not directly. Though I'm sure she has to have an idea by now. "I'm afraid I'll freak her out."

He looks thoughtful for a moment. That's not something I've seen on Connor's face in a long time. "If she does, then maybe you'll get closure and finally move on." He claps my shoulder. "Or maybe she'll give you a chance."

I marinate on what he's said while I head for the bus. Sharing with Layla what she means to me is likely to cause another one of our famous arguments. She'll tell me I'm crazy then I'll get mad and say something rude. Then I'll try to kiss her because I'll feel like crap for being a dick and she'll push me away and tell me to fuck off. It's like I told her before, fighting is kind of our thing. As messed up as that sounds it's the truth. To be honest, there's no one else I'd rather fight with or for than Layla Barlow.

Melissa K. Morgan

After our show in California, we have a few days off to rest before finishing our tour in the Pacific Northwest. Usually I'm pleasantly exhausted toward the end of a tour, but something is off this time. I'm looking directly at her. Layla's on her cell, talking to someone while our managers check us into the hotel. I can tell she's angry as she glares at the potted plant near the oversized lobby couch, mouthing something before lowering her phone and shoving it in her back pocket. I quickly look away so she doesn't catch me watching her. We've been playing this game for the better part of a week now.

When we get our room keys, I purposely take a different elevator than her. I've been trying to keep up my persona the best I can since our last fallout because we're still singing "Waterfall" at the end of her set. Both our managers broached the possibility of us recording a track of the song together to release as a single. I'm hesitant to agree, mostly because more rumors are swirling about the two of us thanks to Max Tate. While it's killing me to distance myself from her, I know it's for the best. Just like I know my bandmates and Aly have to realize what's going on by now. It's kind of hard not to see the sudden separation between us. I'm getting so tired of hiding my fucking feelings all the time.

Once I'm in my room, I decide to take a shower to keep myself from knocking on her door. When I finish with that, I lay back on the king-sized bed, still in my towel. Usually I might join Connor for a night on the town or catch a movie. It doesn't sound that appealing this time. Nothing does. Pulling my phone from the nightstand where it's plugged in, I check some emails which are mostly junk before scrolling through social media to pass the time. A headline catches my eye as I mindlessly swipe, my thumb hovering over the article as I sit up.

Max Tate says Layla Barlow Slept her way to the Top...

Red hot fury boils my blood as I read the headline again. "What the fuck?"

SELF-INFLICTED

Has Layla seen this? Against my better judgement, I type her name into the search bar. Several other articles pop up. Some of which are praising her for being a rising star and others bashing her. There's even one with a photo of her and Max, stating that she broke his heart after learning she'd be touring with her "former flame." Whatever the fuck that means.

I grip my phone hard as I spring from the bed, pacing. This is *my* girl they're shit posting. I can only imagine what she's going through if she's seen it. Closing the app, I go into my texts to reach out before I can stop myself.

Me: *You okay?*

I continue pacing, waiting for a response. Ten minutes go by before my phone vibrates in my hand, but it isn't Layla texting me.

Ty: *Have you seen Layla?*

I get dressed frantically, snatching my room key off the dresser where I set it before racing out of my room to hers. Knocking on the door, I wait for several seconds. *1014*. I know this is her room because I saw it written when Riley passed us our cards. I'm about to knock again when Aly and Ty appear from the room behind me.

"What the fuck?" I demand, glancing between the two of them.

Aly looks concerned which frustrates me further. "She said she was going to meet up with Max."

Rage burns through my chest. "Why would you let her do that?"

"Easy, man." Ty says, placing his hand up. "Aly told her not to."

"She did it anyway." She explains. "I can't get ahold of her."

Some of my rage lessens, replaced with anxiety. "How long has she been gone?"

"Over an hour." She says, pulling her phone from her pocket. "She said he was going to give her back the notebook he stole. Although, I think the damage is already done." She holds her cell up so I can see the screen.

It takes me a minute to figure out what I'm looking at because the photo is grainy. Gradually, I recognize myself along with Layla. We're sitting close to each other, too close for it to look platonic, in the booth of that bar in Arizona.

My eyes close as I pinch the bridge of my nose. "Fuck."

"Someone posted it this morning and it's going viral."

"Good, you're all here." Connor says, coming down the hall. He frowns. "Riley needs a meeting. Where's Layla?"

"She's with Max." Aly says. "Wait!" she peers down at her phone, her thumbs frantically typing away. "She's on her way back."

My shoulders slump. Thank you Jesus! "What does Riley want?" I ask Connor.

"Not sure."

"Can he wait until the morning? I have shit to handle first." Now that a picture someone took is floating around on the internet, I need to talk to Layla.

"I'll tell him it will have to wait."

"Are you going to be an asshole?" Aly asks when Connor walks away. I glare at her. "If you are, then talking is useless."

"God," I groan. "Why am I always the fucking bad guy?"

"She's delicate, Rem. I'm her best friend regardless of us having a little bit of a rough patch. I will always choose her over you, even if it is her fault you two aren't together."

"I wouldn't expect anything less."

She nods once. "I've been trying to wear her down, but it isn't easy."

"I know." Believe me, I found that out a long time ago.

She smiles, placing a hand on my shoulder. "Do you love her?"

A lump forms in my throat. I swallow it down, shifting my gaze to the wall behind her.

"Yeah," I say, before meeting her eyes. "more than anything."

Her smile widens. "You should tell her that."

*

Layla ends up arriving back to the hotel while me, Aly, and Ty are still talking outside her door. It feels good to get some things off my chest with them. Connor said Riley will push the meeting to the morning. At the moment nothing else matters because I need to talk to Layla. Fearing her being gone, if even for a short time, was enough to push me into finally laying it all out to her.

"What are you guys doing here?" Layla asks when she sees us hovering outside her door.

"We were worried about you." Aly says, pulling her into a hug.

She glances between the three of us, her brows raised. "Why?"

"How did it go with Max?" I ask, shoving my hands in my pockets to stave off the need to pull her close to me.

Rolling her eyes, she pins Aly with a glare. "It's fine. I got the notebook back." She pulls it from the oversized purse over her shoulder. "See?"

"Did he say anything?" she asks.

"A lot of things, actually." Her lips turn down.

"Damn, Lay. What happened?" Ty interjects.

"There are bigger rockstars out there. I'm nothing compared to them." She says which incites my anger all over again. Before I can speak, she continues. "Honestly, it's okay though. I don't think I want to do this anymore."

Her words are a blade to my chest. "What?"

She barely glances at me. "Performing is fun, but I enjoy writing more. I'm…well I don't want to be in a position where I'm in the public eye like this."

My eyes narrow as I watch her. What is she saying? She said it was her dream. I shake my head, running a hand through my hair. This doesn't make sense.

"We'll let you two talk." Aly says before they disappear into the room across the hall.

Layla's shoulders drop as she releases a heavy sigh. "Come in."

I follow her into her room, closing the door behind me. "Max Tate is a piece of shit."

"Yeah, well maybe it takes one to know one." She says snidely, stomping over to the mini fridge.

Grabbing a beer bottle out, she twists the top off, taking a long pull. Something snags in my chest at the sight of her knocking back a beer when she's undoubtedly upset. I know what her mother put her through, what I heard when no one thought I was listening.

"Hey." I approach her, gently taking the beer from her hand, setting it on the desktop. She scowls up at me but doesn't protest. "Are you really going to let him win?"

"I don't have much of a choice. You know, I never cared to understand law or follow in my father's footsteps. After the last several months though, I'm kind of wishing I paid better attention to what he had to say. Then maybe I could sue for defamation or something."

"Listen, I know it's not my place, but you can't let Max win. He can't control yo-"

SELF-INFLICTED

"You're right." She says, plucking up the beer bottle before wandering to the small sofa beside her bed. She sits down at the end of it, taking another drink. "It isn't your place."

I deserve that, even if it is frustrating as hell to hear.

Releasing a sigh, I move to sit at the other end of the couch. "Why did he do this?"

Her shoulders raise in a slight shrug. "Who knows, really." She picks at the label on the bottle. "Maybe I hurt his pride by choosing to leave him or maybe Aly is right that he's jealous because I'm doing so well without him. It doesn't matter now." Her eyes lift to mine. "Did you see the picture?"

"Yeah, I saw it." I say, nodding.

"I guess he was hoping we'd slip up or something to give him proof. Thanks to some random fan, he got it. Anyway, It's not worth the fight to me. Honestly when Billy showed me the picture earlier, I felt relieved."

"This is your dream, Bug. You can't quit now just because people know about us."

She frowns. "I don't think I'm cut out for the kind of attention this brings. More than that, I don't want this to tarnish your career."

I blink at her, stunned. "You genuinely think I care?"

Layla rolls her eyes. "Rem, playing music is your thing. It always has been. It brings you closer to your dad. I won't be someone that takes that away from you."

I close my eyes, her words echoing in my brain. I swallow the lump that forms in my throat, opening my eyes again. "You're sacrificing yourself to save me?"

"Don't say I never did anything for you." She says with a smile, punching my thigh.

"I'd never say that." I scoot closer to her on the couch. "Bug, you're always sacrificing yourself. *Always.* I can't think of a time that you've ever once been selfish."

"Really?" she questions with a raised brow. "You and Aly both said it. I use you to disassociate from my problems. If that's not selfish…" she trails off.

"Believe me, I don't find that selfish." My lips tip up slightly. "In fact, I find it incredibly fascinating and thoroughly enjoyable."

I don't miss the way her mouth twitches. She quickly hides the smile by taking another drink of the beer. "I already told Billy that I'm done after the tour. In the meantime, we'll get through this like we have been. Then it will all be over."

I reach behind me, squeezing the back of my neck. "I don't want this to be over." I confess in a quiet voice.

She stares back at me, her hazel eyes searching mine. I'm not going to allow her to make the decision this time. I reach out to grab the beer bottle from her again. I want her head clear, so I know she hears me.

"You don't drink, Bug."

Her throat rolls in a swallow as her gaze falls to our hands, both holding the bottle. Brow crumpling, she releases the bottle so I can set it on the coffee table.

"I'm still mad at you." She leans back against the arm of the couch, drawing her knees up.

I nod. "That's fair. I'm the king of pissing you off."

She chuckles. "That's true"

"And you're my queen." I smile at the way she rolls her eyes. "Do you want me to tell you I'm sorry?" I ask, genuinely curious. "Will that change anything?"

Layla wraps her arms around her knees. "We agreed that what we were doing was temporary. Meaningless-"

"I never said it was meaningless" I growl.

"No." she bites out, her jaw clenching. "Even though you knew you would get hurt again. Then you left…"

"You're the one that told me to leave." I remind her in a calmer tone. "You think that people reject you, that they don't want you. That's not always true."

She falls silent, eyes scanning anywhere except at me for so long that I wonder if she's going to try kicking me out again. I'm not letting her control this even though I give her the moment of space. When she finally speaks, her voice is soft.

"I don't deserve you."

"Bug...that isn't-"

"It doesn't matter." She says quickly. Her feet fall to the floor as she runs a hand through her wavy hair. "The tour will be over next week, then we can go our separate ways."

She makes her way toward the door as if to usher me out. I don't move. "I'm not leaving." I say, earning a look of frustration from her. "Scream at me if you want, Bug. My ass is staying."

She rolls her eyes. "I'm *fine*."

"I'm not."

She folds her arms over her chest, glaring at me. "God, you're difficult."

"Likewise, babe." I lean back on the couch, getting comfortable. "What should we do to pass the time? Do you have any board games?"

She quirks a brow. "Seriously?" I shrug. "I don't even have a deck of cards."

"Lame. How are we going to play strip poker?"

"Nope." She grits.

I laugh. "Never have I ever?"

"I'm pretty sure you'll lose that one." Layla says. She taps her finger to her chin for several moments. "How about truth or dare?"

"So mature." I say, rolling my eyes.

"Okay, genius. You pick something."

We both fall silent for several minutes. I can tell she's tense because we're alone. My gaze drops to her bare thighs. I've only now realized she's wearing a pair of jean shorts that remind me of the ones she used to wear at Happy's years ago. I always want her. Right now is no exception. I flick my gaze up to hers to find her staring at me.

"I dare you to come sit next to me." I say quietly, keeping my eyes locked with hers.

For a moment she doesn't move, then she smirks, rolling those beautiful eyes as she wanders toward the couch. She sits so close to me that I can smell vanilla. I hold back the groan that threatens to surface. I want to bite her again. Eat her up.

"That was dumb." She mutters. She's right, but I don't care. "I dare you to take off your shirt."

I raise a questioning brow at her. "So you can objectify my body?"

She laughs, the sound piercing my heart. I like where this is headed, but I'm not giving in so easily. I oblige her, pulling off my shirt before tossing it at her playfully. Her throat rolls in a swallow as she scans down my neck to my chest, then lower. She trails her index finger along the tattoo on my chest.

"What is this?" she asks, gliding the tip over the insect above my heart.

This is the first time she's asking about one of my tattoos. I've branded myself with a lot of them over the years. I snatch her wrist, bringing it up to my lips. "My turn." I say, resting her hand on my thigh. "What's your favorite color?"

She blinks at me. "Really?"

I smile at her. "Truth. What is it?"

All this time we've known each other, yet there are things we never discovered. The simple things, the little pieces that matter and make us who we are.

"Black. Yours?"

"Like your soul, Wednesday Addams?" She sticks her tongue out at me. I grin. "Blue."

"So basic." She mutters, wrinkling her nose.

I smooth my thumb over the palm of her hand, noticing her tremble. I love it when she reacts to my touch. She has no idea my favorite color is because of her.

"Who is your best friend?" I ask.

"Easy. Aly."

"I take it you two made up?"

"I can't stay mad at her." She confesses. "Yours?"

"Connor."

She looks genuinely surprised by my response. "Seriously? I thought you'd say Tyler."

Shrugging, I say, "I've known Connor longer. He's loyal. He kept me on track after my dad died. We talked a lot during that time even though we lived in different states."

She smiles. "That's sweet. Did you guys always plan on having a band together?"

"Yeah, that was the goal."

"Now it's come true. Look at you living happily ever after."

Almost.

"Yeah," her face falls slightly. "What is it?"

She looks away from me to the drawn shade of the window across from us. "I always thought *this* was my dream. My mom saw the picture of us."

Realization sinks in. "Is that why you want to quit?"

The nod she gives is slow. "That's part of it."

I knew it. She's sabotaging herself again for the sake of everyone else. Her mom is a sad woman who refuses to be happy for anyone else unless it benefits her. Layla doesn't deserve the treatment she endured growing up. If I could, I'd take that pain away from her.

I really don't want to start another fight, but I can't help asking, "Why do you still care what she thinks?"

She surprises me by not getting offended by the question. "It's not that I care what she thinks, it's just that I want her to tell me she's proud of me."

"I'm proud of you. Our parents are proud of you. Hell, more people than you realize probably are."

"I know and that means the world to me." She says. "It hurts though, knowing I'll never have what I want with my mom. There are some days that I feel like I've accepted it, then she'll call me or make a comment that sounds condescending when I'm around, hurting me."

I frown. I don't know what it feels like to have a parent that doesn't love you unconditionally. She's thrown that in my face before and she was right. However, she shouldn't put so much stock into someone that has proven that they aren't worth her love.

"You're one of the most honest people I've ever met." I whisper. She looks at me again. "Stubborn as hell and a pain in the ass sometimes," I wink at her when she laughs. "but honest always and incredibly strong to endure what you have and still stand tall." I tuck a strand of her hair behind her ear. "You're brave and intelligent and worthy of everything despite what she says. Despite what *anyone* says."

I notice a veil of tears forming in her beautiful eyes when she blinks. I wasn't trying to make her cry by telling her how amazing she is. Despite her negative outlook, she has a sweet, compassionate side. A heart of gold wrapped inside titanium.

"I dare you to kiss me." She says, her voice soft and sweet like honey.

I lean forward without hesitation, pressing my lips to hers. I don't expect it to lead anywhere until she grabs my face with her free hand, sweeping her tongue against my lower lip. My chest rumbles in a low growl as I release her hand that I was holding to tangle my fingers in the back of her hair, keeping her close to me. She shifts her leg up onto the couch as I grab her hips, guiding her to straddle me. She grinds against me, making me so hard that if I don't stop now, I won't be able to.

Pulling back, I place my hand around her neck gently, peering into her eyes. "Tell me the truth." I whisper, flicking her upper lip with my tongue. "Do you love me?"

Her eyes widen. "What are you doing?" she whispers.

I feel her start to get up, holding her hip steady with my free hand. "No, Bug. No running."

Her eyes narrow. "What do you want me to say?" she asks in a scathing tone.

This time, when she tries to get up again, I let her. Only because I don't want her to feel trapped. Leaning forward, I rest my elbows on my knees, releasing a breath. She isn't going to make this easy for me, which is one of the many reasons I fell for her in the first place. Layla begins pacing beyond the coffee table. I watch her, seeing the tightness in her jaw, the way her eyes shift constantly as if she's lost in thought.

"Then tell me you hate me." I say.

Her nostrils flare as she stops pacing. "We can't do this anymore, Rem." Her voice cracks.

I stand immediately, marching toward her. She tips her head back to meet my eyes as I hold either side of her face, smoothing my thumbs over her jaw.

"Don't shut me out. *Please.*" I beg.

She places her hands over mine. I can see the indecision in her eyes. I know if she just lets those walls down another fraction, she'll let me in.

"I'm hurting you."

"I told you that I don't care." It's the truth.

I don't care if she destroys my career, if she murders baby ducks, or tells the fucking world a vicious lie about me. I want her attention forever. Nothing is going to fucking change that, no matter how hard she pushes back.

Tears fill her eyes. "That's the problem. You've never cared that I use you. That I seek comfort in you without once ever reciprocating." Her hands drop. I see it then, the defenses lowering. "I know I'm a coward. That I refuse to open myself up to anyone who might get too close. I can't change!"

"That's not true!" I bark. I hate it when she sells herself short.

"Now is not the time for this."

"There never is a perfect time." I release her face, stepping back. "You can come up with a million fucking excuses about why we don't work and every single one of them is bullshit. Because we *do* work, Layla and that scares you. That's why you keep letting me go."

She shakes her head, folding her arms around her waist. "We can't do this."

"Do you know why my favorite color is blue?" I ask, ignoring her.

She releases a sigh, her head tilting up to the ceiling. "Stop."

"You wore a blue dress to our parents' wedding. You wore a blue swimsuit one day at the house when we were younger. I watched you swim like a fucking creep for an hour with Aly. The guitar you broke, the first one I ever bought myself, was blue. I loved it more than anything because it was similar to the one I first played when I was a kid. Like the one that belonged to my dad. When you told me to get on my knees for you and I willingly dropped down, eating that glorious pussy? Those lacy little panties you had on were blue."

I wonder if she's recalling all those memories because her eyes seem to lose focus. She's silent for a long time. When she finally speaks, my control slips. "I'm not good for you. Why can't you see that?"

My jaw aches from the tension of this conversation. "Why can't you see that you're lying to yourself?!" I growl, startling her. "You keep pushing me away yet it doesn't take. Did you ever stop to wonder why?"

I'm done playing this game even if she feels cornered. "All the time." She says, sniffing. She seems to be working something out in her mind. "You like the pain."

I huff out a short laugh. Yeah, that's true, though not the entire reason. "Maybe that's part of it."

She motions between us, "Us together is fucked up. This isn't healthy."

"Do you remember when I told you that I needed grounding? Years ago when I took you out for cheeseburgers and milkshakes?" I ask her, still pressing. When she nods in response, I say, "You ground me, Bug."

I want her to understand how much she means to me. To show her that no matter what she says or does, I'm not going anywhere. She's too fucking important to me to walk away from. Regardless of what people think, I'm hopelessly in love with her. I'll rob a fucking paint store and tag it on a billboard. No other consequence is as harsh as not being in her life every single moment of every day.

Risking a step toward her, I brush my fingers against her cheek, seeing her shiver. "Tell me you hate me." I plead in a thick voice, resting my forehead against hers.

"I can't do that." Her eyes close as I trail the pad of my thumb along her lower lip.

"Then tell me the truth."

A sob breaks loose from her chest as my own heart rises in my throat. "I c-can't." she whispers, sounding terrified.

I know this woman like the back of my hand despite what she thinks. I know she's scared to admit to something so heavy. I brush my lips against hers, feather light, before pulling back slightly.

"Then show me."

I sense the fight withering away when she wraps her arms around my shoulders to kiss me. I take my time, savoring the feel of her luscious lips while she moans softly as I explore her mouth as if this is the first time all over again. My heart wrings tightly in my chest when she tangles her fingers in the longer hair at the back of my head, pressing her chest against mine. Lowering my hands down the side of her body, I curl my fingers into her hips, lifting her so that she can wrap her legs around me. Somehow, I'm able to navigate us toward the bed without barely a glance. I gently lie her on the bed, kissing down to her neck where a faint scar is still visible from when I marked her.

Straightening, I begin undoing my jeans while toeing off my boots. In my haste to get dressed earlier, I never put on socks or underwear and right now, I'm really glad about that. Tugging off my shirt, I kneel between her legs on the bed, placing my palm against the smooth skin of her belly underneath her shirt. Gliding my hand up, the fabric moves higher until the black, lacy bra beneath is exposed. I flick my gaze to hers, shaking my head.

"Do you have any fucking idea how absolutely obsessed I am with you?" I ask, curving my fingers around her left breast. Her eyelids grow heavy as she stares at me, her multi-colored hair wild. "I worship you."

I kiss her again, tugging her bottom lip between my teeth before moving off the bed. She watches as I pull off one of her sandals, then the other, before sliding her shorts down her long legs. Kneeling on the floor, I grip her hips, forcing her closer to my salivating mouth. I keep my gaze trained on her as I glide my tongue over her clit. She cries out, drowning me almost instantly.

SELF-INFLICTED

Clutching her left thigh, I drape it over my shoulder before continuing to feast on her until she's pulling my hair and breathlessly moaning my name.

Standing again, I hold out my hand for her to take. When she does, I ease her up off the bed removing the rest of her clothes. Taking her hand again, I rest it against my chest on the insect tattoo.

"If you've ever doubted how I feel about you, you should know this," I gently squeeze her hand, still holding it over my heart. "I've been in love with you since the moment our eyes met. Fell deeper when you straddled me on that futon. Then realized I would die for you when you ordered me on my knees." Her breath hitches, her hazel eyes pooling with tears. "You're under my skin, Bug. For-fucking-ever."

Layla loosens a heavy breath. "God, Rem…" she sobs, crashing her lips to mine.

I can't speak, can't breathe as she kisses me intensely, climbing up my body which I happily help her do until her legs are wrapped around me again. I turn, sitting down on the edge of the bed so that she's straddling me.

"Like our first time." I say with a wink.

"I love you." She whispers.

My heart stops beating. I don't know whether to laugh or cry. She fucking loves me.

"Holy fuck, that sounds amazing." I growl as I kiss her again.

She lifts up to position herself before gradually slipping over my cock. The feral grunt I release is inhuman, but god, she feels incredible inside.

"Say it like this, Bug."

She moans when I pulse inside her, moving her hips rhythmically. "Rem…I love you." She whimpers, her head falling back as she begins to move faster.

Gripping her hips, I help guide her toward release. "Look at me," she meets my eyes, clutching my shoulders. "Tell me again." I don't want her to ever say anything else.

She shudders, her wet heat coating me. "I love you." She says as the orgasm takes over, sending a shiver down my spine.

The release hits with an intensity that makes my ears ring, catching me off guard. I quickly lift her up, tossing her on the bed, before palming my dick to spill in my hand. That was fucking close! My heart racing, I collapse next to her on the bed, attempting to catch my breath.

"Did I hurt you?" I ask, searching her body for any sign of damage.

She shakes her head, her arms bent, hands resting on either side of her head. "No. We forgot about protection again. I understand why you'd throw me off of you."

"I never want to throw you off me." I say, frowning at my messy hand. Winking at her, I rise from the bed. "Want to help me clean up?"

She bites down on her bottom lip before nodding, following me into the bathroom to shower.

CHAPTER NINE
Layla

    I'm in love with Remington Paulson. Admitting that to him was probably one of the most terrifying moments of my life. Not because it isn't true, more so that I'm afraid of the pain of losing him. Opening myself up to be vulnerable isn't a strong suit of mine. Now that I have, I'm concerned I'll bleed out if we fall apart. He's always been this breath of fresh air in my stagnant life. He's so different than me, so optimistic and ambitious. He's his true authentic self always which makes me want to be that way too. Which is scary, because all I've ever known is the dark cloud of doubt that holds me hostage. He loves me. While I think I've always known it, hearing him put the words together so beautifully last night cracked the final chain around my heart. His patience toward me is literally mind-blowing. Which is precisely why I love him.

    Waking up this morning with his arms around me, my head over his beating heart, felt so natural that I didn't even try to sneak away like last time. We've been awake for a little while now, lying in bed, soaking up the last remnants of our confessions last night before facing the likely hectic day.

    He grazes his long, index finger along my collar bone. "You're not quitting?" he asks with hope in his voice.

    Yesterday, I was dead set on finishing this tour then walking away forever. When Billy showed me the photo of us in

Arizona, I immediately panicked. Even though he assured me that it wouldn't be that big of a deal, I freaked out because that's what I do. I told him I wanted to quit. Then I met with Max to get my notebook back, feeling surer than ever about giving up my dream. Max claimed that he was the reason the label signed me in the first place. Without him, I would be a nothing in Massachusetts still. I didn't believe his words at first. However, after marinating on it, I began to wonder if he spoke the truth.

Regardless, I don't want to give up. Not when my determination to prove him and anyone else that doubts me wrong is humming through me like a cyclone.

Capturing Rem's hand, I meet his eyes. "I know that I might not be the most likeable person in the public eye. I get anxious talking to people and being the center of attention. Plus, I'm kind of my own worst enemy. I have no idea how to navigate bad press." He opens his mouth to speak, so I place a finger against his lips. "I have no idea how to navigate *any* press. It worries me to think that I might say or do something wrong, so I stay silent. Then people think I'm standoffish or mean because of it. It's difficult to navigate if I'm being honest. Although, living with the failure of quitting is something I'm certain I can't handle. So, as much as it scares the hell out of me, not knowing what the future holds or what *us* is all about, deep down, I'm confident in one thing."

"That you love me?" he asks with a smirk.

I roll my eyes, dropping his hand.

"Okay, two things. Yes, I love you." He immediately leans in, pressing his lips to mine. "Also, I can't quit just because things get tough. I might miss out on all the positives."

The dimple in his left cheek deepens as he smiles wide. "That's my girl."

Those insufferable butterflies spring to life with his words. Then my mind decides to remind me that I've never really been a positive person.

"I mean, I guess I have quit things…"

"Nope!" he rolls toward me, using his knee to part my legs. "No negative self-talk." Fire ignites between my legs when he positions himself above me. "You're fierce, independent, beautiful and brave."

Warmth seeps into my chest. "Why are you so nice to me all the time?"

He squints down at me. "Because I love you," he says, kissing me again. "it's my job to make sure you stay away from your dark thoughts. I want you happy, Bug."

I wrap my arms around his neck, squeezing him tight. "I want that too."

His phone vibrating on the nightstand ruins the sweet moment. Remington groans as he lifts himself off me, stretching across the bed to reach it. "I have to meet with the guys for a meeting."

"Okay."

He gets up from the bed, beginning the process of locating his clothes then dressing while I sit up, pulling the sheet up over my chest, watching him. When he begins pulling up the zipper on his jeans and buttoning them, I stare at his hands.

"Layla?" he says in a gruff voice. My eyes flick up to his. "You'll be here when I'm done, right?" the question makes my heart collapse to my stomach.

I hate that he doesn't trust me to stick around, that he's still worried I'll deny him even after last night. I'm the worst person in the world for ever breaking his heart when he so obviously wants me, even after all the pain I've caused.

"I promise." I say, lifting off the bed to approach him. "Rem, I'm sorry that you doubt me. That I've hurt you beyond repair."

He immediately shakes his head, placing his hands on either side of my face. "No, not beyond repair." He says, pressing his lips to my forehead before pulling back to meet my eyes. "I won't say I'm not afraid that you'll talk yourself out of this again, but I know your heart. You wouldn't say you love me if you didn't mean it."

"Yeah," I nod. "I do mean it."

His lips tip up on one side. "Then that's all I need." He kisses me with such intensity that I'm breathless and dizzy when he releases me. "I'll see you later."

I watch him leave, giving me a quick wink. He's too good for me. I'll never stop believing that no matter what he says, but I won't stop striving to be worthy of him. Instead of the black cloud of demise, I feel the eternal springs of hope.

*

While Rem is meeting with his manager, I decide to take a quick shower before texting Billy to see if he's available to chat. I shouldn't have had such a knee-jerk reaction yesterday when I saw that picture. I only hope I'm not too late. That Billy hasn't spoken to anyone at the label yet. He agrees to meet me down in the café at the hotel lobby so we can talk.

He's already at one of the small tables when I arrive, with a tea in hand and a vanilla latte for me. I slide into the seat, bringing the cup to my lips, taking a sip. "Thanks for meeting with me." I say, setting the cup down before wrapping my hands around it.

"Of course," he says with a genuine smile. "Are you doing better today?"

I've always appreciated Billy's kindness. Since being assigned to me, he's not only put up with my sometimes erratic behavior when I get stressed, he's also been a good listener that advocates for me when I'm scared to do it myself. He feels like good family. I say "good," because not all family is. It's okay to separate the two even if you share blood.

"I'm better." I admit, tucking a strand of hair behind my ear. "I'm sorry for freaking out yesterday."

"I understand. You know it isn't a bid deal though."

Lifting a brow, I lean in closer. "What if people hate me now? What if they think we're weird for being in a relationship or Hemingway's Rejects loses fans?"

He shrugs, taking a sip of his tea. "They're a solid band with tons of opportunities still. The label isn't dropping them." Well, that's a bit of a relief to hear. Although, that doesn't mean that people won't be judgy or rude on the internet. "The band doesn't care about the picture. Riley says they all agreed to stay silent about it."

"Really?" Rem hadn't told me that. Then again, we really didn't do much talking after falling into bed with each other. He nods. "What about me? Is the label going to scrap me after the tour?"

One of the positions I agreed to be in was a temporary contract holder. If I don't do well, I could get cut. That's always been in the back of my mind as a stressor even though I accepted the terms because I wanted the opportunity to prove my worth.

Billy's eyes widen. "Are you joking?" he snorts. "Layla you're doing well. Better than anyone anticipated. Honestly, if they don't write you up a full contract then you can tell them to fuck off. You can do this on your own."

Stunned, I feel tears flood my eyes. "You really think so?"

He smiles. "Absolutely. I've worked with a lot of people the last several years. You're unique. People resonate with the message you send in your songs. You have nothing to worry about."

I chew on my bottom lip, letting his words sink in. I could do this on my own? Without the pressure of going where someone else wants me to go or doing what someone else wants me to do? That sounds like a far better future than being tied to some label.

I've always wanted freedom to explore on my own. To be fully independent. Maybe it's the revelations with Remington last night or maybe I truly am growing up.

Blowing out a breath, I nod, sure of nothing while actually anticipating a brighter future.

"I want to quit. After the tour." Billy frowns. "I don't want to work with the label. I want to do this on my own."

"You're serious?" he asks, squinting at me as if to search for a bluff in my expression.

I'm not joking.

"I want to carve my own path. Whatever that is." I'm not stuck how I was when I was eighteen. I have some money saved up as well as a promising career following my dream. Even if it takes me longer to get where I ultimately want to be, I want to try it on my own. I'd much rather die accomplishing something for myself than live following the trend of what someone else wants.

"You've grown a lot from the young woman I met a few years ago." He says, his eyes wrinkling in the corners as he smiles at me. "I'm proud of you."

I can't help the tears that slip down my cheeks. He's proud of me, just like Remington. It's an amazing thing to hear, to know that there are people in your corner routing for you even if others refuse to.

We chat a little more about rounding out the tour. I agree with Billy that Rem and I should record "Waterfall" as a single. It will be the last thing I do as a contracted artist. My swan song as it were - ending one chapter before beginning anew. I'm absolutely looking forward to it. Confident in my decision, I leave Billy to head back up to my hotel room. Aly catches me before I enter, joining me to hang out since the guys are still in their meeting.

"So…" she says with a knowing smirk as she sits on the couch, grabbing a throw pillow to tuck against her. "Care to tell me anything?"

SELF-INFLICTED

Luckily, housekeeping came in to make the bed before I got back, so there's no evidence of Rem staying over, but I know my bestie is no idiot. If I'm going down a new road of being honest with myself, that includes doing the same with others.

"So, what?" I tease, shrugging.

Her eyes narrow. "Lay, don't fuck with me."

I burst out a laugh. "I think me and Rem are…kind of official now."

Her mouth pops open. Springing to her feet, she cheers loudly before tackling me on the bed. "This is the best news I've heard since Ty proposed!" she squeals with delight.

I roll my eyes, moving to sit up. "Really? You're putting us up there with your proposal?"

She shrugs. "Well, I've kind of been pining for you two to get together for a long time. It's like finding a pot of gold at the end of a rainbow."

Shaking my head, I smile at her. "It feels good to finally have everything out in the open." My lips turn down. "I'm sorry, Aly. For whatever shit I put you through over the last several years. I hate when we fight."

She sits up, grabbing my hand to squeeze. "It's okay. I'm sorry too. I shouldn't have called you out so harshly. I know it isn't easy for you to navigate your feelings."

"Thanks." I squeeze her back. "I'm still kind of in shock to be honest. I don't understand how Rem can put up with me the way he does. I've hurt him which I feel absolutely terrible about. It's going to be a long road to forgive myself for that."

"He loves you. He told me that even though he didn't have to. I've seen the way he looks at you and the way he treats you. You're on this pedestal in his eyes, Lay. It's a genuine, unconditional love."

"Such a romantic." I mutter.

"I'm happy for you both. I know that things can still get tough in any relationship, so I'm here for you if ever you need to vent or need advice. I'll never stop loving you. You're my best friend in the whole world. You're the only person I can commiserate with when our favorite person doesn't get to stay married on our favorite show."

"Gil deserves better than her anyway." I say, referencing a particular season.

She bumps her shoulder with mine. "You deserve the best. He's got you, Layla. There's no other man I would trust to steal you away from me than Rem."

"Same goes for Ty." I say, then a thought pops into my head. "Holy shit, you're getting married in like four weeks!"

"I know!" she says, a look of panic flashing across her face.

We begin discussing her upcoming nuptials along with all the things left to cross off the list before the big day. The more I talk to her about it, the more excited I am for her. Apart from my dad and Bridget's wedding, I've never been a part of one.

Shit! Dad and Bridget. Have they seen the picture of us? Do we need to call them? I begin spiraling when there's a knock on my room door. When I answer it, Rem is there gripping the handle of his suitcase, looking as if he's showered and changed his clothes.

"Can I stay with you?" he asks, his brown eyes coasting over my body.

"Sure." I say, motioning him in.

Aly pops up from the bed, giving him a hug. She whispers something in his ear. "I'll see you later." She waves before leaving us.

Rem places his suitcase near mine against the far wall before wrapping his arms around my waist. I automatically embrace him back, letting him kiss me for a few minutes. As much

SELF-INFLICTED

as I want to pick up where we left off earlier, there's a few things I need to get off my chest.
"We need to talk."

Rem

"We need to talk." Layla says, her brow crumpling as she steps out of my arms.

"Okay..." she moves to sit on the couch. "What's up?"

She draws her legs up on the cushion, bending her knees before wrapping her arms around them. "Do you think our parents have seen the picture?"

The thought occurred to me briefly, but I didn't put too much concern into it. We're grown adults, so it's not like they really have a say in our love life.

"I'm not sure if they've seen it. Your dad hates the internet more than you do and my mom, well she's been busy with cases lately."

"We have to tell them about us. I mean, they're going to end up finding out eventually, right?"

"Yeah," I say, moving to sit next to her on the couch. I unhook her arms from around her legs, grasping her ankles. She stares at me curiously as I place her legs over my lap. "You might not know this yet, but you're stuck with me."

Her lips twitch when she narrows her eyes. "Stuck, huh?"

I grin at her. "Forever, Bug. I'm like the barnacle and you're the ship."

"What?"

I lift a hand, cupping her chin. "Part of the structural integrity. You can't remove one without damaging the other."

Her eyes lace with tears as I move in, kissing her soft lips.

"That's...wow." She mutters when I pull away, placing my hand on her bare knee, sliding my finger over the smooth skin. "That's a good line."

"It's the truth. We're made for each other. Nothing can tear us apart."

SELF-INFLICTED

She inhales a deep breath, releasing it slowly. "So, how do we tell them?"

"I was kind of hoping we could wait until the tour ends since we're going back to Massachusetts for Ty and Aly's wedding."

I'm due for a visit with my mom anyway. Plus there's something important I need to speak with Michael about.

"Okay, that sounds like a good plan." She's chewing on her bottom lip again, lost in thought. "There's something else I want to tell you."

"You want to make out with me?" I ask.

She laughs. God, I love hearing her laugh.

"Well, yeah. Let me get this out first though. I met up with Billy earlier with every intention of telling him that I'm not quitting." She pauses. I wait for her to continue. "In a way, technically I'm not. I told him that I don't want a contract with the label."

Stunned, I search her eyes. "You don't?"

She takes a cleansing breath. "I want to do it on my own?" it comes out like a question. Pride blasts through me. "I think I'd like to navigate myself for a while to see what happens. I've been so stuck being other people's puppet. I don't want that anymore. I need to find myself."

"I think it's a great idea." I say. She seems to huff a sigh of relief. "Were you worried to tell me that?"

She shrugs. "I don't know. I guess I'm afraid I can't make it on my own. I don't want you to resent me for giving up on something tangible."

I scoff. "That's never something I would resent you for, Bug. If you want to follow your dream, do it *your* way, not anyone else's. I admire you for that."

"Really?"

"Yeah." I say. "Honestly, there have been times that I've thought about the same thing. I love the guys and creating music with them, but it's not easy being tied to a company that controls your moves."

"I don't want to revert back to the person I was when I felt controlled by my parents. Even if I fail, at least I can say I tried my own way."

I smile, in absolute awe of her. She's come so far from the scowling, beautiful creature she was when we first met.

"I love it. Do that and don't for a second think that I won't support you every step of the way."

"Thanks." She says, tucking a strand of hair behind her ear. "How did your meeting with Riley go?"

"Great, actually." I'm still in a bit of shock with the news he sprang on us even though I'm fucking excited as hell for it. "We get to play at a huge, music festival in October."

"That's awesome!" she beams, grabbing my face to kiss me. "I'm so happy for you guys."

I kiss her back, relishing in the warmth that seeps into my chest with her lips on mine. I don't think I'll ever not cherish every fucking second I get to be close to her like this. Before long, she's sitting in my lap, her legs on either side of mine while I fondle her perfect tits, biting her neck as she rubs herself against my hard length, moaning in pleasure. I work to undo her bra, sitting back to allow her to remove it fully along with her shirt. I instantly capture a nipple between my teeth, rolling the piercing in my tongue along it before moving to the other.

I lift my head, kissing up her chest to her ear, releasing a low growl that makes her shiver. "You going to cum for me, baby?"

She reaches for my hands, placing them back over her chest while rocking against me. "Yes."

SELF-INFLICTED

I kiss her again, letting her rub against my dick until she's panting heavily in my ear, driving me wild when the climax hits her. It's so hot when she dry humps me, but I'm more controlled now that I know what she feels like from the inside, I need to be there.

I grip her ass cheeks roughly. "I want this ass in the air."

Layla doesn't even hesitate. One minute she's on my lap, then the next she's lowering her shorts before getting on her hands and knees on the cushions and presenting her wonderful ass to me. Fuck, she's breathtaking this way. All vulnerable and wanting.

I undo my jeans, grabbing the condom from my pocket, sliding it over my hard length. I push the jeans to my knees after removing my shirt then I kneel behind her on the couch, grabbing ahold of her hips before lowering my face to her pussy from behind. The second my tongue licks over her wet, hot center she sucks in a sharp breath.

I wasn't kidding about wanting to eat her up. I lap my tongue over her slowly, savoring my favorite flavor. *Her.* Oh yeah, she's ready for me again. My lips travel over the back of her thigh to her left ass cheek where I bite it, marking her like I did on her neck. She cries out in pleasure making my heart soar.

I shift, bending over her to speak in her ear. "Let me hear you, babe." I say as I grip myself, sinking inside of her. Her arms tremble as she holds herself up against the arm of the couch. "Fast or slow?" I withdraw inch by inch before pushing in again.

"Fast." She pants.

Straightening, I hold her hips in place to give her what she wants. She moans loud as I keep going, wishing I could live inside her. Wishing I could hear those noises she makes forever. Maybe I'll fuck her in a studio and record it. I continue pounding into her until she bends her arms, burying her face in the couch cushion.

"Oh, God, Rem!" she screams when I feel her inner walls shake.

Gritting my teeth, I cum so furiously that it takes my damn breath away. Blowing out a shaky breath, I quickly deposit the condom in the trash before scooping her up in my arms and lying her on top of the bed.

I slide next to her, placing a kiss against her damp temple, curling my arm over her waist. We lay there silently for a while, catching our breath. She trails her fingers over my forearm, soothing me into a blissful peace.

"I'm so in love with you." I say, nuzzling my face into the crook of her neck.

"I love you, Rem." She says, turning to press her lips to my forehead.

My heart melts with her words, comforting me more than I can ever fully express. Layla is my salve, my solace. She's the only thing that's made me feel at home since losing my father. Falling for her is the simplest thing I've ever done. I'll spend the rest of my life ensuring that she doesn't ever feel like she doesn't deserve me, because she fucking does. She deserves everything life has to offer including the beautiful moments that often get overlooked like cheesy dates and movie nights at home.

"I'd watch paint dry with you." I say, propping my head up on my hand to gaze down at her.

She giggles, "Seriously?"

I smile. "Absolutely. I'd pull weeds with you. I'd refurbish a coffee table, bake cookies, plan kid's birthday parties. All the basic things people do when they're domesticated. I'd even watch your silly reality romance shows."

Her smile takes my breath away, but it's what she says next that captures my heart completely. "I can't wait to do all of those things with you."

SELF-INFLICTED

CHAPTER TEN
Layla

The tour finishes strong with a sold out crowd in Washington State. Before leaving California last week, me and Rem spent time in a studio that the label rented out to record our version of "Waterfall" together. Since its debut on streaming channels, it already has well over one million listens. It was bittersweet to say goodbye to Billy, knowing I may not see him again now that I've officially refused a contract with the label. They own the rights to my album, so I'm working on getting those back. It's fine with me for now because I'm determined to make an even better one next that's all my own.

So far there hasn't been any huge fallout with the image of us that circled the internet. Max has been radio silent since I met him in California. Part of me still wonders why he threatened to reveal my secrets. Some people are just mean. A lot of my fears in being with Rem surrounded the notion that we'd be judged poorly or treated negatively because we're technically stepsiblings. We didn't grow up with each other and are two consenting adults, so I no longer care what people assume. In truth, that wasn't ever my determining factor for being with Rem anyway. It was all based around my fear of falling. Because it's terrifying to make yourself transparent and vulnerable with someone when you aren't even sure if you can trust those who are closest to you. I'm still scared of a fallout. I might always have that fear in the back of my mind, but I'm not letting it beat me anymore. Bearing that burden has been stifling to say the least. Now that we don't have to hide anymore, the freedom I so desperately seek is attainable.

Speaking of freedom, I'm really looking forward to getting off this cramped plane and onto home soil. Aly and Ty will be getting married next weekend, so we decided to come to Massachusetts early. We have to tell our parents about our relationship. Something that I'm still worried about if I'm being honest. Bridget has always been incredibly supportive of her son's endeavors, but what if this is the block that topples all that? There's also my dad who supported me following my dreams yet isn't the easiest person to pull to your side. I'm worried that he'll be angry with me for falling in love with Remington. Will he be angry with *him*?

I'm anxious to get off the plane while also being terrified of what awaits us when we show up at the house to drop this bomb on them. Rem must sense my nervousness, because he places a hand on my knee, stilling my bouncing leg.

"What do you call a factory that produces decent products?" he asks, leaning in to kiss my cheek.

I turn to blink at him. "That's...what?"

"What do you call a factory that produces decent products?" he asks again, his lips twitching.

My brow crumples. "What?"

"A satisfactory." He deadpans. I can't stop the laugh that bursts out of me. It's so loud that I earn a strange look from the people sitting in front of us. He chuckles, checking the watch on his wrist. "Twenty minutes until we land. Are you going to make it?"

"I think so." Flying isn't my favorite thing. "I'm just nervous to see my dad."

He lifts his hand from my knee, cupping my chin before kissing me softly. "It will be okay. I'm sure that even if Michael does have a problem, my mom will talk him down."

"You're not worried that she'll be disappointed?"

"Trust me, there's been times over the years that I've been certain she loves you more. She'll be happy that I finally wore you down." He winks.

"It took you five years." I say in mock disappointment.

He narrows his eyes. "You didn't make it easy."

"Neither did you. King of pissing me off."

"Queen of my heart." I wrinkle my nose. "Too cheesy?" he asks.

I bump my shoulder with his. "I like cheesy."

Rem keeps me entertained with more dad jokes and sweet words for the rest of the flight. By the time we grab our luggage, I'm a little less troubled by the impending conversation. As long as he's with me, I can get through anything.

*

After an hour of visiting with our parents, talking about the tour, my new career path, and Rem's festival show, it's time to confess. Neither of them brought up the picture, so I'm assuming they didn't see it, which is a relief in itself because I would have hated to explain anything over the phone. Especially if they get upset. When we first arrived at the house, we kept our distance from each other. Me sitting next to Bridget on the couch while dad sat in one of the chairs with Rem across from him in the other one. Now, Rem sits straighter in his chair, placing his hands on his knees.

"There's something else we need to tell you guys." he begins, glancing between them. "I'm not really sure how to say it, without just coming out with it so…"

"Is everything okay?" Bridget asks, concern lacing her voice as she looks at her son.

He smiles. "Everything is...amazing." His gaze shifts to me. "I'm in love with Layla."

My eyes dart to Bridget then dad who looks tense as he sits in the chair, his eyes narrowed at Remington. Heat flames my face. I don't know why I feel embarrassed about him professing his love for me. Maybe it's because I'm not sure how dad will react.

"You... what?" Bridget asks, shaking her head before looking at me. "Do you know about this?"

I bite down on my bottom lip, nodding slowly. "I've known for a long time." I say, my voice quiet. "We're together."

Her eyes widen, pooling with tears. I think for a moment that she might scream or rant negatively. Then she turns to my dad, saying, "Michael, are you hearing this?" I bristle, my stomach twisting into knots.

He shifts his gaze to her. "I heard." he says curtly, glancing back to Rem. "What are your intentions?"

I gape at him. "Dad!"

"It's a fair question." Rem says.

"Oh my god." Bridget exclaims happily. "My boy, my girl..." she spreads her arms, pulling me into a hug. I tense, shocked by the display. "I'm so happy for you two. How did this happen? *When* did this happen?"

Some of the shock wears off when she releases me.

"I mean, technically it started over five years ago." I admit. "We kind of met each other before we *met* each other."

"What?" her hand flies to her chest as she looks at her son. "You didn't tell me?"

"Mom, it's not like there was anything to tell at the time." He glances at my dad. "Michael, can we talk privately?"

SELF-INFLICTED

Dad slides his attention to me, his face a stoic mask, yet there's a glimpse of something deeper in his eyes. "Are you happy Layla Bug?"

"Yes," I say. "happier than I've been in a long time."

He nods once before standing. "Let's go talk in my office." He says to Rem before leaving the room.

I swallow the lump that forms in my throat. What are they going to talk about? Is Rem going to asks dad's permission to date me? I'm a free woman who can make her own decisions. Would he break up with me if dad tells him to? Starting to panic, I stand.

"You can't talk to him." I say, stopping Rem when he gets to the entryway of the hall.

He frowns. "Why not?"

"What if he tells you to leave me? What if he forbids you from ever seeing me again or worse, what if he hits you?" I gasp.

He quirks a brow. "Is that where you learned to punch the way you do?"

"This isn't funny." I grit out.

He smiles, bending to kiss me quickly. "Relax, Bug. I'm not leaving you. Nothing can stop me from seeing you, and he won't hit me."

"How can you be sure?"

He rolls his eyes, grabbing my face to kiss me again. "You forget I've know this man for a while. We've had our fair share of conversations."

"What does that mean?" confusion is evident in my tone.

He winks. "Be back soon."

Rem

Michael sits in one of the high-back chairs in front of his desk as I close the door to his office before taking a seat in the other one.

"You know, when she was little, Layla had so many aspirations." He says, crossing his right leg over his left knee. "She was always playing, always happy. Her laughter was contagious. Despite the shit me and Regina went through between each other when raising her, she always gave me a reason to stay. To stick it out for *her*. I only ever wanted her happiness. We have that in common." He says, pinning me with his gaze.

Clearing my throat, I let my arms rest on the sides of the chair. "She deserves nothing less."

He smiles tightly. "She changed a lot from that innocent little girl when she became a teenager. I think she noticed more than I gave her credit for. I was gone a lot due to work. I think a part of me knew a fight would brew at home if I was there too, so I kept my distance. I hate myself for hurting her. For making her believe I didn't want her. When she decided to stay with Regina after the divorce, I figured she hated me. I'm glad we were able to work through all that." He heaves a sigh, standing to his feet before walking around his desk to crouch down, opening a drawer.

"She changed again when she moved in here with us that summer. At first, I thought it was because she had stability, warmth that was so rarely given at home with her mom." He stands again, holding a small, black velvet box in his hand. "I'm not a naïve man and I'm certainly not blind." He says, tossing the box to me.

I catch it, staring up at him. "You knew."

He huffs out a laugh, placing his hands on his hips. "Remington, let me give you a piece of advice, man to man."

"Okay."

SELF-INFLICTED

"A tattooed boy with good looks, charm, and similar interests to one's daughter, makes a man take notice and pay attention. I watched you when she was around. The way you'd follow her with your eyes or go out of your way to be close to her in a room. You're the one that asked us to dance with her at our wedding. Did you forget that?"

"No." I say, chuckling. "I was in love with her then too."

He nods. "I know, son. Which is why I'm giving you my blessing. She changed because of you. You're a good influence on her. I know that you'll never hurt her the way her mother and I have. I know that Bridget and your father made you the man you are today."

A lump forms in my throat at the mention of my father. "Thanks."

"That ring belonged to my great-grandmother. It's unique and beautiful, like our girl."

Opening the box, I peer at the ring, my heart hammering wildly in my chest. It's a rose gold band with a large, round diamond atop it adorned with two black jewels together on one side. "It looks like a ladybug." I say fondly, running the tip of my finger over it. I flick my gaze up to his. "This is perfect, Michael. Thank you."

He claps me on the shoulder, heading for the door. "Thank you for giving my daughter the love she deserves."

Swiping under my eye and sniffing, I stand when he opens the door, tucking the ring box into my pocket. I'm not proposing to Layla anytime soon. That will surely freak her out or possibly make her run. However, when the moment is right, I want to be prepared because I've known for years that she's supposed to be my wife. I've been planning to ask her to marry me since she smashed my guitar to smithereens and told me to get on my knees.

"I think I'm going to throw up." Aly groans, pressing her hand to her stomach.

She does look a little pale. "Do I need to grab a bucket or something?" I ask, backing toward the door.

Layla pins me with a glare. "She's fine." I shrug. Okay, no bucket. "Take some deep breaths, you're going to be okay." She holds Aly's hands in front of her, mimicking slow, tranquil breaths until she follows.

"Okay," Aly sighs. "Okay, I can do this."

Layla smiles. "You're getting married to Ty. He's hot, he's talented and he loves you more than anything on the planet. This is going to be an awesome day."

While I hate that she just called Ty "*hot*," I'm choosing to overlook it because she's being a sweetheart to her best friend.

"He's prepping to head to the altar. I just came by to let you know." I say, opening the door.

"Thanks." Aly says.

"Hey, Bug?" I step into the hall, glancing at her over my shoulder.

"Yeah?"

Smirking, I say, "I can't wait to rip that dress of later."

Her face flames as her lips pop open. I chuckle before closing the door. It's so much fun riling her up. Not that I'm kidding about the dress. She looks fucking amazing in it. I didn't get to spend the night with her last night, so I'm missing her pretty damn bad today.

I find Ty standing near the closed double doors that lead to the room where the ceremony will be held. They found a renovated concert hall to celebrate. Connor slaps him on the back, noticing me approach.

"Looking sexy, Mr. Paulson." Connor says.

I adjust the black tie around my neck. "I hate dressing up." I grumble, looking at Ty. "You're lucky I love you, dude."

He laughs. "How's my bride?"

"Good." I say. "She's anxious to start."

"Me too."

A few minutes later, Layla and Aly's cousins join us while the wedding planner tells us it's time. He opens the double doors to allow Ty to begin walking down the aisle as a soft, instrumental song plays. Loosening a breath, I adjust the tie again, stepping beside Jane. Layla has her arm tucked into the crook of Gavin's. I glare at it. She gazes back as if she can sense me watching. A slow smile forms on her luscious lips as she gives me a slow perusal, warming my blood.

"Later…" she mouths before turning back around.

Fuck, she's sexy. I wonder how long we have to stay at this thing before we can leave. I really want to take her back to the condo we rented while we're here. Better yet, I'd like to take her back to the bridal suite to bend her over the chaise lounge I saw in there.

Biting down on the inside of my cheek, I keep myself in check. We have all the time in the world to be together, this moment is about celebrating our friends. As the music continues, I watch her step into the room, gracefully roaming down the aisle. A surge of love and admiration sweeps through me. I can't wait to be uncomfortable in a tux for her. To see her walking down the aisle to me, becoming mine for good. That'll be the purest form of heaven.

I'm able to remove the tie for the reception along with the jacket. I'm working on rolling my sleeves up at our assigned table when Layla sits in the chair next to me. She immediately takes over the task, somehow making it sensual. Or maybe I'm just always turned on by her.

"I like you in a suit." She says as she uncuffs the other sleeve.

"Do you?"

"Mmhmm." Her hazel eyes lift, pinning me with a sultry look. "It's really sexy on you. But this…" she trails her finger along my now bare forearm. "the rolled-up sleeves are hot."

"Yeah?" I ask, leaning closer to her, inhaling her vanilla scent. "I like your dress. Although I can't help thinking about what would make it even better."

"What's that?" she asks softly, her gaze shifting between my eyes and mouth.

I lick my lips. "If it was bunched up around your waist, while you straddle me."

Heat sweeps through me when she lowers her hand, gripping my thigh. Angling her mouth closer to mine, she exhales softly. "I know a private place."

Nothing else needs to be said after that. Jumping to my feet, I grab her hand before whisking her out of the reception hall. She giggles beside me, interlacing her fingers with mine.

"Where to?" I ask, glancing around the main area.

"Upstairs." She says, angling her head in the direction of a narrow, winding staircase.

Still holding her hand, we head for the stairs together, climbing up them until we get to a small landing with two nondescript doors. "Which one?"

She releases me, stepping to the one on the right. "Aly told me that these used to be offices." She says, shouldering open the door and flicking the light on the wall. "Now they're just empty rooms."

I follow her, closing the door behind me before clicking the lock into place. There's one window in here, covered with a dusty old curtain. Coming up behind her, I wrap my hands around Layla's waist, drawing her back into my body. Her head rests on my shoulder as I nibble her ear before kissing her neck. Spinning her in my arms, I cup her chin gently, kissing her lips. She slides one of her hands down my stomach to my hard length, groping me. I groan into her mouth.

"God, I love when you touch me." I breathe, flicking her upper lip with my tongue.

"Same." She murmurs, trailing her tongue up my neck.

My hands fall to the hem of her thigh length dress, gripping the fabric as I slide it up over her hips. Cupping between her legs, I apply a slight pressure with my thumb over her swollen clit, watching her face contort in ecstasy.

"Bug?" I whisper, loving the way her eyelids flutter while I rub her over the lacy underwear.

Her lashes lift to meet my gaze. "Hmm?"

"Are you wet for me?" I ask, pulling the scant fabric to the side before brushing my knuckles against the sensitive spot. I already know the answer to the question.

"Yes." She hisses when I insert a finger inside, slowly teasing her.

She clutches my shoulders, her nails sinking into the shirt. Removing my finger, she lets out a little whine that nearly brings me to my knees. Grabbing her hips again, I lift her up, turning to pin her against the wall by the window. Holding her up with one hand on her waist, I quickly undo the belt, lowering the pants enough to free my cock. Pulling her panties to the side, I tease her entrance, making her moan for me nice and loud. Releasing myself, I reach into the pocket of my pants, retrieving the condom.

Layla chuckles lightly. "So prepared." She quips as I bite the wrapper open before sliding the condom on.

"With you?" I grunt as I slip inside her, "*always*." Her hips rock back and forth, riding me as I build her up slowly, wrapping my fingers around her delicate throat. "Tell me how good it feels."

"Amazing." She cries, wrapping her arms around my neck, holding me closer.

I lean in to kiss her, careful not to bite since we still have a few hours to kill at this wedding. I don't need Aly questioning another vampire attack or anything. Her legs tighten around my waist when I slide my hand from her hip to her thigh, grasping hard. I move faster, reveling in the way she feels like this. So soft, so tight.

She pants in my ear, nearly sending me over the edge as she bucks her hips. "Oh, god. Oh…"

When I feel her shudder against me, I explode.

Leaning my forehead against hers, we catch our breath together, holding each other close. Nothing in the world will ever compare to these stolen moments we expertly share. With a racing heart and shaky lungs, I clasp her chin, forcing her to look at me.

"I love you, Layla Barlow."

She smiles softly. "You're mine forever, Elijah Remington Paulson."

SELF-INFLICTED

EPILOGUE

Layla

"That's all for today, everyone. I'll see you next week!" I say, waving at the five faces on my desktop screen. I exit out of the video messaging app, rolling back my chair.

I never imagined that I'd use my life experience to help others find their own way in the world, yet here I am doing just that. Teaching teens who love music the basics of playing guitar while lifting them up and letting them know they're amazing despite what others might tell them. It's one of the most rewarding things I've ever done.

It's surreal to know that it's been two years since my first tour as a contracted artist. The summer that changed my life in so many ways, all of them positive. Being an independent artist now, I control my own schedule and get to experiment with different styles and genres of music. Thanks to my hot, rockstar boyfriend, our house is equipped with a music studio where I can play any time I want. It's where I recorded my second album that just released a month ago.

Placing my acoustic guitar on the stand near the array of other guitars belonging to both me and Rem, I glance at the blue electric one nearby. It's an exact replica of the one I smashed years ago when he pissed me off. The smile on his face when I presented it to him last year for Christmas made my cold heart all kinds of mushy and warm, but the spicy reward he gave me that night burned me alive. Even after two years, he still makes me feel like I'm the only woman in the world that matters. He still desires me and tells me I'm pretty every day. I never imagined a love like the one we have. My long-standing cynicism has withered and died, leaving me open and excited for a future with a man I consider my very best friend.

Making my way out of the basement studio, I head up the stairs to the main part of our home. We bought this three story fixer upper together a few months after Aly and Ty's wedding and spent most of last year renovating it to fit our styles. Rem wants to stay in Massachusetts because it's close to our parents and I agreed because I don't hate my home town as much as I once did. Not when this is the place we met, the place filled with our memories, both good and bad.

"I'm not going over this again, Connor. You don't give a girl a fucking engagement ring if you don't intend to marry her." Rem rolls his eyes, standing near the kitchen island.

I approach him, sitting in one of the bar stools. He reaches out to grasp my chin, kissing me. Pulling away, he shoots me a wink.

"That's not a birthday gift, dumbass." He mutters and my brows raise. "I have to go. See you in an hour."

"What was that about?" I ask when he disconnects the call, shoving his phone in the back pocket of his dark jeans.

"He forgot Jane's birthday, so he proposed."

I gape at him, stunned. "What?!"

He shrugs. "My thoughts exactly. Then he calls me because she dumped him…again."

"They're on and off all the time. I'm sure they'll make up by tomorrow."

He smiles, taking my hand and guiding me to stand. "Probably." He wraps his arms around my waist, bending his head to kiss my forehead. "How did the class go?"

Goosebumps form as he begins kissing a path down my temple to my jaw. "Good."

"Did I tell you I'm proud of you today?"

SELF-INFLICTED

I smile then gasp when he bites my neck gently. "Mmhhmm." He says it all the time.

"Well, I'm proud of you, Bug." He flicks my upper lip with his tongue making me whimper.

Lifting my arms, I tangle my fingers in the back of his longer hair, forcing him closer. I kiss him deep, shivering when his hands slide to my ass, tugging me against him. I grind against his hard length, tugging on his bottom lip with my teeth. Rem groans, easing back.

"I wish I had time to fuck you before we leave."

My face falls. "We don't have time?" A smirk forms on his face, showcasing the dimple in his cheek. "Where are we going anyway?"

"Not telling." He grabs my hand, leading me to the staircase that goes up to our bedroom. "Aly will kill me if I don't get you there on time."

"Get me where?" I ask when he releases my hand.

He playfully smacks my ass. "Go get dressed. If I go up there with you, we'll never leave."

I scowl at him. "What are you up to?"

He matches my look. "Go."

Rolling my eyes, I sigh. "Fine." Grabbing the hem of my shirt, I lift it off me, letting it fall to the stairs as I ascend. Then I quickly slide off the loose shorts I'm wearing. Smirking back at Rem, I see him staring at my ass.

"Damn it." He growls.

I shriek when he races up the stairs, grabbing me from behind and carrying me the rest of the way to our room.

✸

"Are we running late?" I ask Rem from the passenger seat of his truck.

Even after all these years, he still has the same truck. I'm sitting close to him, my hand over his that's resting on my thigh.

"Yes," he says, flawlessly turning left with only one hand on the steering wheel. "But that was worth it."

I smile, squeezing his hand. "Where are we going?"

"You keep asking that question."

I glance out the windshield, still not certain where in the hell he's taking me. All I know is that he made dinner plans for us and Aly is somehow involved. He's been acting different since getting home from a European tour last month. I wanted to go with him but I didn't want to cancel my weekly classes with the teens. We're nearing the downtown part of the city. There's a lot of places here that we might go to, so I'm out of ideas.

"Do you remember when we worked at Happy's together?" he asks, heading down a familiar street.

"Yes. You pissed me off a lot back then."

He chuckles. "Same, babe. Do you remember Bryant?"

Narrowing my eyes, I study his side profile. "What does he have to do with anything?"

"He bought the place from Hank when he retired three years ago." He gives me a sidelong glance. "Tried to make the place what it used to be but failed miserably." The arrogant smile on his face makes me roll my eyes.

"I heard that. It's a shame because I loved that place."

He nods, keeping his gaze trained on the road ahead. "Yeah, I remember you telling me once that you briefly considered working there forever and maybe running it one day."

My chest tightens. I peer out the windshield when the truck comes to a stop. We're in the parking lot of Happy's. The back employee entrance door is propped open with a milk crate and I see Bryant, still looking like a ken doll but older, standing there.

"What's happening?" I ask as Remington cuts the engine and unbuckles.

He angles his head outside as he opens the door. "Let's go see."

I follow him out the driver's side, letting him take my hand as we approach Bryant. He's in a light gray business suit, his arms crossed over his broad chest. He shoots me a smile before nodding his head up at Rem.

"You're late, Paulson."

Rem shrugs. "Don't care." He stretches his free hand out, palm up.

Sighing, Bryant uncrosses his arms, reaching into his pocket. My eyes widen when he produces a set of keys, dropping them into Rem's palm.

"Pleasure doing business with you." Rem says.

Bryant gives me another glance. "I'm only doing this because I trust her."

"What?" I look between the two of them.

"Your boyfriend bought the business. Don't let him fuck it up, Layla." He marches toward a white sedan.

"You bought Happy's?!" tears pool in my eyes as I beam up at Rem.

He smooths my hair over my head, grinning. "I couldn't sit back and let this place go to shit. Plus, I'm going to be bored now that we have no tours scheduled for the foreseeable future."

Hemingway's rejects is taking a much needed break after releasing a third album. They've been working a lot and deserve the rest. Plus, Ty and Aly are ready to start a family and he doesn't want to be on the road for that.

"I can't believe this." I mutter, shaking my head.

He squeezes my hand, leading us toward the propped open door. "There's another surprise inside."

Not sure how he could ever top buying a business, I follow him, my stomach filled with butterflies. We walk through the small, empty kitchen where he stops in front of the closed door that leads behind the bar. He turns to face me fully.

"I have a serious question." He says, his face somber. "Do you love me?"

"Of course." I say, frowning.

There's still moments that he asks me this. Despite my love for him, I still get lost inside my own head sometimes. I withdraw because I'm afraid that he'll hurt me. He's never given me a reason to believe that he'll leave and he's never been mean to me, but the fear is still there. Not as present as it once was, but try as I might, I can't fully rewire my brain.

Loosening a breath, he nods. "You know I love you, right? More than anything?"

"Yeah…" I say slowly, curiosity getting the best of me. "Why are you acting weird?"

He bites down on his bottom lip, glancing toward the closed door. "I know you hate attention, that you're better off being in the shadows and not making a spectacle of things. But I couldn't help myself this one time."

He pushes the door open, sweeping his arm out for me to enter. As I step into the bar area, my legs lock up tight. The tears from earlier, spilling down my cheeks. The lights are low in the large entertaining space apart from the mystical twinkling of lights strung around beams and on walls. My eyes stop on the stage where Connor is standing in front of a mic stand, Tyler beside him, strumming the familiar melody of "Waterfall". Movement in front of the stage captures my attention and I see Aly, sitting on a stool next to my dad and Bridget who are smiling at me.

Remington takes my hand again, leading me to the middle of the open floor as Connor begins singing the lyrics. Lifting our joined hands to his chest, he places his free hand on my hip, drawing me in to dance with him.

*Broken roads and empty dreams are all I see ahead of me.
I lost you and I cannot breathe.
I wish you'd come back and haunt me.
They say that I should hold on tight to the best years of my life
But I'm just trying to get by with shaky breaths and bloodshot eyes.
Water crashes down on me, drowning me til I can't see.
It's a damn catastrophe but God, I love a tragedy.
So break my bones and start your call
I'm ready for the waterfall.
Even if I have to crawl
I'll find you again after all.
Loneliness is my best friend and she'll stay with me til the end.
I never want to wake again unless you promise that you'll bend.
Break my heart and chase your dreams
Tear my lungs out while I scream and force me on my bloody knees.
You know you'll be the death of me.
Water crashes down on me, drowning me til I can't see.
It's a damn catastrophe but God, I love a tragedy.
So break my bones and start your call.
I'm ready for the waterfall.
Even if I have to crawl.
I'll find you again after all.*

The guitar continues strumming as Remington places his forehead against mine.

"When I wrote this song, I had no idea the impact it would have on my life. When I realized you loved it as much as I did," he releases a low breath. "God, Bug, it meant the world to me. You get me. Above anyone else, you seem to know me without trying. You love me with your whole heart and hate me just as much." He smirks and I giggle.

"I don't hate you."

"No?" releasing me, he takes a step back. "I dare you to prove it."

Raising a brow, I glance at Aly who's a mess of tears next to an also crying Bridget. Dad smiles at me, winking.

"How do I do tha-" the words die on my tongue when I look back at Rem who is down on one knee, presenting a small box with a beautiful, unique ring tucked inside. "Oh, my god!"

A hopeful look crosses his face, his brown eyes sparkling in the dim twinkle of the string lights. "Layla Darlene Barlow, my beautiful, unique, girl..." he swallows roughly, tears lacing his eyes making me cry more. "Will you spend the rest of our lives fighting with and for each other? In sickness and health, even after death?"

I kneel in front of him, swiping under my eyes before placing my hands on either side of his face. "You're daring me to marry you?" I ask with a smile so wide, my cheeks hurt.

He nods. "Got to keep it interesting."

I glance down at the ring, noting the sparkling diamonds and the shape that looks like a ladybug. Lifting my gaze to him, I kiss him gently. "Yes, I'll marry you."

Lowering my hands, I let him slip the ring on my finger then wrap my arms around his shoulders, squeezing him tight. For a girl who used to be pessimistic about love and thought it sucked, I'm sure looking forward to a lifetime of being in love with Rem.

Maybe it isn't so bad to allow yourself to be vulnerable even if you risk getting hurt. Not allowing fear to determine your outcome makes you grow; it gives you strength and courage. Life would be ridiculously boring if we stopped because of it.

THE END

Thank you for reading Self-Inflicted! I hope that you enjoyed this book and I appreciate your support. Please feel free to leave a review on Goodreads and Amazon as it is a huge help for indie authors like me. If you want to share your excitement over the book on social media, you can follow me here:

Facebook: @ Melissa K. Morgan

Instagram: @melissa_k_morgan

Tik Tok: @melissa_k_morgan

Email: authormelissakmorgan@gmail.com

SELF-INFLICTED PLAYLIST

Self-Sabotage – Maggie Lindemann
DiE4u – Bring Me The Horizon
Lonely Bitch – Bea Miller
Bad Decisions – Bad Omens
Jaws – Sleep Token
Candy Coated Lie$ - Hot Milk
Debbie Downer – L0L0, Maggie Lindemann
Figure You Out – Voilá
Back To You – Our Last Night, Halocene
Bruises & Bitemarks – Good With Grenades
Hatef—k – The Bravery
La La Lainey – Forever the Sickest Kids
A$$A$SIN – Beauty School Dropout
Love Race – MGK, Kellin Quinn
Bloody Knuckles – Sleeping With Sirens
Entropy – Beach Bunny
Hate U – L0L0
Numb – Waterparks
Loved You A Little – The Maine, Taking Back Sunday, Charlotte Sands

ACKNOWLEDGEMENTS

Thank you so much for taking the time to read Self-Inflicted. If you've stuck it out this long, I hope you know how special you are to me and how much I appreciate you. I'm eternally grateful to the readers that take a chance on me and gain entertainment through my stories. I write for me and others out there that enjoy a bit of dissociation to get through life by reading about other people's problems and holding out hope for that happily ever after.

Self-Inflicted is a story that means so much to me. Over the course of the last two and a half years, I've spent a great deal of time trying to wrap my head around Rem and Layla's story to convey it in a way that makes sense. They're the loudest characters I've ever dealt with and I mean that in the most loving way possible. Though, come on guys, can we stop bickering for like five minutes? This author gets exhausted. Honestly, I love these two characters so much because they're not perfect or pretty at all times and definitely not likeable in their worst moments - but they're raw and real, which I'm personally obsessed with.

It all started with a song by Maggie Lindemann called "Self-Sabotage". A banger that really hits the notes of how people who can't make sense of being happy, navigate relationships with those that they can easily attach to. At least that's how I interpret it. I listened to the song on repeat for weeks and peppered in many other songs, creating a playlist that truly matches the vibe of this book. Thanks to several concerts with my husband, and a music festival that I still daydream about, the rock star part of the story was born. If you're keen on music that inspires novels, you can check out the playlist I created for Self-Inflicted.

Giving credit where credit is due, I also have to thank my amazing husband for being my biggest supporter and inspiring the love stories I write. Thanks for letting me steal the things you say and putting them in my books. I love you. I also have to thank my two kids who understand me and my quirks and allow me to take the time I need to write.

Lastly, I want to thank me. I've been through the ringer emotionally and mentally over the last several years and am finally getting to a place where I'm comfortable in my own skin. I still struggle with self-doubt and fears of people judging or not liking me, but I'm learning to not care so much. After finishing this book, I'm just going to say it - I'm fucking PROUD of myself. I did it! No one can take that away from me, not even myself.

Other Books By Melissa K. Morgan

The Silver Series:

Something to Believe In

Something to Hold Onto

Standalones:

Always Beautiful

Let Me Down

Spy

Milton Keynes UK
Ingram Content Group UK Ltd.
UKHW010751010724
444982UK00004B/321